NO MERCY

About the Author

David Buckley is 33 years old and works as a free-lance writer and reviewer. Originally from Liverpool, he lives with his wife and two daughters in Munich, Germany. In 1993, he was awarded his doctorate from the Institute of Popular Music at Liverpool University for his thesis on David Bowie. He is the author of *The Complete Guide to the Music of David Bowie* (Omnibus Press, 1996), and his major cultural biography of David Bowie will be published in 1999.

NO MERCY

The Authorised and Uncensored Biography of the Stranglers

David Buckley

CORONET BOOKS
Hodder and Stoughton

First published in Great Britain in 1997 by
Hodder and Stoughton
A division of Hodder Headline PLC
First published in paperback in 1998 by Hodder and Stoughton
A Coronet Paperback

10 9 8 7 6 5 4 3 2 1

ISBN 0 340 68065 2

Printed and bound in Great Britain by
Mackays of Chatham PLC, Chatham, Kent

Hodder and Stoughton
A division of Hodder Headline PLC
338 Euston Road
London NW1 3BH

For Ann

CONTENTS

FOREWORD

The story that follows is ridiculous. It's about a few people who just wanted to play some rock 'n' roll. Of course, there is a bit more to it than that: there were a few things that happened along the way.

The characters involved are all extremely diverse personalities, so diverse that by any logical assessment the venture should have failed dismally at the outset. Many critics said that it would, and have been repeating the prediction for the last 20 years. Perhaps the single unifying element in the story is sheer determination.

The characters are also colourful, and you will see that they are clever, stupid, crafty, cunning, even wicked at times. Some have described them as talented, others as talentless. But they must have been doing something right, since their tale has few parallels in the history of contemporary music.

The story is also bizarre. It is likely to discourage some who would otherwise consider a career in music. Others will be inspired to initiate such a career all the sooner.

Those at the centre of the story have achieved the admiration of millions, yet they have been reviled, ostracized, pilloried and ignored by the Establishment. Books have been written about the music of the last quarter of a century without a mention of one of its great survivors. How could this be?

There is to many something untouchable about the Stranglers. They have probably been banned more times, and from more places, than any other band in history. It is as though the mere mention of their name invokes in some quarters a hostility that others describe as being manifest within the band itself.

If the band were ever to choose a more appropriate name for themselves, perhaps it would be CONTROVERSY, a subject that has never deserted them.

At long last, the true story is to be told. David Buckley has boldly ventured where others have feared to tread. The band have agreed to endorse the analysis of the career that is the subject of this tale, a tale which should finally put to rest all the conjecture, all the lies, all the assumptions, guesses and put-downs.

All of human emotion is here: elation, disappointment, passion, lust, anticipation, fear, anxiety, stress, fatigue, happiness, disaster, love, hate, apprehension, and death. Yes, this story is ridiculous. It is a tale that many will not believe. I was there, and it happened. Would I do it again? You bet I would.

Jet Black, 1997

PREFACE

Whereas before I only *thought* that the music business was full of egomaniacal people jealously safeguarding their own incorruptible media façades, I can now confirm that this is in fact the case. Unfortunately, for very sound reasons of libel laws, I'm not able to divulge some of the information I've picked up along the way. But the contents of this book are nevertheless wicked enough. Personally, I've never been too keen on 'man (or woman)-behind-the-myth' tabloid-style biographies which seek to spill the beans on the stars. There are a number of reasons for this (not least that I want my myths to remain intact), but I think the main one is that, with only a few exceptions, the tales themselves, and the individuals involved, simply aren't interesting enough. There's no substance, no charisma, and the stories themselves often strain the boundaries of what could be dubbed sensational. But this is a very different type of story in the sheer volume of naughtiness, appalling behaviour, cynicism and nastiness it reveals. It is a sort of rock 'n' roll *I, Claudius* without the poisonings, although the band almost out-did Caligula in some of their sexual exploits. It's a pretty shocking indictment of the rock business that a band such as the Stranglers have actually been allowed to get away with these tactics for so long, and it's a pretty sad indictment of the media that they bought what was very often a complete pack of lies (or at least a very liberal flouting of notions of the 'truth') in the way that they did.

The actual genesis of the book is almost as bizarre as the band's career. In November 1995 they played to a barely quarter-full hall at the spooky Terminal Eins in Munich, housed in the old airport built by the Nazis in the 1930s. I'd heard that Paul Roberts, the band's singer, was a Bowie fan, and when I saw him bare-chestedly strolling around the side of the stage after the gig doing a Vic Reeves-style karaoke to amuse the roadcrew, I thought I'd try and speak to him about a book I was (and still am) writing about the great man, with a view to an interview. Paul was so down-to-earth and friendly that any collywobbles I might have had about approaching the lead singer of a vintage and nefarious rock band soon dissipated. During the course of the chat, Paul let it be known that the band were looking for a biographer. I said, 'I'll do it', phoned up a contact at Hodder & Stoughton and, within two days, I had a publisher. It was nonchalantly bizarre.

Little did I know that it would take months of often extremely petty wrangling for the project to become a cast-iron certainty. For, if I had any illusions concerning the residual animosity between the band and the Cornwell camp, they were soon dispelled. This was the first time that the Stranglers, and ex-lead vocalist Hugh Cornwell, had co-operated on anything since Hugh left the group in 1990. And they certainly weren't going to miss this golden opportunity for a protracted bout of mutual nit-picking.

Not that any of this residual animosity was ever really directed at me. For the most part the band were nothing but totally co-operative. Singer Paul Roberts, without whom there would have been no book at all, was unstintingly helpful and kind, as were the rest of the band. But special thanks must go to archivist, historian, drummer *extraordinaire* and all-round good guy Jet Black, who worked tirelessly to produce valuable information, facts, figures and opinions.

Guitarist John Ellis warned me that there was a negativity within the band and that, now I was connected with it, some of it would rub off on me. At first I was sceptical, but now I almost believe him. There is something dark, even evil about the Stranglers. You can sense it. Collectively they're a disheartening bunch of people. Their negativity did affect me personally in a number of ways, but perhaps the most peculiar, or at least the silliest, event happened when I was writing about the infamous 'Meninblack' phase, when the band went bonkers over sci-fi, ufology, abductions and the paranormal. I went upstairs from my study to get myself a glass of water and when I came back down a toad was sitting on my writing case looking at me with two beady bulging eyes. It was obviously a portent of something genuinely terrible about to happen, like an earthquake, an alien abduction or yet another repeat showing of Bob's Full House on UK Gold. Could I get the bugger out of the room? Could I hell. I barricaded myself in with Jet's huge ledgers full of the cuttings he had been collating for over twenty years, and waited for a less squeamish person (my five-year-old daughter perhaps) to pick up the petrified amphibian and release it into the wild.

Apart from the toad, which gave me the biggest laugh of the project, I would like to thank, first and foremost, the members of the band themselves for their friendliness, co-operation and days (if not weeks!) of interview material. All five are, in their own way, very endearing characters, despite some of the gross lapses of taste they have perpetrated on us over the years. I'd also like to say a big thank you to Mainstreet Management (Sil Willcox and Trevor 'Snogger' Long) for providing me with research materials, drinking my cellar dry and generally being bull-shitting nice guys along the way. At one point they managed to fool me for a whole day into believing that they wanted to call the book *Black Bastards*, thereby reducing me to a shivering wreck.

Outside of the music biz, my biggest debt of gratitude is owed to two people. Firstly, my wife, Ann Henrickson, who read the entire manuscript. And secondly, a certain Garry Coward-Williams, in past incarnations variously a band supporter, photographer and roadie, nicknamed Chiswick Charlie by Hugh, who was a constant source of information and whose journalistic expertise and worldly-wise good humour were invaluable as the work reached its conclusion.

Thanks also to Hugh Cornwell for his help with and advice on a project which touched on areas that he perhaps found uncomfortable. Hugh seems to have nothing but affection for his time in the band. But even so, being confronted with a past he'd done his best to break free from was obviously a trying experience.

I'd like to signal my appreciation of the work of Chris Twomey, who in the mid 1980s wrote a biography of the band which remains unpublished, and who produced the informative booklet, *The Men They Love To Hate*, for the band's four-CD boxed set, *The Old Testament*. Both works remain essential background reading for the first ten years of the band's existence.

I'd also like to acknowledge the cheery assistance of the following, in a sort of cop-out alphabetically-ordered sort of way: John Buckley, Brian Crook, Dai Davies, Paul Du Noyer, Alan Edwards, Dave Fagence, John Gatward, Ian Grant, Laurie Latham, Gareth Noon, Marian Shepherd, Ruth Turner and Alan Winstanley.

A mention must also go to my two daughters, Louise and Elsa, who have spent the last six months wondering if their Dad will ever have time to play with them again, and to my weirdly double-jointed nephew, Peter Buckley, who as our *au pair* was a steadying and calming influence on the whole household, particularly when he poured me the first Weissbier of the evening and cheered me up with his amazing repertoire of burp and 'people being sick' noises in the back garden.

Finally, thanks to my editor at Hodder & Stoughton, Simon Prosser, and his assistant, Anna-Maria Watters, for having faith in me and the project.

David Buckley, August 1997

INTRODUCTION:
THE DISAPPEARED
MEN IN BLACK

The Stranglers are the most despised group in British popular
music. They are, collectively, the Bernard Manning of pop. Just as
Manning, the subject of a recent biography by Jonathan
Margolis, is the alienated man of comedy, marginalized as a
result of his controversial comedic style, which embraces and
reflects society's racism and sexism, so the Stranglers, in high-
lighting similar themes in their work, have been dubbed beyond
the pale. During their heyday they were largely vilified by the
tabloids, critically mauled by the rock inkies such as *Melody
Maker* and *New Musical Express*, and later ignored as irrelevant by
the selectively ageist media culture of the 1990s. They were
outsiders: more technically proficient than all the punk bands,
older than anyone else on the new-wave scene with the
exception of Ian Dury, and more obviously arty and intellectual. They didn't fit in then, and they don't fit in now. To like
the Stranglers was to bear a stigma: they were the rejected ones
of the rock fraternity, easy targets for young journalists eager to
curry favour with their superiors. The Stranglers were the one
major punk-era band to be cast down into hellfire, partly as a
result of their own pig-headedness, preciousness and occasionally violent personalities. But whilst groups from the States such
as the Velvet Underground and Iggy & the Stooges, who
glorified the sewer in their own brilliantly arty way, went
critically lauded but completely ignored by the vast majority
of the record-buying public, the Stranglers, by far the most
commercially successful band from the punk era, have simply
been written out of the official chronicles, sidelined because of
their alleged Cro-Magnon-like unreconstituted attitudes and
overly-sophisticated musical credo. To all intents and pur-
poses, despite being the only major new-wave band to have

lasted almost into the new millennium, they have become conspicuous by their absence: it's like the Men In Black never were. But why?

Writing the Stranglers out of the annals of rock history is merely a symptom of the systematic distortion which has been perpetrated for the last 20 years, as punk has come to dominate all before it. It's well worth pointing out the simple fact that punk was not the only sound of 1977. Take a look at the UK and US bestsellers for that year and you'll find hardly anything resembling a punk record. For the most part, the British Top 40 contained only a few punk records in the lower reaches of the charts. In the period of punk's supposed dominance, between 1976 and 1978, there were no UK Number 1 punk singles. True, 'God Save The Queen', the signature punk 45, actually reached Number 1 during Silver Jubilee week in June 1977, but the chart compilers of the day, the British Market Research Bureau, allegedly fixed the statistics to let cosy Rod Stewart stay at the top with his suitably anodyne rendition of an old Isley Brothers' song. Punk was just part of the total market at the time, and not a very significant one at that. The biggest-selling singles of the 'punk era' in the UK came from Boney M, Olivia Newton-John and John Travolta (then, as now, part of the hipoisie), the Bee Gees and Paul McCartney's Wings. In the album charts, the multi-million-sellers scene was monopolized by Fleetwood Mac, Jeff Wayne's *War Of The Worlds*, Pink Floyd and the *Saturday Night Fever* soundtrack, and certainly not by the Damned or the Clash. Disco, MOR and the final flourishes of progressive rock, not punk, were, in strictly commercial terms, *the* sounds of the late 1970s.

Just as in the seventies and eighties the vast majority of the music press and record-label A&R departments were dominated by white, middle-class males into the Beatles, the Stones, the Who and Bob Dylan (white boys with guitars), so, in the nineties, many of those with their hands on the reins of power cut their teeth not on the Bee Gees but on the Buzzcocks (white boys with guitars). Whilst punk does not seem to have had a huge impact on the record-buying public as a whole, it does appear to have had a very significant effect on that tiny minority of people who actually went on to make a living out of pop music, be they musicians, record company executives, promoters, disc-jockeys or journalists. The punk era is one of the last bastions of rock authenticity.

What punk did do was to suggest that there was, possibly, a real alternative to corporate rock and mass-marketed schlock. It would be over a decade before, with the success of acid house, ambient house and techno in the late eighties, the margins would finally become mainstream, but punk was one of the first indicators that extreme music could also be commercial. Punk tapped into the burgeoning mid-70s pub-rock scene and improved upon it dramatically. Pub rock was full of people who knew how to play but had no idea what to play. Minimalist boogie, loud guitars, often expertly played in sweaty pub venues, were the order of the day but it seemed to offer no real new way forward. Pub rock was the antidote for all those in the audience who wanted music to make a fetish out of its ordinariness (the parallel with nineties Britpoppers Oasis is unavoidable). For those rock and pop fans who wanted their pop stars to be other, to be unapproachably weird and cool, pub rock, and its legacy, were a monumental nuisance. Like pub rock, punk itself was first and foremost a live music. But punk replaced pub rock's honest virtuosity with something altogether more interesting: a spirit of 'malpleasurability', a term coined by postmodernist writer Ron Moy to describe that state of blissful enjoyment in dreadful art. Some of the punks were so bad they were great, and some of the best lead-guitar solos in the history of pop date from the punk era and were played by musicians who contrived a solo by breaking all the rules. Punk replaced virtuosity and technique with an angular quirkiness.

The punk era now appears a mythical, golden period, a touchstone by which to measure the future. Almost every new American guitar band of the nineties has been dubbed 'punk', even if their music sounds more like Bad Company than the Buzzcocks. It's no surprise that, at the time of writing, the UK's biggest group, Oasis, have been able to maintain their credibility because of their impeccable mythological kudos: they are the post-modern combination of the Beatles' tunesmithery and the stroppiness of punk, and so deliberately reference two of rock's most sacred cows. The fact that their music (which for the most part is undeniably good) sounds as much like Slade, or even Mott The Hoople, as the Beatles is always overlooked because, in the Stalinist climate of rock criticism which still pervades much of the music press, Slade, despite their enormous popularity in the early seventies and their often excellent pop records, were never, for reasons which are seldom properly explained, deemed to be 'credible', and few would therefore dare to mention them in the same breath as Oasis.

'Credibility' is that almost indefinable quality which punk has, and disco hasn't, the Manic Street Preachers have, the Spice Girls don't. And credibility, at least in the pages of the music press, is something the Stranglers *never* had.

The popular construction of the Stranglers is that of a bunch of 'old' pub-rockers on a Doors trip who jumped on to the punk bandwagon. No credibility there, as 'young' and 'first' are always best. According to their popular profile, they made a series of nasty sexist records and abused the punk fraternity in the media, before 'blanding out' in the eighties and in the nineties fading out into something approximating a cabaret Stranglers tribute band.

The dilemma for all the Stranglers' detractors, however, is that the record-buying and gig-attending public supported the group through their wallets to a degree the Clash would have given their eye-teeth for. In 1977 the Stranglers sold more records than all the other punk bands put together, and went on to become one of the leading chart acts of their day. They were well-liked by the public but, along with those other big-selling artists of the punk period mentioned earlier, they've subsequently been largely unnoticed and unaccounted for.

However, listening to it again today, it is clear that their back catalogue has a depth unmatched by that of any other punk-era band. Regardless of the Stranglers' media image, which was a product of tabloid sensationalism, trendy journalism, brilliant packaging by PR people and gross (though often witty) self-publicity on the part of an outrageously manipulative and mischievous band, it's the music which, in the end, carries the day. The Stranglers could be fun and disposable ('Go Buddy Go'); gorgeously melodic ('Golden Brown'); sing-a-long ('Always The Sun'); topical and politically sussed ('Nuclear Device (Wizard of Aus)'); barbed ('Duchess'); sinister ('Waltz In Black'); thunderously rousing ('Hanging Around'); disco ('Thrown Away'); reggae ('Nice And Sleazy'); ornate and ambitious ('Down In The Sewer'); breezy ('Nice In Nice'); parodic ('Don't Bring Harry'); anthemic ('Heaven Or Hell'); and heart-rending ('Let Me Down Easy'). They had hits with three cover-versions, which first matched, and then improved on, the original ('Walk On By', 'All Day And All Of The Night' and '96 Tears'). They recorded some of the most impressive instrumentals of their era ('Longships', 'Waltz In Black', 'Turn The Centuries Turn', 'Love 30', 'Yellowcake UF6'). And in concert, they have a power and presence which few can match.

Another reason why the group were a curio in the seventies and early eighties was that their themes were both international (global and European political and social themes recur), as well as universal (love, death, race, religion and the paranormal) and parochial. There's also a richly singular eccentricity running through their music which marks them out as one of the missing links between Bowie and Ferry in the early seventies and the Smiths in the early eighties. Their best records are full of a strange quirkiness and eccentric wit, and embody that dark, naughty underbelly of urban/suburban tension and violence which can now be found on those bizarre instrumentals by Britpoppers Blur and in the *mise en scène* of Pulp's bedsit dramas.

Most significantly of all, despite having a punk in the guise of JJ Burnel, and being bracketed along with the punk bands, the Stranglers themselves weren't really punk at all. Their music didn't actually fit in anywhere terribly comfortably. They were both forerunners of punk and separate from it. They were the link between pub-rock and punk rock. Punk gave them their big break, but the impetus behind the band was not punk in origin. They were up and running over a year before the first punk bands were formed, and they played in what were later to become punk venues a year before the punk bands did, helping to create a network of viable venues for them later in the decade. Musically they were different too. As Hugh Cornwell comments: 'We weren't competent enough to be Brinsley Schwarz and we weren't bad enough technically to be punk, so we were sort of awkwardly placed.'

On top of all that, they didn't really look punk either, and their credentials weren't exactly helped by the fact that by the time they broke big in 1977 their members included an ex-research biochemist in his late twenties, an ex-French teacher and economic history graduate in his mid-twenties, a prog-rock virtuoso in his late twenties, and a soon-to-be forty-year-old businessman and inventor.

The Stranglers were also somewhat different from the punks in that, rather than hiding behind the chimera of punk's alleged ideology of 'direct action' and glamour of violence, the band, especially bassist JJ, were extremely violent *in actuality*. As a result, their career was undoubtedly the most controversial of any of their contemporaries. *No Mercy* tells the tale of violence, drugs, comatose journalists, Russian roulette with crazed Hell's Angels, black magic, ufology, imprisonment, further imprisonment, chart-riggings, kidnappings, record label fuck-ups and fall-outs, interpersonal bust-ups and punch-ups and, in amidst it all, some of the best music of the time. There was little need to embroider stories of what the band got up to. That was the way they lived their lives, positively courting controversy in any way possible. Their media-manipulation skills make Malcolm McLaren's look reasonably genteel. Wind-up merchants *extraordinaire*, their career, certainly up until the mid-eighties, when they began to lose direction and focus, was one long media runaround. And all four members of the original line-up were, to a greater or lesser degree, difficult, uncompromising and wilful individuals given to outrageous tantrums and bolshy behaviour of John McEnroe-like proportions. All this made them one of the most consistently talked about (and feared) bands of their day. But it also drew attention away from their music, and has meant that a whole generation of journalists cannot as a result even pretend to take them seriously as musicians or people. Their career has been made remarkable by the extent to which the Stranglers flouted legal and moral codes and, for the most part, got away with it all.

Both the Clash and the Sex Pistols have had their apologists, and rightly so, as their contribution was crucial. But the Stranglers were undoubtedly one of the best bands to emerge in Britain in the 1970s, and were perhaps the most talented of their day. *No Mercy* is not another punk book. It follows the band into the late nineties. It is the story of a great, but flawed, band which never quite made it in the way they perhaps should have done. But they have lasted well beyond their notional sell-by date and remain, at the time of writing, the only major commercially successful band from the punk era still touring worldwide and making records. They are the third part of that great British trio of new-wave bands (the other two members of which are the Clash and the Sex Pistols) which transcended the mundane and banal nature of much of punk and made records which we still play and talk about today. *No Mercy* tells you why.

PART ONE

Infamy (1974–1978)

1: THE ICE-CREAM
MEN COMETH

JJ Burnel: Three of us went to direct-grant grammar schools. Jet didn't, but the Education Act hadn't been invented then.
NME: Exactly how old is Jet?
JJ: Have you read Stephen Hawking's *A Brief History Of Time*? I think it's nearer four digits than three.

Author: So you're the progenitor of the band then, Jet?
Jet Black: Yeah, yeah, I'm the fucker!

The Stranglers' drummer and co-founder, Jet Black, is the self-styled 'oldest man in British rock'. Now that Bill Wyman has retired from the Rolling Stones, Jet reckons that, at 59 years of age, he is the oldest rocker still active in the business, constantly gigging, writing and recording music. True, there are older show-singers and cabaret acts still treading the boards, older jazz and country musicians on the circuit and the odd American rocker still cutting the mustard, such as the maverick guitarist Dick Dale, but, at almost 60, Jet is a unique commodity in British pop.

Like all the best pop artists, the Stranglers have surrounded themselves with myth, and it's been part of their appeal for almost a quarter of a century. In the youth-obsessed pop world, Jet, who was already close to 40 when the group made their initial impact on the charts in 1977, famously lied about his age, often knocking a good ten years off the true figure. But the downscaling of the true enormity of his real age was done, so Jet adamantly states, for professional reasons rather than personal vanity:

> I knew that historically, especially in England, it was almost unheard of for people at the age of 35 to emerge in a new pop group. I knew that it perhaps wasn't helpful to tell people I was 35,

36, 37 and I used to knock ten years off and I seemed to have got away with it most of the time but I did it for commercial reasons. It was nothing to do with vanity, it just made good business sense to appear to be younger. The band knew I was an old man. Once you've been around for this long it's pretty remarkable and people come to see you just for the mere fact that you're still there!

A secretive, slightly eccentric man, and a believer in the maintenance of a certain personal mystique, Jet also spun the media a series of yarns about his name, variously claiming his real name was Jethro Whitethorne and Jethro Black. In September 1996 Jet explained to me how he had re-invented himself well over two decades earlier:

My father was an Irishman and I feel a bit Irish, and when I was in Dublin on one occasion I was looking into some Irish literature about the Gaelic language and I discovered that 'Duffy' in Gaelic or Celtic, or whatever it is, means, or is derived from, the word 'black'. So I've always been 'Black'. I was born Brian Duffy and I used Whitethorne for a while and thought it was silly. I hated the name 'Duffy'. It emanates from my basic insecurity as a child, I suppose. 'Duffer' and 'dud' were words which used to torment me at school. In the early 1970s, when I started meeting people in the music sphere, I started saying I was called Jet Black, and eventually the amount of people who knew me as Brian Duffy declined into oblivion. Now nobody refers to me as Brian Duffy and I'm pretty angry with them if ever they do. Your name is what you say it is. I've tried to retain a bit of mystery I must say, but now you've blown the gaff, you bastard!

So Jet was born plain Brian John Duffy on 26 August 1938 in Ilford, Essex. Today he is a big man in more senses than one. Corpulent, but remarkably strong (his forearms and biceps are still wondrous to behold), Jet is thoughtful and considerate, interested and interesting. He is the band's historian, their letter-writer and organizer, the practical, capable one. He is also a perfectionist, never satisfied with his work, restless to move on and do different things. Jet is the person who holds the band together: without Jet, more so than any other of the original band members, there would be no Stranglers. He also has a hard-headed, no-nonsense approach to business, and what he some-times lacks in tact or in the ability to see shades of opinion he more than amply makes up for with his willingness to make tough decisions. The hiring and firing, the general course of the band's career, is ultimately bound up in the person of Jet Black. And for Jet, art and commerce are inextricably tied together as single entities. Whereas JJ Burnel has an endearingly naïve approach to money-making, ruled more by his passions than his purse, Jet, one suspects, is the band member to put cash before kudos every time. His fellow band members also point to his sporadic gruffness and vile temper but, for the most part, he is one of the friendliest and most down-to-earth people around. Today, Jet is something of a rock colossus, but, as a child, everything was very different:

I hardly ever went to school. I was a chronic asthmatic as a child and whenever I managed to go to school I was so far behind everybody that I didn't know what the hell was going on and I was treated as a backward kid. It probably wouldn't be going too far to say that I was considered the dunce of the school. But the one thing that always puzzled everyone was that I won the school chess championship! School was a living hell until the 18 months I spent in a school on the Kent coast in Broadstairs which was called, to my eternal embarrassment, 'The Holy Cross Convent School For Delicate Boys'! They were the happiest 18 months of my school life and my asthma almost vanished. It wasn't until my early thirties that I realized that my asthma might have been a nervous reaction to my domestic environment. I was the son of a schoolmaster who was an Irish immigrant who had come here completely uneducated. He studied at night school and qualified and became a teacher and was very proud of that all his life. He was a Catholic, and he married a Catholic, but he had some psychological problem. I don't know quite what it was, but he hated his children and he seemed to hate his lot in life. We were all thrown out of the house (the three of us) when in our teens and had to fend for ourselves. However, by the time we were middle-aged, it was as though nothing unpleasant had ever happened and he died a changed man.

Anyway, I left school with no qualifications, and I think it was probably true to say that I was illiterate. Towards the end of my school years I got this real interest in music. First of all I played the clarinet, piano, and violin. I learnt the violin when I was at school in Kent, and in no time at all I was the best in the school. But there was no enthusiasm or encouragement back home. When I got home from school and put the radio on to hear the music of the day, my Dad used to tell me to 'turn that row off!'.

The 'row', of course, was the music which would soon become
known as rock 'n' roll. It was Jet's generation, rather than those
born in the post-war 'baby-boom' (the people whom popular
myth has portrayed as being at the vanguard of rock 'n' roll when
in fact they would have been still in short pants), who were the
first to consume then act upon this new music. Jet remembers:

> I used to listen to pop music as it was in those days (when I could)
> and it was absolute drivel. The early days of rock 'n' roll, however,
> were immensely exciting, and I remember Elvis coming on to the
> scene and everyone going apeshit. Before then jazz was all there
> was. Pop music was regarded by most people as a joke – 'How
> Much Is That Doggy In The Window?' and all that nonsense. Jazz
> was the serious musician's music but it wasn't really appreciated
> by the masses.

Ever the autodidact, Jet soon gravitated from clarinet, violin
and piano to the drums. His first drum kit – 'some 1920s rubbish'
– he bought 'for about a quid'. Towards the end of his school
career, Jet was playing in an amateur swing orchestra at school,
and then briefly 'graduated' to the proto-punk musical style of
skiffle, popularized by the homespun sound of the likes of Lonnie
Donegan. After leaving school, Jet's fascination with the drums
intensified, and it was at this early stage, mindful of his inter-
rupted schooling and lack of any formal qualifications, that he
decided that he wanted to become a professional musician, whilst
simultaneously serving an apprenticeship as a joiner and cabinet-
maker: 'But then I looked around me and I realized that you had
to be damned good to make a living playing the drums because in
those days the situation wasn't the way it is today. Today, if you
create an image, and a different sound, you've got a career.
Maybe a short one, but you've got a career. In those days, you
had to be the best *technical* performer to get the job.'

Apart from the skiffle boom, which democratized music-mak-
ing to an extent and was encouraged by the establishment as a
'safer' form of musical expression after the media moral panic
over the evils of the Devil's music, rock 'n' roll', public performance still demanded technique, virtuosity and all-round proficiency. Likewise, throughout the sixties and early seventies,
virtuosity was king and the guitar hero's extended freak-out

and the drummer's five-minute tub-thumping solo 'extravaganza' became the currency of the rock spectacle. It was not until punk that competent, enthusiastic non-virtuosos like Jet could really make an impact on the scene. But, on a small-scale local level, Jet soon found himself amply employable as a gigging session musician. During the period of his seven-year apprenticeship as a joiner, most nights of the week he was playing a gig in a pub and, by the end of those seven years, he had learned a lot about life, music and showmanship. In fact, one of his first public appearances, at the age of 16, was a night to remember for this pubescent purveyor of the paradiddle:

> I got this gig in the Isle Of Dogs at a pub called 'The Pride Of The Isle', a stone's throw from today's Canary Wharf. It was packed to the rafters with these dockers. We played our cabaret thing, which consisted of standards and at a certain time in the evening I had to do this drum roll and then this fan dancer came on. I didn't know what a fan dancer was, but I soon learnt. It's when a naked lady comes on with these enormous ostrich feathers which always covered the vital parts. It's a tease, and when she moved around of course, they always covered the naughty bits. But I was behind her and I saw it all! And I thought to myself, this is quite a good way of making a living! Just before the end of the evening, the police raided the joint and threw everyone out, and I thought, this is living a little bit close to the margin, this is quite exciting. The pub was demolished a few years later.

Jet is in fact so old that he has played drums for Julie Andrews' mother! He lived in Walton-on-Thames in Surrey for a time in the 1960s and Julie's mother, Barbara Andrews, was a not very far away neighbour. The two often used to meet up for a social down the local boozer. Barbara lived in a rambling great mansion and used to throw parties three or four times a week, and Jet would play drums during the many impromptu musical evenings. In her day, Barbara was a talented pianist and performed in cabaret with her husband. Jet worked out that, unbeknownst to one another, they had actually played on the same bill some time during the 1950s. Jet reminisces:

> I got to know Barbara very well, and after becoming aware of Ted and Barbara's cabaret act I recalled an occasion when I had been

hired as a semi-pro drummer to do a night at some club or other's annual bash. Their act was so distinctive that it had stuck in my mind until one day Barbara was playing something on the piano that rang a bell with me.

We were great friends and I knew her right up to when the band started and I brought her along to see the band rehearsing and she was well impressed! But she was getting a bit frail and she moved to Los Angeles to live close to her daughter. She died, probably in the late 1980s, and it was the end of a lovely friendship, but I've never met Julie. I'm sure Julie has heard of me.

Jet became a part-time journeyman musician, learning the ropes as he went along. He also learnt the art of showmanship:

I remember one particular occasion, in the late 1950s, playing at a club in Soho. I'd had a phone call saying, 'We're a German band and we desperately need a drummer, can you come?' When I got there it was this Bavarian oompah band and they pulled out this costume and they said, 'You've got to wear this.' It was lederhosen and I thought, fuck, do people really walk around wearing this stuff! Anyway, I did this gig with them and they were talking about going back to Germany as conquering heroes and how they were going to make the big time and I thought, you've got to be joking playing all this crap music. This must have been in the late 1950s. Anyway, it was a valuable experience because it taught me what it feels like to feel an absolute prat up on stage in front of people. By the time we formed the Stranglers I had this wealth of experience which the others hadn't had.

But Jet, now married for the first time ('some time in the 1960s, I try to forget'), never made it professionally as a drummer. By the mid-1960s, he had set up his own business, or rather businesses. Apart from music, his abiding passions have always been cookery and booze. After the Conservative Chancellor of the day, Reginald Maudling, introduced legislation to abolish excise duty on domestic brewing, Jet started to think about ways of making money which nobody else had. He was one of the first people in Britain to start up a domestic brewing equipment company, the Wine and Beer-Making Centre in Guildford. First Jet ran a retail domestic equipment shop and, after that business grew, he moved operations to a huge Victorian off-licence owned by the Courage brewery, where he established a successful wholesale company. Already showing the eccentric's propensity for inventions and novel schemes, he marketed a patented domestic brewing equipment sterilizer, AC200, thus providing a curative for all those interesting infections such as the delightfully evocative 'Ropes Of Sulphur' which still charm amateur home-brewers to this day.

It was around about this time that Jet also secured his impeccable nutty credentials by becoming the first professional rock musician with a background in ice-cream. Jet Black is rock's 'Mr Whippy', a man who, by the early 1970s, had a flotilla of ice-cream vans at his disposal. So, by the early seventies, Jet had three businesses on the go, and an off-licence full of ice-cream. But he also had major marital problems. His second wife, Helena, had just left him, although they would be re-united, sporadically, over the next couple of years. During one of her early absences Jet decided to take some bold, direct action. The ice-cream man himself takes up the story:

> Up until that point I'd been expending all this energy for *us*, me and the missus. I suddenly thought, 'well, hang on a minute'. I sat down in the off-licence after it had closed. I was having a drink (and listening to some current music on the radio), and I thought, 'the rules have changed now because I'm sort of single again, and whatever happened to my ambition to be a drummer?' So I spent a few days thinking about it, and then I said, 'I'm going to burn my bridges and make the commitment.' I was about 33 or 34 by this stage. So I went out the next day and bought a new drum kit and I spent a couple of weeks doing one of the rooms up on the top floor of the off-licence, and turning it into a studio. I said to the guy who was managing the business for me that I was putting him in charge. He said, 'Well, what are you gonna do?' and I said, 'I'm gonna go upstairs and bang my drums.' He said, 'Do what! Have you been drinking or something?' And I said, 'Yes!'

The music of the Beatles and the Stones – R'n'B/pop – seemed easier to play along with than the jazz music of the fifties, when Jet had been frustrated in his attempts to break into the big time. Soon Jet started getting local gigs in pubs again, and then a few nights in a holiday village on the south coast playing 'classics' like 'Hi-Ho Silver Lining'. Jet Black:

Well, I thought, I'm at least as good as these people and some of
these were pros. Then I suddenly reached the point when I said to
myself, 'Now I've got to form a band of my own', because I knew I
didn't want to work for someone else, and that was about late
1972. I advertised in *Melody Maker*, and I got phone calls from all
over the place. I conducted auditions in the off-licence. But they
were all Rod Stewart look-alikes and they were all dressed the
same. I was searching to find someone with ability and ideas who
wanted to try something different. But all of them wanted a
guaranteed gig, money in their hand, and they wouldn't take
any risks. Eventually, I was still gigging around doing the odd
show just to keep my hand in when, one day, I was flicking
through the *Melody Maker* and saw an advert, 'drummer wanted
urgently'. I phoned the number, and it was a London number, and
it was Hugh Cornwell, and he said, 'Oh yeah, we've got this band
and our drummer's split. Can you come down and help us out?
We're rehearsing tonight in Camden.'

The band was Wanderlust, and their guitarist was none other
than a 24-year-old dropped-out research biochemist named
Hugh Cornwell.

Whilst it is true that Jet Black provided the thrust to form a band,
and the hard-headed business acumen to back this up, Hugh
Cornwell provided the real maverick musical creativity which Jet
needed. Already in his mid-twenties, Cornwell was, as Jet
remembers, an ambitious, enthusiastic and driven young man,
hilariously funny and full of ideas:

> All of a sudden I could feel a buzz around me, there was something
> that was making me excited and I couldn't put my finger on it at
> the time. But later I realized it was Hugh's influence, because as I
> got to know the band, I realized whose input was what. It was
> Hugh's songwriting ability and his quirky guitar work which stood
> out. Everything he did was so unconventional. If he'd applied for a
> job as a guitarist he wouldn't have got it. And that was what I was
> looking for. I didn't want to do what everyone else was doing; I
> wanted something different and I'd found it.

Hugh Alan Cornwell was born in London on 28 August 1949
and lived around the Parliament Hill Fields area until he left home.
His father was a draughtsman, his mother a full-time housewife.

The Cornwell family were comfortable with the rurality of Hampstead Heath, the largest area of green in London. Hugh had all the benefits of the countryside without the disadvantages of being cut off from the pleasures of city life. In later life he would split his time between the urban bustle of London with its cinemas, clubs, and art galleries, and the quiet countryside of the Bath area, where he set up home during his Stranglers days. This urban/rural tension is played out in his music, his wistful, pastoral ballads set against the highly-charged crackle of urban *angst*.

Hugh went to Burghley Road Primary School, passed the eleven-plus, and moved on to William Ellis School, a direct-grant grammar school. In the year he took his A levels, well over 90 out of the 100 pupils, including Hugh, won university places. Hugh became interested in film while in the sixth form: 'I suddenly discovered that films weren't just James Bond and *The Magnificent Seven*. There were other things going on too. I saw all of René Clair's work and Buñuel and Cocteau, and I was seeing all these at 16 and my mind was getting boggled.'

Unlike Jet's home background, there was plenty of music in the Cornwell household. Hugh's eldest brother was into jazz, his second-eldest brother was a fan of the progressive rock of Cream and Jimi Hendrix, and his father listened to classical music: 'Throughout the years I was at school I was getting bombarded by music all the time and I got a better musical education than if I'd studied the history of music at a university. My eldest brother had this amazing blues collection. I was listening to Art Blakey along with the Cannonball Adderley Quintet and Mose Allison when I was fifteen.'

Hugh came from an archetypal lower-middle-class background, the same social set which provided the motor for so much of the best post-Beatles music. These were the disaffected, arty rebels who reacted strongly against the ennui of suburban life: 'I used to sneak down to the Marquee when I was 15 and watch the Yardbirds, the Who and the Spencer Davis Group. Two or three times a week I used to go down to the Marquee. No one would bother you, it was cool.'

Hugh started playing on his brother's guitar and soon became reasonably proficient. At school he formed a group, Emile & The Detectives, later given the almost punky name, the Germs. The band included the highly-regarded singer-songwriter Richard

Thompson, soon to be of Fairport Convention, who taught Hugh how to play bass guitar. The highlight of the band's career was a support slot for Helen Shapiro in the mid-1960s.

Hugh was a bright, resourceful pupil, particularly talented at botany and art. He stayed on at school for an extra year after his A levels, but failed the Cambridge entrance exam. He then had nine months to kill before university, which he filled in by working in the research hematology department at St Bartholemew's hospital. After a few months he was offered the opportunity to work in Sweden as a lab assistant, where he remained until it was time for the 'joys' of hall life at Bristol University. Initially he read Microbiology, but after a term switched to Biochemistry (he apparently couldn't stand the smell of the agar plates!). As an undergraduate Hugh reviewed plays and exhibitions for the student mags, played music, got involved in acting and fringe comedy, and even developed an interest in brass-rubbings, selling his work for '£50 a rub'. Formal study went on the back-burner, and as a result the talented, though undisciplined, undergraduate could only manage a disappointing third-class honours degree.

But Hugh thoroughly enjoyed his time in Bristol, then in some respects the party capital of the south-west. It was at this time that he met cook and restaurateur Keith Floyd, later to become the famous toff-punk cook, broadcaster and writer, and the two struck up an immediate rapport. Hugh would play guitar to late-night revellers in one of Keith's chain of Bristol eateries and be fed and watered till dawn for his pains.

Hugh then took up an offer to study for a PhD over in Lund in the southernmost part of Sweden. It was at this stage that he formed his first semi-professional band, Johnny Sox, with the talented guitarist Hans Wärmling, bass player Jan Knutsson and two American draft-dodgers: a drummer called Mike, originally from Chicago, and Gyrth Godwin, 'a poet', soon to become the band's chief lyricist and singer. Johnny Sox quickly built up a repertoire of over one hundred two- or three-minute rock songs which they played in clubs and discos on the local circuit around 1973. One of their songs, 'Country Chaser', would be one of the Stranglers' first live numbers, and was demoed at TW studios in London with Alan Winstanley.

Whilst he was in Sweden Hugh got caught up, willingly, if only peripherally, in a very heavy scene indeed. He had befriended a guy he met in the student union called Axl C, who was half-Swedish, half-Hawaiian. Axl was another draft-dodger, and also something of a man of mystery who used to disappear for periods without warning. Soon Hugh and the band found out what he was getting up to. Hugh explains:

> Earlier that day there had been an armed robbery at a post office and they were looking for this guy and it was this guy who had jammed with us. I got out to my house and here he is in the kitchen with a can of cat food saying, 'Hugh man, where's your fucking tin opener? You never feed your cats, they're starving.' He's wanted by the police and he's worried about feeding the cats! So this guy was hiding out at my house. I didn't know what to do, I liked him and he hadn't shot anybody. And he said, 'Sorry Hugh, do you mind if I just stay overnight, I promise I'll be gone in the morning; I've got all my transport arranged for tomorrow.' He was a very charming man so I said reluctantly, 'Oh all right then, all right.' So then he said, 'Let's have a party!' I'm fresh from the laboratory and I've got to go in at 8 a.m. in the morning. And he said, 'Well I've got tons of money!' He'd probably got twenty or thirty grand from this post office. So they went out and got loads of booze and loads of drugs. About one in the morning I went to my room but I couldn't get to sleep, so I ended up in the garden in a sleeping bag. About 6 a.m. he said, 'Thanks Hugh, we're off.'
>
> About two weeks later I get up in the morning and look in the garden and there's a soldier with a machine gun. I thought, it's a raid, so I put the dope I had in the bottom of a bag of coffee and went down and opened the door. It was the head of Lund police. Then twenty of these guys came in like the SAS with machine guns and they were looking for Axl. And they asked, 'When did you last see Axl C?' and we said, 'Months ago'. And it all held water. Basically they'd missed him by about two weeks and they left. They never found him, the guy had disappeared touring round Europe. Then we got a weighty envelope through the post one day and it was from him. Inside were some car keys and a note saying 'Thanks very much for looking after me that night. Please accept this as a gift to help the band. If you go to Copenhagen airport you will find in the car park a blue Ford Transit van and I'm giving you this as a present.'

This wasn't the last Hugh and the band saw of Axl C either. About a year later, the central bank in Lund was robbed and an elderly customer was shot in the leg and seriously injured. It was Axl again, and after the heist he appeared at Gyrth's house requesting Hugh and Jan's company for a jam. Reluctantly again, Hugh went round:

> I'd had a few drinks and I said, 'Look, Axl, you're a nice guy and all that, but there's one thing I don't approve of. Why did you shoot that guy?' He said, 'I had to, Hugh, he got in the way. I told everyone not to take part in this and this guy came for me and I had to shoot him.' And I was really pissed off. But I was really curious about this guy and I'm interested in ideas and different viewpoints, so my view is that you don't judge people because you want to find out. Then we get very drunk and he says, 'Do you want to see the money?' So he gets out tons of this stuff. Then he said, 'I wanna get some publicity!'

Hugh had the perfect scheme. He knew a very ambitious journalist in Malmö, and arranged for him to interview Axl C, for the scoop of the year. 'Axl then went off on one of his prolonged holidays and he left us all these new notes which he had which we used to buy petrol at the late-night automatic petrol pump. He contributed a lot to Johnny Sox this guy, one way and another.'

Axl was later wrongly suspected by the police of another bank robbery in Stockholm. He was later arrested after he had, in an effort to embarrass the police, with amazing cheek called them to say that he was in Hawaii, not Sweden.

These episodes in Sweden are important in that they reveal much about Hugh Cornwell's character. Hugh had harboured a criminal, had probably received stolen goods in the guise of a van, had then had a jam session with someone who had just shot an innocent member of the public and had used stolen money to put petrol in the tank. But, although Hugh certainly did not condone the use of violence, the fact that Axl C was a violent criminal was secondary to Hugh's passion for ideas and excitement. Part of Hugh's personality relished Axl's sense of daring, and viewed the brush with the law as adventurous and thrilling. He liked Axl and considered him a man full of ideas. Oscar Wilde wrote, 'Education is an admirable thing. But it is well to remember from time to time that nothing worth knowing can be taught', and this dictum applied to Hugh's world-view too. He lived for inspiration through experience, and Axl C personified both intellect and danger. Axl's personality and his criminality aligned him, in Hugh's mind at least, with forces for change: 'Most people who you find interesting in your life have done dodgy things in the past. People who obey rules tend not to have any ideas. Unfortunately if you're going to have a civilized society, you've got to have guidelines, and the people who follow guidelines don't seem to have any ideas. Because ideas are dangerous.'

Hugh's research was not progressing well at the university and after being called in by the professor for crisis talks he decided to leave academia once and for all and to give professional music his best shot, leaving 'with a guitar in one hand, and a bag of clothes in the other. It was very romantic.' The band finally left Sweden for London at the end of 1973, having realized that, in terms of the international music scene, Sweden was hardly the epicentre of the world.

During a period of about a year Johnny Sox, or Wanderlust as they were now called, would eventually metamorphose into the Stranglers. Hans Wärmling decided to stay in Sweden after falling out with the emotional Gyrth. The band played a number of pub and club gigs and attracted the attention of the manager of the pub-rock group the Winkies, Paul Kennerley, but the erratic and anti-social behaviour of the lead singer, including attacking pub landlords, was not endearing the band to any future employer. In 1974 the moratorium on draft dodgers was lifted by the US government, and Mike the drummer returned to the States with his family. His replacement was, of course, Jet Black.

It was obvious, at least to Jet, that the band was never likely to succeed in its present line-up. Jet made it plain to Wanderlust that, whilst he admired their spirit, they were an under-rehearsed and unprofessional unit. He invited them to stay and rehearse in Guildford, upstairs at the off-licence. The initial response was one of reluctance: the capital was where the gigs, the excitement and the opportunities lay, and the band were loathe to up-root to the 'sticks', 26 miles south-west of London. But after they heard that Jet ran an off-licence there, they soon decided that a move might not be such a bad thing after all. So, by spring 1974 the group had decamped to Jet's place to booze their way through his assets.

After a brief period it became obvious to Jet that Hugh was the only enthusiastic and dedicated one amongst their number, and soon enough it would be just the two of them writing and rehearsing above the off-licence, with Jet as beneficent provider of accommodation and food to the near-penniless beatnik Cornwell. Jet gave Johnny Sox an ultimatum – put in a professional commitment or quit. He wasn't prepared to finance a holiday in Guildford any longer. Jet's dream of a whole band of mavericks had yet to be fulfilled. Hugh had more obvious musical talent than Jet, and was brimming over with concepts and ideas, but they needed to be sure that fellow recruits would be kindred spirits, could bounce off Hugh's intelligence with complementary ideas and could translate these ideas into solid musical forms.

It was at this time that nutty singer Gyrth, who had been hitching back from London along the A3, was given a lift by a good-looking man in his early 20s called John Burnel, then working as a deliverer for a local firm, Brown Brothers. Gyrth invited him back for a drink at the off-licence, and this karate-obsessed biker interested Hugh. He was also a gifted classical guitarist.

John was born Jean Jacques Burnel on 21 February 1952 in Notting Hill, London. His Norman parents were restaurateurs who had been living in the London area for a number of years. Coincidentally, in his business days, Jet had actually dined *chez* Burnel in Godalming in Surrey, and remembers that the meal was excellent (but pricey!). At school the young JJ, at pains not to be different from his classmates, anglicized his Christian name to John (and for a while in the mid-70s spelt his name 'Jon') in order to cover up his Frenchness. It was only when his future manager Dai Davies noticed on his passport that his real name was in fact Jean Jacques that he persuaded him to revert to his more alluring and more marketable original name. He was thus the second member of the band to adopt, if only to a degree, a moniker as a defence mechanism, thus hinting at a basic psychological insecurity. Although not exactly bullied at school, JJ was considered different and was often set upon by his peers: 'There weren't any coloured kids at school and I was the nearest thing. I was the only child with shorts on, which marked me out, and my mother used to kiss me goodbye as well.

English mums didn't kiss their children in those days. I do remember being beaten up and kicked on a cinder track. My dad put a steak on my face out of the fridge at the restaurant. I must have been 10 or 11.'

This incident, according to JJ's best mate, Brian Crook, who later became the Stranglers' second manager, had a marked effect on JJ. Crook remembers the young JJ had shaven, spiky hair and was immediately known as 'puncho' at school because he wanted to fight everyone! JJ was mothered to bits and that, combined with the obvious discomfort JJ felt about his French parentage, goes some way to accounting for his often explosively temperamental personality.

JJ's Dad was a remarkable man. A short, stocky, extremely tough individual, he was a real gentleman. Apart from being an exquisite cook, in his time he had also been a talented sculptor. In the 1930s he worked as a chef on the French shipping line from Le Havre down to Buenos Aires. During the war he was arrested by the Gestapo in Moulin for carrying messages for Jews. Like JJ's mother, English was his Dad's main language. JJ remembers him with great fondness: 'He sold his motorbike to give me my first guitar when I was 12. It's still the instrument I write on. He was a good Dad.'

According to Brian Crook, the Burnel family home was very des res. One particular bath-time incident sticks out: 'They had a lovely house with an *en suite* bathroom. One day JJ was lying in the bath and he shouted out to his mother to come and look because he'd got his first erection. He had to show his mother!'

As a teenager, JJ lived in Godalming, attending a local all-boys' school, the Royal Grammar School, Guildford. Charterhouse public school was nearby, the *alma mater* of Peter Gabriel, Tony Banks, Anthony Phillips and Mike Rutherford, who would in the late 1960s form the nucleus of the supergroup Genesis. JJ was also a talented musician and learnt classical guitar, reaching Grade 6. His interest in the contemporary music scene was already in evidence in his early teens. He used to frequent the Gin Mill club run in a local pub in Godalming called The Angel, where at the age of 14 and 15 he would groove to Ainsley Dunbar's Retaliation, Free, and Peter Green's Fleetwood Mac. Like Hugh, JJ was hooked on the blues as a teenager, particularly the newer wave of British R'n'B revivalists.

Before he left school to read for a degree in Economic and
Social History at Bradford University and Huddersfield Polytech-
nic, JJ had also developed an interest, soon to become an
infatuation, in motorcycles: 'At the age of 17 I had already fallen
in love with motorcycles. I hardly had any mates at school and I
loved the idea of belonging to a gang. I wanted to have a group of
people whom I could identify with. I worked my balls off and I got
a Harley-Davidson and I joined the Kingston-on-Thames Hell's
Angels. I left after a couple of years, though. Beating up (or being
beaten up by) skinheads wasn't my idea of cool.'

Whilst at school JJ ran a magazine called 'The Gubernator'
(Latin for 'helmsman') and was dubbed a trouble-maker by the
school authorities. He was also a member of the rather grandilo-
quently titled British League Of Youth, a debating society, not a
far-right group. Contrary to subsequent reports, JJ was not
expelled from the grammar school, as it was anxious to avoid
bad publicity. JJ claims that, imbued with the anti-establishment
campus angst of 1968, the 'Gubernator' was little more than silly
situationist rants about school life and conformity. But in 1977
he made what at best could be called an extremely injudicious
remark in the *NME* to Tony Parsons: 'So because I was *different*,
because I was *French*, I couldn't make friends. I find it very hard to
make friends and I was always getting beaten up. So by the time I
was 17 I was a Nazi.'

Confronted with this twenty years on, and with Simon
Reynolds and Joy Press' section on the Stranglers from their
book *The Sex Revolts*, which based some of its arguments on this
NME original, JJ is bewildered and repentant: 'I don't remember
saying that to Tony Parsons at all, but that's no excuse. You're
asking me to justify something I don't remember saying. Even
worse, if I had said it, I'd still have no justification for saying it
apart from provocation, which, as we all know, was/is one of my
fortes. However, in this case, it's just plain dumb. Sounds like to
me that 20 years ago I might have been trying to show that I had a
massive chip (sorry, French fry) on my shoulder.'

But Brian Crook recollects that JJ's pamphlets were actually of
an incendiary nature, and that his trouble-making used to run to
epic proportions: 'Without a doubt he was responsible for putting
a lot of neo-Nazi propaganda together. I can tell you this with
certainty because he used to show me his diaries. I think he was

plotting all the time in that school. I know he raided the school weaponry department and at one stage held one or two people at gunpoint!'

JJ's teenage experiences set the emotional tone for the Stranglers during the band's first few years. JJ was an outsider, a loner who craved the feeling of belonging in society which he felt was his due. He was an alienated figure, placing his trust in the camaraderie of males within a fairly well-regulated pack structure. The Stranglers' famous mascot, the rat, is a metaphor for JJ's sense of isolation – the atomized individual moving along with the gang, the outsider as part of a society of outsiders. Even now, in his forties, JJ is an imposing figure both mentally and physically: personally charming, likeable, original, intelligent, informed and with a surprisingly self-deprecating sense of humour, he is also emotional, reckless and combative, always probing his opponent in any conversation for weakness, always playing games and testing the interlocutor until he susses him out. Talking to JJ is the verbal equivalent of a karate bout, with JJ always trying to make the first move, to turn a chat into a show of intellectual strength and skill. He's also pop's self-styled man-of-action. Other pop stars might brawl in a drunken stupor, tote guns or abuse their wives, but JJ is more discriminating with his shows of male strength. For him, physicality is a philosophy, an ideal and the best means of self-preservation: 'I've always believed in direct action. I've always believed that no one's going to get you out of the shit, or into the shit, other than yourself. Rather than pay the lackeys and the flunkies and security men to do it, I've always done it myself.'

During his university years his life revolved around women, drugs and the beloved motorbike. He failed to finish his course, and, according to Brian Crook, 'If he had stayed there any longer he would have killed himself – he spent his time tripping on LSD.' JJ was also becoming very sexually promiscuous: 'He was initially very naïve as regards women, but when he discovered it, he used to go for it big time. He was proud of sleeping with women who were twice his age, and he made a point of mother and daughter scenarios. But he was very intelligent and charming, and that's why he was successful.'

Brian Crook also remembers some far from sedate excursions with the young JJ:

We used to go on trips to Normandy, take a bit of LSD, then trip around on the boat. There was one occasion when we were in this little village in Normandy and JJ drove the bike right into the bar, parked it, went to a table and screamed 'Beer!' In the end we were chased out of there by a gendarme who held his machine gun up to him! When we got out of the bar we found ourselves surrounded by about eight Algerians who were acting really threateningly. JJ used to carry a chain down the frame of his bike. He pulled it out and ran down the road after them trying to chain them all. They ran off pretty quickly, needless to say.

When he met up with Jet and Hugh in early 1974, JJ was saving up to fund a trip to San Francisco, where he would work as a motorcycle mechanic before moving on by ferry to Yokohama, Japan. He already had a letter of introduction to a certain Mas. Oyama, and he hoped to win his black belt in the homeland of the martial arts. Hugh takes up the story: 'Suddenly Jan and Gyrth upped and left, rather like I left the Stranglers, and I went round to see Jon about 10 o'clock at night or something and was really pissed off. I didn't know what to do. He was the only person in Guildford I knew. We started talking and getting drunk and I said, "You can play the guitar, why don't you join the group?" I talked him into it. When I first met him he was a really nice bloke.'

JJ's first rehearsal with the group in April 1974 was notable only for the fact that he had attended a karate tournament that day and was sporting a heavily bandaged wrist after an ill-timed chop. Hugh sold JJ his old Fender Precision bass guitar, which he had bought in Sweden, for the princely sum of £35. Jet remembers the JJ of the time as being:

completely mad, but we all are, in different ways. JJ was completely irresponsible. I think I was the only one who had any sense of responsibility, because I had lots of responsibilities. One thing JJ didn't lack was enthusiasm, or ability. And from a performance point of view he was an asset because he was quite a good-looking young lad. We invited him round and he moved in. He knew the hardship he was going to have to suffer – that was spelled out to him. We used to spend the afternoons rehearsing and writing, and after about two or three months we had a whole string of really interesting songs.

Jet made the lads work for their board, and soon Hugh and JJ were manning the off-licence or out on the road selling choc-ices and 99s. (Hugh even wrote a song at the time called 'Ice Cream Salesman' – sadly it's gone unrecorded!) Hugh remembers Jet in the early days as still very much the businessman in his Bri-nylon shirts, tie and suits, and there was even a suggestion that Jet might simply become the band's manager. But, despite the obvious age gap between Jet and the rest of the band, his enthusiasm overcame any ageist concerns. Besides, technically Jet was an accomplished jazz drummer and could also keep time. Musically and financially he was indispensable. JJ remembers: 'Jet was something of a father figure to us. Hugh and I found this old 50s-style Ford Pop in his cellar and we got it going again. We drove down to a pub in the country and on the way home we ran out of petrol. So eventually we got hold of Jet and he came in his dressing-gown four or five miles down the road. He was really pissed-off with us and he was telling us off like he was our Dad! He's quite formidable when he's uptight.'

Single again, Jet devoted all his energies to the band. But there were yet more tensions. Hugh remembers that Jet and JJ appeared to be in a constant state of open warfare: 'JJ and Jet didn't get on well together at all. There was a lot of bitterness and a lot of rows. They got to tolerate each other.'

Temperamentally Jet and JJ had, and still have, very little in common, and, whilst they respect each other's talents, they give the appearance of being not particularly close. They are, in fact, the polar opposites in the band: JJ physically daunting, emotional, romantic, political, educated; Jet physically daunted, rational, pragmatic, apolitical, largely self-taught and a natural loner. JJ loved the pack mentality, Jet was a solitary man. That they ever got together in the same group, let alone remained together for almost a quarter of a century, is remarkable. But accident certainly played a central role in the formation of the Stranglers and it was this combination of completely different temperaments which gave the group its distinction and its drive.

The band soldiered on as a three-piece for some months, rehearsing in a local Scout hut. Jet gave expression to his newly-won bachelor status through a sort of sartorial melt-down. After daring Hugh to dye his hair (a dare which Hugh, probably wisely, chickened out of), he himself adopted platinum blond hair and drainpipe trousers – the grandad of punk to be sure. Jet also sold all but one of his fleet of ice-cream vans in order to fund the band's expenses. The one he kept became the band's battle-bus, clocking up 77,000 miles in under two years before it finally ground to a halt in early 1977. (Jet, incidentally, still has this now 'legendary' automobile.) At Hugh's suggestion, Hans Wärmling was invited to join the band after Wärmling had come over to England to make contact with his old mate, and, as a guitarist, keyboard player and talented writer, he was initially thought of as an asset. They were already writing together well, and their earliest repertoire included the now famous 'Go Buddy Go', which JJ had written (middle eight aside) around 1967, 'Strange Little Girl', with music by Wärmling and lyrics by Hugh, along with unrecorded songs such as 'Bouncing Man' (thought of by Jet as the first ever punk song), 'China Town' (a pleasing, cinematic Wärmling instrumental), 'I Know It', an old Johnny Sox number called 'Country Chaser', and 'Charlie Boy', written about the band's unofficial first manager, who according to the lyrics of the song used to like getting drunk and sitting in trees.

Hugh explains: 'There was a bloke called Charles Edwards who used to come off the train. He used to work in the City and he hated it. On his way home he used to come in and have a chat and a beer. He got interested in us, so he managed us for a while. But he couldn't really do very much. I wrote this song "Charlie Boy" because he used to get drunk and sit in trees.'

Listening to these earliest Wärmling-era songs now, one is struck by how doggedly slow they were. This was rock rebellion at walking pace, a mixture of the rock sounds of the early 70s – a bit of Free, a smattering of the Faces, a sliver of Beatles, a dusting of the Velvet Underground – all underpinned by Wärmling's deft and often haunting guitar-playing.

'Go Buddy Go' was a prime example of how adept the band were at the art of musical pastiche. The bass line was a steal from Jimi Hendrix's 'Hey Joe' (another pop song in the key of E), and the chords for the song's chorus were also identical to those in 'Hey Joe''s verses. The middle-eight by Hugh used exactly the same chord sequence as the Beatles' 'Nowhere Man'.

By the end of 1974 Jet and the lads had left the off-licence. The lease on the building was not only limited – thereby diminishing the business's value – but the entire property and adjoining buildings were due for demolition in the near future as part of the modernization of Guildford's town centre. In late 1974 the group moved at Jet's suggestion to a furnished house in the Surrey village of Chiddingfold, which would be their home for the next two years, first as tenants and then as squatters. Although initially flush from the sale of his business assets, Jet impressed on his three confrères the need to bring in some ale money. JJ and Hans worked as bouncer and dishwasher respectively in a local club, whilst Hugh signed on. In the meantime Jet set about the onerous task of finding a deal for the band, but without success. Over the next months the band, who still didn't have a fixed name, were rejected by Island, Courtney Music and Bell Records. Interestingly, Jet was obviously still mid-way through his personality change, and was still referring to himself as Brian Duffy in these formal correspondences. He didn't want to make it obvious that he was actually *in* the band.

These were hard times financially, but musically things were quickly coming together. The band gigged extensively in local pubs and clubs during the summer and autumn of 1974, but many of the performances were technically disastrous, as a combination of clapped-out equipment and lack of basic technique scuppered the shows. At this point they were calling themselves anything that sprung to mind (including the suitably daft proto-punk-sounding Oil And The Slicks!). On one particularly bad night an embarrassed JJ stormed back into the dressing-room and shouted 'Well, the stranglers have done it again!' and soon the name stuck. The foursome first went out as 'The Guildford Stranglers' (or occasionally as the Chiddingfold Chokers), and then simply as the Stranglers. The band name was registered by Jet on 11 September 1974. The Stranglers were born.

2: SOFT ROCK COMBO

MOR stalwart Tony Orlando is, by an amazingly silly quirk of fate, responsible for the addition of Dave Greenfield's 'massive swelling organ' to the band set-up. Unlike some rock artists who positively revel in baffling their audience with a set of largely new or obscure material, the Stranglers have generally given their audiences what they wanted. And back in 1974 it was deemed necessary, merely in order to get on the gig circuit, to play a mixture of original material and cover versions. In 1974 and 1975 the Stranglers performed such rock 'n' roll standards as 'Rock 'n' Roll Music', 'Fun Fun Fun', 'Jeannie, Jeannie, Jeannie', and 'I Saw Her Standing There' (with Hugh singing 'I couldn't dance with her mother – ooooh!'), as well as Dionne Warwick's 1964 classic 'Walk On By' and more recent songs such as Slade's 'Flame'. Jet 'who loves ya baby!' Black was also wont to take the mic and burst out into David Gates' 'If'. The song, a recent UK Number 1, had been reconstructed into an unintentionally hilarious narration, intoned in a deep Bronx jowly growl by Telly Savalas – TV's lollipop-sucking, follicly-challenged crime-buster, Kojak. And, showing no shame, another occasional 'favourite' to find its way into the set was the genuinely excruciating 1973 monster UK hit, 'Tie A Yellow Ribbon', recorded by Tony Orlando and Dawn. But the addition of this 'classic' to the band's repertoire put Wärmling into overload. He promptly 'got on the bus' to indeed 'forget about us'. Already disillusioned by the fact that the band were wont to drop covers into their set as sweeteners, Hans could take no more and, on the way to play at a high-prestige wedding gig, told the band that he couldn't go on one more second. 'So we told him to fuck off,' JJ recalls, 'and stopped the ice-cream van and he got out there and then.' Hugh remembers Wärmling, who tragically drowned in 1995, with respect:

Hans taught me a lot about writing. He was very talented, very enthusiastic, a great player. He wasn't scared of singing backing vocals. He had a great ear for commerciality. The reason he left was that he was fed up with playing other people's songs. He said he couldn't be bothered learning 'Tie A Yellow Ribbon' because it had too many chords! He had the dogmatic approach, and we had the pragmatic approach. We thought it was better to be playing some music rather than no music. When he left I was a bit pissed off because he left us in the lurch, so I didn't really keep in touch.

If the intricacies of Tony Orlando were the ostensible reason for Wärmling's exit, the deep-seated reason was that old chestnut of band politics. Wärmling simply didn't fit in, and the rest of the band had been looking for a way to manoeuvre him out. Wärmling's dogmatic approach to the non-playing of covers was the episode which enabled him to be isolated and eventually removed from the starting line-up. Jet remembers with some sadness that many years afterwards, Wärmling came backstage to meet the Stranglers, who had, by then, entered the big time, to admit that they had been right and that their more flexible, realistic approach had been justified.

Back in 1975 the Stranglers had no pretensions that what they were doing was art. They had no allegiance whatsoever to the burgeoning progressive rock scene, which was characterized by technical virtuosity, lofty sentiment and original material. The Stranglers, at least initially, were a rock 'n' roll band interested in action, energy and a bit of fun along the way. They were keen to learn their craft. If they had to look to Telly Savalas or Dawn for inspiration for popular material in order to get a gig, then so be it. In this they were little different from many other punk outfits such as the Sex Pistols, who cut their teeth live on old Monkees, Small Faces and Who songs, although the Stranglers were even more populist in their choice of material. Covers, however badly played, were almost guaranteed to get people up dancing, and once they were up strutting their stuff, a few new songs could then be slipped in along with the 'palliatives'.

Before Wärmling's departure the band had its first sniff of stardom, teaming up with Reg McLean, owner of the reggae label Safari. They recorded three songs with Alan Winstanley (later to work on some of their classic material) at T.W. Studios in Fulham. 'Wasted' had an almost Eurodisco Abba style, the ballad 'My Young Dreams' was eventually re-recorded and released by Jet and writer and Stranglers fan, Chris Twomey, in 1985 under the name 'A Marriage Of Convenience', and the third was the elegiacally beautiful 'Strange Little Girl', later to become a Top 10 UK single in 1982 in re-recorded form. 'My Young Dreams' became the first choice for single release. As well as paying for the recording of the single, McLean also promised to get the band gigs if they would hire out their PA. Hugh explains:

> John and I would take the PA out with the speakers and set it all up for three black singers in Acton Town Hall. And on one occasion we were in this place and we were the only white people in this club and we came back and wrote 'Peaches' that night. We had been listening to reggae music the whole night. Reggae was big at the time, with Burning Spear and Bob Marley. It was everywhere. When you hear something all the time you've got no choice. So 'Peaches' was our attempt at rap/reggae.

But it eventually became clear that Reg McClean and Safari were far from being a bona fide operation. Jet Black:

> Safari was technically a record company but it wasn't really. It was one little guy sitting in an office looking for an easy way to make a fast buck. He was signing up artists and doing nothing with them until he saw somebody else taking an interest and then hoping he could steam in and make some money. We were offered the chance to make these demos and after that he did nothing with them. Eventually we found a way of getting away from him and going with somebody else. As soon as we had a proper deal he got straight on the phone and wanted his money!

Hans' departure reduced the group to a 'power trio', who gigged on for several months. They started getting occasional work through a booking agency called Savage–Ayris Associates Ltd, run by Derek Savage and Doug Ayris, and began to set up something approximating a team of helpers and advisors. JJ's friend, Brian Crook, was drafted in as the band's part-time manager, whilst another drinking pal, Dick Douglas, who was a jeweller by trade, helped out as a roadie. It was all very amateurish, but, for the most part, loads of fun too. These were mates of the band who thought they had talent, not professionals doing a job. They worked with, not for, the band. Unfortunately,

Crook was having a very hard time trying to convince anybody that the band had even a smidgin of talent: 'I touted "Strange Little Girl" to every single record company I could find, and I was thrown out of every door. I was getting nowhere.'

According to Crook, it was glaringly obvious that Hans had been the stumbling block: 'Hans used to sit down and practice guitar for eight hours a day, trying to play as fast as he could. He was withdrawn, had no sense of humour and was stony cold. He was a damned good guitarist, but there was definitely a missing ingredient in that band.'

In May 1975 they decided to try and replace multi-instrumentalist Wärmling, and advertised in *Melody Maker* for a saxophonist and a keyboard player. They found a saxophonist who played one gig with them, but it didn't work out and he left after a matter of days. The ad for the keyboard player in *Melody Maker* gives an indication of the band's self-image at the time: 'Keyboard/vocal man for soft rock band. Mostly original material. Good gear essential. Accommodation available. Recording contract.'

Considering that less than a year later the band would be performing such 'soft rock' classics as 'Down In The Sewer' it is bizarre that at one time they considered themselves a soft rock combo. But, as Hugh points out, their music was, at least in part, more musically complex than simple rock 'n' roll: 'There were major sevenths in some of the songs – sweet chords – and minor chords too. Hard rock was all major chords.'

Taking the whole of their recorded output into consideration, it's plain to see that the Stranglers were never just a hard-rocking new-wave band. As far back as 1974, 'Strangle Little Girl' hinted at a soft-focus style, a whimsicality which couldn't really be defined as a ballad style, because virtually none of the Stranglers' slower numbers were ever really love songs, and most ballads are constructed around an emotional dialogue between singer/icon and addressee. Whole albums, such as *The Raven, The Meninblack, Aural Sculpture* and *Dreamtime*, moved well away from power chords and 'good-rockin' beats'. When the band returned to rock for Hugh's last stand, *10*, the result was leaden and plodding.

Dave Greenfield, the third keyboardist to be auditioned, had been holidaying in Germany when his aunt rang up with the information from the *Melody Maker* ad. He was the obvious candidate for the gig. Jet Black: 'Dave arrived looking like a hippie, with long hair and high boots, and he went through these numbers like "Hangin' Around" as though he knew, as though he'd been rehearsing for six months. He was so right for the band.'

Dave possessed a technical proficiency and musical purism which, back in 1975, was a huge advantage to the band's sound. As the years rolled by, the same purism estranged him from the band sonically, and by the 90s had begun to marginalize him. But back in the 1970s and 80s Greenfield was utterly essential to the band's musical identity. Not only was he a very talented player in his own right, far and away the most proficient member (JJ, who was just starting out on the bass, and Jet, who hadn't played in public for years up until the early 1970s, coming a distant joint second), he was also the band's musical director and interpreter. As time went on their respective roles became more well-defined: Jet was the businessman, the hirer and firer, the backbone of the band both emotionally and, in musical terms, rhythmically. Jet used to contribute musical ideas, but his lyrics tended to be rejected by the band: 'My lyrics used to sound like business letters and used to get vetoed! But Dave used to throw in the odd word. Or the odd grunt.'

Hugh and JJ were the creative duo and originated the vast majority of the songs, with JJ singing around a quarter of their total output. Dave was the musical frame-maker, chipping in, along with Jet, with suggestions and musical sections. Unlike many hugely successful rock bands, all four put something into the creative soup. But it would be the arrival of Dave which would make the band into a force to be reckoned with. Brian Crook: 'Dave Greenfield's influence on the band was major. He made them all gel without a doubt. His playing ability was stunning. They couldn't fail at that stage. The day he was hired was the day you could tell quite clearly that they were going to do something.'

David Paul Greenfield was born on 29 March 1949 in Brighton. Like Hugh and JJ, he came from the lower middle classes. His father was a talented pianist and clarinettist who toured the world, although Dave remembers that he was never actively pushed by his parents towards a musical career. He attended Varndean Grammar School in Brighton, and around the age of 13 developed an interest, like JJ, in classical guitar, persuading his sister to fork out a few pounds for a guitar to practise on. After that there was no stopping him; by his late teens he had become a precocious musical talent, had taken a theory of music course at school, and had taught himself piano in his spare time.

Dave left school at 17 before his A levels, and spent the whole of his 18th year in Germany playing covers at gigs in American bases and civilian clubs. The next half-a-dozen years or more were spent travelling to and from the continent, working in England to raise the capital to finance a music career in Germany. In the late 60s and early 70s, Germany was home to some of the greatest talents in the pantheon of rock – Kraftwerk, Can, Faust, Cluster and Tangerine Dream – and it has taken 25 years for this Krautrock scene to be paid the respect it deserves. But Germany was also an important market for more mainstream pop acts and had a booming club circuit, ideal for both the journeyman professional or the *ingénue* keen to learn his or her trade. Back in Brighton in the frequent gaps between tours, he earned some extra cash tuning pianos and mastering the now out-of-date technique of compositing for his Dad's printing firm. Like JJ, he also developed something of an infatuation with motorcycles, although his interest has not maintained the Burnel proportions of idolatry still in evidence to this day. Dave was the only one of the band who was a true musician before becoming a Strangler and, in his spells in the UK had worked professionally in groups such as The Initials, Rusty Butler, and Credo.

Significantly, one of Dave's favourite bands from the 1960s was the Beach Boys, and their tunesmithery has undoubtedly influenced his melodic sensibility. This melodic gift was augmented by his admiration for the intricacies and technique of progressive rock, particularly early Yes and the keyboard work of Deep Purple's John Lord, and the baroque flourishes which Dave would later build into the Stranglers' music reflect this early interest.

Surprisingly, given the amount of media coverage devoted to the similarity between Dave's playing style and that of the Doors' Ray Manzarek, it was Hugh and JJ in particular who were the Doors fans, not Dave, who claims only to have been aware of the three Doors' songs which had charted in Britain, 'Hello, I Love You', 'Riders On The Storm' and 'Light My Fire'. Dave: 'I tried not to be influenced by any one style or type or one particular keyboard player, even though subconsciously you find yourself doing the same thing, which doesn't really help. And no, I've never listened to the Doors too much, before you ask!'

But there were undoubted similarities between Dave's Hammond-organ style and that of Ray Manzarek's, particularly on the band's cover version of 'Walk On By'. 'Walk On By' was the one big bonus to emerge from the days when the band were forced by circumstance to play covers. After being 'strangulated' by the band, the song grew into an improvisatory monster, and showcased how adroit they were becoming at extemporization: the Hammond-organ instrumental section in particular brilliantly pastiched 'Light My Fire'. The choice of a Bacharach and David MOR classic and its extension, through extemporization, into a seven- or eight-minute live track, was the very antithesis of new wave's 'back-to-basics' anti-commercialism and musical minimalism. Dave: ' "Walk On By" started basically as the song, then it progressed, then the solos grew, then there was the interactive solo. We tried to re-create it just before Hugh left, but it had lost it somehow. We just couldn't get the feel back.'

In the early days the Stranglers were blighted by (almost always) unfavourable comparisons with the Doors: 'sub-Doors', 'on a Doors trip'. There are obvious similarities between the two groups which it would be churlish to deny. But it is as well to remember that back in the mid-1970s the Doors had not attained the god-head status in the UK rock pantheon they have today. In fact, many of their records were very hard to find in the record stores, having been deleted in the early 1970s. Most of the teenagers who bought Stranglers records would never have even heard a Doors record at the time, and for them such comparisons were meaningless.

Dave Greenfield is, in fact, the band's great unfathomable. Traditionally reticent with the media he is, like JJ, the sum of two very different character traits. Whereas at the time JJ was politically confusing, 'very right- and very left-wing simultaneously', as Stranglers' publicist Alan Edwards aptly put it, Dave is both supremely rational and logical *and* a mystic. An intelligent and gifted musician interested in the technological aspects of recorded sound, his logicality is evidenced by his love of cross-words, puzzles, computer games and the gadgets carried around in his legendary, and inseparable, black shoulder bag. At one point he also joined that exclusive club of rock aviators as a junior partner to Mike Oldfield and Gary Numan, with a view to piloting the band from gig to gig. But this practicality is tempered by a mysticism, a love of fantasy, and an interest in the occult. Dave says that his interest in the occult is now 'theoretical rather than practical' but, as JJ remembers, it wasn't always so:

> I wasn't as involved in the occult as the others, and I'm not sure Hugh was either, but Dave was seriously involved in it at one point. I was wary because I was sure you could summon forces of energies which you were totally not in control of. When we were living in Chiddingfold we met this very weird Canadian guy who was about 21-years-old but looked about 40, very imposing with a white streak in his hair. But I was very wary. I think you can summon up forces which move into other dimensions which I wasn't prepared to explore.

Although in person he had none of the negativity of Hugh's darker, sometimes spiteful wit, JJ's seldom concealed aggression and political schizophrenia, or Jet's combative defensive aggression, Dave gave the Stranglers much of their dark power, and it is through him that their sonically scatty and idiosyncratic music best expressed itself. As Dave became sonically distanced from the band in the late 80s and early 90s, the Stranglers' music lost much of its oddball playfulness.

Dave made his début a week after the successful audition, and for the rest of 1975 the Stranglers wrote literally hundreds of songs together in Chiddingfold. In the absence of regular, well-paid live work, the band were forced to take part-time jobs again for a short period. Jet and Dave worked as a piano tuning/repairing duo, JJ began to give private French lessons and Hugh taught biology at a local sixth-form college (he was later sacked for lunchtime fraternizing with the girls down the pub).

Around the end of 1975 the band were, nevertheless, building up the very beginnings of a fan-base. Garry Coward-Williams, who lived with them at Chiddingfold for a short time in 1976, is perhaps uniquely placed to give an insight into the pre-fame

Stranglers. Nicknamed 'Chiswick Charlie' by Hugh, at fifteen he was still at school and far from being worldly-wise or a culture vulture. But he took a keen interest in both music and photography and his year in the inner sanctum of the band afforded the opportunity to put his twin obsessions to good effect. Coward-Williams remembers his first Stranglers' gig, a support slot for the late, great Vivian Stanshall at the Nashville in November 1975:

As a band, they were the biggest bunch of scruffs I had ever seen and they had all this clapped-out equipment. But when they started playing I was mesmerized immediately. With the black leather jackets (Hugh and John) and their irreverent and ambivalent attitude to the audience, they immediately made me think of the Beatles in Hamburg. They had an aura about them, particularly Hugh, who appeared to be the central focus of the band – John had yet to develop his stage craft. I'd taken my camera along to photograph Viv, but the Stranglers were so interesting I thought I'd take some pictures of them as well. At the end of the gig, Hugh approached me as I was leaving and said, 'We're after some photos of the band. Can we see how yours came out?' Well they must have been desperate if Hugh had to approach some 15-year-old kid who was taking pictures in the audience. Anyway, we exchanged telephone numbers and that was the start of my relationship with the band.

My hero at the beginning was Hugh. He appeared to be the most dominant personality, with talent and charisma. He looked like the one who could make it. I remember foolishly saying something like, 'You're the one with the talent, I'd get rid of this lot' to him at one point. However, it was not long before I realized how good the rest of the band were and how well the four individuals were synchronized into a musical unit.

Garry also had a unique insight into the developing personalities of the four musicians struggling for the big time:

In terms of stage-craft and stage personae the band contained two very young and exciting characters, and two very unexciting characters! But the medium that they were in required that *everyone* should look exciting. It was not so bad for Jet, as the anchor-man behind the drums, no one expected more than his rhythmic ability, but they were always trying to come up with ideas to make Dave more visually interesting. I think the funniest idea was to dress him up in a sailor-suit with pigtails! Dave was the quieter of the four, the consummate professional, friendly, but not very accessible. He was into the magick arts and I remember him once telling me that someone was sending him waves from another country and he was bouncing them back and it was going to really hurt him when he got them back. But I never quite understood what it was all about. It was very difficult for me to communicate with Dave on this level.

Garry remembers Hugh at the time as developing a combative streak:

Hugh was bright and articulate on one level and yet awkward and gauche on another. The others would try to avoid letting Hugh drive the ice-cream van because it took him three goes to get his licence. His co-ordination, or lack of it, is represented in his quirky guitar playing which was his own unique style and a vital part of the band's sound at the time. On stage, Hugh would say things like, 'Are there any students in the audience tonight?' There would be a cheer and then he'd sneeringly say, 'Well come up here and show me what you've learnt.' He could be verbally very hard on stage and off.

He was also taken under JJ's wing, given fashion tips and was made to feel part of the 'Stranglers family' by supposedly the most unaccommodating member:

Whereas Jet was always very fatherly towards me, John [JJ] fulfilled a different family role. His media image is nothing like what he is actually like in person. His girlfriend at the time, Suzie, who was a nurse, told me that he considered me as a younger brother, which was so touching. JJ's got a very feminine side to his personality and he also had an outrageous amount of charm, and that missing ingredient which the girls go for – mystery. He had seriously gorgeous girls doing anything for him. Suzie was the classic very, very nice girl, and she fulfilled the need for him to have a nice girl who was always there, but he was cheating on her and she ended up emigrating to South Africa or Rhodesia, I can't quite remember. She went back a long way because she used to call Jet 'Brian', which is seriously taboo. John, Hugh and Jet were incredibly kind, and incredibly forgiving. They used to drop me back home after their gigs! They were really lovely blokes and never seemed to mind that I was a fifteen-year-old pimply nobody. I still don't know why they were so kind to me.

Coward-Williams remembers the Chiddingfold house as being 'very squat-like, very *Young Ones*'. John's bedroom was on the ground floor towards the middle of the house. His room was very spartan and contained few possessions, mimicking his almost ascetic philosophy. Jet and Dave were on the first floor, and Hugh, ever the loner, up in the loft. Although life in Chiddingfold obviously helped the band to gel into a unit, only Jet remained there on a day-to-day basis. Most of Dave's mates were in the Brighton area, and he used to spend a lot of his spare time there with his girlfriend. In fact, in these early days, Dave brought in many Brighton-based groups to open for the Stranglers. Again, it was Jet who held everything together, paid the bills, did the shopping and cooking. Garry Coward-Williams: 'I never knew anyone who could make a great meal out of virtually nothing as well as Jet. He could turn his hand to anything and was totally unflappable. He was also ace at slicing bread straight too!'

The band were keen to show Garry Coward-Williams, hitherto into pop acts such as the Sweet, Slade and Gary Glitter, their own, more 'refined' musical world. JJ's favourite album was *LA Woman* by the Doors, and Coward-Williams remembers that in 1976 the band wrote a song called 'Highway' which was almost a musical homage to *LA Woman*-era Doors, but it never got recorded. For Coward-Williams, the links between the two groups were strong:

I think it was more than just Dave Greenfield's keyboard sound or their arrangement of 'Walk On By' which made them like the Doors. It was a mixture of their sound *and* their aura. Hugh's quirky guitar style was not dissimilar to Robbie Krieger's early work, and Jet and Dave – the anchormen of the Stranglers – performed a similar role to Densmore and Manzarek in holding the band together. The brooding, malevolent and far too good-looking Morrison could be compared to Burnel.

Both bands have a strong sense of melody in their compositions; neither were afraid to throw in the odd waltz. Both courted controversy by attacking the taboo subjects – political and sexual – of their respective decades, in many cases pushing the establishment too far, with disastrous results. Morrison was arrested for the infamous on-stage Miami dick-flash, whilst the Stranglers spent time in prison too. In the late sixties, the Doors were accused of inciting riots at their concerts to the degree that they found it difficult to find venues that would take them, much like the Stranglers.

The strange thing is that any likeness between the two groups is purely accidental. To my knowledge only John was actually interested in the Doors, and his influence focused on *LA Woman*, their last album before Morrison's death, a most untypical Doors work. To me there is a link, but it is one born of spirit rather than kinship.

Other musical influences included the Kinks – Hugh was a fan, whilst both Hugh and Jet were great admirers of Arthur Lee's Love. Indeed, a lot of the melodic pop of Love, as evidenced on the 1968 flower-power classic *Forever Changes*, which included songs such as 'Alone Again Or' and 'Andmoreagain', proved as much a blueprint for the Stranglers' style as the Doors' broody, Hammond-sopped angst.

Meanwhile, life out in the sticks was not without its difficulties, and top of the list of problems were the Stranglers' neighbours, Mr & Mrs Rubens, who apparently regarded the band as the neighbours from hell. The situation soon developed into a sort of surrealistic episode of a bad 70s sit-com, a sort of 'Stranglers versus Terry and June' scenario. Jet explains:

> They didn't like our music at all. It's not like we made a lot of noise but we used to play acoustic guitar in our back garden and piano in the house or in the garden too. On a nice sunny day we'd be in the garden singing and strumming away and Mr Rubens used to get his dustbin lid and started banging away too saying, 'If you can make a bloody noise, so can I.' It was all very funny until we used to see the council people walking up and down the street. Mr Rubens organized a meeting in the village hall to get us evicted and nobody supported him! They all thought it was rather nice to have some artists living in the village.

In terms of their career, the main problem for the band was not so much getting well-paid gigs in rock venues, but getting any gigs anywhere. As soon as Hugh, or more likely Jet, rang up a local pub, club or promoter and let slip the band's name, the result was often a mixture of affront, hilarity and incredulity, followed by the sound of the receiver being slammed down. However, the band soon developed a successful ruse. Jet Black:

> Those very early gigs were hilarious. We couldn't get a rock n roll gig because we didn't look right: we didn't have the platform

shoes, we didn't have the long hair. So we just tried any gimmick, and Hugh and I worked out this plan and what we'd do is, we'd play anywhere so we'd be practising our art. We'd try all the working men's clubs, the football clubs, even weddings. Hugh would phone up and say, 'Oh, we've got this band here. Any chance of getting a gig at your club?' They said, 'Well you know, we might give you a try, what are you called?' and Hugh would make up some name and they'd ask, 'What music do you play?' and he'd say, 'Rock'n'roll' and the reply might be, 'We don't do rock'n'roll here, only country and western.' So we'd leave it a couple of days then I'd phone back and say, I've got a country and western band, any chance of a gig?' And so we'd be doing Stranglers stuff at country and western pubs, or at sixties clubs, or seventies pubs. We made a couple of concessions to popular taste by playing one or two famous songs but mostly it was our own stuff. The consequence of this was that if you book a country and western band, you expect them to look like a country and western band and to sound like one, and of course we never did. After a few numbers they'd come up and say, 'Turn it down!' and we'd turn it up and they'd say 'Turn it down!' again and we'd turn it up even higher just to get noticed. There was always a row at the end and people used to throw things at us and they'd say, 'Play something we know!' and we'd steam into something we knew they didn't know. There were so many arguments and when it came to getting paid I'd be the one to go up and ask for the money and there'd be steaming rows and we never used to get booked back. After many months of this we played at hundreds of places and everyone who came to those gigs never forgot this band who wouldn't turn it down and wouldn't play anything they knew. I'm sure that contributed to why the first album did so well, people all over the country used to say, 'I remember that band!' They were hugely exciting days and very funny. Often the police were called and we'd do anything to get noticed. As soon as the punk thing came along we'd then be accused of jumping on the bandwagon, but we were already doing all the outrage back in 1974, but of course, nobody was writing about it.

In 1975 the band gigged exhaustively in the Guildford area, and then further afield in the Home Counties. This was very much a pre-punk scene: the average concert goers were Status Quo rejects, long-haired, in jeans and cowboy boots, no-nonsense rockers doing, as Hugh remembers, 'formation Status Quo dancing' at the front of the stage, mimicking the group's promo for their recent UK Number 1, the mind-numbingly repetitive, though maddeningly catchy 'Down Down'. The earliest bootleg of the band dates from 15 November 1975 and was recorded by Hugh himself using a small cassette player which he left in his coat pocket at the bar at a venue in Redhill endearingly entitled *The Nob*. *The Stranglers at The Nob* shows the band navigating their way uncertainly through a set of covers and originals to spatterings of applause from the assembled 'masses'. But as an artefact from these neophyte new-wavers it's a priceless memento. It has to be said that very little on that recording hints at the greatness to come. It was still very much up for grabs whether the band would ever make it and break out of the club and pub circuit.

The band certainly must have cut a very stylish jib dashing through the countryside in their clapped-out ice-cream van. But there wasn't much money in the kitty for any of those regular little expenditures. Hardly a week went past without Dave's organ packing in mid-chorus or the van itself conking out in some uninhabited part of the Home Counties. Dave remembers that Kent in particular was a bogy-county for our fabtastic foursome: 'We always had bad luck in Kent. Gigs would go wrong, or not happen and once when we were coming back from one gig the van broke down. There was nothing unusual in that. We pushed it up to the top of the hill, got to the top, jumped in, started going down the hill. Would it start? Would it hell. Then halfway down the hill we left Kent and it started instantly, no word of a lie.'

These were desperate times for the group financially. Often they didn't have enough money for a decent meal and the band used to live on toasted cheese, tomato and Marmite sandwiches. JJ remembers that on one occasion the band left him alone in Chiddingfold for three days with just a few pence and a couple of packets of Paxo in the cupboard! JJ: 'I used to walk four or five miles to a sewage farm near Guildford and pick loads of tomatoes to eat. The sewage farm had several acres of tomato plants growing there. As long as they didn't touch the ground they were fine!'

In the end they would play a gig anywhere for a few quid, as little as £35 for a night's work, hardly enough to put petrol in the tank. On 1 May 1976 the band were booked to play a gig for those stalwarts of the punk era, the Young Conservatives, in Purley. Jet Black tells the story:

> There must have been this one person in the entire population of London who'd been to see us somewhere and thought we were sensational and he apparently happened to be a Young Conservative. Anyway, he was obviously a very forward-thinking and radical Young Conservative and he booked us for this Young Conservatives' annual ball. We didn't really think that much about it, we just knew we had this gig at Purley Halls. We turned up and we thought, 'What are these people doing in these penguin outfits?', and it's this really formal ball. We got up on stage and set the equipment up. When they came in after dinner we thought, 'Oh my God, look at this lot, they're going to be expecting Victor Sylvester!' I thought, 'Bollocks', and went up to the mic and said, 'Listen, you're not going to like us, so you may as well fuck off now.' After that first number, it's totally true about half of them walked out the door, and by the third number there were about three people left.

Also in May 1976, the Stranglers supported that personification of punk angst, Ricky Valance (whose calling-card was his 1960 hit 'Tell Laura I Love Her') in front of an audience of half a dozen at Kettering Central Hall. But perhaps the apogee of inappropriateness was reached later that autumn when the band were booked to play at Roehampton convent! Knowing no shame, they played their increasingly lewd and fleshly set to an audience of the chaste.

In addition to playing these farcically inappropriate venues, the band were also beginning to make it on the London club and pub scene in a major way, thanks to the efforts of Albion Agency in Wandsworth, London. Derek Savage had formed Albion with Dai Davies, an enthusiastic young Welshman who had worked for Tony Defries' Mainman organization in the early 1970s and had helped break the decade's most influential pop star, David Bowie, in the States. Davies had also managed pub-rockers Ducks Deluxe and Brinsley Schwarz. He enjoyed the pub-rock scene, seeing it as an energized alternative to the excesses of prog-rock. Prior to the Albion connection, the Stranglers had relied on friends to manage their affairs part-time. First came Charles Edwards, a drinking partner of Jet's who was one of the few people at the time to spot the huge potential of the band, and later Brian Crook, who also had faith in a band few held out much hope for.

However, these well-intentioned men were handling the Stranglers' affairs in their spare time and could not devote all their energies to making the band a success. But Albion could. The agency itself wasn't exactly situated in the most salubrious of locations. Dai Davies remembers that working all day in an office above a ladies' hairdressers and next to a Chinese takeaway made for a stunning combination of smells: 'Cheap lacquer, MSG and noodles, it was a "lovely" smell, but it was only £12 a week!' Nevertheless, in 1975 Albion were starting to flex their muscles. They began booking bands from the burgeoning pub-rock scene, and by 1976 they had some big names on their roster, including Roogalator, the Jam, the 101'ers and Elvis Costello, and virtually controlled the London pub-rock scene. The Stranglers had been petitioning the agency for live work over a period of several months without success, until Hugh hit upon a typically novel idea:

> Dai was this eccentric, really very charming Welshman, and Derek was the wide-boy from the East End, balding with a big beard, jeans and braces. They thought we were very weird, and we thought they were very weird. They were such characters that I made up this comic strip about them, 'The Adventures Of Dai and Derek', and I used to send it to them every week. In the end they called us and said, 'We obviously can't get rid of you, why don't we manage you?' They were the first professional managers we had. Crook had gone by then, and Reg McLean had disappeared. I think he'd had some dealings with some people in south London and he suddenly disappeared, but *really* disappeared.

Dai Davies had been in the States when the groups which would later influence the British new-wave such as the New York Dolls and Iggy Pop and the Stooges were rising to prominence. Davies liked what he heard, and when he first encountered the British punk bands he immediately saw the connection between the two scenes, the shared excitement and danger, and orientated Albion towards this new, more demotic, and certainly more outrageous sound. It was hard, however, to get decent bookers and, since Albion couldn't afford to actually pay a wage for someone to do the onerous task of phoning round venues for gigs, Davies and Savage brought in Ian Grant as a partner. Davies: 'Derek and myself were the founders of the company and equal partners. Ian was definitely a good catch for us at the time because he also had some experience as an agent. I think we gave him a share of the management company and the agency, but, although I can't remember the actual proportions, he didn't get a share equal to ours.'

So it was Ian Grant, who joined Albion as a partner in July 1975, who took on the job of getting the band live work. Grant had run an arts lab in the 1960s in Worthing on the south coast and had fallen into managing local bands too. In his early 20s he was asked by Dai and Derek to build up a stable of acts they could promote at the Nashville. Their first two acts were Roogalator and Rocky Sharpe and the Razors (later Replays), and as 1976 progressed their stable of acts included Neil Innes, the 101'ers, the Jam, Eddie & the Hot Rods, the Sex Pistols, the Damned, the Vibrators and Johnny Thunder & the Heartbreakers. Ian Grant recalls: 'Derek and Dai said to me, "Look, we've got this band coming to us on and off, we don't see it really, but they're clever, they don't just send us tapes, they take the piss, they send cartoons."

Grant could readily identify with another ex-Hippy like Hugh, and Dave he had already known and booked when he was in the Brighton-based band Rusty Butler. Hugh remembers Ian Grant as 'a complete acid head, into drugs and dope – a real hippy. But he was very efficient. Some people call him the John Major of the music business. He was the one who did all the work in there. He used to sit in a little cupboard at the back of their office and they used to say, "You're not coming out until you've got ten gigs for the boys."'

One of Ian Grant's first moves was to bring in Alan Edwards to do the publicity: 'I'd known him since schooldays when I used to sell him "quid deals", little lumps of hash, outside his school in the late 60s. He was five years younger than me and at the time was selling advertising space in *Sounds*.'

Alan Edwards played a crucial role later in 1976 and throughout 1977 in breaking the band into the big league. He had developed a strong interest in the incipient pub-rock scene in the early 70s and began freelancing for *Sounds* and *Record Mirror*. He then worked for top publicist Keith Altham, dealing with the Who and T.Rex. More than anyone else within the Stranglers' camp, it was Alan Edwards who pushed the band closer to the punk scene media-wise:

I was into the rebellious side of it. I had a real gut feeling for it. You see, when I was working at Keith's office he used to have all these over-the-hill rock stars like Alvin Lee, Ten Years After, the Moody Blues . . . and they'd come in with their fur coats and long hair and I really grew to dislike these people, to be honest, because they were wealthy and they made horrible records and they were arrogant and they had loads of girls. I was looking for something of my own, something I could relate to. We really didn't have anything else going on in our lives, we'd be hanging around the Nashville on Sunday lunchtimes taking speed, all the normal stuff, and bit by bit the pub-rock scene evolved into the punk scene. But for the people inside the scene it happened organically and it was never actually premeditated.

I met the Stranglers in late 1975, liked them straight away and naturally became part of it. We all grew up together in some weird way.

The band played an astonishing number of gigs during this period. Although the figure for 1975 is unknown, in 1976 the band played a fret-snapping 191 gigs, and hardly a single one passed off without an incident of some sort, whether it be a spectacular equipment failure, a riot, a brush with the law, or some bizarre on-stage antic by the bassist, fast becoming the Eric Cantona of the new wave. Garry Coward-Williams:

John was a very flexible performer, he got up to all sort of tricks. I would imagine that some of them were generated through sulphate or some sort of amphetamine. Now, I'm sure you remember, the Stranglers always had their set positions on stage. As you faced them Dave would be at the far right, Jet in the middle, Hugh on the right and John on the left. At one of the double-header Nashville gigs with the Vibrators, John was playing in his natural position on the left of the stage. Alongside him, running high up the wall was a stack of empty beer crates. Suddenly, John decided he was going to run up the crates, whilst playing the bass! The band were in the middle of a song, when he walked past Jet, Hugh and Dave, turned towards the crates and then ran at full-speed, partially achieving his intention before gravity put him down on his back with a thump! Another time in the middle of a song, again at the Nashville, he decided to run off to the right of the stage past the other band members and into the tunnel which led to the dressing-room. The only problem was that he was still plugged into his amp, which flew off the speaker cabinet, hit the floor and followed after him! John also had a thing about peeing in public, so he used to pee in a beer jug. There was a sort of off-shoot room from the dressing-room at the Nashville and I remember him coming out with a jug of piss looking quite pleased with himself.

JJ could also be knowingly silly and, as Coward-Williams recollects, this would annoy Dave, who regarded gigs with more serious intent:

I also remember one night at the Red Cow, it must have been January 1976. John was cold when he got on stage to start the first set (they would do two sets at the Red Cow), so he kept his scarf on, which was wrapped around his neck and lower face, obscuring his nose and mouth with just his eyes popping out. Their first song was a John number, but that didn't matter to him at all, he just sang through his scarf and, of course, you couldn't understand a word. He used to do that sort of thing and then smirk like a *Just William* character. He could be a bit childish, he was like a *provocateur* leading the pack. He was so idealistic and had this death or glory thing about him, he didn't seem to care. This used to upset Dave quite a lot because he considered himself a professional musician. I remember another gig at the Red Cow when John decided to mix up the lyrics of a song and generally mess around for no apparent reason. Dave, who had clearly had enough, just pulled down the lid on his piano, walked off the stage and never came back for the rest of the gig.

I know that there was an open feeling that Dave was giving them only so much time (this was in 1976) and if they didn't make it by a certain point then he'd go off and do something else and look for another vehicle, which was fair enough. In picking Dave for the band they'd picked up a professional musician who'd been on the circuit since he'd left school, done the Hamburg trip and was looking around for the right band. The other three were totally committed to the cause but Dave was a professional, and if they didn't go anywhere then he would have to go somewhere else, he would go on to another band, whereas the others might go back to their former professions and teach or whatever.

Jet has some 'fond' memories of those early gigs. The Stranglers happened to have the misfortune to play a gig at a venue where, only the week before, a member of the audience had been killed. When the Stranglers played, competing factions in the audience were ready to continue the gang warfare: 'I remember one gig at Friars in Aylesbury very well. They hated us, as did everyone at the time. Anyway I was playing and a bottle landed on top of my head, in the middle of a song, on its side. It shattered into millions of pieces. In a way I was lucky. If it had landed end-on, it might have killed me. I just kept on playing though!'

Perhaps the most frequent occurrence at mid-70s Stranglers' gigs was spectacular equipment failure. Of course, the band were never going to let that get in the way of a good time. At one gig JJ's bass packed in, so he 'sang' his lines into the microphone instead! At an early gig at the Hope and Anchor, the microphone broke down during 'Go Buddy Go' and JJ actually walked off the stage and round the audience, shouting the lyrics to them individually!

The Stranglers were developing a musical style which set them apart from their pub-rock confrères. Their original compositions were not really akin to the r'n'b being played on the pub-rock circuit, and at a time when progressive rock was still the dominant musical mode within rock, the Stranglers largely went against this grain too, producing hundreds of quirky three-minute songs. Their only concession to prog-rock mores was their seven-minute-plus epic, 'Sewer', premièred in early 1976, which grew and grew in live performance, with the addition of the rousing, militaristic instrumental section and Hammond organ run, into their early signature song, 'Down In The Sewer'. Sartorially, they were also a race apart, as JJ explains: 'Dave had the pony tail, Jet had peroxide blond hair in 1974 well before the rest of the punks, Hugh had wavy hair and I had my short fringey thing which everyone seems to have copied these days, my "Oasis" haircut. You didn't wear leather jackets and drain-pipe trousers in those days. It was just not on, but we did. And we just played rock 'n' roll music, which was so unhip.'

There's a bit of typically naughty historical revisionism going on here by JJ. When Garry Coward-Williams met him in 1975, JJ apparently had the biggest pair of flares you could possibly imagine! But the spirit of what he says is spot on (and he's dead right about that Oasis haircut!). Today Jet is in bullish mood about the place of the band in the historical scheme of things:

The chronology is misunderstood here by everyone in the media. *We* were the fathers of punk, because the Pistols used to come to watch *us*! I had some money but the others were totally penniless and dressed like it, so I kind of dressed down as well. We had this image like we were bums. We wanted not only to look different but to *sound* different as well. While everyone else had these really long guitar solos ours were the opposite. Hugh was perfect for this because in fact his natural bent was to play two notes and call it a solo!

Hugh was developing a novel way of playing his Telecaster, thinking up guitar parts which were wholly idiosyncratic and immediately memorable. In the mid-70s the Stranglers were evolving a musical idiolect which would make them instantly recognizable on the airwaves in the years to come.

Slowly but surely, the Stranglers were raising their profile, helped considerably by Albion's cartel on the London pub-rock scene. In late 1975 the band started a weekly residence at London's prestigious pub-rock venue the Hope and Anchor, Upper Street, Islington, run by music nut and band-supporter Fred Grainger. It was here that a myriad of bands later to make it big honed their performance style, playing in a converted cellar with the lowest of ceilings to no more than 100 sardine-packed punters. Fred had a band playing every night of the week, except on Sunday, his night off. But having heard the band play he was willing to give them a chance in front of the few punters in need of a stiff drink after *Songs Of Praise*, and eventually they were first booked to play on the manifestly low-prestige Sunday night slot, the deadest night in the boozing diary, and typically a graveyard for bands trying to make it. On their first Sunday night appearance, they were all set and ready to play but there was only one problem. There was nobody to play to! By now it was nearly 9.30 p.m. and Fred Grainger was urging the band to start their set. But they refused to play until at least one paying member turned up. Jet continues the story: 'Eventually just one guy turns up, so we gave him a crate of beer and said, "You're our customer for the evening, we're going to give you the full works." And he sat there and we played to this bloke all night long. He went away and he came back the next Sunday with a few of his mates and then the next Sunday and the next Sunday and after about five weeks the place started to get packed every night.'

This was the very beginning of the Stranglers' success story. One of the first journalistic pieces written about the band by Mick Brown for *Sounds* from April 1976 gives an indication of the sheer hard graft needed to put on a pub-rock group and the serendipity and improvisation involved. Brown tells how the equipment, including Dave's seriously heavy Hammond, is hauled down the chute where beer-deliveries were made, how there's a mad scramble to find various electrical odds and sods and how beer crates and barrels are used as speaker stands. Wembley Stadium this was not; but it soon would be.

Despite later claims by the leading punk protagonists, the Stranglers were a much-admired band in the months before the Sex Pistols broke punk in late 1976. The Vibrators, whose lead guitarist John Ellis would become a Strangler in 1990, were often the support act: John Ellis: 'The first-ever Vibrators' gig was supporting the Stranglers at a place called Page Green School. There were three people in the audience – and a dog.'

The Vibrators supported the Stranglers regularly at the Nashville and the two bands were initially very well disposed to one another. They were a great double act – the Vibrators an energetic, fun pop band setting the stage for the heavier main act. Later both bands would be regarded with disdain by the punk fraternity, the Stranglers because they were musos, old, and deemed misogynistic, the Vibrators because they had signed a one-single record deal with Micky Most's pop-oriented RAK label, home of the very uncred Suzi Quatro and Mud. Punk was nothing if not conformist and Stalinist in its philosophical outreach, as John Ellis remembers: 'One of the terrible things about punk was that we all threw the baby out with the bathwater in a way. You weren't allowed to admit the fact that you liked Abba or Genesis. It wasn't a cool thing to say.'

The band also regularly toured with Joe Strummer's pre-Clash band, the 101'ers, and Hugh and Joe soon became good pals. In fact, Strummer obviously regarded the Stranglers as the yardstick by which all other competitors had to be measured: 'I remember after the Patti Smith gig at the Roundhouse, Joe Strummer coming up to me after a gig – I think they were playing first and we were playing later, and he started crying on my shoulder,

"Hugh, why can't I have a band like yours, it's fuckin' great!" I mean, it was real emotion. I was saying, "Don't worry, Joe, your band's great." This was when he was in the 101'ers. They were good, they were great at what they did, but it wasn't very organic.'

Lead guitarist Steve Jones and drummer Paul Cook from the Sex Pistols also attended Stranglers gigs during this time. Hugh remembers that Jet in particular was something of a focal point: 'Paul Cook, the drummer from the Pistols, used to come in afterwards and he was almost sitting on Jet's knee, saying, "How d'ya do that bit when you do that bit?" and Jet would say, "Well, Paul, what you do is, you know, you go like this." It was like father and son, talking to him, telling him how to do stuff. They used to come round to our gigs all the time. We never used to see Rotten, but Steve Jones and Paul Cook used to come down all the time.'

Apart from Garry Coward-Williams (Chiswick Charlie) and his schoolmate, Duncan (Duncan Doughnuts), the band were also attracting the idolization of a Mancunian in his late twenties called Dave, who once worked at the Ford plant in Dagenham and was now a scaffolder, and his girlfriend, Brenda, who was an illustrator. The two lived in a hotel in Sussex Gardens, off the Bayswater Road. Predictably Hugh soon nicknamed them Dagenham Dave and Bren Gun. Dave was a music aficionado (he had a love for classical music and jazz in addition to pop – his hero was Charlie Parker and his three favourite rock bands were the Tubes, the very un-cool Genesis and soon, obviously, the Stranglers) who instantly fell in love with the band, forming an intense and ultimately tragic liaison. Dave was also a militant socialist with very firm views on the wrongs and ills of society. He was a man of extremes; in fact he confessed once to having been diagnosed as paranoid schizophrenic. But, by all accounts he was, for the most part, an entertaining, well-read rogue, with plenty of disposable income for the odd pint or fifteen, or for the highest quality joints. He kept the band's spirits up during a period where they might make as little as £25 a night for a pub gig, telling jokes and anecdotes. His party trick was to take his front false teeth out! And he worried on behalf of the band and took each reverse personally. He even went so far as offering the band free use of his girlfriend. And he had no doubts that the Stranglers would make it, and he kept telling them so. Jet Black:

'He was a loveable bloke and he followed us wherever we were. But he was a deeply frustrated man because he had a lot of ability but he didn't know how to channel it. He was certainly more capable than his job allowed him to be. He couldn't do anything in moderation, whether it be drink, or drugs, or sex – he was a man of gross extremes but he was a tremendous comrade and supporter.'

Garry Coward-Williams, now working for the band as a roadie, remembers that Dagenham Dave first made contact with them after a gig at The Golden Lion in Fulham:

> He was a stocky, half-caste guy with very short hair and one of those faces that had been in many bar-room brawls. He was the sort of guy that if you hit him with an iron bar he'd smile at you. He was totally into music. He'd had a very hard life and learnt to hit first and ask questions later. Dave and Brenda would travel to all the gigs. He took over from me in a way as the fan central to the band – Dave became the new one-man appreciation society. But we all got on well. John in particular was into Dagenham Dave because he respected hard men. You never bought a drink when Dave was around. He was a sunshine man, very up.

During the first half of 1976, the band, with Albion's help, began breaking into the bigger venues, making the transition from the metropolitan pub-rock circuit of the Nashville, Red Cow, and Hope and Anchor, to bigger gigs such as support slots at the Round House or the Hammersmith Odeon. Their first major support gig was on 29 February at the Roundhouse. The Stranglers were fourth on the bill to Deaf School, Nasty Pop and Jive Bombers. Their main problem that night was a simple, but fatal one: the PA wasn't switched on! Midway through the second song, they beat a retreat to the intended 'celebration' gig at the Hope and Anchor (or the 'Grope And Wanker' as Hugh was now wont to call it!). However, all was not lost. The usual promoter at the Round House, one of the most influential of the day, was John Curd. If he liked you, then the shift from small-scale parochial pub act to the big time was possible. Curd hadn't promoted this particular gig, but quite liked the band, so gave them a second chance, this time as the support for Patti Smith (or, if you were Hugh, 'Smatty Pith') in May.

Patti Smith, like Bruce Springsteen (or, as he was known in the

pun-tastic Stranglers entourage, 'Loose Windscreen'), came over
to the UK with plenty of kudos but minimal record sales. Her
début album, *Horses*, had been released in 1975, its cover pictur-
ing Patti in a white shirt and tie, a gender-bending feminist
heroine for the new-wave age. Hugh, however, was singularly
unimpressed: 'She confused me a bit, Patti Smith, because we
were told, here is this liberated woman, very feminist. And yet
she's writhing on the floor pretending to be fucked by a guitar. I
thought, That's not very liberating, is it? That looks very sexist to
me.'

Garry Coward-Williams remembers that during a sound-check
Smith yelled back to her lead guitarist: 'Hey, Lenny, do you know
the *Strangers* have got a seven-man road crew?' The band were so
unknown at the time that even the main act couldn't get their
name right!

There was obviously a big media buzz about Patti Smith at the
time. Granada's new-wave show, *So It Goes*, hosted by Tony
Wilson (later Anthony H. Wilson, doyen of the Hacienda and
owner of Manchester's Factory records), hired the legendary
Adam West, the original caped crusader of Gotham City and
star of the kitsch 60s television version of *Batman*, to do some
locational links dressed in his full batman regalia.

Garry Coward-Williams again:

> I was standing next to Hugh and Joe Strummer watching *the*
> Adam West and I thought, Wouldn't it be great if he'd do the bat
> dance during 'Sewer'? Hugh and John used to do this darker
> version of Chuck Berry's duck-walk – a kind of a creepy crawly
> thing. They used to hunch shoulders, their whole bodies would be
> quite low and they'd be looking at the floor or slightly up from the
> floor and move around from side to side. It was really quite a
> menacing weird thing they were doing. I said wouldn't it be great
> if we could get Adam West to do this bat dance during 'Sewer'. It
> would blow Patti Smith out of the fuckin' hall. Hugh knocked on
> the door of his dressing-room and asked him, but he couldn't do it.

These gigs saw Hugh and JJ in make-up. JJ in particular would
play the part of punk-rock beauty, claiming that the girls loved it.
With hindsight JJ admits that at the time he had bisexual
tendencies although never acted upon them. His punk androgene image was as telling as any from the era.

As was frequently the case, the first night at the Round House, 16 May, the Stranglers were given a really hostile reception, and the second night provoked much the same reaction until, that is, the introduction of one song, the charmingly titled 'Tits'. 'Tits' was the band's premier novelty number with the sing-a-long lyrics: 'She's got 36, 24, 36 hips [5 times]/That was the size of her tits'

Mid-song, in a deliberate spoof of prog-rock virtuosity, the band would do the naffest, and funniest solos imaginable – easy enough for Hugh, Jet and JJ, but quite a task for muso Dave, who found it genuinely difficult to play even the occasional bum note. Amazingly, this would be the song which, according to Jet, made the band's career: 'I remember that, up until that show, at every gig we did, we'd be booed at, have bottles and chairs thrown at us, anything, and at that gig we were getting a similar reaction until we thought, "Bollocks to you" and started playing our joke number, "Tits". From that point on, they suddenly realized that all the stuff they thought was very heavy, was actually tongue-in-cheek, and from that minute they loved us. That was the turning-point of our career.'

There was certainly an air of celebration at the backstage party that night. Hugh got horrendously drunk and collapsed, whilst Joe Strummer, also the worse for drink, suddenly found himself in love. Garry Coward-Williams:

By the time I saw Joe at the party he had got himself into a right state. There were three of us in a group: me, Joe and Nick Garvey (ex Ducks Deluxe and later The Motors). Strummer had decided he was in love with Patti Smith and was just telling us all about it when she happened to walk by. Joe made a lunge for her crying, 'Patti, Patti, I love you!' The poor bloke had to be restrained and needless to say Patti was bewildered – this was pre-Clash and Joe was a 'nobody'. Nick and I tried to calm him down. I remember him looking at me with tears streaming down his face and froth gathering in the corners of his mouth saying, 'The problem is I've got too much soul, man – I feel too much.' What a performance, it was the talk of the party. We liked Joe, he was one of our friends. I don't know why, but when he joined the Clash he suddenly became anti-Stranglers, whereas I know for a fact that he really rated them as a band.

The Round House gig may have significantly raised the band's profile, but the group were still without a record deal and, despite regular live work, were still in a financially precarious position. It was still by no means certain that the band would go on to break out of the pub-rock scene and make it in the mainstream. But there was one obvious precedent; United Artists' pub-rock band Dr Feelgood crashed into the UK album charts at Number 1 with their live album *Stupidity* in the October of 1976, and it was Dr Feelgood who emerged as the benchmark by which many of the bands, including the Stranglers, measured their own success. It was to securing a record deal that they and Albion now devoted most of their energies.

3: MEN BEHAVING BADLY

Although the Stranglers would never become a punk band, it was the burgeoning punk movement which would eventually make their career. An integral part of the new wave were shock tactics, affrontery and taboo-breaking. When the Sex Pistols appeared on teatime television and were goaded into swearing by TV presenter Bill Grundy, their words challenged the norms of acceptability. Punk allowed the hitherto inadmissible, and violated 'correct' language. All the punk singers of the time turned their back on the idea upheld by the likes of Elton, Rod and Mick of singing in a mid-Atlantic drawl, and sang using the voice of parochial Britain. Punk helped British pop to decouple itself from the notion that British pop should pay lip-service to its origins in black America. Punk rock was particularized and provincial. Overwhelmingly, the new-wave groups spoke not of love, relationships and heartbreaks, but of hate, alienation and the functionality of sex without feelings, or 'squelching' as it became known in punk lingo. The Stranglers tapped into this nihilism but added a twist which was all their own – a moody, dark misanthropy, a cutting cynicism and a penchant for the tasteless.

In the nineties, it is very hard for anybody working within the popular media of television, film and music to shock anybody. In the UK, perhaps only writer and comedian Chris Morris appears to be able to scandalize the establishment. In 1997 one of his TV sketches, 'Sutcliffe–The Musical' about the Yorkshire Ripper, aimed to satirize television's 'celebretization' of criminality, but was deemed too controversial to broadcast. But in the less media-saturated seventies, it was easier to be offensive, and punk was constructed to be just that. The Stranglers courted controversy from the very outset, and their outrageous exploits were fashioned as media charades, often embroidered upon by scandal-mongering copy-editors, but largely planned, nevertheless. Jet in particular saw that all the stage mishaps, the punch-ups and the wilfulness were creating a terrific buzz around the band, and as long as it got punters through the door he was happy. Some of the band rhetoric, the casting of themselves as the Dick Dastardlies of pop, was plainly deliberately silly and cartoonesque. But, from the beginning, there were darker, more violent, more forbidding themes. The band talked up the idea of the group as a bunch of sexual predators. The band name itself, although coined initially in a half-jokey manner as an attempt to *épater les bourgeois*, has obvious connotations with violent crime: strangulation is a murder technique used almost exclusively on women by men. Although in fact the greatest stranglers of all time were the Thugs (from Sanskrit 'sthag'), a secret organization of robbers in India and devotees of the goddess Kalia who raised strangulation to an art form, regarding it as a religious rite; their penchant for murdering rich businessmen exclusively by means of strangulation (interestingly, the strangulation of women was forbidden) was finally put a stop to in the early nineteenth century.

On the subject of punk 'naming', pop historian and semiotician Dave Laing in his book *One Chord Wonders: Power And Meaning In Punk Rock* writes:

> In an inversion of the other earlier practice of group naming which signified success or status, the Damned and the Stranglers highlighted the socially undesirable, sinners and lawbreakers respectively. Both, too, were *excessive*. To say 'Damned' rather than 'Condemned' was to invoke an extra layer of the supernatural and in a media context to invoke the 1969 film by Visconti which caused a ripple of excitement or censure for its lurid presentation of Nazi decadence. 'Stranglers' goes further than 'Killers' would, in its specifying of a particular method of assault. It also invokes a well-known film, the dramatization of the real-life career of the *Boston Strangler*.

The publicity poster, designed by Kevin Sparrow, an artist whom Ian Grant knew in Brighton and had decided to bring into the Stranglers' entourage, featured a true-life photograph of a strangled woman lying in a pool of blood. This was rock rebellion in the worst possible taste, and it suited the Stranglers' Mansonesque image perfectly. They certainly weren't alone in deploying such shock tactics. Almost two years later the Sex Pistols scraped the barrel of bad taste with their song 'Belsen Was A Gas', but it would be the Stranglers who would become the kicking boys in the media. The band soon realized that death was a powerful sales pitch, and that the evil and the sinister provided a potentially endless variety of selling-points and dynamic images. The ad for their appearance at The Hope and Anchor on 1 February 1976 ran: 'Fact: Stranglers seen leaving 3.00 a.m. with 17-year-old nympho schoolgirl!!'.

Quite what this rather puerile exercise in sexual mastery was meant to convey now appears unclear. It's certainly hard, looking back from the standpoint of the late 90s, to think anyone would find this amusing, even if it was intended as a joke. But the fact of the matter was that a joke was what it was intended to be. Today it's easy to get a lot of the tabloid imagery out of context. It was a very sexist society. The photo from John Peel's column in *Sounds* depicted him with his eyes-closed, wearing his rightly beloved Liverpool FC T-shirt and grooving along to the music in his headphones, while a topless woman lies on his lap looking yearningly at said DJ as if about to shove her chest into his face. But for the first four years of the band's existence it suited them, and those around them, to sell the Stranglers as libertines in a world of sequentially fuckable women.

One song in particular, the live favourite 'School Ma'am', was viciously voyeuristic. This was quintessential Cornwell: an imaginative reconstruction of a sex act witnessed on short-circuit TV by an archetypal 'old maid' (represented by the headmistress) who climaxes for the first time and dies as a result. It's a song which deals with the sexual repression of an older generation in a cruel and mocking way. There's no irony or lightness of touch on evidence here, and Hugh's sexual peccadillos are paraded for all to see. The listener is manipulated to laugh at the repression of the headmistress, although she herself could easily represent Hugh's own male gaze. There are two very interesting things about 'School Ma'am'. Firstly, the form of the song is quite peculiar within the pop of the day – it is a long, narrative recitative delivered against a discordant, repetitive guitar riff, almost like a Home Counties version of 'Venus In Furs' by the Velvet Underground. Secondly, on stage, at the climax of the song, when the old mistress dies after her first-ever orgasm, Hugh would grab his throat, pump his hands up and down and spit out the mother of gobs into the first row. Jet explains, hopefully with a touch of irony:

The story was about his days as a teacher, and the narrative of the song is about the mistress who spies a bit of sex going on and starts masturbating. And Hugh does this symbolic masturbation of his throat and at the climax there's all this froth in his mouth and there's this ritualistic ejaculation. It wasn't designed as gobbing into the audience, it was supposed to be a dramatic wank in an artistic way, and he didn't know how to do it without getting his todger out. I think Mr Rotten got to hear about it.

And so, through Hugh, one of the tributaries of snot which became the collective 'punk gob' was being spat out into the audience in early 1976 (in fact, the journos at the time called it 'flobbing'). He wasn't the only punk to be forgetting his handkerchief, though. Johnny Rotten also loved a good old spit on stage, but claims this was due to a chronic sinus infection. But by 1977, 'goading and gobbing', as Dave Laing puts it, was a staple of punk performance, as showers of spittle were shot by both band and audience, covering the stage in slime and reducing the average punk gig to a slippery mucous-bound re-enactment of a heat from 'It's A Knockout'. Even children's television got in on the act, with the brilliant *Tiswas*, itself a reconstruction of a punk gig in its general mayhem, featuring Bob Carolgees and 'Spit, the punk dog'. (Incidentally, the Stranglers must hold the record for being the only group to have been banned from appearing on *Tiswas* after angering presenter Sally James). Before punk, the rock spectacle depended upon sincerity and reciprocity, as *artistes* ingratiated themselves and fans roared back their delight. But with punk the bands taunted their audiences and the fans returned the compliment. Bottles, cans and mucus became tokens of affection. Punk revelled in a general disgust for the body, its functions and its secretions: just as sex was mere 'squelching', so approval was inverted to the taboo of spitting in public.

The Stranglers' collective view of women as objects wasn't anything out of the ordinary: their brand of misogyny was echoed almost throughout the new wave in the next few years. The publicity poster for the Damned's first album ran the legend, 'Album out now. Play it at your sister', whilst Mark P, the famous punk periodicalist, wrote in his fanzine *Sniffin'*

Glue: 'Punks are not girls, if it comes to the crunch we'll have no option but to fight back.' Dave Laing argues that punk's alleged taboo-breaking in relation to the permissibility of language, which found its apogee in the name of the most famous punk band, the Sex Pistols, actually changed nothing at all: 'The lifting of the taboo on the unsayable in rock discourse ended in a new way of saying something quite old: a celebration of male sexuality as essentially aggressive and phallocentric. The phallic motif, incidentally, is echoed . . . in punk names: the Buzzcocks, Hot Rods, Throbbing Gristle, Screwdriver . . .'

The Stranglers were simply the most visible element in a new wave scene which remained almost wholly un-reconstituted.

Whilst it is true to say that the Stranglers pre-dated most of the punk bands by a year, and that there is something undeniably *ur* about the aura of violence and domination which attached itself to the band, it is also true that they responded to the new wave musically and allowed themselves to be packaged as a punk act. Albion received £1000, then a substantial sum of money, from Andrew Bailey at Bell records, and on 11 and 12 July the Stranglers demoed 'Go Buddy Go', and 'Bitchin' at the Pebble Beach studio in Worthing. The songs' structures are essentially the same as those which would later be released on United Artists the following year, although the arrangements are very different, with 'Go Buddy Go' complete with backing vocals and Gary Glitter-style glam-rock handclaps (Hugh called them 'gargantuan claps'). The most striking feature, though, is how *slow* these songs are. 'Bitchin' really does sound like a long-lost cousin to Oasis' 'Roll With It'. Around this time the band demoed two new songs, 'Grip' and 'Peasant In The Big Shitty', at Riverside Studios in Chiswick. Again, the tempo is incredibly plodding. Six months later, however, when it came to the band laying down tracks for their first album, their songs were souped up and speeded up in response to punk's freneticism. Garry Coward-Williams:

The punk groups considered that the Stranglers were bandwagon-ing, and . . . to a degree they were. When the punk thing really started to happen, a lot of the songs started to speed up. The original demo of Grip was half the speed! A lot of the slow, melodic songs like, 'Strange Little Girl' and 'I've Got Myself To Blame' were dropped from the set. If you'd been a punk and gone to one of their gigs in the first half of 1976 you'd known that they weren't part of the scene. Then if you had gone six months later you'd have heard everything speeded up.

Another indicator of the band's distance from punk was their choice of recreational drugs. Apart from Dave, who was into acid, the communal drug most used by the band was dope – the quintessential hippy drug. The rest of the punks were into speed and various other uppers, but the majority of the time the Stranglers were content to indulge in some serious flower-power stupefaction.

The band's publicist, Alan Edwards, was instrumental in packaging them along with the other new-wave artists, no easy task given the rather aged hardware he was working with. Even the band's *bone fide* punk, JJ, was five years older than most on the scene. 'I was one of the forces pulling them into punk because I was hanging out with Billy Idol. I had known him when he was William Broad from my school days near Brighton. I was doing his publicity and I'd bring him along to Stranglers' gigs. I remember JJ didn't like him and thought he was a poser, which was the worst thing you could be in 1977. I instigated that fanzine, *Strangled*, the first one was written and designed by me in early 1977.'

Throughout the second half of 1976 and 1977 Edwards worked assiduously for the band. As Garry Coward-Williams remembers, he definitely tried to sell them as punk hunks to that section of the audience which was guaranteed to put them in the singles charts – teenage girls: 'They were trying to get a teen-appeal thing going with the band, and I had a couple of pictures of John at Dingwalls before the punch up with Simonon and JJ. Alan Edwards looked at them and said, "They'd be great for a girls' magazine."'

Like Edwards, Albion's Ian Grant, himself an ex-member of the Angry Brigade and the White Panthers, warmed to punk's 'in-yer-face' anti-establishment rhetoric. However, if one third of Albion agency was willing to ride the commercial crest of the new wave, Derek and Dai were, according to Ian Grant, already feeling semi-detached: 'Dai and Derek hated the punk thing; they got intimidated by it. This is not to say that I revelled in it or enjoyed it, because I didn't, I hate violence. I remember arguing with Mitch Mitchell and Phil Lynott in the early days at the

Nashville and the Speakeasy when they said, "This is rubbish music and they shouldn't be playing", when they were taking an almost parental attitude. We understood punk, me and Alan. We were loving every minute of it.'

It was during the steaming-hot drought of the summer of 1976, with West Indian Michael Holding terrorizing the English batsmen on the cricket field and Elton John and Kiki Dee terrorizing the charts with the 'incendiary' sounds of 'Don't Go Breaking My Heart', that a recognizable punk scene began to emerge. The Stranglers, despite all their badges of difference from the vast majority of practitioners, were active on this circuit. A little piece of pop history was made on 17 June when the Stranglers shared the bill with Ian Dury and the Kilburns, and the *enfants terribles* of punk, the Sex Pistols. Garry Coward-Williams remembers the Walthamstow gig well. It was 50p to get in, and 25 people turned up!:

I remember seeing the Sex Pistols for the first time, standing by their van outside the gig. They were all wearing leather and looked really moody and hard. I subsequently found out that they weren't hard at all, but they had this atmosphere around them. Steve Jones came into our dressing-room and chatted with the band. I remember John telling me that Jones was the hard one and the rest weren't worth bothering with. John was always interested in who was physically tough and would afford them a certain respect commensurate to their hardness. There was definitely an element of competition between the Stranglers and the Sex Pistols – both bands realizing that they had the potential to be the top dogs in the new movement. Although musically very different, the Pistols were the Stranglers' greatest rivals in that summer of '76. I remember John and I watched some of their set and were both impressed with how powerful they sounded.

In truth the Stranglers seldom occupied the same territory as the Pistols. The differences between the two groups were both musical and ideological. The Stranglers were, even during their first years together as a band, far and away technically superior and musically more intricate than groups such as the Pistols. The Pistols made two singles, 'Anarchy In The UK' and 'God Save The Queen', which musically photographed 1976–7 more succinctly than any band of the era. But the Stranglers were, in traditional terms, more '*musical*', more melodic, and less concerned with energy and attack, a reminder of the psychedelia of the sixties, whereas the Pistols' music dealt in volume and power, in forcing rock out of the navel-gazing progressive era by means of a sonic reconstruction. Never have guitars in pop sounded as nasty as they did on Pistols' early records. The noise became the concept and the pleasure. And, in this, they were perhaps closer to reggae and dub than to rock. Echo, noise, distortion and volume were more important than melody, harmony and structure.

In addition, the Stranglers had an ideology of anti-fashion. With the exception of JJ, they played up the image of being working-class scruffs, streets away from King's Road chic. You certainly wouldn't see a Strangler with a safety pin through his nose. JJ told the *NME* in 1976 that the band had been slated: 'For not digging Iggy and the Stooges and telling them so . . . and not going down King's Road to the Roebuck and the Sex Shop. That's why we've been ignored a lot.'

The motivation behind the Sex Pistols was patently different. Their initial band of followers, the Bromley Contingent, which included Billy Idol and Siouxsie Sioux, were the disenfranchised sons and daughters of Bowie and Ferry. They saw music and fashion as inseparable wholes, as did the punk gurus Malcolm McLaren and Bernie Rhodes. For them punk was conceived as a situationist scam: they lived punk as much in *theory* as in practice. The Stranglers were initially punk's prosaic flip-side. Like prog rock and pub-rock bands, they 'paid their dues' by gigging up and down the country, while the punk *artistes* remained largely localized in Manchester and London. The Stranglers were a demotic band and built up a huge following, not through the *NME* but through sheer hard work. They were the last pub-rock band to break out of their *locale* and build a career.

The only Strangler to consider himself a punk was JJ. But, as he explains, he thought of himself as a free-thinking radical, completely separate from the herd-mentality which character-ized the scene:

> I was a punk rocker, yeah. I immersed myself in the whole thing. It was very tense, because there were very few places where we thought we could go and hang-out, but they were our temples. One thing I didn't agree with was the manipulation of politically

ignorant people. Just following slogans I always thought was pretty naff anyway. So the Clash posing by the barriers in Belfast wound me up a bit, and we refused to get involved in Rock Against Racism because I just thought it was racist. We were involved with reggae bands such as Steel Pulse and we helped them out in real racist situations. I thought, 'Well, drainpipe trousers are in again, cool, because we'd been wearing them anyway. Leather jackets are in again.' I didn't have to buy any new clothes, it was perfect. And I loved the style of the girls and I liked the anger, although I didn't realize that most of the anger was phony anger from the other bands and that they were told what to say politically. The Clash were totally programmed by Bernie Rhodes, you know.

Punk undoubtedly broke the band, as JJ admits. And he liked the perks that went with his new role as pop-star punk-rocker!: 'Suddenly, whereas 18 months before we'd been turned down by 24 record companies because they didn't want short pop songs, now they did. Suddenly girls were queuing up to sit on my face which I thought was really pleasant, if they'd washed beforehand.'

Although punk broke the band, the Stranglers were always different. Rather than stay in London, the Stranglers were a provincial phenomenon. JJ again:

Punk was full of missionary zeal. The other bands were playing in London getting front covers and we were the band playing up in Grimsby or something, having punch ups with dockers who thought they were going to destroy this punk menace from London they'd read about in the *News Of The World*. We were in the front line, the other bands weren't. That made us stronger. We were getting beaten up and attacked, and giving beatings, and it was all very exciting, I thought. And we were being paid for it.

Musically, they considered themselves very much as separate entities: Dave: 'We were part of the new wave, but not specifically punk rock, because we had a different line-up and more musicianship. I liked most of the punk bands, though, for certain tracks. It was useful to be classed as a part of them because it helped the band.'

Punk certainly appealed to Jet's crusty sense of humour, particularly the contribution of the Sex Pistols: 'Well, I started off thinking they were hugely funny. I thought these lads are taking the piss out of everything and getting away with it and when they brought out an album, *Never Mind The Bollocks*, I cracked up laughing. It wasn't until some years later I'd sit down and seriously listen to this music that I thought this was bloody good, powerful rock n roll, so I would say they made a serious contribution to British musical culture.'

So, for the most part, the band were happy to be bracketed along with the other punk acts. In truth the punk scene in Britain was talked up by a very small coterie of writers and fashion designers. In the music press, punk's major apologist was Caroline Coon, who revelled in punk's anti-rock establishment pose and kept the torch burning, despite the hostility of her editor Allan Jones, who regarded punk's 'we hate everything' stance as unsophisticated and nihilistic, unpoetic and pointlessly depoliticized. During 1976, the Stranglers themselves began to attract the attention of a small bunch of journalists writing about the pub-rock circuit. Their most vocal supporter was Chas De Whalley, the *Sounds* grass-roots man, keen to pick up on emerging talent in the pubs and clubs. He dubbed them 'Punk Floyd', picking up on the Syd Barrett-era psychedelic shadings of their early material. To reinforce their punk credentials, the band were chosen to represent Britain for two gigs with the Flamin' Groovies and the Ramones at the Round House on 4 July and at Dingwalls the next evening to commemorate the American bicentenary.

These concerts were by all accounts hugely enjoyable and a real education: nobody had heard anything quite as fast and as brutal as the Ramones before. Their thrashing guitar style, volume, energy and sheer unstoppability dazed their audience as their set was played at break-neck speed. It had taken Genesis thirty minutes to perform one song, 'Supper's Ready', on their first post-Peter Gabriel tour that year. In the same time the Ramones could pack in fifteen, maybe twenty. And although many of those involved in the New Wave would secretly go back and listen to *Foxtrot* on their headphones when they thought no one was around, for the most part it was blasphemous to admit to liking any track which lasted longer than the time it took to have a pee.

But on the second night, after the Stranglers had played their support slot, there was some serious trouble. Dagenham Dave had 'made' JJ drink two bottles of red wine in quick succession, a synaptically-challenging load of alcohol even for most people, but for JJ potentially devastating. At that time JJ hardly drank at all, and could become a little faint after a half of lager. So the red mists had descended on JJ's world and as he made his way rather unsteadily to the bar he came within 'spitting distance' of Paul Simonen from the Clash. JJ now takes up the story, tail fairly well tucked between legs: 'I saw Steve from the Pistols and Paul from the Clash and just as I walked past Paul spat on the ground because he had one of these nervous mannerisms. I thought he was spitting at me, so I punched him. He fell backwards and spilt a drink all over Steve's head. Next thing we knew we were thrown out by the bouncers. It was kids' stuff really. No one would apologize – it wasn't real fighting.'

The action then moved outside to the car park, and soon a grand face-off occurred between the Stranglers' entourage and Dagenham Dave, and an assemblage of the Clash, the Sex Pistols and Chrissie Hynde, with a luckless and blameless Paul Simonen and a pissed JJ at centre stage. Garry Coward-Williams explains:

I remember Johnny Rotten was leaning with his back to the door of the Pistols' transit van. Dag Dave, Jet and I were standing together and there were assorted members of the opposition hanging around. A classic 'Mexican stand-off' – straight out of a spaghetti western – with John and Simonen in the middle facing each other off . . . I looked to 'uncle' Jet for guidance, his response was, 'Just wait till it starts then get stuck in.' As far as Jet and Dag Dave were concerned if John and Simonen were going to fight, then that was their business, but if anyone else was going to have a go, then we would all pile in. With the atmosphere in this highly charged state, Rotten decided to make a remark – I forget what he said, but it was probably uncomplimentary. Dag Dave, seeing this as an opportunity to show that we meant business, thumped Rotten squarely in the chest with the flat of his hand, smashing him against the van door, and on the rebound he grabbed Rotten by the throat telling him in no uncertain terms that no one else was to be involved. Rotten was shitting himself big time, and rightly so – Dave would have beaten him senseless if he had retaliated. This act broke the tension and John and Simonen decided to call it 'quits'. Throughout the whole episode, Hugh watched the proceedings from the inside of the ice-cream van with the girls – he wanted to have no part in the punch-up, which at the time really shocked me. However, with hindsight, he was probably being sensible.

This whole incident was important in that it began the stigmatization of the Stranglers. Before this point the band were on relatively friendly terms with many of the punks. Chrissie Hynde, later of the Pretenders, used to ride in the famed ice-cream van, and even asked the group if they'd like to be her backing band (she was christened Chrissie Hindleg for her pains by Hugh). However, from this tiff onwards they would be barred from the punk 'club' and would be viewed with contempt. True, all the rest of the bands tended to view one another with a very public disdain – there was a covenant of mutual hatred, a code of loathing which bonded them together. But the Stranglers were now outside this mutual-(non)appreciation society and they really only had themselves to blame.

The Dingwalls ding-dong demonstrated JJ's seriously high testosterone levels. JJ had a temper that at times was impossible to control, and, in the next decade, he would follow the law of the jungle, many times matching verbal taunts with physical action. JJ saw no fundamental difference between the violence inherent in the words of a critical review and the physical violence of a 'provoked' reaction. The incident also demonstrated Hugh's innate self-preserving tendencies. Hugh was not a physically violent man. He didn't need to be: his tongue could be cruel enough. But he considered JJ's penchant for giving beatings immature. Faced with 'sticking up' for his pissed mate or keeping a low profile in the van with the girls, Hugh chose the latter course of action. Hugh remembers the incident as another example of JJ's needlessly aggressive mentality:

We arrived at Dingwalls very elated from the gig. I saw Joe Strummer at the bar and was very happy to celebrate and listen to his opinions as a friend. In mid-conversation Joe grabbed me and said, 'Uh-oh, looks like our bass players are having a barny!' We looked on aghast, and saw them both being thrown out. Joe and I tried to calm the situation down, but I gave up when I realized JJ was manipulating things to satisfy his own ego. There was never going to be a punch-up outside, just a few drunk musos posing in a car park. Nobody was going to risk getting damaged by Dagenham Dave. What should have happened was that everyone should have had a drink together and enjoyed the evening. After all this I went to the van to make sure that a girl I had been chatting up all evening hadn't got away. I was disappointed that a potentially great evening had been sabotaged.

The rest of 1976 saw the band courting violence in ever more direct ways. One of the components of the punk movement was its air of mindless, male-dominated violence, which was more prevalent in football hooliganism or moronic right-wing groups such as the National Front and the British Movement. As the band broadened its appeal, it attracted any number of undesirables. Some were harmless hard-nuts, some outrageous pranksters (one of the punk fraternity, a bloke called Martin, in an effort to outdo his mates in acts of depravity, used to climb on stage and stick his fingers down his throat to make himself sick) but some were less benign. For the next few years the Stranglers would attract these homosocial types and the first wave of lads made their appearance on the scene one autumn's night in 1976. On 14 November 1976 the band were playing a gig in a London pub called The Torrington when they were subjected to a full-scale invasion by a posse of likely lads in mysterious garb. Hugh:

I saw all these heavy-looking geezers coming into the gig. There were loads of weird-looking people around. That, in itself, didn't surprise me. Anyway, I saw them all troop in like a squad and all suddenly go to the loo and I thought, 'This is looking serious, this is looking like something has been prepared here. I don't know what the fuck is going to happen.' And the loo door opened and they all came out in all this bondage stuff and they looked really really menacing and frightening and they just jumped on the stage and I thought, 'Oh fuck, this is it, we're going to get completely slaughtered'. But they just started dancing and they didn't attack us at all.

After the gig they said, 'You guys were great!' And I thought, 'Thank fuck for that,' I said, 'Why did you all file into the bathroom?' And they said, 'Because we're not allowed to come into the venue dressed like this.' So they'd all brought their stuff in plastic bags and changed into all this punk gear in the loo!

JJ developed the closest relationship with the Finchleys and is still in contact with a few to this day. He remembers them as 'lovely, really sweet, down-to-earth people from the council-estates of Finchley' although he concedes that originally he had to put straight one Finchley who was a NF-supporter and was giving Pete, a black Finchley Boy, some stick. Afterwards the aforementioned Finchley was strongly against the NF. So there was certainly some political naïvety within the grouping.

For two years the Finchleys were the band's praetorian guard, travelling from gig to gig in their minibus 'Rod' (named after the first three letters of the registration number), and were always on call to meet might with might. Jet Black:

> They became first of all a sort of mobile fan club, and then a sort of army, as they started having aspirations toward protecting us. JJ used the term, 'our private army', I think, and they were very close to the band for a couple of years and then they went their separate ways. Some of them were pretty nefarious characters, but some of them were absolutely charming. They were just out to have a good time, and if anyone stopped them they might get a bit violent. Kids latch on to something which is fun, like raves, and its only when people stop them having fun that it becomes violent.

These were violent times for the Stranglers and a gig could easily get very nasty indeed. Garry Coward-Williams, however, takes a less charitable view of the Finchley Boys, or the Finchley Freds as they were originally called. He comments:

> Finchley Boys were John's new crew. I never got involved with them, and I didn't really like them. I found them aggressive and unfriendly, so I ignored them. Although a hard man, Dag Dave had soul, he was actually quite a gentlemen in a way, he was a nice, friendly guy totally into the band. The Finchley Boys were classic skinhead-types with the gang mentality. When they came on the scene it was time for Dave to move over, but it didn't work out that way because he took tremendous exception.

To say that the Finchley Boys were into violence would not, perhaps, be an earth-shattering overstatement. These were violent times and laddish thuggery was part and parcel of it. They were also wont to get up on stage with the band for a sing-along and one of their number used to particularly enjoy having a noose slipped round his neck whilst a mate pretended to hang him. The Finchley Boys were undoubtedly more punk than the band they followed and found the band an enigma – middle-class rebels with more intellectual might than they could perhaps handle.

The situation with Dagenham Dave came to a head at a gig at the 100 Club, just over two weeks after the Finchleys' first appearance, when Dave challenged them *all* to a fight! Coward-Williams:

> I remember that the Finchleys were pogoing aggressively and being a pain in the arse to those trying to stand and watch the gig. Dave decided to dance and started pogoing amongst them. Something happened – I don't know what, but the next minute fists were flying and he was fighting them – Dave versus about eight or more Finchleys. It was a really nasty brawl with chairs and tables. They were usurping him as band mascot and he didn't like it. Eventually an ambulance turned up. Dave had fractured his skull, but ran out before any medical help arrived. The Finchleys were in a dire state. In fact I think Dave ended up getting the better of all eight of them! I don't think they realized what they'd got themselves into. It was the most blood-chilling, most frightening fight I had ever seen. The band kept playing for a bit and JJ tried to break it up from the stage.

It all went wrong for Dagenham Dave after this point. His long-standing girlfriend, Brenda, left him and he felt increasingly sidelined from the band's activities, particularly when he was asked to leave the recording sessions for the band's first album, *Rattus Norvegicus*, because he was deemed to be interfering too much in giving producer Martin Rushent the benefit of his opinions. He pleaded with Brenda to come back, but to no avail. He became extremely depressed and threatened suicide, and on 9 February 1977 he jumped off Tower Bridge. His body wasn't recovered from the Thames for another three weeks. JJ immortalized him in song on 'Dagenham Dave' for the *No More Heroes*, album and Coward-Williams guesses that would have pleased him: 'I think he would have been absolutely delighted by that, being immortalized by the band he loved. He was so into music.' But ultimately JJ's lyrics, although intended as heartfelt, ring slightly hollow: 'I'm not going to cry, I bet he hit that water high' . . .

Jet has pointed out that this lyric was intended to be inter-

preted as, 'I'm not going to cry about your death, 'cos I know you
wanted to die while high on drugs!!' But the truth was that he
was a broken man. He had lost his franchise as the band's
confidant and true supporter, and he had lost simultaneously
his girlfriend, who was the main emotional crutch of his life. It
marked the beginning of a history of death and misfortune which
would attach itself to the band during the next four years. It also
marked the end of an era of innocence. Dave did not live to see
his favourite band so successful, which is probably the ultimate
sadness. But rather than heeding the warnings and distancing
themselves from violence and aggression of all forms, the band
continued to be embroiled in it, and to court it. And they began to
live out their own publicity, as Ian Grant and Albion ultimately
began using violence as a selling-point: 'I often couldn't get gigs
for them after a while, because they were so bad I couldn't get
them rebooked. Either they'd play bad or they used to cause too
much trouble. They ended up living out their publicity and
believing it all. I suppose a publicist's and manager's role is to
act on it.'

The band have always had a very uneasy relationship with the
media, and the trouble started as early as 1976. From an early
stage in their career, the band would look on with incredulity as
gigs which had actually been cancelled were reviewed negatively
in the pages of the rock inkies. Jet has always viewed the media
with a certain disdain, treating the odd informed interviewer with
respect and friendliness. Dave has simply decided not to talk to
the press at all (the easy option), viewing the whole profession,
with the exception of specialist publications, as dishonest. It
would be JJ and Hugh who would give the bulk of the interviews, and their approach, after several unhappy experiences,
was often combative to the point of bullying. Hugh: 'We were
distrustful of journalists because they were always misrepresent-
ing us. You'd do an interview and you'd be thinking, "Oh what a
nice chap, that's gonna turn out to be a really great piece" and it
would come out a complete disaster. You'd be really disappointed
because you'd think that you had points of agreement in tastes
and thoughts and ideas and then it turns out that you hadn't at all
and it was just a big con to get you to relax and drop your guard.'
   In addition, both had a penchant for telling outrageous lies and

getting away with it (Hugh told the *News Of The World* that December that the leather thong he had taken to wearing round his neck was for auto-strangulation on stage: 'I'll tighten this knot to give me more blood in the head. Like a shot of adrenalin.') This pattern was already set by the end of 1976. The Stranglers were not a media-friendly band, often reacting wildly to criticism. Because of their outsider position in relation to punk, they were viewed as musically carpet-bagging opportunists, as frustrated intelligentsia, by a media which had seldom witnessed quite the level of articulateness, manipulation and aggression in one package before. The *NME*'s Phil McNeill was the first journalist to lock horns with the band after he reviewed their gig on 7 November at the Marquee. McNeill liked the band a lot, and said so vociferously ('They are a terrific band'), but found some of their songs 'aggressively sexist', called Hugh 'old even by my standards', and found the band's exhortation to 'smash the place up' (because the venue was deemed to be an anachronism and lifeless) rather puerile. McNeill could be cleared on all charges: some of the songs were indeed misogynistic (whether the Stranglers themselves were is another matter which will be addressed later). Hugh did look a little older than his 27 years (although, remarkably, he's barely aged since). The band were violent and wilful – inviting the punters to tear down a crap venue is simply stupid, and such incidents ultimately backfired on them in a big way. The reason for the band's vocal put-down of the venue appears to be quite simple: it was an act of solidarity with Albion. The Marquee had broken Eddie & the Hot Rods, one of the leading new-wave acts, and it was the only major London venue not controlled by the Albion hot-shots.

For his pains, McNeill was harangued by the band about the minutiae of his Marquee review when he interviewed them in the December of that year. This set the tone for many exchanges between band and media, as any criticism was taken so personally that the journalist concerned was cowed into surrender. McNeill found the Stranglers infuriating: they espoused rebellion but appeared apolitical and uncommitted to any firm beliefs. Then there was the matter of the band's failure to condemn Nazism outright. 'Nazi fetishism,' opined JJ, 'is the only vibe that is united . . . we're due for tyranny. People laugh at that, because England is the last place for that, but I really think it could happen.' And Hugh chipped in with similar newsbites: 'I'd like to make enough money to buy a large mansion and put all the politicians in separate rooms so they can play with themselves . . . What we desperately need is a Robin Hood character.'

Here JJ and Hugh were reflecting a rock *Geist*. A year earlier a coked-out David Bowie had uttered almost identical sentiments predicting the rise of a Hitler figure in Britain. The UK was shifting right-ward, with the increasingly unsocialist Callaghan Labour government of the late seventies leading to the monstrosity of Thatcherism in the eighties. JJ was hip to what was happening, but couldn't decide whether it was for good or ill that Britain was calling for a 'strong man'. 'Leftist heroes are very much middle-class heroes. They [the people] want warrior heroes.' As history would show, they only had two-and-a-half years to wait for their own Boadicea. But it would be intellectual laziness to brand JJ (who was well-informed, deliberately provocative and extremist), or any of the Stranglers, as Nazis. In fact Jet Black has had a long-standing hatred of the Far Right: 'It sickens me that people can do to other human beings what the Nazis did. When I see the kids today going round with their short hair cuts, their aggressive stance and their swastikas then it sickens me. I was born at the tail end of an absolute nightmare and those kids have no respect for, or comprehension of, the evil they're getting into.'

The Stranglers were merely picking up on very heavy vibes and could, perhaps, feel that the country was drifting towards a political revolution. But it's as well to point out that nobody connected with the band at the time thought that Hugh, and more importantly JJ, harboured Nazi sympathies. Alan Edwards: 'JJ wasn't a Nazi. If he'd had a heavy Nazi thing going, I think I would have noticed. In fact I don't remember him being heavily political at all. JJ was more a hedonist. He was into the buzz of riding motorbikes, doing the gigs, going to the parties, with babes everywhere. He lived the life. He was a great bass player; not a good bass player, a *great* bass player. He was, to use a term that would have gotten you shot in 1977, a star performer.'

JJ was a very bright bloke, interested in political debate, but still a little green, with a tendency to see things in black and white terms. He had fun playing devil's advocate, and he simply enjoyed winding people up. But the Nazi tag stuck, and a section of the media insinuated that JJ harboured far-right sympathies.

The Stranglers were obviously a very talented band, but having started off before all their competitors, they were the last of their generation of new-wave acts to secure a record deal. For most of 1976 they had been working their bollocks off playing to ever more enthusiastic crowds on the London pub-rock scene, a workload which eventually led them to move out of their Chiddingfold squat to make their own individual accommodation arrangements in the capital. Whilst they knew that visibility in London was a prerequisite to being signed, they also played a number of gigs in the provinces. On 30 July they played Chelmsford Prison. Taking a leaf out of their book, the Sex Pistols appeared at the same venue that September.

But the main concern was to find a record deal. CBS had already conducted some market research into the band and had concluded that they were simply too old and too unfashionable to succeed in the punk rock era. Although publicly the band always gave the impression of being extremely confident, privately they countenanced the unthinkable: that they would miss the boat and fail to win a recording contract. Jet: 'We had absurd amounts of self-confidence. Too much in fact. We were so confident that we couldn't understand why anybody could dismiss us. But I think there was always some doubt in our minds that we would ever get signed, although we would never admit it and there was no way we were going to give up. Historically it was a two-or three-year period, but when you're going through it and you're starving and you can't pay the bills, it's heavy.'

Dai Davies knew Andrew Lauder, the A&R chief at United Artists, and invited him to attend a number of Stranglers' gigs. Lauder was a wise choice as a contact man, having already signed the pub-rock supergroup, Dr Feelgood. But, perhaps more importantly, he also had an ear for the bizarre, having been instrumental in breaking krautrock in the UK by having the foresight to sign up Can and Tangerine Dream in the early 70s. There was quite a buzz about the Stranglers by the autumn of 1976. They were now being regularly reviewed in the music papers, John Peel had said some nice things about their demo tape and, with the Damned signed to Stiff and the Sex Pistols being snapped up by EMI, the time was surely right for the

Stranglers to be signed up too. New-wave music was perfect for a music industry sliding slowly into recession: it was cheap to make and cheap to put out, and UA wanted some of the action. Alan Edwards says Lauder was 'a really lovely music guy. They don't have many people like that left at record labels these days.'

But every time he went to see the band it was a disaster. They had been asked to support Patti Smith again on her short British tour that October, and it was again a chance for the band to gain experience at 2,000-capacity venues such as the Hammersmith Odeon in London and the Birmingham Odeon in the Midlands. But on the night Andrew Lauder turned up (the second of the Hammersmith Odeon gigs), the PA turned bandit and there were so many technical problems that the gig was a farce. Finally, it was arranged for the band to play a live gig for Lauder in a rehearsal room on 4 December 1976. Presented with a great band, at full-throttle and with decent equipment, Lauder had no hesitation. United Artists signed the band on 6 December 1976. Their leading label stablemates were the very un-punk Electric Light Orchestra and Slim Whitman (twenty years before he attained hip status as the alien-killing country singer in *Mars Attacks!*). Their advance was £40,000. The Stranglers were on the threshold of stardom.

4: RAINING SWEAT

1977 was the Stranglers' year. It was they, more than any other
new wave act, who impinged on the record-buyer's conscious-
ness to the greatest effect. The cultural clout may have belonged
to the Sex Pistols, but in terms of record sales, it was the
Stranglers who made the bigger commercial impact, with two
Top 5 albums and three hit singles.

The main consideration once they had been signed by United
Artists was to get some product out quickly. UA were obviously
keen on packaging the Stranglers as a top pub-rock band and, in
an attempt to ape the success of Dr Feelgood's live album,
Stupidity, suggested that the Stranglers' vinyl debut should be a
no-frills live recording. The band's performance at the Nashville
on 23 December 1976 was taped, but nobody was happy with it,
and so a conventional studio album was planned instead.

Another priority for the band was to replace the legendarily
unreliable equipment with some gear that might possibly get
through a set without malfunctioning. To that end much of the
advance was spent on updating the band's kit and a new PA,
while Dave had his Hammond serviced.

UA's in-house producer was Martin Rushent. Rushent at this
stage was a pop *ingénue* and had virtually no track record (his
recording credits had been with Curved Air and that stalwart of
the new wave, Shirley Bassey). But Rushent was young and
enthusiastic, and obviously had talent (his later work with the
Human League on the brilliant *Dare* codified British synth-pop for
the decade to come). The band decamped to their favourite TW
studios in Fulham to record the first single, the set-opener 'Grip',
before laying down enough tracks for not just one but almost two
studio albums. The atmosphere was good-natured and fun;
Rushent's brief was to capture them as they were with the
minimum of actual production, to get the guys to play and to
make the best of still shaky musicianship. The band knew next to
nothing about the ins and outs of a 24-track recording studio and
were happy to let Rushent get on with the job. The group's dark

power and sinister prowl, and the neophyte mix of Stranglers and Rushent, was a success. Hugh Cornwell recollects, however, that it was Alan Winstanley, the in-house engineer at TW studios, who really impressed with his technical know-how. Hugh: 'In those days you were a good producer if you could tell a good joke and Martin always had loads of jokes. You see Alan would do all the work, Martin's position was just to oversee it all. He was like the nurse maid. Martin would get the beers in, or order the food, or tell a joke: he would look after us.'

Listening to '(Get A) Grip (On Yourself)' 20 years on, it's hard to think of a more impressive début single from a rock band in that era. Every major artist of the sixties and seventies from Dylan to Bowie, from the Beatles to the Who, took at least a few releases to get into their stride musically. But, along with Roxy Music's epochal début, 'Virginia Plain' in 1972, 'Grip' sees a band hitting top form straight away. Too slow in tempo to be classed as punk, the masturbatory-punning 'Grip', written by Hugh, is a sanguine tale of the mundanity of being in a rock band, the struggles and the financial bummers. It's a summation of Hugh's rock life up to that point and ends with world-weary sci-fi trappings which would later resurface on their *Meninblack* album four years down the line:

> Stranger from another planet
> Welcome to our hole
> Just strap on your guitar
> And we'll play some rock'n'roll

Dave Greenfield's arpeggiated keyboard figures tumble out of the speakers. JJ's bass growls, an incongruous sax line further distances the sonic territory from punk, and the whole is a gorgeously infectious pop song. That it failed to set the charts afire was less to do with a lack of publicity or real support, and perhaps more to do with the machinations and designs of the chart compilers, the British Market Research Bureau, and the official chart publishers, *Music Week*. The single was mysteriously left off the chart for one week (due to a clerical error) and replaced by Silver Convention's 'Everybody's Talkin 'Bout Love'. The band suspected foul play, as the Silver Convention *meisterwerk* was allegedly hyped into the chart and there was an

A youthful Brian Duffy (a.k.a. Jet Black) on stage in the mid-50s. (*Photograph: courtesy of Jet Black*)

Hugh (far right) in Johnny Sox. (*Photograph: courtesy of Hugh Cornwell*)

REGISTRATION OF BUSINESS NAMES ACT, 1916

as amended by the Companies Act, 1947

CERTIFICATE OF REGISTRATION

I hereby certify that a statement of particulars furnished by

THE STRANGLERS

pursuant to sections 3 and 4 of the above-mentioned Act was this day registered in London.

Dated the   11th September 1974

(R. W. WESTLEY)
Registrar of Business Names

Regn. No.   1886366

This certificate is required by the Act to be exhibited in a conspicuous position at the principal place of business. Notification of changes in particulars or cessation of the business should be sent to the Registrar, Companies House, 55-71 City Road, London, EC1Y 1BB

The Stranglers' Certificate of Registration. (*Courtesy of The Stranglers*)

Telephone: GUILDFORD 76147

The Winemakers Centre (Guildford) Ltd.

61 WOODBRIDGE ROAD · GUILDFORD · SURREY

YOUR REF   GO BUDDY GO   OUR REF   KEY E   DATE

the boys and the girls were dancing around
danceing all night to the crazy sound
its the newest thing to hit this land
the boys and the girls are all holding hands
i said go buddy go buddy go buddy go buddy go go go

im with my friend bob having a good time
ive got me a girl and im feeling fine
but bobs not dancing nosiree
hes got alively eye on a little lady

     CHORUS
cant she ~~seepse~~ see that hes giving her the eye
       see
wont she stop cos hes giving her the eye
wont she stop and give her a little of her time

     2 CHORUS
****
    SOLO
****
     REPEAT 3 VERSE

i see were changing partners but thats not for me
i notice bobs joining the party
hes standing on the outside looking in
wishing that little lady were with him
     CHORUS

'Go Buddy Go' lyric typed out by JJ on Jet's typewriter at the off-licence. (*Courtesy of Garry Coward-Williams*)

Original scribble for 'Sometimes'. (*Courtesy of Garry Coward-Williams*)

The band's first publicity photo, 1975. (*Photograph: courtesy of The Stranglers*)

Portrait of JJ backstage at the Nashville, November 1975. (*Photograph: © Garry Coward-Williams*)

Garry Coward-Williams (a.k.a. Chiswick Charlie).

The house in Chiddingfold.

The legendary ice-cream van, 1975. (*All photographs this page: © Garry Coward-Williams*)

The band with Hugh's home-produced banner at the Red Cow, Spring 1976.

Dagenham Dave, 1976.

'Where's the beer Dai?' JJ supping beer on stage, 1976. (*All photographs this page:* © *Garry Coward-Williams*)

Jet at the Hope and
Anchor, Summer 1976.

A shifty Hugh at the
soundcheck for a gig at
the 100 Club, Summer
1976. (*Photographs this
page:* © *Garry Coward-
Williams*)

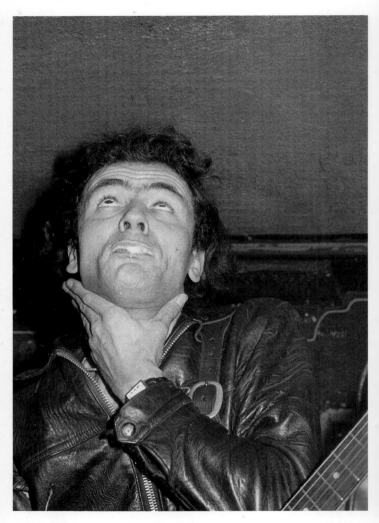

Hugh's 'dramatic wank' during the climax
of 'School Ma'am', 1976. (*Photograph: ©
Garry Coward-Williams*)

anti-punk feeling in the establishment at the time. For whatever reason, retailers failed to re-order the single, which had been selling well, and the result was that it peaked at a respectable, though under-achieving, Number 44.

But momentum was building up behind the band: their gigs were now sell-outs, and a media machine was sweeping them along. Alan Edwards: 'My strategy was this. I said to myself: "I'm going to put the group in the music papers every week for a year." To do that I had to be getting the stories, developing them, inventing them, exaggerating them. It became a mission. "And I succeeded."

The band was packaged and branded perfectly: they had an instantly recognizable sound, two oddly distinctive front men, an easily saleable group ethos of intellectualized violence and rebellion, and one of the most individual band logos in rock history courtesy of the late Kevin Sparrow. Hugh: 'It reminded me a bit of Walt Disney. That was the curious thing about it. It was this heavy name but it was in this Walt Disney writing!'

The album was originally given the typically macabre title *Dead On Arrival*, and was set for May release, but with a real buzz developing about the band, this was brought forward to April 17. There was a last-minute change of title after UA's art director Paul Henry found the perfect image for the band in the shape of a rat scuttling off into the sunset. 'Down In The Sewer', the band's live *tour de force*, had been slated to finish the album, and the recorded track itself ended with the squeals of rats and the drip, drip of water in the sewer. So the rat became the album's remarkable cover shot, and the band's lucky mascot. In the words of writer Simon Reynolds, the rat was 'sewer survivalist in a world turned shitty', and mirrored the way the band viewed themselves: as lone rangers in a corrupt society.

The album was therefore re-titled *Rattus Norvegicus – Stranglers IV*. The 'IV' bit was a characteristic scheme to mislead the public, whilst the intellectual gravitas of the Latin name for the brown rat hammered home their know-it-all predilections. It was an unforgettable title and brought yet more attention to an already notorious and nefarious collective.

For the front cover shot, the band visited a suitably creepy mansion in Blackheath which was the frequent haunt of horror movie film-makers. The front cover itself shows JJ plastered in make-up – a true punk androgene – whilst the inside cover, according to Hugh, still a great believer in fate and destiny, predicted the future of the Stranglers in a most eerie manner: 'That house in Blackheath was full of relics. Dave found a black cat which he put on his lap (*Feline*), we found a Viking chair with spears (*Raven*), I had a plastic kid ("Bring On The Nubiles"), there was a statue (*Meninblack*) and then there was the tubing in the ear (*Aural Sculpture*). All those motifs ended up on Stranglers records.'

During the winter of 1976–7 the band fitted in gigs between their recording commitments. There was now a media outcry wherever they went. Like the mods and rockers in the 60s, and acid house and the ecstasy culture in the late 80s, punk provided the fodder for moral panics, media outrage at disaffected youth, and a tabloid debate about the morality of British youth. The Stranglers were co-opted by the forces for the promotion of moral righteousness and used as a test-case. On 30 January they were due to play a slot at the Rainbow in London supporting the headlining act, the Climax Blues Band. The Tory-run Greater London Council had been made aware of a Stranglers' gig the previous week at the Red Deer in Croydon, where Hugh had allegedly worn an obscene T-shirt and had repeatedly sworn at the audience. The T-shirt in question has now gone down in punk folklore (for example, reproductions of it were sold by traders at the Sex Pistols' reunion gigs in 1996). It was a spoof of the Ford logo, with the word 'fuck' substituted in the style of the original lettering. As a swipe at corporate big business it was an effective (and rather innocuous) parody. The GLC at the time were rumoured to be operating a blacklist following the death of a fan at a recent David Cassidy concert, and were looking for the opportunity to ban as many punk acts from the capital as possible. They had a clause written into their licensing deal with the Rainbow venue demanding an assurance from the Rainbow that certain words 'would not appear on their apparel or over the amplification'. Jet Black takes up the tale:

> We got on stage and Hugh's got this 'fuck' T-shirt on which he'd been wearing for months, and to our utter astonishment some GLC inspector at the back of the venue happens to see it through

his binoculars. He sent word to Dai Davies to tell him to get it off immediately because it might provoke a riot. We're steaming away and our manager is crawling along the back of the stage on all-fours saying 'Jet Jet Jet, tell Hugh he's got to get the T-shirt off immediately or they'll pull the power!' So Hugh puts it on back to front, then of course he turns round and they pull the switch! I keep playing, and of course all the punters went berserk. I thought, 'We've got a big, big story here.' It was at this point that I realized the power of the media and how to use the media. We saw they were using us for their own ends so we thought, 'Two can play at this game', and we've had them many times.

The GLC finally got the excuse they wanted early in 1977, following violent incidents at a Clash gig, and promptly banned many of the leading new-wave acts from the capital. Later that year, after the massive success of their debut album, the Stranglers were forced into the ludicrous tactic of advertising gigs at very short notice and performing under pseudonyms such as the Old Codgers, the Shakespearos and (brilliantly) Bingo Nightly and the OAPS. True, there was violence at some punk gigs caused by the audience, but very often the violence was directed at the punks themselves either from non-punks looking to teach them a lesson in hardness, or from the establishment. The Stranglers were often having to battle with the audience, or with security people, just to get through their set. Punk's leading polemicist Johnny Rotten who saw through much of punk's phoniness and pitiful aggressive poses, was himself attacked in 1977 by a thug, and the Sex Pistols' anti-Jubilee boat trip down the Thames that June was savagely broken up by the police using violent tactics. Many of the protagonists, including Malcolm McLaren, were arrested for no apparent reason whatsoever other than as a show of strength by the powers that be. Ultimately, there was no real difference between the violence inherent in the sporadic outbreaks of lawlessness from the punks and that of the establishment jealously protecting its hegemonic position. Throughout 1977 the Stranglers were having to deal with ever more violent situations. And in June of that year, with seven of their planned *Rats On The Road* tour gigs cancelled by local authorities, there was an escalating pattern of violence and disorder. On 28 May there were violent scenes after a gig in Canterbury. Stranglers' fans had been hassled in the queue before the gig by some local hardnuts and at the end of the gig 50 or 60 of them were there waiting for the band to come out. JJ:

> So myself, a Hell's Angel, and Dennis Marks from the Finchleys went out and confronted them. I went berserk and went for them with a mike stand and initially they all backed off. But when they realized there were only three of us they started getting stuck in. By that time quite a few Finchley Boys had come out of the hall to help us and eventually it all broke up. But I remember one of the Finchlies telling me that a guy was just about to stab me in the back and he just managed to stop him.

The gig in Guildford the very next night resulted in £700-worth of damage when chairs were wrecked by fans. Incidents like this became a regular occurrence at Stranglers' gigs, and soon prompted them to play almost exclusively non-seater auditoria. Matters came to a head at the Winter Gardens on 23 June, subsequently given the endearingly bathetic McGonagallesque title 'The Battle of Cleethorpes'. The Stranglers had been warned that 15 or so dockers from Grimsby would be attending the gig with the express purpose of 'teaching these London punks some manners', using brute physical force if necessary. The support band, London (which included the future Culture Club drummer Jon Moss), fell foul of a contingent of local dockers who began hurling glasses and beer trays at them. The dockers continued the barrage when the main act took the stage. They also thought it would be a great wheeze if they beat up two teenage girls dressed in the chic schoolgirl garb of the day. Ironically, the Stranglers had opened the set with 'Sometimes' ('Beat you honey till you drop'). The *NME* reported the incident

> Looking towards the back of the hall, Hugh Cornwell said: 'If there's anybody out there who's into beating up women, why don't you go down the beach and make sand-castles?'
> Burnel then stepped forward to say that 'if anyone really wants some aggro, I'll take on any two of you at once!'
> An *NME* reader witnessed what followed: 'This last statement was no bluff. Burnel took the strap of his guitar over his head with his left hand and simultaneously turned down the volume with the right. He had barely rested the bass against the stack when a fat and total moron came on (apparently) from the side of the stage, and attacked him.'

JJ continues the story:

I saw this huge fucker and I kicked him but he kept moving towards me, so I had no choice but to rush him and trip him up. I was battering this guy when all hell let loose. More dockers piled on stage and there was this huge fight. I remember Jet swinging his cymbals around. Eventually the police were called and we went backstage. I think one person needed hospital attention for a gash in the face caused by a cymbal, although I'm not sure if Jet was responsible. It could have been anyone. As far as I remember, we then finished the gig.

But the fun didn't stop at the gig as Jet recalls:

We came back to our hotel after the gig and asked for some sandwiches. They told us to go into this room and they would bring us some. Anyway this room was like a phone box, so we decided to go back to the bar, but they said, 'You can't go in there' and we said, 'Why not?' Well, all the posh people were in the bar, you see, and we didn't look right obviously. But we said, 'Bollocks, we're going into the bar, please bring our sandwiches in there, we're paying good money.' So the next thing is, they've called the police and the hotel management has told them that we've been trying to start a riot or something. Anyway the police came and started bossing us about and we told them there was no need for this as all we wanted was something to eat and to go to bed. But they were obviously seized by this paranoia and believed everything they'd read about us in the papers. At one point I was standing at the top of the staircase and this copper pushed me back down the stairs! The result was that I fractured a finger and we had to call off the next show.

Jet maintains the tabloid media deliberately stirred up a campaign of hatred and directed it against the band: 'The first two or three years there were fights almost every night, because people used to read this stuff in the newspapers and they used to come along looking for a fight. We had to defend ourselves and in those days we couldn't afford security, so we had to do it ourselves. But when we were defending ourselves, the press used to say we'd started a riot!'

That said, the Stranglers, and particularly Hugh, deliberately reviled the audience. A prime example came that April when the group played a gig at the Roundabout in Newport, South Wales. Cornwell, angered by the lacklustre audience response, tried to provoke some reaction with a spot of taffy-bashing. Ian Morse reported the following in *Sounds*:

> 'Why are you sitting there like dummies? Why don't you come up here on the floor?' Pointing to the small dance area between him and the front line of tables. 'Or ain't you got legs? I suppose you all got your passports to come and work in England?
>
> 'All live in the same flat down here do you – and work in the steelworks?' . . . Cornwell . . . carries on with his torrent of abuse until he gets some response. It comes in the form of a well-aimed nob of gob that started its life in the throat of some well wisher in the front row of tables. This pleases the man – at least someone's woken up. 'Try again,' Cornwell retorts, holding his leg nearer the would-be assailant.

This 'goading and gobbing' tactic is given an extra spice by Hugh in the form of a barely concealed racist overtone. In an era in which jokes about all sorts of stereotypes were part and parcel of everyday life (mother-in-law, 'Paki' and Irish jokes abounded at the time), Hugh was not immune from using such tactics himself. It may have all been tongue-in-cheek, but Hugh was playing a dangerous game.

Equally, Hugh could be hilariously funny on stage, as the recording from The Hope and Anchor from the autumn of 1977 shows. His band introductions, his asides, his punning sense of humour could work brilliantly well. But, given the odd heckler, or a cryogenically static audience, Hugh's caustic side would emerge.

Rattus Norvegicus was released on Friday 18 April 1977. Reviews were generally very positive (*Record Mirror* gave it five stars), with only *Melody Maker* raising a dissenting voice. However, one review in particular, by the Stranglers' old sparring partner Phil McNeill, savaged the band for the stridently misogynistic tone of many of the lyrics.' I'd have to think hard before I could name an album as grossly sexist as this . . . Don't tell me it's just The Rolling Stones and 'Brown Sugar' however many years on, because that was pretty pathetic too.

This is an album that can move people to tears – female people to tears of humiliation, that is.'

In July 1977, Julie Burchill in her live review of their Round House performance picked up on similar themes. She wrote: 'I don't find "Peaches" offensive because girls feel the same way about men, too . . . I'm not bothered by general abuse, because women get that from the cradle to the grave . . . What I object to is the playground bully mentality paraded in "London Lady".'

'London Lady', a JJ lyric, had been written, in part, about the 'unsatisfactory' nature of a sexual liaison with *Melody Maker*'s Caroline Coon: 'I thought the days of the public pillory in the market-place were over,' wrote Burchill.

Of the nine tracks on the Stranglers' début album, five deal specifically with women, and all five contain lyrical material which could certainly be deemed sexist. The opener, 'Sometimes', had lyrics written by Hugh. Here's a taste:

> Someday I'm going smack your face
> Someday I'm going smack your face
> Somebody's going to call your bluff
> Somebody's going to treat you rough . . .
>
> You're way past your station
> It's useless asking you to stop
> I got a morbid fascination
> Beat you, honey till you drop.

Twenty years on Hugh explains why the lyrics were so unashamedly violent:

The lyrics I write are all about things that happen to me, and people I know, and things I think. With 'Sometimes', I'd just split up with a girl who I had been seeing for a while and I went round to her house to find her one day and she's spent the night with someone else. I could smell sex on her and I hit her. I was livid and I was emotional and I felt ashamed too. It's terrible when you get to a state where you're so cut up emotionally that you use violence. So I thought that was worth writing about. And suddenly it became, 'Oh he hates women because he's writing about when he hit a woman! I thought it was a bum rap actually.

I've never hated women and I've never mistreated any I don't think.

Even in the 1990s, mainstream pop acts are still writing these kinds of songs: 'Smack My Bitch Up' is the opening track on the Prodigy's 1997 album *The Fat Of The Land*.

Another *Rattus Norvegicus* song with lyrics by Hugh, 'Peaches', went on to become the band's first big hit single, coupled with 'Go Buddy Go'. Its closing section graced dozens of Keith Floyd cookery programmes from the mid-80s onwards. There's a great bass line from JJ that almost, but not quite, pushes into reggae territory, some cheeky keyboard playing from Dave, and an outrageously over-the-top vocal from Hugh. Whereas 'Sometimes' was a brutal piece of reportage, 'Peaches' was simply a bit silly, more Benny Hill than anything else. True, not everyone went round ogling women, not everyone possessed Hugh's cynical, leering tone, and not every musician felt cool about writing about it even if he did, but the phenomenon of the male ogler existed and still does. Jet Black: 'If you picture the situation where you've got Placido Domingo in the studio and he's singing this great piece, then he's desperately serious, but it's not like that with the Stranglers. We've got the vocalist in the booth. He's with his mates and he's trying to entertain us. It's an act, it's not serious. He's talking about women in that lusty way that young men like to when they are amongst themselves. And if that's sexism then let's have more of it!'

It's difficult to take 'Peaches' seriously. The problem is that the lyrics come somewhat predigested, a little too in-yer-face. There's no subtlety, no irony, no 'benign' or subtle sexism as displayed today by that funniest of cultural commentators, the American writer Bill Bryson: 'Copenhagen is also the only city I've ever been in where office girls come out at lunchtime to sunbathe topless in the city parks. This alone earns it my vote for European City of Culture for any year you care to mention.'

The tone and register is different, but the meaning is the same. Garry Coward-Williams recollects:

> I have to say that I don't think they were sexist at all. I didn't think of them as treating women badly, or being sexist, till I read a review of the first album, *Rattus*. I don't know whether this was

because I was naïve or just simply because they weren't. To be quite honest they were just like any bunch of blokes who were in a band would have been at the time. There were girls around, and obviously John was the one who got the most, and then Hugh. Dave had a regular girlfriend in Brighton, and Jet had a couple of girls who would come and go, and they'd all be perfectly charming with them. I didn't see anybody being mistreated. I didn't see that they were in any way derogatory to them other than what one expected at the time in a band. I mean girls were 'chicks'. John was in a long-term relationship at the time and the fact that he was seeing someone on the side wasn't any different from what many others would have done. There was more obvious sexual libera-tion at the time in the 70s. I think that once the first album came out and they'd got that review, everyone jumped on the band-wagon. Bands had to have a selling feature and the Stranglers have several, and one of them was that they were mean and moody and broody, and that they considered women as objects who were only there for one reason.

Band publicist Alan Edwards puts it another way: 'Hugh and JJ did make what could be construed as sexist comments, but they weren't actually sexists themselves. Twenty years ago attitudes were different. Generally, a lot of men were quite sexist because that was the atmosphere they were brought up in and nobody knew any better. It was ignorance rather than anything else. And, in the Stranglers' case, they kind of grew out of that, but they were very much tarred with that brush.'

It is as well to remember that Anglo-American pop was incredibly sexist at the time. It was predominantly owned, run and made by white, middle-class men. And many of the lyrics were alarmingly sexist too. The Rolling Stones' 'Under My Thumb', 'Brown Sugar' and 'Honky Tonk Women' dealt with women as sex-objects to be dominated, with none of the over-the-top irony which can arguably be read into the Stranglers' music. And contemporary black dance music was little better, as the Gap Band's 1978 hit 'Oops Upside Your Head' evidences: 'Jack and Jill went up the hill to have a little fun/Stupid Jill forgot her pill and now they have a son'.

'Peaches', however, is also famous for that rather perplexing delivery given to the line: 'Is she trying to get out of that clitoris', which made those of us too young to know what a clitoris was think it was some kind of wet-suit or tight-fitting jumper.

Confusingly, Hugh pronounces it 'clit-aris'. He recollects that people thought he was singing 'Is she trying to get out of that guitarist', which would indeed have been a better line, but the original was intended to censure women afraid of their sexuality. But why 'clit-aris'? Jet has a ready explanation:

> It was a new word in pop lyrics and he probably didn't know how to pronounce it. You've also got to remember that Hugh was a very eccentric person. Like later on in the Eighties he pronounced 'Big In America', 'Big In Ameri*cor*'. He was a very unconventional character with a strange way of doing things. For example, he left strings dangling on his guitar on stage, whereas any other guitarist would neatly cut off the excess wires. He'd walk down the street and he'd strike up a conversation with a complete stranger and be very funny with it.

Hugh went out of his way in interviews to say that his art was merely a quotidian reflection of society and to define that society in a way which portrayed women as happy with the status quo of sexual inequality. He told Caroline Coon in May 1977: 'Well, it has always been a male-dominated society. And it still is. And the majority of women accept that and they don't want to change it . . . We're not criticizing women . . . We are just observing behaviour. And sure, we have a vested interest in not changing. Men do think of women as sex objects. That's just an observation.'

And here's Hugh on women musicians in the same interview: 'I don't think I want to play music with women. They always end up getting involved with someone in the band and then the band is finished . . . And I think women are more emotional than men. Much more emotional. And emotional people are very difficult to work with. I'm a real chauvinist. Totally.'

Three other songs from *Rattus*, 'London Lady', 'Ugly' and 'Princess Of The Streets', all sung and with lyrics by JJ, also dealt with the opposite sex. 'London Lady' tells the tale of a sexual encounter which reminds JJ of the famous 'joke' about women and the dreaded 'loose fit' during the sexual act:

> Making love to
> The Mersey Tunnel
> With a sausage
> Have you ever been to Liverpool?

In 'Princess Of The Streets' JJ writes about a girl who's gone and left him and made him cry, 'a piece of meat', who'll 'stab you in the back', whilst 'Ugly' starts off with a totally over-the-top description of a shag with a woman with acne whom he should have 'strangled to death' before she 'laced my coffee with acid', and goes on to attack the fat, rich businessmen who attract beautiful 'chicks'. 'Ugly' ends with the ominous chant of 'Muscle Power', a musical quintessence of male domination and an ominous prediction of the rise of that most loathsome of musical movements, the far-Right-leaning Oi, later in the decade. Today, JJ denies that the lyrics on *Rattus* are misogynistic:

> I think they're much broader than that. I think they're misanthropic. The lyrics are meant to be sketches. With 'Sometimes' Hugh found out that his girlfriend Caroline was going out with someone else so they had a row and he slapped her. I'm not condoning it, but it happens between people. So from that particular episode to being treated as a kind of philosophy, 'This is where we stand in relation to women' is ludicrous. I mean people must be dying to be shocked. Does this mean that he's a woman-beater and that he hates women?

Jet Black:

> Our lyrics are usually written in a very ambiguous manner, sometimes tongue-in-cheek and rarely seriously. If people think we're misogynistic or women-haters, let them think that. We don't care. We're just making an observation in an art form which allows you to do what you want. We live in a culture which allows you to assume the mantle of a misogynist to express a viewpoint. The next day you can assume the mantle or demeanour of an intellectual, or an archbishop.

Women were very much part of the Stranglers' set-up during this time: 'There was masses of sex, bus-loads of it,' concurs Jet, 'and a lot of the lyrical content was a detailed account of the previous night's sexual encounters.' As with every other heterosexual male on the planet, it obviously wasn't all plain sailing for the lads. Caroline Coon in an interview with Hugh in May 1977 wrote: 'One can only feel compassion for him, and the sexist tone of his songs, since his stance must be the unfortunate result of the unhappy state of his affairs.'

Their violently sexist pose has to be seen in the context of British society in the late 1970s. Unlike punk bands such as the Clash and the Sex Pistols, who attempted to reject this *status quo*, the Stranglers reflected it, and at times came to glorify it, which was ultimately their mistake. But in glorifying it, the Stranglers also mocked it, and in so doing mocked themselves too. If sometimes their sniggering and cruel lyrical put-downs are nothing less than obnoxious, they simply represent the views of the average boorish male of the late 1970s. Dai Davies: 'It was a different era really, and they were written to shock. Things that were pushing the boundaries of sexual expression in the 1970s would be regarded as offensive and anti-feminist now, and rightly so. But people were on a learning curve then. There was a complete cultural shift and the same people thought two completely different things between 1976 and 1986. I know I did.'

The Stranglers were not alone in having difficulties relating to 'chicks'. If their problem was their propensity for generalizing out of the particular, and reducing womankind to an objectionable and objectified mass, than the Clash and the Sex Pistols were having their fair share of problems too. The Clash's first album is remarkably homosocial, revealing a world populated by would-be freedom-fighters with hardly a woman in sight. For the Sex Pistols, sex seemed an absolutely terrifying act, with the sensual body reduced to gob, mucus and various bodily secretions. Rotten was no misogynist, but rather came across as someone disturbed by the corporeality of feminine desire. This was the era of the 'squelch' (a term coined by Rotten), the impersonal fuck in the toilet during the gig. The punk world espoused not simply a world of sex without love, but a world of sex without much pleasure too.

It should be pointed out that the Stranglers' lyrics which were written by JJ were sung by him in an affected, self-mocking manner (particularly live). When JJ sings: 'She's gone and left me I don't know why' it's like a cartoon hooligan on stage parodying an MOR ballad, drawing out its stupidity rather than its phoniness.

The real shame is that the lyrics, and the discussion of them, have diverted attention from the fact that the music which

houses these splenetic outbursts is of the highest order. 'Sometimes' is a solid rocker, 'Princess Of The Streets' has a strong
melody, and 'London Lady' is racy and catchy. The Stranglers'
music was outrageously danceable, melodic and poppy, but with
a real edge. And their aggressive stance, as American critic Kurt
Loder wrote, was nothing if not remarkably well done: 'The
Stranglers have a vision – a nasty, sometimes appalling vision,
granted, but it's their own, and they weave it through their songs
with remarkable lyrical facility . . . the Stranglers conjure up the
hissing, hateful rage of this particular urban state with a knowing
incisiveness that may leave some listeners gasping. (William
Burroughs would give a knowing nod.)'

Three songs on the album contain true quality: 'Goodbye
Toulouse', co-written by Hugh and JJ, started the tradition of
the Stranglers' rock waltz and is tremendously catchy, with its
lyrics concerning the city's imminent demise predicted by that
sixteenth-century physician and astrologer Nostradamus, cur-
rently back in vogue in the hippy-trippy counterculture. Since
Toulouse is on a fault line and has a nuclear reactor close by,
Nostradamus' predicted apocalypse is given a macabre edge.
'Hangin' Around' is the true gem, far and away the best
Stranglers' song of that time. The way in which it builds
musically from the little organ lick at the opening to its rousing
finale, with all the quirky guitar runs in between, is a thing to
savour, and illustrates how musical this rock band was. The group
had a brilliant grasp of dynamics, knew about tension and release,
and how a rock song could stir and rouse the emotions. And lead
guitar and keyboard interconnect and answer each other's riffs
beautifully. The lyric itself, co-penned by Hugh and JJ, is full of
little pieces of reportage from the London scene:

> I'm moving in the Colherne,
> With the leather all around me,
> And the sweat is getting steamy,
> But their eyes are on the ground,
> They're just hanging around

One of the venues mentioned, the Colherne in Earl's Court,
particularly attracted JJ: 'I had a girlfriend called Choosie Suzie
who was living round there. Once I went into this pub and

suddenly I realized that there weren't any girls in the pub at all. I was very pretty in those days. I had a little earring, tight jeans, short hair, and a leather jacket, and I used to wear a bit of make-up. Suddenly I turn round and there are these fuckin' blokes with moustaches and leather jackets.'

JJ's lyrics capture the inner-city vibe of metropolitan London and also hint at his own voyeuristic tendencies. JJ liked taboo-breaking, and in the 70s gay subculture still carried with it a strong oppositional force, an air of the forbidden.

'Down In The Sewer' was the band's epic. Clocking in at nearly eight minutes, in form it obviously had little in common with the crash-bang-wallop approach of most of punk. Most of the original ideas for the music were JJ's, although the cross-rhythm section and the symphonic endings were Hugh's, as were the lyrics – a curious blend of the genuinely sinister and the preposterously jokey. The Stranglers' outsider pose was put across here to telling effect: they envisaged a rhizomatic society, a society based on the intelligence of the pack, which moved with individual grace in a shit-stained world:

> I tell you what I'm gonna do
> Gonna make love to a water-rat or two
> And breed a family
> They'll be called the survivors.

On one level this was mere pretension. On another, the Stranglers were again reflecting what they saw happening around them, as British society had regressed from harnessing Wilson's white heat of technology to a suburban/urban night-mare of high-rise dereliction and gang lawlessness. And all things apocalyptical were in the air. In the mid-70s the BBC ran a telefantasy series called *Survivors* about a band of people reduced to barbarism after a nuclear war. Leftist politics increasingly concerned itself with the establishment's nuclear war-monger-ing, whilst the Right were preparing to dismantle the Welfare State and to institute a return to insanitary 'Victorian values'. The problem with the lyrics here is that they come completed: there's no room for the listener to infer or to complete the picture. It's the same when Hugh bawls: 'Use your twentieth-century imagina-tion/If you've got any' on 'School M'am': in reality nothing is left to the imagination with the majority of these early lyrics, everything's so brute, so graphic.

If the best pop songs are simple, or simply ambiguous, then the Stranglers' early work suffers from being too literal. Hence the badgering vocal delivery. There's no point being vocally subtle with such overt lyrics – better scream and shout them rather than sing them. But Garry Coward-Williams, who had seen the song develop over a two-year period, was disappointed with the vinyl 'Sewer':

> I watched 'Sewer' develop as a song and grew to love it. I remember one night Jet telling me that they had added a new piece to the end, which I think is the part subtitled 'Rats rally'. I remember hearing it and being totally blown away. They then started using it as the final song in their set, so it was fitting that it should be the last track on their first album. Unfortunately, in my opinion it didn't record very well. I remember listening to it at the time and being really disappointed – every other song came out great, but they just didn't manage to capture the live feel of 'Sewer' in the studio.

Rattus Norvegicus débuted at Number 46 on the album charts after just two days in the shops (this was in the days before record companies got wise to the charts, which ran from Monday to Saturday, and began releasing records on a Monday). The next week the album had climbed 42 places and the Stranglers were stars. *Rattus* stayed in the album charts for the rest of the year. But the days around its release were a dicey and nervous time for the band, as Hugh remembers:

> The album was coming out and we had done all the press for it. I was really on tenterhooks because we didn't know what it was going to do. I thought, I'm gonna go to the countryside and I'm gonna trip. I went down to this cottage in Somerset with a friend of mine. I was getting over the trip the next day and there's this phone call. They're trying to get hold of me because the album had taken off. I just did not want to be disturbed. But they said, 'You've got to come back.'

The double-A-sided single – the newly edited, cleaned-up version of 'Peaches' along with 'Go Buddy Go' – reached Number 8 and hung around the charts for over three months.

Unlike the Clash and the Sex Pistols, who made a trademark out of their non-appearance on *Top Of The Pops*, the band made their début on 18 May, JJ strumming a lead guitar and Hugh playing the bass for a joke.

The Stranglers' overnight success was, of course, no such thing; the band had been playing up and down the country for over two years before this, slowly building up a huge grass-roots following. They played it clever by being sufficiently outrageous to capture the media interest in punk (thus propelling themselves into the tabloids virtually every week), and also sufficiently musical to be 'the acceptable face of the new-wave'. Their music, therefore, appealed both to punks and to that huge community of record-buyers who valued such old-fashioned notions as melody and lyricality. Crucially, according to Dai Davies, their music also appealed to those people who were influenced by punk, 'but who wouldn't go the whole way and pierce their nose with a safety pin. These people bought the Stranglers, but they didn't buy the Damned.' The Stranglers also did quite a quaint thing: they brought back the song. Hugh said in 1977:

> There has been the odd thing, like Bowie producing *Ziggy Stardust*, but that was very isolated. When that came out in England, it was the only thing that was happening. *One album* . . .
> . . . I knew the Stranglers was going to be a success but we didn't know what form it was going to take. I knew it was going to be different. I knew it was going to be more song-oriented or melody-oriented.

If the Stranglers were a song-oriented band, at the time they also had a powerful groove, courtesy of JJ's extraordinary bass sound: toppy, urgent and melodic. These early Stranglers' songs had wonderful bass lines. For a time in the late 1970s JJ was *the* bass player every would-be guitarist dreamed of being. In short, he made the bass guitar cool. JJ:

> My bass sound was down to three main things: the way I played, the strings I used, and the fact that there was a tear in one of the speakers, which distorted it a bit and gave this growl, this rasp. The bass guitar I was using, the Fender, had a unique quality. There was also some serious compression when I played the bass in the recording studio, because I didn't know how to control the bass, I

just played it as hard as possible. It went against the rules of a bass guitar because it wasn't very bassy.

After a sell-out British tour, the band decamped once again to TW Studios, with the same team, to record material for the next album. Several of the songs slated for the second album were old live favourites left over from the TW sessions earlier in the year, including 'School M'am' and the catchy 'Bitchin', which centred on the bar-room back-biting and petty hostilities the band encountered on the pub circuit. Some of the newer material was deliberately provocative and obviously designed to really get right up the nose of the critics. 'Bring On The Nubiles' first hinted at paedophilia: 'I want to love you like your Dad/And be your superman', before this charmingly understated couplet, 'I've got to lick your little puss/And nail you to the floor', and that most retiring of chat-up lines:

> Lemme, lemme fuck ya! fuck ya!
> Lemme, lemme fuck ya! fuck ya!
> Lemme, lemme lick your lucky smiles!

Live, Hugh and JJ were wont to chant the title 'Bring on *ze* nubiles' in a cod-German accent, bringing to mind the Nazi Joy Division – the brothel for commanding officers. Hugh now claims he was provoked into writing the song by the rest of the band:

That lyric was very tongue-in-cheek. That was really written to see what I could get away with, what would really freak people out? I mean I was goaded into that by the rest of the band. There were a lot of girls hanging around at the time, and we were having a great time, so it was a celebration of that. It was an erotic fantasy put into song. Most men entertain sexual fantasies and most men love the idea of young women. So all it is is putting into words something people think about. But it's a song like 'Peaches', it gets misrepresented. Just because you're the messenger bringing something, don't shoot the messenger. These things exist. You don't deal with something by ignoring it.

It was a powerful song musically, but the end result was simply confusing – if their music reflected gender/racial stereotypes, how much did they concur with these sentiments? The evidence at the time suggests that they themselves were part of the problem. In a 1977 interview, Hugh defended this paean to the fleshly as follows: 'Men are like red wine – they get better with age. Girls are like white wine – they only taste good when drunk young.'

'I Feel Like A Wog', an almost free-form, faintly jazzy song, was anti-racist in intent, but performed with all the nastiness of a raving bigot. Like the Clash, who were jealous of black activism and called for a 'white riot . . . of my own' after first-hand experience of the run-ins between blacks and a bullying police force at 1976's Notting Hill Carnival, Hugh was desperate to link his own alienation with that of ethnic minorities. And this alienation also extended from the individual to the collective: the Stranglers were by now completely *personae non gratae*: 'We were alienated not so much by the musicians but by the pressure put on them by the media. And if they were associating with us, then they were tarred with the same brush, so they were pretty scared of getting involved – and probably scared of being beaten up!'

And, at the same time, Hugh wanted to reassert his own attachment to some of the new-wave ideals the Stranglers espoused, despite the emotional apartheid apparently operated by the rest of punkdom. The Stranglers, like most of the rest of the new-wavers, hated the establishment with a vengeance, and felt marginalized by it:

> I feel like a wog
> Got all the dirty shitty jobs
> Everybody's got to have something to
> do with their time . . .
>
> I feel like a wog
> I don't wanna go home
> I just got a lot of life to live through
> through, through, through
> I feel like a wog
> I don't mean you no harm
> Just don't ask me to shine your
> shoes, shoes, shoes, shoes.
>
> Golly gee!
> Golly gosh!

Interestingly, the Beatles' original title for their 1969 hit 'Get Back' was 'No Pakistanis', a send-up of the then current Powellite repatriation scheme. But the Beatles obviously got wise.

'I Feel Like A Wog' also deliberately alienated the Stranglers politically in that it indicated the band's desire to distance itself from the Rock Against Racism movement, which JJ thought racist. The band claimed to deal with racism in real-life situations, such as when their support act, the black reggae group Steel Pulse, whom they had good relations with and had befriended, were the subject of racial abuse from the audience at a gig in Birmingham. Jet took to the stage during Steel Pulse's set and dealt with the bigots there and then. JJ also remembers another incident during this period at Bath Pavilion, when JJ 'sorted out' a skinhead giving a Nazi salute. The Stranglers could not be said to be racial bigots.

Songs such as 'Wog' and 'Nubiles' brought downright nastiness to new rarified heights. The music was less melodic than on *Rattus*, more insistent and forbidding, the tone more glaring and maniacal, and, beneath it all, was the feeling that the Stranglers were deliberately casting bait for journos in a hurry to condemn the Stranglers' lack of moral rectitude.

In the summer, the band embarked on their first tour of the US, which drew a mixed reception. The band had been signed to A&M records by Martin Kirkup and it appeared, by mid-1977, that the melodic though hard-edged pop of the biggest-selling British new-wave act might translate to the far more lucrative American market. The interest was certainly there, but the main problem was, as Hugh succinctly told one American critic: 'You're all too well-off in America.' The kind of angst shown by the new-wave in Britain was a product, in part, of feeling marginal to the future of the nation, of being sidelined economically, of not sharing the aspirations of the establishment. In America, white youth was largely well-off, or at least not marginalized. This was the era of the great North American supergroups – the Eagles, Kiss, Rush, Journey, Foreigner, Boston – of faceless stadium rock, where jeans and T-shirts were the order of the day, not day-glo hair and a face like a pin-cushion. British punk was simply incomprehensible to the majority of Americans. And the New York new-wavers such as Blondie, Television and Talking Heads were considerably more quirky and arty than their British cousins. It wasn't until the recession-hit nineties that America finally had the right conditions for its own 'punk' movement.

In between recording albums the band also developed a sideline in production. Celia Gollin, a torch singer from London, had been spotted by Albion's Dai Davies in a local club and was teamed up with the band for the cover version of 'Mony Mony'. Jet remembers: 'It was a publicity stunt which might have worked, but Celia was incredibly shy and shunned all interviews. But that record's worth quite a lot of money now, if you've got one.'

Dai Davies suggested that JJ write some new material with Celia, after her first single flopped and JJ and Celia slept together, literally: 'I was round at her flat one night and we wrote songs and I distinctly remembered it was very late and she said I could stay and there was nowhere to sleep but the bed. So we slept in the same bed together . . . but we didn't . . .!'

But a follow-up single recorded with the help of JJ, Wilko Johnson and Terry Williams of Rockpile also stiffed, and soon Celia & the Mutations were nothing more than a footnote in the annals of punk.

The gap between albums also saw JJ travel for the first time to his beloved Japan to do a promotional tour and to train under the originator of kyokushin karate, ole 'God Hand' himself, Mas. Oyama. JJ came back with a pair of black MacCampbell's jeans which, when worn with his black leather jacket, provided the first hint of a move towards an all-black uniform for the band. JJ was called upon to put his fighting skills to real effect when he received instructions from the French Consulate in London to report to the 39th Infantry Division in Rouen 'immediately and without delay' to do his national service. JJ had both British and French passports and was reluctant to give up his dual nationality. Eventually, after months of wrangling, Albion managed to get him excused from what would have been a career-wrecking stint in the army. Look what it did to Elvis . . .

In the summer the band released their third single for UA – another double 'A'-sided effort, 'Something Better Change'/ 'Straighten Out'. 'Straighten Out' was archetypal Hugh, whilst the poppier 'Something Better Change' was the band's only stab at writing a punk anthem. The song became a sort of blueprint for later punks, such as Sham 69 with the shout-along 'If The Kids Are United'. It was, however, a strong song, powerful and, like virtually all Stranglers' songs, infectiously danceable. The band recorded promos for both songs in a cul-de-sac just off Ladbroke Grove in West London. Jet Black: 'In the opening shot of the "Straighten Out" video you can see a house across the street through the archway and you can see a window. Somebody was telling me only a couple of weeks ago that they'd been down there recently and they still had the same curtains up!'

Even though the single was soon Top 10, the band were having a major promotional problem. Not only were they prevented from lining up a string of dates in London but their records, despite selling well, were simply unheard on daytime Radio 1, then the most important cog in the promotional wheel. Heavy rotation on Radio 1, together with fortnightly exposure for a climbing single on *Top Of The Pops*, maximized sales. But Stranglers' records never got the backing from radio they were entitled to, given their often impressive sales. John Peel did play the record on his show, however: 'Now here's something from the Stranglers. "Something Better Change" into the singles charts at No.15. They're also there with "Peaches" at No. 28. Two in the Top 30. Funny, I haven't heard any of my "colleagues" playing either track . . .'

Apart from Anne Nightingale and Alan 'Fluff' Freeman's shows, Radio 1 was largely a 'Stranglers-free zone'. Never have a band built up such a great chart profile with so little air-play.

The Stranglers were now riding a massive wave of commercial acceptance. After playing a thank-you concert for the Finchley Boys that August, in the autumn they embarked on a British tour to promote their new album, entitled *No More Heroes*, which culminated in a record-breaking five nights at the Round House that October.

The *No More Heroes* tour saw the band introduce the first, and most famous, in a long line of unusual opening acts. The Stranglers had, and continue to have, support bands opening the evening's entertainment. But they wanted something more novel than simply more pop before their grand entrance, and down the years a number of weird and wonderful entertainers have taken the stage for the thankless task of entertaining an audience psyched up for the main attraction. This wasn't an entirely new idea: the veteran Max Wall opened for Mott The Hoople earlier in the seventies. In the 1980s the band have had comedians such as Keith Allen; a tap-dancing spoon-player who used to mime to old Noël Coward-type records; a completely crap ventriloquist; Paul Davies, who used to do a surreal imitation of a roadie; and the odd female mud-wrestler. However, two entertainers have gone down in Stranglers folklore. Bambi was a transsexual from San Francisco. JJ: 'Everyone thinks I shagged her. I was in my room with Bambi. She was in my bed and I was lying on the outside of the bed. Then, suddenly, the whole band piled into my bedroom with girl-friends, wives, managers, you name it. Suddenly Bambi said, "Life has been so much better for me since I got *these*," and she got out of bed sporting these massive knockers, but of course, her cock was in full view as well. Well, everyone was frightened and rushed out!'

But perhaps the doyen of the Stranglers' warm-up acts was the intentionally crap Johnny Rubbish, the not terribly demanding creation of twenty-year-old John Gatward. Gatward recollects how his character, rather miraculously, became an unintention-ally big hit:

I was a fan of the band and I started hanging out backstage. Then I had this idea for a punk comedian called Johnny Rubbish, the idea being that I was rubbish before he was Rotten! He was supposed to be rubbish, I mean real rubbish. He wasn't supposed to be funny, he was supposed to be crap. It was all written by me, but it didn't take a lot of work! I used to come on in a dustbin and say things like: 'This is a party political broadcast on behalf of the Conserva-tive Party: James Callaghan's a cunt.' It was stupid and insulting. The idea was that he [Rubbish] would sort of die a death, but this was not how it worked out at all, because what happened was that people started to take him really seriously. United Artists signed me up and I did a single, 'Living In NW3 4JR', which was essentially a piss-take of the Labour government set to the Pistols' 'Anarchy In The UK', with Martin Rushent producing and Herbie Flowers on bass! I used to say, 'I'm an alternative comedian because I'm not funny', but it all started to get far too serious. I had Alexei Sayle and people who would later form the *Young Ones* coming down to check me out. Soon they were calling themselves 'alternative comedians'. Then there was John Cooper Clarke, a punk poet. The second they got the idea of it, it became so contrived it was extraordinary. After a while you couldn't even get backstage to talk to these new 'alternative' comedians.

Gatward also remembers that, at the height of his notoriety, the punk audiences could be rather less than altogether charitable:

The atmosphere just before the band comes on is absolutely electric. They're not interested in anything other than the band coming on, and the last thing they want is some idiot drooling on about some old crap. A performance could last one minute, like in Cardiff, when I walked on and said, 'The problem with Welsh people is that you can't play rugby!' What the audience would do would be to open a can of lager and throw it at me immediately. It was quite a weapon. You could see it spinning through the air like a meteor from the back of the hall. I used to wear a waterproof suit and carry an umbrella because I used to get spat at so much. I also took to wearing a crash helmet. At one gig in Dunstable, when I took it off backstage I noticed it had three darts stuck in it!

Gatward, who was by now building a successful career in industry, was keen to keep Rubbish very quiet from his friends and acquaintances. It wasn't the right image at all. But he looks back on his time with the Stranglers with a great deal of affection, and recollects that they had one particularly well-developed passion:

When I first met them they were the most ordinary stars I'd ever met in my life. They were so pleasant and they were so, 'What's special about us? Come and have a drink in the pub.' After *Black And White* came out it all started to become very serious, at the beginning they were like big kids at a party. The thing I remember most of all, particularly with regard to John and Hugh (and to a lesser extent Dave), was their absolute obsession with shagging anything that came near the dressing-room. Some of them were absolutely appalling. I remember once in Llandrindod Wells, Hugh was shagging in the broom cupboard before we went on stage. We all looked at each other with this terrible bonking noise coming from the broom cupboard, thinking, what the hell is going on here, this is really stupid!

These were indeed heady times. The album itself reached Number 2 in the charts and the title track was yet another Top 10 UK hit. Indeed, 'No More Heroes' has been a live favourite

ever since. In a curious display of pop kismet, just as superstar
David Bowie was singing 'We can be heroes, just for one day' for
his first live performance on *Top Of The Pops* for five years, the
Stranglers were in the charts bemoaning the lack of role-models,
urging their fans to be their own heroes. JJ to the *NME*, 1976:
'They're picking out old heroes because at the moment they're
still trying to get new heroes together. That's why Iggy . . . is
becoming a cult figure.'

It was the new wave's most eloquent put-down of the cult of
celebrity. It also name-checked some suitably trendy revolution-
aries: Leon Trotsky (with an ice-pick 'that made his ears burn'),
Lenny Bruce, Sancho Panza and the Great Elmyra, an artist who
brilliantly defrauded the world with amazingly true-to-life reproductions of the old Masters.

But, as ever, there were problems behind the scenes, most
notably concerning the cover art work. The original shot by John
Pash, a striking colour photo of JJ lying on a reconstruction of the
tomb of Trotsky, was rejected by the band because it was thought
that a picture of just one member of the band, even the most
conventionally photogenic, was anti-democratic. As 1977 progressed JJ emerged as one of the leading pop icons of his day.
Initially the Stranglers had been very much Hugh's band. He had
the pedigree, had played hundreds of gigs and had already
written some interesting material in his pre-Stranglers' existence. He was also older and wiser than JJ and simply had a
more well-developed aesthetic sensibility. But he was challenged
now as front-man by JJ, and the dispute over the *No More Heroes*
cover shows the band dynamic was altering. Hugh: 'I thought,
What the fuck's going on here? It's a band, how can you have a
shot of one person? Everyone's supposed to be of equal merit,
how can you have just one shot of somebody on the cover? And
John actually went and did a photo shoot for it with him – a
tribute to his cupidity. To try and build up one person by doing
solo photo shoots on group albums wasn't helping the situation. I
mean, I would never have considered something like that.'

Reviews of the album were mixed. With hindsight it was
thematically and musically a little too similar to *Rattus* to be a
total artistic success, and overall the standard was less consistent.
One critique, penned by Jon Savage, actually provoked JJ into
direct action. The review itself, which ran in *Sounds* that

September, was not wholly uncomplimentary (in fact the album won a respectable, and probably accurate, rating of three stars). Savage wrote:

> Who needs them as moralizers? Agreed that having your face rubbed in a cess-pit can, on certain occasions, be salutary (shock/emetic). Beyond a point, reached on this album, it seems more redundant, self-indulgent. I mean we know that England's going down the toilet, we've been told often enough. What to *do* about it? Because the Stranglers offer nothing positive, not even in their music. Look: the Pistols tell you we're being flushed too, but their music has kick, a bounce, a tension that gives you energy, makes you want to do something. Some sort of life out of decay . . .
>
> I suppose they got up my nose, didn't they? So they win in the end. Some pyrrhic victory, though. The music's powerful enough to get some reaction (always better than none) but what comes off this album, with its deliberate unrelenting wallowing, is the chill of death. No life force, nothing vital. Not so that it's frightening, just dull and irritating, ultimately. And it doesn't even make it as a statement, even though it's all taken so seriously.

Savage certainly hit a raw nerve: it wasn't so much that the Stranglers were sexist or racist – they were deadening and boring with it, and intellectually substandard too. And Savage had been distinctly unimpressed by the album's cover, which he called 'chintzy chocolate-box style'. This was probably the straw that broke the camel's back, considering the vastly superior cover-shot featuring JJ had been rejected. JJ himself picks up the story:

> I was looking for him round town and I knew that there were lots of gigs where he might be. I happened to go to the Red Cow one night and there he was with Jake Riviera, Nick Lowe, Elvis Costello and Andrew Lauder. I was with a Japanese girlfriend at the time and one of the Finchley Boys and I thought, 'This is the guy I've been looking for all around town.' I wasn't going to let him get away with it. So I went up to him and said 'Are you Jon Savage?' He said, 'Yes', and I said something like, 'You're an enemy of the revolution!', or 'You've spoilt my revolution!' and I threw a coke in his face. He made some sort of dodgy attempt at hitting me, which was the excuse to sort of just go for him. The bouncers threw me out.

Giving beatings to critical journalists was obviously not outside the norms of common decency for JJ at the time, who admits to being 'seriously aggressive'. This was appalling behaviour, but not unexpected or out of character either for JJ or for a few of the other leading punks such as the extremely violent, bicycle-chaining Sid Vicious. JJ took criticism of the band extremely personally and believed that aggressive words should be countered with aggressive deeds. He hated people whom he thought of as in any way phony or cliquey, and thought Savage fitted the bill perfectly – a middle-class law student hob-nobbing with the punk intelligentsia. According to JJ, these incidents had the result of partly writing the Stranglers out of the punk script:

> He's made a lot of money from the punk period. But he seems not to have forgotten this incident. In all the portrayals of the seventies we're not there, which is a bit silly, since we outsold nearly everyone and were quite an important band. It's a bit Stalinist, isn't it? You read articles on punk in the pictorials and it's always got Jon Savage's name under it. I was watching a punk documentary on the television with some friends and we're not there. At the end of it they were looking at me and said, 'I thought this was quite a busy period for you?' I said, 'I bet it was written by Jon Savage, or had Jon Savage as consultant', and the titles roll up and it says, 'Consultant: Jon Savage'. I rest my case.

Beating up the 'enemy' was hardly the way to further endear the band to an already hostile press. Dai Davies points out, however, that the band had very good reason to think of the press as a lower form of life:

> You've got to remember the mind-set really, because the Stranglers were rejected before they became successful. Critics like Jon Savage and Julie Burchill came along in the wake of the Stranglers and the Sex Pistols. They weren't there before. Up until the point when these bands were successful, most people were against them. They had very few allies. Chas De Whalley was one of very, very few. *Melody Maker* and *New Musical Express* hated them because they were still writing about Genesis and Yes at that time. So the Stranglers felt that if they could upset the breed of person who had spent two years making their life a misery and writing them off, then all the better. There was a bit of a bunker mentality in the band by the time they were successful.

By the end of 1977, however, even those working for the band were beginning to see that the devilment and rather light-hearted pranks which they were indulging in were starting to backfire a little. An incident on their sell-out UK tour that autumn showed the lighter side to their law-breaking. It was a rather innocent skirmish which is significant in that it showed how much fun the band's brushes with the law were initially. When they heard after the gig that one of the Hell's Angels who had attended that evening's show was being held in police cells, Jet and JJ hot-footed it to the local nick. Jet takes up the story:

> I said to the policeman, 'I'm not leaving until I know whether you're holding him or not', and they banged us in jail for the night. So, I got released in the morning and of course we got outside and there were cameras and everything. There was a court case about a month later. We got this hot-shot barrister in and we beat the police, we won the case! The crux of their argument was that we were drunk and disorderly, and so their barrister had to find some way of proving that I was drunk. So he said, 'I could smell it on his breath', and I said, 'Until the moment I was arrested he was never close enough to me to smell my breath, because the counter was about this wide'. I had to show the jury how wide the counter was and the jury believed me and we won the case! We were consciously milking the media time and time again. There was half a truth in all of it.

One particular incident from the *No More Heroes* tour showed how aggressive JJ could be when provoked. The band, sick and tired of the whole ethos of heroism within rock and keen to promote the original levelling instincts of punk, adopted a policy of not signing autographs on the tour. They still had a close relationship with fans, and often allowed them backstage or into the venue during sound-checks, but, as a point of principle, autographs were out. One particular guy began hassling JJ backstage after a gig, and in the end JJ's resolve cracked: 'He kept asking so I just "swept" him – I just kicked his legs from under him so he landed on his bottom. I lost it, I kind of lost it. I do regret things like that . . .'

JJ having karated a fan, the last thing the band needed was more high-testosterone shenanigans. But the Stranglers' adventures on tour in Northern Europe confirmed the general feeling that their activities were attracting violent behaviour wherever they went. A major incident occurred in Klippan in Sweden that September, when members of the far-right Raggare, an organization of marauding male nutters into Americana such as old-fashioned cars, graffiti clothes and rock'n'roll, decided to try and destroy the Stranglers' equipment and trash the venue before the gig could take place. About 120 of them in a procession of 40 or 50 cars drove to the venue, crashing through a police barrier and beating up two policemen in the process, before attacking the road crew as they were setting up the gig, and causing thousands of pounds worth of damage. The band were advised to remain in their cellar changing-room by a white-faced promoter left with a trail of destruction in the hall above. It was estimated that the Raggare wrecked £20,000 worth of equipment, and JJ returned home with his old bass guitar now in two pieces instead of the customary one.

This was a frightening and financially damaging incident, but the real fun came later that year, at the last gig of 1977, when the band played two nights at the infamous grot-hole, the Paradiso Club in Amsterdam. This was the moment when the Stranglers brushed up against some *bona fide* heavies. The band were now being courted by another far-right lads-together organization, namely the Hell's Angels, who began to usurp the Finchleys as their bouncers. One of the most prestigious chapters was in Amsterdam. Publicist Alan Edwards, eager to make media capital from the final Stranglers' shows of a triumphant year, brought a posse of journalists along to cover the shows. The Hell's Angels' clubhouse was situated out of town and, it was hoped, out of harm's way. The chapter had actually been given a £150,000 grant by the Dutch government to set up shop. State-subsidised mayhem was therefore permissible, as long as they kept out of everyone's way. The clubhouse had its own disco and bar, sleeping quarters, a garage and a makeshift shooting range. A machine gun stood in the garden. Each of the 25 members received an annual grant of £2,000. During the night when the Stranglers and their entourage went back there for a bit of a social, the Angels were busy getting up to some alarming 'pranks'. One of the Hell's Angels was driving his motorbike along the bar (as you do), whilst another was showing a home-movie of a woman lying on the club pool table in various stages of undress. The next home video consisted of the Angels pulling guns on people. Then another guy occupied himself in the garden firing round after round into the building site of a new prison under construction, which the Angels were busy destroying in their spare time. And a gang-bang is going on in the back room for good measure. Alan Edwards takes up this increasingly bizarre and sordid story:

> There's some really heavy people there and gun runners, drug-dealers, and someone said there was some sort of gang-bang going on in the back. I'm with Bob Hart from the *Sun* and suddenly they're playing Russian Roulette and they've put the gun to Bob's head! Then this guy comes up to me and puts this gun to my head and pulls the trigger. Nothing was in it, but I didn't know that. It was all really freaky. It was so surreal it felt like it was a movie. I didn't get scared, it was like it wasn't happening, or it was in slow-motion. It's possible that we had a good few drinks down us. Funnily enough, being in Holland it could have been Dutch courage! I know the *Sun* did a big story on it.

It was at this point that the chimera of violence and criminality which had attached itself to the band suddenly transformed itself into something more threatening altogether. There was a real miasma over the band now, and for the next three years they seemed synonymous with evil and mayhem.

However, 1977 ended in triumph for a band which had been largely unknown just twelve months earlier. Both Mick Jagger and Pete Townshend had been sufficiently riled by the band to express their disgust openly to the press, thus securing the Stranglers' anti-rock aristocrat credentials. That autumn their popularity was demonstrated in their strong showing in the readers' polls in the rock inkies. The Stranglers won the 'Brightest Hope' section in both *Melody Maker* and *New Musical Express*, beating off their nearest punk rivals, the Sex Pistols. In the *Melody Maker* they were voted third best live act behind Genesis, who had won it since the Ark. 'Peaches' was well-backed in the best single category, as was *Rattus* in the album poll. All four instrumentalists were also heavy pollers in their respective instrument categories (JJ was voted top bassist and Dave Greenfield's swelling organ was second only to Rick Wakeman's in the *NME* poll). Interestingly, JJ got 10th in the *NME*'s best songwriter poll (Bowie had a monopoly on this in the seventies and early eighties), whilst Hugh was nowhere to be found (providing an interesting insight into the public perception of the band at the time, and particularly curious since no individual songwriting credits were ever given on a Stranglers record). *NME* readers deemed the chintzy chocolate-box *No More Heroes* cover the sixth best of the entire year.

The band had been a commercial, as well as a critical success, with *Rattus* the 21st biggest-selling album of the year and the recently-released *No More Heroes* the 32nd. The year also ended with JJ winning the epithet 'Stud Of The Year' from the *NME*, thus confirming him as *the* master punky hunky.

In November 1977 the band were disappointed to learn that Andrew Lauder and Martin Davis were leaving UA. They had been instrumental in signing the band, so their loss removed its most vocal supporters from the label. This was the beginning of an unfortunate pattern of events which kept on repeating itself throughout their career. As soon as the Stranglers signed on the dotted line, then personnel would change to such an extent that it was almost like dealing with a new, and very often less-supportive, label. This is something which happens to many bands, particularly major acts, and is one of the reasons why relations between labels and stars can be so transitory and impersonal.

Also in November, the Stranglers played at the Hope and Anchor Front Row Festival, opening a three-week stint of gigs set up to bail the venue out of financial difficulties. Ian Grant had the idea to record and film the gig and, together with Clive Banks at Warner Brothers and Dave Dee at Atlantic, began the onerous task of securing permissions and copyright. Dai and Derek wouldn't have anything to do with it, as they deemed the project too complicated and a potential legal minefield. But the resulting album sold in the region of 40,000 and went Top 30 in the UK, thus vindicating Grant's decision.

The band themselves were always willing to help out publican Fred Grainger, who had given them such support during their lean early days. Other luminaries on the bill included Steel Pulse, the Saints, XTC, Roogalator, X-Ray Spex, the Tom Robinson Band, future stadium-rock snoozers Dire Straits, and a Welsh

'Elvis impersonator' who would become one of the top-selling singles artists of the next decade, Shakin' Stevens.

Just before Christmas 1977 Albion announced that the band would be going back to their roots early in the New Year with a string of small-scale gigs, to be announced only hours beforehand so as not to hassle publicans with mile-long queues of fans. Afterwards the band would retreat to record their third studio album and prepare for world domination. They also had a new single, the robotic, hard-hitting 'Five Minutes'. This gave a strong indication of a change of musical direction, away from the melodic pop of their previous singles and towards a starker, more experimental sound. It boded well for the future. The lyric by JJ re-told a horrible incident which took place in his flat while he was away in Japan that summer:

> I shared a flat with Wilko Johnson, who founded Dr Feelgood, and occasionally Steve Strange and/or Billy Idol. A girl called Suzie lived in the middle room. While I was away she was raped by five black guys and they threatened to kill her cat. After that the place was tainted and we all moved out. Motorhead took over the flat after us. It was five minutes by motorcycle from where we were to Bishop's Avenue – just about the richest street in England with £2–3 million mansions. Five minutes from security walls and cameras and Rolls-Royces to where we were.

As the single climbed the chart that February to become another sizeable UK hit (the single finally peaked at Number 11), the band stormed into their surprise pub gigs. It was the end of an era. The Stranglers had always eschewed the trappings of stardom: the limos, the fancy hotels, the outrageous fan-fleecing ticket prices. They liked the money, for sure, but they weren't going to screw their fans for every last penny. They were entering a phase when their popularity might have dictated, on purely financial grounds, that they upscaled from medium-sized venues such as the Hammersmith Odeon and the Round House to bigger venues such as Earls Court, or even bigger outdoor gigs. That the band decided to scale down for this pre-songwriting warm-up shows an endearingly personal approach. They valued the closeness to their fan-base (something shown by the institution of the *Strangled* magazine by Alan Edwards). Jet remembers in particular their return to one of their favourite pub venues, the

Duke Of Lancaster, whose owner Bill Phelan, like Fred Grainger, was another band supporter and nice guy, and also written into 'Bitchin':

> When we played there originally we were totally unknown and we used to play to a few locals. Then we went away for a year and all of a sudden we became famous. We phoned him up and said, 'Would you like us to come and do a gig', and he said, 'Oh we'd love it!' When we arrived at the pub there were about 10,000 people outside and about 150 inside. We squeezed through and there was this riotous applause. We started playing and they were squeezing through, climbing through the windows and it was boiling hot and we were doing these 200 mile an hour songs. You could see the precipitation of the sweat going up and forming clouds and literally raining! The pub was a microcosm of the atmosphere, and when it hit the floor it obviously fell on to my drum kit. As I hit the tom-toms, all the water would flop about on top of them! It was absolutely amazing, everyone was having the time of their lives. *It was raining sweat!*

But from now on, the Stranglers had to look to bigger territories, bigger venues, and new ideas. It was time to move from the pub cellar to the stadium. The Stranglers had made it.

PART TWO

Blasphemy (1978–1983)

5: RECKLESS IN
REYKJAVIK

It's the photo shoot for the band's new album, *Black & White*, and Jet can hardly move his head or focus at the camera. His hair tousled, his mouth like the inside of a birdcage, he is unsteady on his pins. His bog-eyed stare to camera, captured for immortality by photographer Ruan O'Lochlainn, is the result of the mother of all hangovers. In fact it signalled the advent of almost a month of non-stop liver-crunching for that far-from-temperate band. For the Stranglers had planned a 72-hour media meet-and-greet in one of the silliest venues possible – Iceland.

There's nothing inherently silly about Iceland apart from the fact that, in strictly commercial terms, it's hardly central to the global music industry economy. A big hit in Iceland is hardly likely to make you rich. Iceland was out-of-the-way, a backwater, a siding, and that fitted perfectly with the band's strategy of remaining outside of mainstream ligging and loveydom. A volcanic rock with over 200 active volcanoes, lava fields, and geysers, with an economy almost entirely dependent on cod, and with six months in turn of daylight and darkness, Iceland is the only country known to be able to regenerate itself; a new bit of it, Surtsy, popped up in time for the Beatles in 1963. And that's not everything that pops up at regular intervals. Iceland in the seventies had the highest incidence of illegitimacy and venereal disease in the world. Trivial Pursuit aficionados (or anyone who has watched the Ben Elton-penned sitcom 'Filthy, Rich & Catflap' in the eighties) will also know it has the most northerly capital city in the world ('Reykjavik comma Iceland full stop'). At that point it was the home of just one popular cultural 'icon' – Magnus 'I've started so I'll finish' Magnusson – although eleven-year-old Björk had just released her début album!

The band arrived at Keflavik airport on May Day with a plane load of journalists, record company executives and other assorted business illuminati for what became, by all accounts, three days of solid drinking and frolicking, all in the name of launching their

third, and, as it turned out, best album to date. For one particularly pissed journalist it would actually end a career. But, in the
meantime, there were promotional photos to take (the four lads
looking suitably menacing against the volcanic splendour of this
tiny island), more booze to drink, civic dignitaries to meet, and an
actual gig to play.

Incredibly, the show at the Exhibition Centre played to an
estimated 3 per cent of the adult population of the entire country.
As Jet remembers, the atmosphere was positively Bacchanalian.
In the absence of beer, the fans turned to the harder stuff with
instant results:

> Some of these young 16- or 17-year-olds came in with at least a
> whole bottle of spirits each. When we started the gig we thought,
> 'These people are really pleased to see us!', and there was a lot of
> excitement, but by the end there was a war on. They were
> smashing bottles over each other's heads. There were kids lying
> all over the place drunk and throwing-up. It was a picture of total
> devastation. I said to one of them after the gig, 'Are they doing this
> just because of our music?' and he said, 'No, it's like this every
> night!'

The band used the promotional trip as an opportunity to settle a
few scores. There were some unfortunate little 'accidents' in store
for those journalists who had been foolish enough not to fill their
reviews over the previous two years with unequivocal praise. JJ:

> It was our chance to get our own back on a lot of people. I
> remember Tim Lott had been giving Hugh a bad time, so Hugh
> humiliated him in front of the assembled journalists in some
> studio during the reception we were having (which I missed
> because I was so out of it). Then we arranged for one journalist
> not to have his saddle fastened properly on a pony-ride, so he fell
> off and hurt himself. Another journalist fell into a geyser – some
> mysterious hand just pushed him in.

For one particularly snooty journo from the *London Times*, there
was serious trouble on the coach back to the airport at the end of
the visit. Unwisely, this particular scribe, whose name has
fortunately been forgotten by everyone involved, challenged JJ
to a drinking competition. Now, given JJ's land-lubbered alco-

holic capacity of yore (a mere sniff of booze was enough to send the cherubic bassist out on a road which would almost inevitably end in tears), it was remarkable that he would ever make, let alone win, such a challenge. However, as Alan Edwards, who was on the Iceland trip, remembers, JJ merely decided to let the said reporter 'go first' by physically holding him down and pouring the best part of a bottle of VAT 69 down his throat:

> That bloke was a twat, a real upper-class twit. I think he had a monocle or something. Anyway, he thought he could keep up with the punks and he said, 'I can out-drink you punks!' So JJ decided to teach him a lesson. We're coming back to the airport and JJ physically holds him down and literally pours a bottle of spirits down his throat. The guy gets off the bus at the airport, and I'm not exaggerating, there's sick coming out of this guy's ears and he's passed out by now. But, being the Stranglers, instead of calling an ambulance, what they do is that they get this wheelchair. He's covered in puke, and they get all the press (and there's 40 or 50 journalists and photographers) and they get him there for a photo-call and the band line up behind him. It's pretty sick stuff.

The journalist, who was still completely comatose, was not allowed to board the plane, as his passport, which was in one of his cases, had already been checked-in. He followed on the next flight to England three days later. Ian Grant picks up the increasingly sorry tale: 'Me and Alan [Edwards] saw him some time later on Brighton beach and he was a tramp. He'd lost his job because of that incident and he just dossed around on Brighton beach. We all felt really guilty.'

Confronted with this for the first time in the twenty years since the event, a horrified JJ told me: 'I didn't do it maliciously – he wasn't even targeted. He was a journalist who was having a drink with me on the bus. I didn't have anything against him. Man . . . what a terrible story. It's not right is it? I don't wish that on anyone.'

The Stranglers were operating on the very thin line between buffoonery and tragedy, and as the years rolled on, the fun was increasingly replaced by disaster and disharmony. JJ's behaviour was upsetting a lot of people, and his violent conduct was now the stuff of legend. In the space of a year or so he had attacked journalist Jon Savage for a three-star review, karate-chopped a phone in TW studios during the recording of *Rattus* so that it hung by a wire by the end of the session, karated a fan asking for an autograph, bashed his way through the dressing-room at the Paradiso, beaten up various unsavoury people at gigs and chucked a bottle of wine at journalist Mike Nicholas in the dressing-room at the Glasgow Apollo. Later in the decade he kicked a hole in the door of Alan Edwards' office in Edgware Road. There was probably a lot more that has been consigned to the incinerator of history. JJ was untamable. Even at this early stage, Hugh had grown tired of JJ's antics:

> JJ was dangerous. He was out of control sometimes because he couldn't handle the alcohol. There are two types of people who drink: there's the person like me who goes silly and starts laughing, and there's the person who gets very belligerent. JJ's aggression did get in the way sometimes and it did get tedious, particularly later on. You'd have interviews with people and all they'd want to talk about was how many people got injured at a riot at a gig, or how many times we'd been arrested. And you'd think, 'Hold on. Isn't this all supposed to be about the music?'

Jet is typically rather more blunt: 'JJ was a complete pain in the arse, a nightmare. He didn't want to play this gig, he didn't want to play that gig. It was all to do with his image. He was a ranting, raving loony.'

But at least there was more than the odd funny moment or two thrown in. JJ was never, ever boring. If rockers are supposed to be menacing, aggressive and 'out there' doing it, then JJ was certainly *the* frontiersman of punk.

During a recording session in the States, Jet in the control room spied JJ entering the drum booth with a girl. Jet remembers with obvious glee:

> Somebody said, 'Where's JJ?', and I said, 'He's in the drum booth with that tart.' The engineer, who was a woman actually, fiddled about with the controls. She turned the mike up and it was like, 'Uh, Uh, Uh', so she quickly turned on the tape machine and recorded it. 20 minutes later, when they walk out, we pretend we don't know anything about it, and suddenly she turns on the tape, and the pair of them are pretending nothing's happened and then they suddenly realize they've been caught.

But there was even worse to come: 'It was hugely embarrassing for JJ, and then everyone got over it. It was a big laugh, and then everyone went home. But we heard a few months later that this engineer had apparently copied it and it had gone all round New York!'

During this period, the Stranglers saved some of their more outrageous pranks for the Nordic countries. Jet Black is, once again, the man in the know:

> I remember in Oslo we'd come back from the gig and JJ had a young lady with him. The management of the hotel wouldn't let her in, so he arranged for her to go round the back of the hotel and he'd get her in through one of the windows. Anyway, they caught him trying to smuggle her in and decided to call the police. So JJ goes down to the foyer of the hotel where all the people had returned from the opera with their theatre gear on and moons at the punters in the lobby! Sure enough, the police turn up and JJ comes running to me and says, 'Jet, Jet, the police are after me. What should I do?' I said, 'Where are they?' JJ said, 'I don't know but they're searching all the rooms.' I said, 'Right, JJ, get under the bed and get Dave in and put his table up.' So there's three of us sitting round the table and Dave always has a pack of cards, so we made out we were playing a game and having a drink and soon enough there was this knock on the door. I said, 'Who is it?' And the reply comes, 'It's the manager.' So I said, 'Sorry, we're not doing any more interviews tonight!' And the reply came, 'I've got the police here.' I opened the door and they said, 'We're looking for someone'. And I said, 'Can't you see we're trying to have a quiet game of cards?' In the end they go away and JJ gets away with it.

But it was Sweden that time and time again witnessed the Stranglers at their most mischievous. The band's introduction to the country at the hands of the Raggare had not been the smoothest, and the Stranglers' entourage always feared the worst when crossing over the border. After one gig in Stockholm, the band reached their hotel to find the usual problem – they couldn't get a drink, or anything to eat, and JJ and Hugh were barred from bringing girls back to their rooms. JJ: 'It was late at night, so Hugh and I tied up the receptionist with gaffer tape and put him in the broom cupboard. There was no one around so we got away with it and just took the two girls back up to our rooms.'

Of course, this little prank worked in the band's favour. Jet: 'The next morning when he got out he made a big stink and it was front-page news. So the gig sold out!'

At another gig in the border town of Örebro, Jet was so annoyed that the restaurant was closed (it was a Sunday) that he hurled a table across the bar. He retired grumpily to his room to wait for the obligatory police presence. Jet: 'The policeman turns up armed and says, "Are you Mr Black?" And I said, "Yeah, I'm Mr Black, now fuck off, that's what you can do." And amazingly he did!' Later, in the 1980s, Jet also quizzed an unsuspecting copper as follows:

'What would you do, Officer, if I called you a cunt?'
Copper: 'Well, sir, I would have to arrest you.'
Jet: 'What would you do if I only *thought* you were a cunt?'
Copper: 'Well, I couldn't do anything, sir.'
Jet: 'Well, Officer, I think you're a cunt!'

The band seem to have a special affinity with Sweden, the only country, so the song goes, 'Where the clouds are interesting'. 'Sweden (All Quiet On The Eastern Front)' was actually re-recorded in Swedish and released as a single, but failed to set their charts alight. The original version was on the *Black And White* album released in May 1978. Work on the album had begun in December 1977 at Bear Shank Lodge in Oundle, Northamptonshire, where the young Billy ('I've had rely-shuns wiv gawls frum many nyshuns') Bragg made the acquaintance of the group. This was a big test for the Stranglers: the songs on *Rattus* and *No More Heroes* were drawn from the band's songbook, built up over a three-year period and honed in live performance. For the new album they had to start from scratch, and the pressure was on. The songs being developed during that period were altogether more experimental. Most of the older songs were fairly conventional rock ditties – quirky, but essentially sing-along numbers, with the odd exception such as 'School Ma'm', which was musically more unconventional. But the newer material explored the chemistry between the band to a fuller extent and took more risks along the way. JJ remembers staying at the Lodge over Christmas, laying down some ideas with Finchley Boy Dennis Marks on drums while the others went back to family and friends. JJ's stock-in-trade was the melodic, almost symphonic, sweeping musical *leitmotif*, which is shown to full effect on one of the album's strongest cuts, 'Toiler On The Sea'. JJ: 'In those days Hugh and I used to spend a lot of time together. I was really into these longish, quite well-arranged songs, with a kind of surf guitar thing for the melody which Hugh would play. I'd hum out the melody and he'd play it.'

After several weeks of biting cold, Hugh upped and left for a holiday in his beloved Morocco (even now he sometimes wears a badge of the Moroccan flag on his jacket) where he wrote the lyrics to many of the songs, including those for the sea-swept grandeur of 'Toiler'.

The original intention was to have one side with John's music and Hugh's lyrics and singing (this later became the material for the 'White' side) and the other side with Hugh's music and JJ's vocal and lyrics (the 'Black' side). It didn't quite work out that way in the end, but roughly speaking Side 2, with songs such as 'Threatened', 'Curfew' and 'Death And Night And Blood' (Yukio), showcased JJ's obsessions at the time. 'Curfew' in particular was typical JJ. It was a doom-laden, dystopic account of a political shutdown, set against some wonderful music from Hugh and a brilliant riff from Dave. 'Death And Night And Blood (Yukio)' was JJ's paean to the Japanese writer Yukio Mishima, who committed ritual suicide during a live broadcast in 1970. JJ was not the only rock star to have an interest in Mishima. David Bowie's portrait of Mishima was mounted above his bed in his Berlin flat. Like Bowie, JJ was fascinated with Japan. But JJ's interest in Mishima went considerably deeper. Mishima's writings were proto-fascistic, and he himself was a homosexual who had a bodyguard of gay Samurai warriors. What appealed to JJ was his intellectualism, his physical strength and beauty, and his serenity. In Mishima, JJ saw perfection – the ultimate in mental and physical prowess. JJ explains:

He wrote in the modern version of the Samurai bible, the Hagakure, that the way of the Samurai is death. If you have the choice at any one moment, you must choose death. It's the belief that if you know you can die at any one moment then you have to live life to the full now, which means everything has to be beautiful. So the Samurai used to put make-up on so that he wasn't grotesque in death. They'd disembowel themselves and then, five seconds later, were beheaded by their best friend. So this was deemed to be an act of courage. But it's been illegal since 1945, when lots of people were doing it. They believed that you had to die like cherry blossom – with a bit of rouge on your face and lipstick. So you'd do the bizz, and then someone would behead you to stop your face being grotesquely distorted. Mishima believed that you had to die creatively. He thought he'd written his best work and he'd been planning it for months. And he was physically middle-aged and didn't want to see his body deteriorating any further. So, on the day he finished his last manuscript, he killed himself.

Of the other tracks, 'Tank' powered along at high speed with some of the fastest keyboard riffs you'll ever hear in rock. Another waltz, 'Outside Tokyo', possessed, as *Record Mirror*'s Tim Lott put it, a 'funereal fairground riff' whilst 'Nice 'N' Sleazy' centred on the band's visit to the Hell's Angels in Amsterdam the previous autumn. This is the cleverest song on the album: it was another stab at white reggae, with another outstanding bass line from JJ. According to JJ, they 'fucked it up' on 'Peaches', but on 'Sleazy' there's a definite reggae feel. Musically, the best bit comes when Dave's moog synthesizer sweeps randomly from speaker to speaker in a sonic frenzy. And, like so many great moments in pop, its origins lay in accident. Producer Martin Rushent told *Trouser Press* in 1981: 'At the end of "Nice 'N' Sleazy" there's a synth solo that goes crazy. It was due to my plugging in the wrong socket; the whole system fed back . . . Dave Greenfield heard it and he said, "Great! That's unreal! I'll do it again and make it a bit longer."'

Lyrically, the song is a pastiche of a biblical parable – a clever device which worked. Hugh wrote:

> An angel came from outside
> Had no halo had no father
> With a coat of many colours
> He spoke of brothers many
> Wine and women, song a plenty
> He began to write a chapter
> In history
> Nice 'n' sleazy

'Nice 'N' Sleazy' was the only UK single 'proper' from the album, reaching a creditable Number 18 in the charts. It was the first single to really break free from the tradition of conventionally melodic

Stranglers songs and suffered commercially as a result. The single's sleeve resurrected the old 'Strangled woman' photo from 1976, showing that the band were still in need of a massive overhaul in the good-taste department. A studio version of 'Walk On By' was included as a free white-vinyl EP with the first 75,000 copies of the album, and was backed by the pub-rock numbers 'Mean To Me' and a live 'Tits', which also hinted at old-style Stranglers (refreshingly, *Black And White* itself had none of the hectoring tone in relation to the 'chicks' of the first two studio albums). This giveaway EP was, according to band legend, JJ's idea, and when later in the summer they decided to release 'Walk On By' as a *bona fide* single, sales naturally suffered. That said, it still sold well enough, reaching Number 21 and remaining in the charts, like 'Nice 'N' Sleazy', for 8 weeks. However, it would surely have been Top 5 had it not been for JJ's altruistic proclivities.

'Walk On By' also had a noteworthy 'B' side. 'Old Codger' was sung by Liverpudlian jazz maestro and hep-cat, writer and broadcaster George Melly, who had recently featured the Stranglers prominently in a BBC2 documentary on the impact of surrealism on contemporary art. Suitably flattered that their activities had been endorsed by the cognoscenti (his 1972 book *Revolt Into Style: the Pop Arts in Britain* was one of the most influential of its day), the band asked Melly down for a spot of brandy-drinking and crooning, and he obliged with a great vocal for the 'Old Codger' track. It was a footnote in the band's development, but a genuinely silly one and a light-hearted counterpoint to the increasing gravitas of their newer work.

Dark, sombre, and reflective, *Black And White* showed that the band had matured as songwriters and performers. Lyrically the songs were more reflective, more European, and less parochial. Musically, the album moved the band into a different terrain from that of their major-league new-wave contemporaries. 'In The Shadows', originally the B-side to the 'No More Heroes' single, gave a hint at a new style to come, and represented a more experimental approach which would be synth- rather than guitar-led. *Black And White* manoeuvred the Stranglers into the vanguard of the new wave. Their Hammond-organ style toned-down, and their punky freneticism re-designed, the Stranglers emerged with a rather hip sound. By the middle of 1978 with the Pistols' original line-up shattered, and most of the original energy of punk dissipated, British pop was heading towards a more experimental approach based on the synthesizer. Groups such as the Human League, Cabaret Voltaire, Joy Division and Throbbing Gristle led the way. The Stranglers were still a song-based pop act, but they were moving with the flow and were actually helping to define post-punk music. Very few critics have given them the credit for this that they deserve. The gloominess of *Black And White* was one of the influences on the miasma of Joy Division, a group which contained, in bassist Peter Hook, a player with a style not so distant from JJ's own.

The bold approach paid off. Whilst not quite scaling the commercial heights of *Rattus*, *Black And White* was still a more than respectable seller, reaching Number 2 in the British album charts and becoming the third Stranglers' album in a row to be certified gold. It was far better received critically than the rather formulaic *No More Heroes*. *Sounds'* Donna McAllister gave it five stars, and even Tim Lott, recently targeted for some ritual humiliation by Hugh, found the grace to award it four in *Record Mirror*. The album's release also saw the return of Phil McNeill to the fray. In an astute review, McNeill pointed out that the band had become *artistes*. The misogyny on *No More Heroes* had been less vehement and more self-parodic. On the latest offering, however, it had been replaced by a 'fierce dynamism and studied power'. The only mildly dissenting voice was that of *Melody Maker*'s Harry Doherty, but even his was, on balance, a positive review. Predictably, anything less than unbounded acclaim was enough to give the band a collective apoplectic fit. JJ told *Melody Maker*'s Chris Brazier that Harry Doherty, 'will go the same way as Jon Savage – tell him to stay out of town, keep out of my way'.

Finding major gigs in the capital to support the album was a continued headache. Alexandra Palace (12 years later to be the site of Hugh's last appearance with the band) was mooted, but soon quashed by a GLC still out for the band's blood after the Rainbow incident. Albion found it simply impossible to get the band booked into any venues in London. However, four British shows were fitted into the European dates. On 7 June the band played a benefit gig for PROP at Leeds University. Jet:

We've supported PROP (Preservation of the Rights of Prisoners) for many years. Having been imprisoned as innocents ourselves, we appreciate that some prisoners are themselves innocent. Of course, a lot of them are guilty, but nevertheless people who are put in prison are supposed to have certain basic rights, and we know that, very often, they're denied them. It's not a popular thing to help people in prison, because people assume that they're all nasty. That isn't necessarily the case. We did a number of gigs for that support group down the years.

At the Glasgow Apollo, incidentally one of the band's favourite venues ('Our love-affair with Glasgow started there,' remembers JJ), the Stranglers once again took the law into their own hands. They were less than impressed by the violent conduct of the security people, whose heavy-handed tactics with a volatile crowd simply exacerbated the tension. Midway through one song, Hugh cut off, had the stage lights directed on to the phalanx of security people, and publicly humiliated them. JJ decided to take some direct action himself: 'The bouncers were like fucks at the time. They weren't professional, they were just beating people up! I saw one kid, a small little thing, being beaten up. So I jumped into the audience, grabbed hold of the kid, went out of the building, round the back, through the stage door, put him back in the audience and climbed back on stage!'

The bouncers retreated outside the venue, leaving the unrestrained audience to invade the stage and cause the hackneyed x-thousand pounds' worth of damage to the structure of the hall and to themselves. Before the second night's gig the bouncers were filed into the Stranglers' dressing-room and requested to cool it with the fan-bashing, but, after a good few milligrams of alcohol had percolated around their bulky bodies, they decided it would not be a bad idea if they simply attacked the band instead. Eventually the band made it to the safety of waiting cars, after a meagre police presence kept the boozed-up bouncers at bay. But the band were reluctant to call the police on this second night of frolics, after a culinary-induced brush with the law on the first . . .

The band were having a seriously bad time of it in Glasgow. After the first gig Jet had another spot of bad luck with his eating arrangements, this time at the Central Hotel. Of the three restaurants on site, one was closed, the second refused to admit the band, and a third, *La Fourchette*, denied Jet a meal when he arrived 10 minutes after the kitchens had closed (even though they were busy preparing meals for the rest of the band). Jet once again entered his own personal culinary Groundhog Day. He tried to get a meal, failed, and everyone got stroppy. The police were called, and Jet ended up in custody (this time with JJ, who always wanted a piece of the action), until he was bailed out by the management. He eventually pleaded guilty and was fined £25. Jet liked his nosh on the road, but there always seemed to be some strange outside force preventing it reaching his stomach. These unhappy gastronomic experiences eventually led Jet and his girlfriend of the day, Sue Prior, to plan what would have been one of the handiest volumes ever to find its way into the 'Food & Drink' section in WH Smiths – *Black's List: The Bad Food Guide*. That November Jet told the *Daily Express*, 'More bands break up because of bad food than bad management'.

At the gig at Leeds University in June, the band were surprised to see a female stripper take the stage during 'Nice 'N' Sleazy'. This started a pattern for young women in the clichéd garments of male desire willing to 'get their kit off' on stage during this particular number, and gave the band a cheeky idea for their London open-air gig in Battersea that September. The Battersea gig was an important one for the band as it was their first major London date for nearly a year. They had managed a few pub gigs earlier that month, again in their pseudonymous guise, but the Battersea gig was their official metropolitan re-launch and the band were determined to mark it with something spectacular. Ian Grant decided to hire a real armour-plated Sherman tank, to be placed on stage as a prop for a song called . . . wait for it . . . 'Tank'! But JJ wanted even more in the line of big surprises for the show:

I was living with three girls at the time: my girlfriend, her gloriously beautiful sister called Jane and a friend called Lynn. Lynn was a stripper (I think it was £9 for gyrating about and £14 if she took her top off). At this time we were getting so much stick for being misogynistic because of the lyrics, which wound- up the liberal community. But it's always a good thing to wind them up, so I was pleased about that. Lynn had asked to do a strip at a show in Brighton. We never thought of it as sexist or anything, we just thought of it in terms of some girl wanting to do it. And she's a tough girl – she's not going to take any crap off any bloke. Jane, who was the girl with very long blonde hair, was 16 at the time. She said; 'Let's do it. Let's show these wankers who's boss.' They were on my side saying, 'This is bollocks, you hating women.

There's nobody who loves women more! You're not exploiting us. We're letting you do what we want with us. 'So Lynn got a few women from the profession to do it with them. It's a caricature, isn't it? It's a piss-take. People wanted to take it the wrong way.

True to form, Jet, who had distant memories of playing in East-End pubs accompanying the local fan-dancer, was definitely up for the strippers too, while Dave was too busy being Dave to notice. As ever, Jet could see pound-signs imprinted on every buttock as they wiggled their way through the song: 'After JJ's dodgy friends had come on and done their bit, the police came backstage to take down their particulars! To cut a long story short, the police were going to prosecute us for lewd behaviour, but they found that before they could do that they had to prosecute the GLC for allowing this to happen in the first place. So, in the end, nobody ever got prosecuted. But it was a huge publicity stunt and hugely beneficial to the progress of our career.'

The striptastic Battersea gig has been immortalized on video and, nearly twenty years on, makes for rather perfunctory viewing, as several strippers (including a flaccid Finchley Boy with a whip) gyrate in time to a seriously extended instrumental section. It's not really erotic (the belly dancer on U2's *Zooropa* tour was far more effective, even more so as she remained fully clad throughout), and it's ultimately more silly than outrageous. So if this was the intention, it was undoubtedly a success. But the routine seemed so clichéd, so obvious and ultimately rather boring. The Stranglers-as-sexist tack had surely played itself out as a selling-point by now. Hugh, talking in 1997, tired of the line of questioning about the sexism inherent in a strip, testily commented: 'It adds to the spectacle. I don't see it as an unhealthy activity. It's a dramatic turn. I don't see it as degrading to anyone. They're only doing it because they enjoy doing it. I don't think women are forced to strip to music – they're doing it because they're exhibitionist.'

The autumn UK tour passed off without further incident, save at a gig down on the south coast in Bournemouth. The band had been persuaded to play a fund-raiser for one of the Wessex chapters of the Hell's Angels, who needed a new club-house. Hugh remembers that this gig was something of a turning point in relations between the band and the Angels: 'They insisted on doing the backstage security themselves, and as we walked to the stage there were two of them trying to kill each other with knives on the floor, and I thought, Oh God! This is marvellous. Then they started kicking our fans from the front of the stage and JJ had to say something.'

The Hell's Angels' presence was simply alienating large sections of the Stranglers' audience, who were sick and tired of being muscled around by these huge, bearded colossi everywhere they went. And the Finchley Boys had not taken kindly to being shoved down the pecking order. But the Angels, like Dagenham Dave and the Finchley Boys, had served their purpose: they were the last in the lineage of band protectors. The band were genuinely grateful to them for helping them out of several violent situations, and had befriended some of them, but now they thought they were becoming part of the problem. The Stranglers weren't the only band at the time having problems with the Angels, either. There was violence at a 999 gig around that time, and a little later both the Pretenders and the Stray Cats were adopted by the movement. The Angels' tactic was always the same: befriend the band, 'protect' them, ply them with bags of Class-A drugs and then ask for payment for these 'gifts' a few months down the line. And they were enormously powerful. After making an ill-judged comment about them at the Paradiso in the seventies, Iggy Pop was forced back on stage to make a public apology after the gig.

One final incident further queered the Stranglers' pitch as far as promoting the band on British television was concerned. The group had appeared on a variety of programmes, but were always rather a handful to deal with. They had an uneasy relationship with the *Top Of The Pops* production team, who found their behaviour a problem. Before their slot the band used to tell the audience of assembled teenagers dirty jokes, and JJ is rumoured to have opened the dressing-room door with his boot, much to the chagrin of the powers-that-be. On one occasion the band appeared for rehearsals, asked the bemused staff for a mop and bucket, and proceeded to clean the dressing-room in an ostentatious display of good behaviour. But one incident in particular helped reinforce the corporate image of a band of mischief-makers.

That autumn the Stranglers were booked to appear on BBC2's

Rock Goes To College, which every week showcased a live act from a student venue. The Stranglers were to play Guildford College, on the understanding that sales of tickets whould be split evenly between students and local fans, who had been prevented from seeing the group live because the Guildford town council had banned them from the local Civic Hall. Jet:

> When we got there we saw the audience and we thought, 'These look like a bunch of students', so we sent people all along the queue asking them if they were students. Every one apart from a couple were students. No tickets at all had been sold to the public. We were outraged. We said, 'This is a fundamental breach of the deal we struck,' so we fucked off. And this was all captured on film and has been hugely damaging to our career amongst the straight people at the BBC, who still think we're a bunch of loonies.

In one sense the Stranglers were right to feel aggrieved, having been told that only half of the tickets would be sold to students. It was only years later that they found out that no such arrangement had actually been made with the BBC and that their wishes had not been communicated to the authorities. On the other hand, they had been hypocritical. Ex-PhD student Hugh had the audacity to shout, 'We don't like playing to an élitist audience!' before throwing his mike stand across the stage in a huff. Producer Michael Appleton, who controlled the *Old Grey Whistle Test*, made sure that the group were permanently banned from all programmes he was involved in.

The year 1978 saw the group trying to widen their commercial horizons. Jet Black: 'This was a wild, crazy, successful era for the band and there didn't seem to be anything stopping us. But we realized that it couldn't go on forever. We couldn't keep chasing round Britain because people would go off us. So we tried to extend ourselves abroad. We obviously weren't as well-known outside the UK so we really had to work at it.'

In 1977 and 1978 the band had toured Europe reasonably extensively, without much success. What success they did have in terms of record sales, air-play and tours came almost exclusively in the UK. Of course, their reputation went before them. Of the many cancelled gigs on the continent during this era, perhaps the most infamous, and most frightening for those involved, happened in July 1978 in Cascais in southern Portugal. There was a real buzz about the band in Portugal at the time, and, after the Salazar years of dictatorship, rock gigs by major bands were few and far between. When the Stranglers entourage arrived on the steaming hot afternoon of 14 July to set up the equipment at the venue, a huge sports arena near the coast, they found that the promoter and all those concerned were completely green as to setting up a large-scale rock gig. The stage was still being built and the crew found that the electricity supply was woefully inadequate for their needs. Despite numerous attempts to arrange for more juice, it was obvious by early evening that the 7,000- strong contingent of fans waiting ever more impatiently to get into the gig would be leaving disappointed. The decision to pull the show was made for reasons beyond the control of the Stranglers themselves (the promoters simply didn't have the necessary expertise), but the baked and baying fans did not take kindly to their non-appearance. Jet Black takes up the story:

> The road-crew started breaking down the equipment and loading it back into the truck. Somebody made an announcement that the gig was off, and the crowd went berserk. They hurled bricks at the driver as the truck with all the equipment was heading off, and he got hit on the head. So the crew are thinking, 'Shit, this is getting a bit heavy – we can't all walk out the front door. We'd better get out the back door.' So they get out the back entrance and they immediately find themselves in this alleyway with this big 10ft brick wall in front of them. One of the crew shins up the wall and sees this football pitch. So they say, 'Quick, let's nip across here.' So all of them are climbing over this wall, getting their bags over and they're about halfway across this football pitch when a section of the fans sees them and the word goes round and about 7,000 people start running across the pitch towards these terrified 15 crew members.

It was time for a sharp exit:

> They scramble over the wall and over the other side and they're in this deserted street. Two go one way, two go another, and our manager, Ian Grant, jumps into a hayrick and makes his escape that way! Another bloke goes up the road, and suddenly there's hundreds of fans chasing him. He sees this huge mansion with huge gates. He runs up the path and bangs on the door, and there's

no answer. So he bangs again and still no reply, and this mob is only a few yards away by now. Finally he tries the lock and it's open, so he runs in and there's this family of six eating their dinner. 'Help me! Help me!' he cries, but of course nobody can speak English. All of a sudden there's hundreds of people in the grounds of the house, some inside, some in the garden putting bricks through the window. All hell's let loose, and eventually they call the police to help quash this riot going on in the grounds of someone's house!

Jet and the rest of the band were out of harm's way. They had been waiting all day at the hotel for news of the gig. But some of the road-crew weren't so lucky. Two had head injuries and had to be treated in hospital. Of course, to Jet's glee, it was big news:

We turned it to our advantage, as we always try and do. At the very next opportunity we went back and made sure it was organized properly. We took with us a pyrotechnics expert and shipped over thousands and thousands of pounds of fireworks, and we put on something that they'd never seen before. We had rockets going along ropes [Flying Pigeons] and at one point we made it look like the stage had blown up. In fact the fire services were really worried! But the gig was a huge success.

For the Stranglers to really become a major-league act, they now had to break globally and be a success in the Far Eastern, Australasian and North American markets.

America at first proved receptive to the band's melodic new-wave music, and an initial tour in 1977 aroused a certain amount of interest. Hugh comments drolly that the first tour of the States was coast-to-coast – New York and LA! Unfortunately, the LA gig coincided with the first press reports of the gruesome Hillside strangler. There were curfews in the LA region, and massive police presence. Everyone thought the Stranglers were opportunists and had acquired their name expediently as a sick joke. According to Hugh, this did the band great harm.

Then there was the famous incident in Lansing, Michigan, in April 1978, where the band ran up against dozens of very vocal female protesters, the self-styled 'Housewives' Movement', who were handing out leaflets urging people to boycott the gig, to be held at a club called Dooley's. The leaflet itself, 'Punk Rock/

Dooley's – Partners in Sexism' reads like it's been written by a man trying to give the impression that all radical feminists are unhinged. Here's a brief extract:

> Punk rock is overtly sexist. Men who write, perform and listen to punk rock are sexist. The Stranglers perpetuate the philosophy that is inherent in Punk Rock with lyrics that are 'clearly contemptuous of and offensive towards wimmin' . . .
> The area wimmin's community is outraged that Dooley's would invite these men [the Stranglers] to East Lansing to spread their misogynist (womyn-hating) propaganda. The motive is clear. Punk rock is now big money, and Dooley's, as a capitalistic establishment, wants to cash in on that new gold mine.
> Punk rock debases wimmin. The analogy can be drawn that Dooley's is a womyn-hating establishment . . . Boycott punk rock and Dooley's until they clean up their act!

JJ remembers that their response to the demo backfired rather drastically: 'All I remember is that we thought we'd grab hold of one, kidnap her and take her on the tour bus with us. And then we started to get whacked on the head with these placards and we didn't quite manage to get one. We got beaten up!'

Later Hugh commented to the *NME*: 'There was a big fracas and she got away unfortunately . . . but I bet she was really excited and turned on by it.' That night on stage Hugh read out the following statement: 'The Stranglers have always loved women and their movements, and will continue to do so.'

The major stumbling block to American success lay with the band itself. They simply didn't like the place, and for JJ, American imperialism represented one of the world's unquestionable evils. Ian Grant remembers a meet-and-greet given by Dutch EMI in 1977 which provided a strong indication of JJ's antipathy: ' 'Peaches' was Number 3 in the Dutch chart and we were going to meet the managing director. Suddenly we noticed that JJ wasn't there. There was an American flag on the wall and JJ was really anti-American because of what they'd done to Japan, and he was heavily into a United States of Europe. JJ had set fire to the flag and had left the room. The fire spread to the curtains, then the stereo, then the carpet. Needless to say we never met Dutch EMI again.'

The band had signed a deal with A&M, who were showing

considerable interest in them. But JJ wasn't exactly endearing himself to Uncle Sam. In June 1978 he gave one of the weirdest interviews in the history of rock to one of *Melody Maker*'s best writers of the day, Chris Brazier. JJ's chip really was on overload for whatever reason that day. He twice threatened journalist Harry Doherty with physical violence for his review of *Black And White*, praised the Hell's Angels ('cool guys'), defended their indiscriminate violence at a recent 999 gig, attacked the 'hi-faluting liberal ideas' of the women's movement ('I like women to move when I'm on top of them,' chipped in Hugh), spoke about the 'usefulness of violence', and ended with an endearing little swipe at the whole American nation: 'There was nothing there we could appreciate, nothing in the American culture that appealed to our superior Europeanism. They had nothing to offer us and we had so much to offer them . . . Everyone knows that Americans have smaller brains. Fact of life, you know – they're just inferior specimens.'

Reminded of this quote nearly 20 years on, JJ is adamant that it was a calculated wind-up, and not actually meant: 'They were entirely premeditated provocations. I didn't believe what I said.' JJ was a strong supporter of artisanship and also spoke in the interview with Brazier about how Europeans should rediscover their common roots, draw strength from a shared cultural ancestry, and reject the economic determinism of the EC. But his Europeanism was selective: Dai Davies remembers that he refused to fly Lufthansa during the European tour, so deep was his dislike of Deutschland.

The executives at A&M were hardly pleased with these high-profile instances of anti-Americanism. And it was the failure to crack the States which brought increasing tension to the relationship between the band and Albion, particularly Dai Davies. Davies was becoming less supportive of the band in general, and disillusioned at the band's (and maybe his own) lack of determination to succeed in America:

> I think the American tour made me really fed up with them because America was going to be a real hard grind. I learnt this during my time working with David Bowie in the early seventies. You go to one town and pull 30,000 people and you go to another and you pull 60. And for that reason the US has to be treated as a

continent, not a country. The Stranglers, because they had a bit of this bunker mentality and were already successful in Britain and parts of Europe, found the idea of slogging away in America for a couple of years too hard for them. It pissed me off but at the same time, I probably felt a bit the same way myself.

Matters came to a cataclysmic head that December. The band were outraged by A&M's plan to cull an album of material from the first two albums as a sampler for the American market. They thought it was sacrilegious to chop and change their material and saw this as unwarranted interference from their US record label. In truth they were not taking the reasoned, pragmatic approach. In fact, rather the opposite. Just before the festive season the band sent the following telex to A&M: 'Get fucked, love, The Stranglers.' This far from conciliatory missive had the immediate effect of getting them kicked off the label, and, basically, destroyed any chances of breaking America. It was a wilfully silly act, but totally in keeping with the band at the time. It was also something which JJ came, in part, to regret:

We shouldn't have fucked up our relationship with our American record company, A&M. I suppose it was a good and a bad move in a way. We wouldn't have existed so long if we'd been successful in the States, without a doubt. I think we would have lasted another two or three years at most. It was a big commercial mistake at the time, though, because we would have been financially secure for the rest of our lives. We really were on the verge of cracking the States. We were selling out medium- to large-sized clubs at the time. On the other hand, we wouldn't have had such a rich seam of music to discuss – we simply wouldn't have existed. The *Meninblack* album wouldn't have been allowed to be released in America. And Hugh would have done his little thing much earlier than he did.

The main problem was that JJ could never make his mind up whether he wanted to hold on to his fame or destroy it: 'I was never really sure what I wanted. I was a bit maverick about the whole thing and still am to a certain degree. I'm not a career-minded person.' This made him, at times, virtually unmanageable. How do you manage a rocker who sporadically does his best to fuck up own his career? JJ was a rock 'n' roll kamikaze, a genuine anarchist.

The Stranglers didn't have the stomach for the regime of touring and promotional work which was a prerequisite to success in America and it was at this point that they lost the chance of becoming a really major stadium act. This was not necessarily a bad thing, as the vast majority of bands who make the transition from cult act to stadium act rarely survive with their artistic integrity intact. With the notable exception of a band such as U2, becoming a stadium draw means becoming a musical bore. A whole range of artists from Bowie, Simple Minds, and Genesis, to the Rolling Stones, Prince and Madonna lost their artistic credibility when they became arena acts. Only Bowie was able to pull back from the lure of corporate rock and re-find his cutting-edge. So although the Stranglers failed to make the transition into the big league, this 'failure' allowed them to remain true to their own idea of the sort of group they had to be. The band were moving into the most creative phase of their career. And a new team of people were necessary to carry this through. In 1979 it was all-change for the Stranglers.

6: MY FRIEND, YOU'RE BLACK

Black-and-blue, black magic, blackball, black book, black box, Black Death, black flag, blackleg, Black Maria, black mass, black sheep, Blackshirt, black spot, black economy, black widow, black hole, blackmail, blackguard. The word 'black' in the caucasian English-speaking world has always carried with it pejorative connotations, whether of danger, pain, illegality, lawlessness, the forbidden or the occult. The dictionary definition of black is 'of the colour of jet or carbon black, having no colour due to the absorption of all or nearly all incidental light'. It is a 'non-colour', it is lack, it is absence, it is negativity but it is also power. The association with the colour black and primordial disharmony stretches back far into antiquity; in Greek myth Erebus was 'the god of darkness, the son of Chaos and the brother of Night'. In folklore and fantasy, black is associated with evil and punishment: 'Schwarzer Peter' (Black Peter) was good St Nikolaus' wicked partner, beating naughty children with his stick and capturing them in his sack at Christmas. The Black Death, personified in paintings by a scythe-wielding skeleton shrouded in black, was the popular name given to the Bubonic plague (an almost always fatal disease spread, fittingly, by rats) which ravaged medieval Europe. Lepers were forced to ring bells and move from place to place in groups in order that people might avoid contact with these unclean people, shrouded in black. Black is the colour of mourning, of ritualized grief. In spiritual and religious terms, if God and his angels are the forces of good and light, then the devil and his devotees, with their black masses and spells, are the ones who have been cast down into the darkness. People who speak of near-death experiences, of having technically died before being miraculously resuscitated, tell of witnessing an intense white light – a heaven, an intensely powerful rhapsody of welcoming.

Historically, it has, paradoxically, also been the colour of legality, ceremony and law-enforcement, from the ceremonial power of Black Rod and the black attire of the law-courts to the referee on the football pitch and the modern-day UK police constabulary. Black is also the colour of domination, of will and desire, from the fascist Blackshirts in the 1930s and '40s to the garments of eroticism and sexual fetish. In twentieth-century popular culture, through the media of radio and television, the colour black has been associated with evil, and infamy. Valentine Dyall's post-war radio broadcasts earned him the epithet, the 'Man In Black'. In *Dr Who*, the Time Lord's evil adversary was the Master, played originally by Roger Delgado, in a uniform of black, whilst later in the Seventies, in *Star Wars*, Darth Vader (his first name a corruption of 'dark' and 'death') was the evil alien dressed in black. And in advertising, black has always been used to signify temptation. What could be more self-indulgently wicked than sitting on the sofa enjoying the dark pleasures of the Black Magic box?

From 1977 onwards, the Stranglers began their inexorable progress towards the association of their image with this most potent of colours. Already outsiders, ostracized from their punk brethren through their dealings in the currency of the sexually taboo, black was the perfect colour for the band. They were indeed the black sheep of the punk flock. Of course, they already had a drummer with perfect non-colour credentials. The photo session for the *Black And White* album, as well as the publicity photographs from around that time, saw the four songsters more often than not dressed in black. Soon, wearing black would become the closest to a uniform or 'look' they would ever get. It was an anti-fashion statement, stark, monochromatic and threatening. JJ:

> Black was the nearest thing to a corporate image the band had. I came back from Japan in 1977 with a pair of black McCampbell's jeans and had loads more sent over. By the end of 1977 I was dressed all in black. In 1978, when we were preparing the *Black And White*, album, everyone thought it would be cool to wear black. In those days everyone was wearing very bright Day-glo clothes, and we wanted something distinct from that. I thought black was a good colour for loads of reasons: it was heavy, it saved you the bother of having pink this, or green that. And I always believed that the baddies had the best clothes. But they do say that

black clothes create negativity, so I always make sure I wear some
non-black just to fight it off.

It was the practical nature of the colour which appealed to Jet
the most: 'It was a badge of identity for a while. But now I only
wear black because I've got black clothes. And you know, when I
go to the wardrobe I never have to say, "What shall I wear
today?" After 20 years chasing round the world and living out of
a suitcase, it's very handy just to have one colour. There's a very
practical element to it. I've got the odd red or white shirt that I
might wear when I cut the grass, but generally speaking, it's
black!'

Dave too wore black most of the time: 'I had loads and loads of
black T-shirts. It wasn't a band policy to wear black though,
although Jet always wore black. I remember him telling me that
he had this big cauldron and dyed all his clothes black, but I didn't
go quite that far!'

In 1979 the band's 'black phase' began a two-year period
which would bring unhappiness, violence, tragedy, and bizarre,
almost supernatural occurrences. Also, the band were now being
looked after by Ian Grant's Black And White management. Their
Albion connection was over.

Albion had made the Stranglers stars. For two years theirs had
been a successful, dynamic team. Derek Savage was the hustler,
Dai Davies a skilful manager, and Ian Grant the band's confidant.
But by the second half of 1977 it was obvious that there were
tensions. Dai and Ian actually quit during their first promotional
tour of the States in 1977, only to be persuaded to stay following
the band's effusive apologies for their poor behaviour. By 1978,
Dai Davies in particular was beginning to lose confidence. It was a
culmination of three factors: internal disagreements within the
hydra-headed management set-up, the quixotic personality of JJ,
and a lack of enthusiasm for the band's new, more experimental
material:

It was a terrible mistake for the three of us to be involved in their
management. You can't manage effectively by committee. In the
early days I'd been doing it, and Derek and Ian did the gigs. Derek
was involved on a business level because he was a very good

negotiator. Ian was a really good agent and was getting to be a good manager. But, didn't Napoleon say, 'It's better to have one bad general than two good ones'? In the end, one person's got to be firmly in charge.

The other problem was JJ. Charming as he was half of the time, he enjoyed mind-games. The fact that there were three people in the management company gave him the opportunity to wind people up and work one against the other. He did this amongst the band too. He could never decide whether he wanted to destroy the Stranglers. He actually left a couple of times, he just stormed off, but he was back within the week.

According to Dai Davies, the Stranglers were beginning to resemble that which they had set out to replace:

They were becoming unmanageable and losing direction. In fact, I thought they were beginning to become a prog-rock band! I didn't like *Black And White* much and I thought they were losing that thing of the three-minute pop single and the direct, dynamic message.
In the end they were always looking for us to be wrong. For example, JJ wouldn't fly Lufthansa so if they had to be up at 7 a.m. to catch a plane, then it would be our fault. It got to the point where we were looking for faults in one another and we were getting more and more fed up. And, as a result, I got less and less interested in them.

The set-up within the Stranglers, the fact that the band had two focal points demanding attention, was, in Dai Davies' mind, what made them special, but was also the factor which ultimately led to disunity and discord. Like Roxy Music, who in Bryan Ferry and Brian Eno had two band leaders both striving for their dominant share of the limelight, so, within the Stranglers, having two such forceful personalities was always going to lead to conflict: 'Hugh had this ability to write really good pop songs – he was the songwriting talent. But JJ was the energy and drive and image of the band. It needed both these guys for it to succeed. In pop you need to find one person with these two skills, or you have to find two people. But if you have two people with those different skills there's also conflict within the band as well as the dynamism to make it successful.'

Dai Davies sensationally asked the band to split up after the

Black And White album, thinking they had totally lost direction. Suffice to say, the suggestion was viewed very dimly by the band themselves, who were undergoing a painful artistic transition from new-wave popsters to moody, dramatic songwriters with a more left-field appeal. The band wanted to leave the raucousness of the new wave behind. Furthermore, they were also beginning to suspect Derek and Dai of using the success of the Stranglers to expand and consolidate their own position as pop managers and entrepreneurs. Tired with, as he perceived it, doing all the work, Ian Grant proposed that he become the band's sole manager: 'Dai and Derek were empire-building. I was not involved in Albion Records or in Albion publishing at the time. Once the Stranglers related to me and I to them, I thought there was no way I was going to do all the work and let Derek and Dai take an equal percentage.'

Jet Black on the split: 'They were charming people to do business with, but at the end we began to see them for what they were, shrewd businessmen who were ultimately more interested in their own careers than ours. They started making demands that we should split up and re-form in some other guise, and it all ended quite sourly. So we soldiered on with Ian Grant for a while.'

So the end of 1978 saw the termination of the Stranglers' association with Albion and the beginning of a new era under Ian Grant. This was followed a short while later by the end of the band's professional relationship with Martin Rushent. Rushent had been booked to work on the planned, and subsequently never released Stranglers' single, 'Two Sunspots'', at Eden studios in Chiswick. Hugh: 'The tape of "Two Sunspots", was being played at the wrong speed and we said, "This is great. Lose the vocal and let's work on it at this speed." The result was really quirky, a sort of lunar landscape with western, Ennio Morricone music on top of it. It became "Meninblack". We preferred that to "Two Sunspots".'

Unfortunately, Martin Rushent didn't. Like Dai Davies, Rushent was fast losing patience with the Stranglers' new, less pop-oriented, material. Jet remembers: 'We started doing stuff that he didn't like at all and he started getting headaches. One day he said, "I'm not into this." We said, "Why don't you bugger off." So he buggered off. It ended on a sour note.'

Rushent duly buggered off to become one of the most creative and successful producers of his day, working with the seminal synth-pop group Human League in the early 1980s. His place in the Stranglers' producer's chair was taken by a promoted Alan Winstanley, who was asked to make the band's next studio album. Early 1979 saw the release of *Live X Certs*, the last album to be produced by Martin Rushent, which was culled from two shows at the Round House in 1977 and the Battersea stripathon in 1978. The sixties and seventies were the golden age of live albums. Some, such as the Rolling Stones' *Get Yer Ya Ya's Out*, actually usurped the original studios tracks and provided definitive versions of individual songs. Peter Frampton's *Frampton Comes Alive* and Thin Lizzy's *Live And Dangerous* in the seventies were huge commercial successes. Pub rockers Dr Feelgood contemporaries of the Stranglers on the same label, UA, had claimed the UK top spot in 1976 with their *Stupidity* live album. In the Nineties, live albums are considered virtually redundant, but twenty years ago, when a sizeable part of the record-buying public still regarded the live rendition, not the vinyl track, as the most authentic version of any particular song, the appearance of a live album was something to get worked up about. *Live X Certs* fails to capture the Stranglers at full throttle, but it's a listenable enough record, and caught the band as they were, with no overdubs added in the studio to paper over the cracks. It was something of a stop-gap, but its Number 7 chart placing showed that the Stranglers had lost none of their commercial appeal. Reviews, predictably, were mixed: Nick Kent at the *NME* remarked, 'Those who have all three studio albums don't need inferior versions of the same.'

Live X Certs marked the end of an era. The cover pays homage to the band's sexism and notoriety, depicting as it does a black fist scrunching up a newspaper bearing one of the most priceless headlines of the Stranglers' career, the *Stockport Advertiser's* 'Stranglers In Nude Woman Horror Shock', which must surely have been a spoof. It was the end of the first phase of the Stranglers' musical development. From now on their music would become seriously experimental, certainly in terms of the pop genre they inhabited.

This more experimental approach was nowhere better evidenced than in JJ's solo album, *Euroman Cometh*, released in April 1979. In a short lull in band duties, JJ set about constructing a quirky, though strangely melodic piece of state-of-the-art electro-pop indebted to Krautrockers such as Can and Kraftwerk. On

tracks such as the single 'Freddie Laker (Concorde & Eurobus)' and
'Jellyfish' it works remarkably well and underneath the surface
frippery are some really good pop tunes. Lyrically JJ is unfettered,
opining on the European condition in French, English and German. 'Deutschland Nicht Über Alles' is the most pointed track, and
'Crabs' the silliest. Yet again, it's the woman to blame:

> The girl she's got them crabs
> And she gave them to me
> I got some crabs
> I just don't know where she's been
> And she hasn't been fishing in the sea

The album reached a respectable Number 40 in the UK charts
and has sold around 60,000 to date. Not everyone found JJ's
prototype techno to their liking. Alan Winstanley:

> I thought it was awful! It's not one of my favourite albums, I have
> to say. He did a tour after that and he asked me to record one of
> the shows in Hemel Hempstead. I turned up and the guy who was
> setting up the equipment said, 'Where would you like me to put
> the audience mic?' I said, 'Hang on and I'll find out how many
> people are here', and I found out that they'd sold 10 tickets! So I
> said, 'I think you'd better put the audience mics pretty close to the
> audience.' There were a few more people who came in at the
> door, but it wasn't full by any means.

For the tour JJ was supported by Blood Donor and John Ellis'
group REM (unconnected with their contemporary namesakes),
which included several members of the risqué dance-troupe Hot
Gossip. Ellis chanced his arm as JJ's lead guitarist for the main slot too.

Ronnie Gurr, a 20-year-old journalist working for *Record
Mirror*, and hitherto a fan, wrote a particularly negative review
of JJ's show at the Pavilion Glasgow entitled 'Euroman boreth
something awful'. It wasn't brilliant journalism: the young Scot
was no great stylist, and it read as snide and petty. Gurr had
actually been befriended by JJ a couple of years earlier, and this
critical *volte face* was regarded as a stab in the back:

> There was a young guy outside the hall at the Round House, I
> think, with a rucksack, and a Scottish accent, asking if he could

leave his stuff somewhere. I said, 'Sure, leave it in the Stranglers'
dressing-room. Here's a couple of pence, go and get yourself a cup
of tea.' This was about sound-check time. After the gig he picked
up his rucksack. I think he met some people backstage and he got
put up in London for the night. Over a period of time I remember
letting him sleep on my floor in Hamburg. He started offering
articles to music papers. He also asked me if he could have a job
roadying for the band, but I said no. But when I read his review of
my gig, I felt betrayed by a friend.

JJ's retribution, however, was little short of startling. He asked
publicist Alan Edwards to ring Gurr up and invite him to the pub
for an exclusive interview. But JJ never showed up. Alan
Edwards: 'So I innocently phone this guy up for an interview
in this pub. He shuffles in and the road crew, the Finchleys, have
got this transit van, and they tie him up and throw him in the
back of the van!'
JJ continues the saga:

We took him up the A1 to the next gig. I got Ronnie to be
placed in a room with one of the Finchley Boys, Dean, with
express orders not to speak to this guy. So he was a prisoner in
that room. The intention was to seat him in front of the
audience and then put him back on the train. So we've got
him there on stage. But during the support group, Blood
Donor, he rushed off and straight to the police station. I ended
up hiding in Hot Gossip's dressing-room to escape the police
who were looking to arrest me.

Press reports at the time quoted JJ as admitting that he had
kidnapped Gurr, but that 'he reacted to what was intended as a
good clean joke'. Then JJ reveals his true intention: 'So I decided
not to strip him and hang him up.'
It was at this stage that Alan Edwards began to seriously
wonder whether JJ was now totally out of control. Beating up
journalists was pretty heavy, but kidnapping them was in a
different league: 'They kept him tied up, and I heard the
intention was to lower him into the audience, during the
middle of the performance. Since I had arranged the initial
interview, this was a bit delicate for me because it was looking
like I was someone who had got a journalist abducted, which,
unwittingly, I suppose I had.'

Events such as this were fast turning 1979 into the most heinous of the band's career. During a recording session in Paris, JJ decided once again that these news-hungry hounds should get the best story possible. And if he could scare them shitless in the process, then all the better: 'During the making of *The Raven* album, Philippe Manoeuvre, now a famous journalist and rock newspaper editor, was being very pushy. He kept hovering round our hotel in search of a story; he was obviously a very ambitious guy. So I took him up to the first floor of the Eiffel Tower, it was only about 300 feet up, took his trousers down, strapped him to one of the girders with gaffer tape and said, "Bye-bye."'

The band were also coming up with ever more fruitful ways of dealing with the spitters in the audience. On one occasion Hugh decided to haul the guilty party on stage and administer a beating with his shoe. Word soon got round at Stranglers gigs, and a section of cheery punters would shower the stage in spittle and beg to be brought up on stage to be spanked. Wearied by these exhibitionists, Hugh, goaded on by JJ, decided to take more drastic measures. At a gig in Lyon in France, Hugh forsook the boot for the banana, inserted it up the naughty fan's arse, and removed the shit-covered object only to see the audience head for the exit in droves. Media outrage ensued, along with decreasing media confidence in the band. According to Jet, bananas were going up bums at regular intervals during the early 1980s, but a recent attempt to resurrect this eye-watering 'trick' by JJ was quashed by the band's management.

The two front men themselves were making sure that they remained as newsworthy as possible. Hugh, for example, was making some high-profile connections on the dating front, stepping out with 20-year-old Kate Bush, who had recently embarked on her first and, sadly, only solo tour to date. Jet called her 'Squeaky' (to which Kate apparently countered, 'Oh don't be cheeky!'). Hugh still remembers her with affection:

> I almost got it together with Kate Bush, but the timing wasn't right. I was going off to Germany and she went off to Japan on the same day and we saw each other the night before. But we both had to get up early the next day. And if anything was going to happen it would have happened that night, but there just wasn't

time. We liked each other. She used to come to a lot of the gigs. I remember we went to see *Monsieur Hulot's Holiday* at the National Film Theatre. That was our first date. She was a lovely girl.

Later in 1979, Hugh had a scene with a Japanese girl called Shoko, said in initial press reports to be 14 years old, although this was subsequently upped two years to a legal 16. JJ had this to say about the Jerry Lee Lewis-like sexual proclivities of his older partner: 'Hugh happens to have this thing towards under-age girls. He'll get arrested for it one day, but that's his quirk.'

Jet also remembers that Hugh's predilection for young girls was in evidence during the off-licence days: 'I can remember in the early days in the off-licence Hugh used to have young ladies popping round at 8.30 in the morning on their way to school. I'm not sure if he was coaching them in their studies or was meeting them for some other reason.'

Through songs such as 'Bring On The Nubiles' and his openly stated attraction to young teenage girls, Hugh was pushing the bounds of sexual tolerance to the limits in a society in which different-sex, same-age relationships were the norm. Hugh told the *Daily Mail* in 1978: 'We offer a challenge, we make people challenge their own ideas. They look at us, and that makes them look at themselves. If they don't like what they see when they look at themselves, they change. If they do, they're stronger.'

Hugh wasn't alone in acknowledging the phenomenon of adult desire for under-16s. His one-time paramour Kate Bush wrote a song in 1980, 'The Infant Kiss', which dealt with similar emotions, but in a more poetic and nuanced way.

Hugh was not the only Strangler courting sexual outrage. JJ was also wont to stoke the fires of sexual outrage himself, as this quote from 1979 fully evidences: 'I just wanna fuck my mother basically. Always have done. Not so much now as she's getting older, she's losing her grip on her looks. She's a cute little French girl.'

Both Hugh and JJ were revelling in the taboo, and rejoiced in portraying themselves to the media as objectionable and morally corrupt. It was a dangerous game and reflected the arrogance of the pop world, in which a space is created by the media for rock stars to make private peccadillos public, and to sell records along the way.

It was around this period that the band started to become heavy drug-users. Hugh remembers that cocaine was ubiquitous:

> We were all smoking dope, and we were all taking cocaine. This was normal for bands in those days. You started making money and you took what you could lay your hands on. It's always around. It's terrible really. I knew where to get the good stuff, so I was the mug who used to get it and carry it around and have it on me. It got to the stage where it was no coke, no gig, and we would see what we could get away with. We'd have the promoter running around trying to find a dealer so we could have some cocaine and there'd be 2,000 people in the hall. We were holding him to ransom and seeing him running around. And you knew that he'd find some. It was a silly game – you'd find things to entertain you.

Producer Alan Winstanley adds that the recording of *The Raven* album was a very druggy time indeed: 'We recorded the album at the Pathe Marconi studios in Paris, and in the studio next door were the Rolling Stones recording *Emotional Rescue*. I kept thinking that Hugh was going off with Keith Richard! I remember after we'd done the drum tracks, Jet would sit at the other end of the console and every time you'd stop the music you'd hear the razor blade tapping on the side of the desk!'

The Stranglers were moving into a far heavier, darker, and more hedonistic scene. It was to be a kaleidoscopic existence, one which would produce their finest work. At the same time they were also becoming a cliché, a parody. Sex, drugs and rock 'n' roll, the axiomatic rock n roll 'nirvana', dominated them. They had become part of the whoring, drugging and boozing rock establishment, despite the oppositional stance of some of their music. There was too much money, too little moral restraint, too great an opportunity to 'go for it'. Like thousands of bands before them, and thousands since, they embraced chaos, relished it, but ultimately paid the price.

Before the recording of *The Raven* that summer, the band turned their attention to the potentially lucrative Japanese and Australasian markets. Their first tour of Japan in February 1979 was a howling success, 'howling' being the operative word, as Jet recalls: 'They used to scream at us, and we used to find this really amusing, so in the end we used to scream back at them, and that totally threw them!'

JJ was the perfect rock icon for the Japanese market – dashingly good-looking, physically perfect, a devotee of all things Japanese (karate, Yukio Mishima), and elegantly aggressive. The Stranglers were the first new-wave act to be packaged in Japan, and their success was startling, if short-lived. A second Japanese tour later in the year was less well-received and ended in financial disaster for the band. The tour manager, Paul Loasby, who worked for rock impresario Harvey Goldsmith, unwittingly accepted the mother of dodgy cheques – drawn on a Japanese bank for pounds sterling – from a Japanese promoter. When the cheque bounced, the band were informed that they had lost their share of the revenue from the shows and had to foot the £18,000 freight bill. Jet Black: 'When he cashed it, the Japanese promoter had gone bust and vanished. We never got the money out of Harvey Goldsmith, and we've had rows with him for years over it. But we did manage to sting him for a few grand recently and we got our own back!'

Australia was a different prospect altogether. This would prove to be a seriously sticky reception. The stunts began immediately as Jet remembers: 'We were due to meet up with some journalist and photographer in the street. JJ mooned at them. I must say, I was totally amazed at the reaction. It became a massive news story; the headlines were all of the "shock, horror" nature.'

The first gig at the Queen's Hotel in Brisbane saw some more 'direct action' from JJ. After being repeatedly spat at by a local punk by the name of V2, JJ jumped into the audience and put V2's head on more than nodding terms with the side of his bass guitar. According to *NME* reporter Kevin Meade, they almost never took the stage in the first place: 'Five minutes before they were due to begin their set at 10.30 p.m. the Stranglers demanded four bags of lollies (sweets) and refused to go on until they got them.'

On the second night at the same venue, Hugh was struck on the head by a beer bottle, and halfway into the set the band decided to smash up their instruments in a Townshendesque fit of stroppiness. They were really getting into this rock 'n' roll lark by now, the motto being to behave as wilfully as possible to every-one, and be as rude to the promoter as time would allow. The band suspected that they were being set upon by local plain-clothes' police. *Record Mirror* carried the following quote from Jet: 'They seemed to have come with the intention of smashing up the gig . . . We thought they were local heavies, and had no idea they might be police. Hugh was hit by a bottle and Jean managed to flatten a couple of them.'

The Stranglers regarded Queensland as something of a police state, and were particularly charmed by state president Joh Bjelke-Petersen, later to be immortalized in one of their best tracks from the seventies, 'Nuclear Device (Wizard Of Aus)'. Back home in England, Alan Edwards dressed up the story for the British press, claiming that the band, or at least one of them, had to flee from the Queensland police in the middle of the night on the backs of motorbikes.

During the promotional visit the band also used their appear-ance on Channel 7's talk show, *Willesee at 7*, to re-enact their version of Bill Grundy's lager-lout performance with the Sex Pistols from the *Today* programme in 1976. A ten-minute inter-view was edited down to barely 90 seconds, and the band, goaded into saying something 'provocative', duly obliged by telling Australia's youth that drugs were great. It was a classic rock interview and it did the trick. The group were duly dropped from the high-rating *Countdown* programme on ABC TV, thus ensuring a huge demand for tickets for the tour. Jet describes the very sordid scenes of mayhem and depravity which ensued:

I remember that at this point we got the best news headline of our career: 'STRANGLERS: COPS SET TO MOVE'. Along with the commercial advantages that resulted from that, it also attracted just about every nut in Australia. There was this sex maniac, an Aborigine, who was constantly out of her head on drugs. She just wanted to shag the band. We couldn't get rid of her. So, one night, after we had been unable to get her out of the dressing-room, we decided to tie her up with gaffer tape and take her on stage which was usually the best way of getting rid of pests. Anyway, we were steaming into our set in this packed club. The stage happened to be very low, only about 18 inches or so high. The audience were pressed right up against the platform and we could see the whites of their eyes, so to speak. Very soon the gaffered girl, in her dazed condition, was hanging half on and half off the front of the stage.

In the process of her rolling around, her dress had been pushed up beyond her waist and she wasn't wearing any knickers. The bloke jumping around in front of her whipped out his todger and gave her one right there and then! I believe that is called rape. If he ever had any guilt about his actions what he probably didn't know was that she would have been more than happy if the entire audience had given her one. After this incident, she still hung round the band. Eventually she sussed out that the crew had this big bus which got them around Australia. One of the crew later confided to me that they had all had sex with her until she was too sore to carry on. When they got home the crew had a reunion at the clap clinic.

These incidents again confirm that the Stranglers' 'jolly japes' were now becoming far from innocent. But, in the rock business, morality, sexual or otherwise, appears to be a shaky concept. Other Oz-style pieces of 'fun' included having a female journalist from the *Australian* newspaper gagged, bound and dropped into the audience on the opening night on the tour; a near riot at the Monash University in Melbourne; and an anti-Stranglers demo by feminists in Adelaide. The legend on their leaflet ran: 'Why The Stranglers Are Rats And Should Be Treated As Such', before listing the band's crimes to womankind and exhorting: 'Boycott and picket them! Don't go to see them! Or if you do, throw things at them – take ammunition!!' At the Adelaide gig there was another face-off between the band and the police. The police's old sparring partner, fearless Jet Black, describes the scene:

The papers were full of stuff which they'd nicked from the British press. The police obviously thought that they were going to make sure there wasn't any trouble with these limeys. We played in this huge square room. Right across the back, shoulder to shoulder were all these police, about 100 of them. After the first number I got down to the snare drum microphone and said something like, 'What do you guys at the back think this is, a fancy dress party? Why don't you just fuck off, you're not wanted here!' And the punters went 'woooarrh' and they all turned round and the police sheepishly walked out of the hall. Now they weren't going to leave this unchallenged, of course, so after the gig we went back to the hotel and two fucking coach-loads of them turned up. So all four of us got into this small bedroom, because we knew there was going to be trouble – which we'd all engineered, of course. We thought we would play this for all it was worth. Eventually the tour manager's knocking on the door saying, 'Lads, you've got to come out and talk to the police.' We said, 'No, we're not coming out, we're tired and we want to go to bed.' The next thing we heard was a knock on the door and someone shouting 'This is the police, open up!' So they broke down the door and they steamed in, about 60 of them, and we couldn't move. The papers were there too. We'd just been banned from this TV show and we could do no wrong. We were having a ball with the authorities and they couldn't see it was all one big game. They go to arrest me, and everyone says, 'It can't be him, he's the drummer!' And then they go to cart Hugh off. In the end they realized that they didn't have anything to stick on us. But we made sure it was a major incident, and it led to a sell-out tour.

Asked to assess their back catalogue today, the Stranglers are often quite vague about which song was on what album, and even about the order albums were released in! But the one that all members of the original line-up unequivocally praise is 1979's *The Raven*.

JJ: '*Black And White* was musically quite adventurous compared to *Heroes* and *Rattus*, but it was quite stark, as we were trying to be much more artistic. *The Raven* is much more successful and it's much more listenable, because *Black And White* is a hard album.'

Jet: 'I have great memories of the satisfaction I got from doing that, because when we started doing the album it was pretty much an unknown quantity and I was so pleased with the way it turned out. I thought it was a tremendous achievement. I cite that purely and simply because I remember the great feeling of elation when we went on to premier it at Wembley Stadium with the Who. It was the first time that we got major critical approval in the newspapers.'

Indeed, when the Stranglers were added to the line-up of Nils Lofgren and the Who for that concert on 16 August, the hatchet-burying must have been audible given Townshend's reportedly less-than-chuffed remarks about the band in the music press the previous year. The Stranglers were literally explosive: a barrage of mortars courtesy of *La Maître* fireworks caused such a commotion that the Who were forbidden from using their normal pyrotechnics by the local constabulary later that evening. The gig was a major triumph, and the album was only prevented from débuting at Number 1 in the UK album charts by a clerical error : the Police's

Regatta De Blanc was wrongly credited with the sales from *The Raven* album, and installed at Number 1. This was, indeed, a curious state of affairs, given that the Police album had still to be released.

Written in Italy and recorded in France, this was the Stranglers' most cosmopolitan album to date: 'Shah Shah A Go Go' was a quick-on-the-draw comment on the Iranian Revolution – an event predicted by Nostradamus in the sixteenth century (according to the band), 'Dead Los Angeles' was a mordant put down of phony Americana, whilst 'Nuclear Device (Wizard Of Aus)' was a barbed political satire of their beloved Joh Bejelke Petersen, the rather 'charming' right-winger who ran Queensland like a private fiefdom. 'Ice' revisited Mishima territory, 'Longships' was a typically eccentric waltz, whilst 'Genetix', with its odd-sounding 4/4 beat played on every drum by Jet, discussed tampering with the gene pool, and humans playing God in a strangely disinterested tone. Musically, the band had never been so seamless and so assured, with Hugh echoing his riffy neo-Beefhartian work from *Nosferatu*. *The Raven* also plays around with form: *Black And White* had been stark and forbidding but it still dealt in the currency of the four-minute pop song. On *The Raven* around half the tracks have long, intricate instrumental sections before the first verse, pushing the band's style closer to prog-rock than to punk. It was a strange mix of registers, but it worked. The finest track on the album, and arguably the finest of their career, was the title track, a gorgeously melodic piece of music with a romantic, sagaesque lyric from JJ, sung in his best, breathy, punk-Charles Aznavour style, sweeping, swooping synths from Dave, which boom out at the song's dénouement like the call of the raven itself, and some wonderfully understated choppy guitar from Hugh. The opening lines: 'Fly straight with perfection/Find me a new direction' carry an almost manifesto-like quality, before JJ conjures up the folkloric symbol of the raven, the figurehead in Nordic saga:

> My friend you're black and when you fly you're wild
> I am white sometimes I behave just like a child
> The northern seas are cold but they're our own
> We'll sail your southern seas before too long
> When I was a Viking
> My friend he was the raven

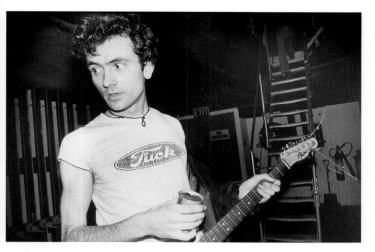

The T-shirt that stopped a gig, 1977. (*Photograph: © Garry Coward-Williams*)

'Oooooooooh!' The opening of 'Grip' recorded at Riverside Studios, Summer 1976. (*Photograph: © Garry Coward-Williams*)

Photoshoot for the *Rattus Norvegicus* album, with JJ as android androgene, Spring 1977. (*Photograph: courtesy of The Stranglers*)

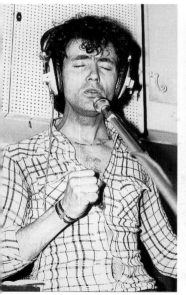

The band sign to UA, December 1976. From left: Hugh Cornwell, Alan Edwards, Ian Grant, Dave Greenfield, JJ Burnel, Jet Black, Andrew Lauder and Derek Savage. (*Photograph: courtesy of Alan Edwards*)

The rejected artwork for the cover of 'No More Heroes', 1977. (*Photograph: courtesy of The Stranglers*)

High-jinks at the Paradiso Club, Amsterdam, 1977. (*Photograph: courtesy of Allan Ballard*)

Jet outside the off-licence, Guildford, 1977. (*Photograph: © Peter Harding*)

At the Hell's Angels' clubhouse, just before a round of Russian Roulette, November 1977. (*Photograph: courtesy of Allan Ballard*)

The fab-four captured mid-mayhem during the launch of 'Black And White', Reykajavik, 1978.

Comatose journo after 'drinking contest' with JJ, Keflavik airport, Iceland, 1978. (*Photographs this page: © Jill Furmanovsky*)

Opposite page: Bare bums and male nudity shock-horror for 'Nice 'n' Sleazy', Battersea Park, September 1978. (*Photograph: © Pennie Smith*)

JJ with his beloved Triumph Bonneville on the Euroman tour, Spring 1979. (*Photograph:* © *Gareth Noon*)

Still from the gloriously silly 'Duchess' video, Summer 1979. (*Photograph:* courtesy of *The Stranglers*)

SOUNDS May 21, 1977

New wave paranoia strikes

SEVERAL acts suffered gig cancellations in the anti-punk backlash following last week's hysterical press reactions to The Clash's Rainbow concert.

Two dates have been struck from the current Stranglers itinerary — Leeds Town Hall ("Not prepared for New Wave . . .") on June 13 and

Cancellations backlash after Rainbow damage

EVENING POST & CHRONICLE
WIGAN, LANCASHIRE
ISSUE DATED 21 JUN 19

TOP POP GROUP HELD IN FRANCE

A TOP British pop group were arrested by French po

ANGLERS HELD AFTER RIOT IN FRANCE

Arrested— British punk group

Four

THE STRANGLERS punk group, the most controversial British band since the Sex Pistols, were arrested today by French police after a

JJ in classic leg-cocking pose, Manchester Apollo, 1980. (*Photograph:* © *Gareth Noon*)

The band post-'Golden Brown', 1982. (*Photograph: courtesy of The Stranglers*)

The Nordic theme was JJ's and it was a clever device on which to hang all the pieces of worldly reportage which made up the album. Like the raven, the Stranglers were seeking out new vistas: 'I named that album. The raven was a very potent symbol in Nordic mythology. Odin, the king of the gods, had two ravens and they were his eyes and they would fly out to the world and come back and report to him and it all fitted in with the subject matter of the album. The Raven was a symbol of flight because the Vikings used ravens aboard ships to find new territories.'

A startling 3-D raven graced the first 20,000 copies of the album, whilst the back cover shot showed our intrepid seafarers on a Viking ship. If the iconography, like many of the band's lyrics, was uncomplicated and a little too literal (like having a raven on the cover of an album called *The Raven*), it was a powerful image all the same. And Jet had already made the acquaintance of that same longship many years previously:

> The replica Viking ship was built around the late 1940s and sailed across the North Sea. I was one of the many thousands of kids on the beach (Broadstairs in Kent, I believe) who were there to witness the re-enactment of the Viking invasion of whenever-it-was. The event was sponsored by a national newspaper – I don't recall which one. The replica can be seen to this day, mounted on concrete blocks at Viking Bay which is close to St Lawrence near Ramsgate, Kent. The red-and-white sail of the ship was – when it was erected – found to be badly decayed and torn to shreds. If you look closely, you can see that it is retouched. I could never have imagined all those years ago that one day I would be standing in this ship promoting a rock album. Indeed, rock hadn't even been invented then!

However, it was 'Meninblack' which pushed the Stranglers in a bizarre new direction: a slow-paced track boasting an ominously insistent drum figure, a big booming bottom-end, and Hugh's aforementioned Spaghetti-western-style lead-guitar riff, and a recitative which allowed the band full rein to create a more sinister version of Uncle David Bowie's 'Laughing Gnome'. It was creepy and silly at the same time, portentous and powerful. The Meninblack, now immortalized in a 1997 Hollywood blockbuster, were either government agents, or aliens, or figures from a parallel universe, who visited those individuals who had gone

public about their experiences with UFOs and other extraterres-
trials. These black-suited, fedora-wearing agents, reported to
have no facial hair, to wear lipstick, to speak in an 'expressionless monotone', to display psychic tendencies, and to move with
an unnatural stiffness, would call upon their targets in a huge
vintage limo which would mysteriously disappear as soon as the
message to keep shtoom about their experiences was delivered.
The Stranglers thus had an interest in what in the nineties would
be *X-Files* material a good fifteen years before it became mainstream. The song also showcased one of JJ's obsessions at the
time – cannibalism:

> We have come to make you function
> So we can eat you at our functions
> We are the Meninblack . . .
>
> Healthy Livestock so we can eat
> Human flesh is porky meat hee hee heeeeeeeeeeeeeee . . .
> We are the Meninblack

JJ explains: 'For me cannibalism is sexually erotic. When I was
really young I started getting interested in women's legs and
thought, "I just wanna eat them," you know, as you do. Then I
read some interesting things about castaways and people eating
each other. Apparently human flesh tastes a bit like pork. It's a
great concept but it is just an erotic fantasy, no more than that, I
may add.'

The Meninblack material was introduced into the band's
collective creative soup by Jet, who had a long-time interest in
Ufology. Jet was fascinated by the 'mysteries' of life. He wanted to
see a ghost and he'd travelled to Scotland in search of the Loch
Ness monster. One evening he was looking out of the kitchen
window when he saw a brilliant light in the sky, which he tracked
for several minutes before it zoomed up out of his field of vision.
According to Jet, it was a UFO. The whole Meninblack philosophy became more than an interest. It became, as such things
often do, an obsession. The band began discussing the phenomenon with leading authorities on the subject such as John Keel,
and film-maker Lindsay Clennell. They learnt about such phenomena as the Frank Fontaine abduction. A young Frenchman

who disappeared after he and his friends had noticed a 'brilliant light, about the size of a tennis ball' in the sky reappeared a week later (dressed in the same clothes) at exactly the same spot as he was last seen by his two friends. The Meninblack became the band's alter egos. Dystopic, gloomy, frightening, corporate: the band had found their most resonant image to date. But it started a pattern of events which the band firmly believe was a direct consequence of them, as public people, making the phenomenon a media talking-point. For the next two years they would be surrounded by death, tragedy, misfortune and negativity. JJ: 'The whole association was very negative and very bad, and bizarre things happened. It's a taboo thing with us now, and things have been much better since we looked the other way. I'm not armed for that kind of struggle and I'm not sure anyone in the band is either. In the end you'll always be the loser.'

Obviously the whole Meninblack vibe was made more real and more frightening by the drug-induced states of psychic disturbance that the band were regularly experiencing. The third single off the album, the Lou Reed pastiche 'Don't Bring Harry', is a clear indication of the band's reliance on Class A drugs. JJ was by now close to being an addict, and felt himself physically wasted, whilst Hugh was going for it in a big way: 'I got into speedballs, which is mixing a line of heroin with a line of cocaine. You get the up from the cocaine and then the heroin calms you down, so you don't get paranoid.'

Hugh remembers that the song itself, with a rolling piano part which would later be echoed by Marillion in their 1985 hit 'Kayleigh', was written when the two songwriters were 'out of their faces.'

In 'Duchess' the band had written a classic pop song, possibly the best single of their career. Breezy, intelligent, anthemic. The fact that it peaked at a slightly disappointing Number 14 in the UK charts bespoke a certain cooling-off in public acceptance of the band. (Though in 1997 the single hit the charts once again, covered by My Life Story.) The song struck a blow at the 'chinless wonders' (the Rodneys) and the upper classes:

> Duch of the terrace knows all her heritage
> Says she's Henry's kid
> Knows all the history in the family
> Needs a man God forbid!
> God forbid!

The video was a cracker too. The band, complete with obligatory dark glasses, dressed themselves up in cassocks and
looned around in a local church, whilst shots from aristocratic
Ascot were intercut with this knock-about footage (the Manic
Street Preachers included similar tofftastic library film in their
Number 2 hit 'A Design For Life'). The video was a hoot to make,
as Jet Black fondly recollects:

> I actually had the idea to do it in a church in cassocks. We even
> walked down Oxford Street in them as a publicity stunt! We tried
> to find a church to let us film the video, and we managed to find
> one up in Hampstead, where there was this very modern-thinking
> cleric [a certain Fr R.A. Coogan] who thought it was a great idea.
> So we made this video, which was huge fun. There was this funny
> little incident which people who have seen the video a million
> times have probably never noticed. Just as Hugh was about to do
> one of his shots in the pulpit – he was doing it unshaven and
> wearing dark glasses to get the contrast between the choir boy
> image and the nasty rocker image, the lens fell out of his
> sunglasses and broke. He couldn't fix them, so he said, 'I know
> what I'll do. I'll get some silver paper', so he found this cigarette
> packet and ripped it up and got the silver paper and stuck it over
> the lens! The video was banned by the BBC of course. We were
> told later on that there was no way we were going to get it on *Top
> Of The Pops* the same week as Cliff Richard. I don't know if that's
> true or not!

The banning of a video which was simply light-hearted fun was
an indication of the media profile the band had: even the hint of
devilment was regarded as beyond the pale by the 'moral
majority' at the BBC, who were notoriously obtuse when it
came to censoring pop songs – disallowing a genuinely funny
Carry On-style Stranglers' video, whilst allowing Lou Reed's song
'Walk On The Wild Side' ('But she never lost her head, even
when she was giving head') to blare out before *Junior Choice*
earlier in the decade. Now, whereas the banishing of a song from

the nation's airways merely has the effect of increasing demand for a 'naughty' record, the removal of a video from a show like *Top Of The Pops* was bad news. In the seventies there was precious little pop on television unless you were po-faced and credible enough to get a slot on *Old Grey Whistle Test*, or poppy enough to chance your arm on *Tiswas* or Noel Edmonds' *Multi-Coloured Swopshop*. If you got played on *Top Of The Pops* you were almost certain to go up the charts the next week, but without that exposure your single was pretty much doomed.

The second single from *The Raven*, 'Nuclear Device (Wizard Of Aus)' had an equally daft video with the band dressed in khaki, sporting Nat Lofthouse-length shorts and Aussie-styled hats with corks dangling fetchingly on string in front of their faces. Jet can be seen banging a billy-can in time with his drum part, and all four get to show what great legs they've got (not). Whatever, it was another splendid video and prefigured the brilliantly silly videos by Madness in the 80s. It was shot in a small patch of deserted scrubland in Portugal. Several tonnes of high explosives were driven by a roadie named Blue, without a licence, at great personal risk down from the UK (through Basque territory!) for the explosive parts of the promo. The video might have been a laugh, but the attentions of a journalist, Deanne Pearson, who was pressing for a news story, were, for some reason, regarded with a certain amount of disdain. Suitably riled, the band again decided to 'teach her a lesson'. The original intention was to tie her to a tree and simply leave her overnight whilst the band packed up and flew back to Britain. In the end, they made sure that her lift back to the airport left without her. The result was Pearson was left stranded in the middle of nowhere, with barely an hour to find her way to the airport. Unfazed by this less-than-charitable behaviour Pearson, who decided to try and hitch to Lisbon and was making her way though the scrubland which lay between her and the main road, managed to blag a lift from a complete stranger in combat clothes toting a gun, before reaching passport control with only minutes to spare. Ian Grant and Alan Edwards arranged for a posh limo to pick-up this freaked-out journalist back in London but Pearson was not impressed by this show of good-will. As a result of this escape she joined the huge army of detractors in the press, savaging the band whenever she could. And who could blame her?

'Nuclear Device (Wizard Of Aus)' was, rather surprisingly, the band's first single since 'Grip' two and a half years before to stall outside the coveted Top 30. It would begin a run of poor-selling singles which would not be broken for another two years. But the band toured the album with much success that autumn, confident in their new, more accessible material.

November saw the release of Hugh's collaborative effort with Robert Williams, *Nosferatu*, named after the 1922 silent vampire classic by F.W. Murnau. Work on the album had begun the previous Christmas, in a lull in band activity. Hugh had been introduced to Williams, the drummer with Captain Beefheart's Magic Band, at a gig and the two immediately developed a personal and musical understanding. Once they had decided to lay down some tracks, however, progress was fitful and slow. Hugh jetted out to LA on Boxing Day 1978 at very short notice, but the whole project was a rather *ad hoc* affair, as the two were forced to work in a variety of studios at most unsociable hours. The album therefore achieved a rather quirky, vampirish quality, as Hugh and Robert would write and record through the night, often with a little help from 'Harry' and various other recreational aids. The single which led the campaign that autumn was a spanking version of 'White Room' which had all the prog-rockiness kicked out of it, and included a great guitar sound and some grandiose percussion from Williams. Hugh himself appeared in the expressionist video in make-up and huge billowing trousers. It was a difficult, but interesting album: expressionistic, ambitious, but rather doleful. Musically the record fitted in well with the then burgeoning American new-wave scene and there are distinct similarities between *Nosferatu* and the music of Devo and Talking Heads. *Nosferatu* is a private world of neo-Gothic horror: of magic transformations, freaks on display at circuses (and here MGM's 1932 film *Freaks* which used men and women with frightening real-life deformities, was an obvious influence), of insectoid habitats. But the public were singularly unimpressed and critics bemoaned the lack of Hugh's tunesmithery and pointed out the dull, flat, expressionless vocal. Unlike JJ's solo effort, the album failed to chart, and the whole project was a substantial money-losing exercise for Hugh's miffed record company, United

Artists, who hadn't even been informed by Hugh that they had to foot the bill.

But the Stranglers' autumn shows had done well, culminating in a gig on 1 November at London's Round House, the scene two years earlier of the band's record-breaking residency. The penultimate gig was in Cardiff. The band intended to stay overnight in Wales and travel back to London the next day. But Hugh changed his plans and hitched a lift back with tour promoter Paul Loasby and three teenage French fans whom Hugh had arranged accommodation for that night at a friend's house. In the early hours of All Saints' Day their car was stopped at a road block on Hammersmith Broadway. It was the start of the band's Nemesis.

7: ANNUS HORRIBILIS

Instead of getting rid of the few lines of coke he had in his shirt-pocket as soon as he saw the police presence, Paul Loasby got out for the meet-and-greet with the coppers knowing that if he was searched he'd be nicked. To Hugh, this seemed a rather ill-advised manoeuvre, given the fact that his own bag, stashed in the boot of the car, resembled a small chemistry set. This is a slight exaggeration: what Hugh lacked in quantity, he made up for in variety. This was the end of a tour, and Hugh had picked up a variety of stimulants along the way, some from welcoming fans keen to ingratiate themselves with the band. His bag contained two packets of coke (one gram and half a gram), a packet of heroin (90 mg, enough for one hit), half-an-ounce of dope, resin, some grass wrapped in tissue paper, and two packets of magic mushrooms for good measure. It was the presence of the heroin, according to Hugh, which angered the authorities the most – the naughtiest of the rock-star narcotics, and the one bound to raise the establishment's shackles. But initially it was the French fans (two girls and one boy) travelling with Hugh and Loasby who aroused their suspicion, as they looked under-age. Loasby was searched, charged and taken to the local nick, whilst Hugh was requested to follow on to get his belongings from the car boot which were to be confiscated and searched. It was obvious that he was going to be nicked when they searched his overnight bag, and nicked he was, with suitable irony, by a friendly police officer and Stranglers fan, who asked for Hugh's autograph (which read 'This is for the copper what nicked me, who thought he was pursuing justice'). And, just to turn the whole escapade into a tragi-comedy, Paul Loasby happened to have the following book in his possession: *How To Sell Cocaine In Bulk – How To Be A Success In Dealing Without Really Trying*. Short of displaying a 'Class A drugs in this car – please nick us' sticker on the windscreen it's hard to think how anyone could have been less discreet about his recreational foibles. Loasby also had £2,000 in receipts from the previous night's gig in his bag, and this immediately made the police suspect he was a dealer. After counting all the money, the police finally released the two in time for breakfast at 8 a.m. Hugh must have wished he'd stayed in Cardiff for a few pints of 'Skull Attack'.

Drugs and rock 'n' roll are, as we all know, close chums. According to Jet (who at the time was known by the rest of the band as 'The Hoover'!), the only real difference is that drug-taking in the rock world is less clandestine:

> We'd all seen drugs coming and going. They were around then, and they're around today. You go to any rock concert and you'll always see drugs in the dressing-room. Some do them, some don't. Everyone around us was taking drugs in those days, and a lot of people are today. I don't think the band do, but everywhere you go in rock 'n' roll someone is taking drugs. In rock 'n' roll everyone knows about it. It's endemic within society. It's just that in rock 'n' roll it's more open. In the end there's no real fun in drugs. They cost you a fortune, do you no good and can do you time.

But Hugh liked taking drugs, and had been a user for a decade. Indeed, he was by then obviously something of a drug gourmet, the Keith Floyd of the celeb drug-world. He knew a lot about them, how to combine them, how to experiment. He'd come close to OD'ing too, but he claims never to have been an addict. Here's an extract from Hugh's book, *Inside Information*, published in November 1980, a year which would become something of an *annus horribilis*, a year of disasters and cock-ups to make the Monarchy's record of infidelity and vice in 1992 seem puny by comparison: 'I used to smoke mostly to go to sleep, because I'm a bit of an insomniac. It's the best type of sleeping draught, a joint. Coke I used to work with. It improves memory powers, work motivation: you want to do it better when you're coked up. Also, it keeps you awake. Various dabbles in smack . . . I reckon it's the best drug in the world because it's so euphoric . . . I'm talking about snorting, I'm not into needles.'

Loasby and Hugh were asked to face charges at West London Magistrates Court on 6 January 1980. Everyone in the Stranglers' entourage expected a hefty fine, a suspended sentence and a ticking off – this was, after all, Hugh's first offence. But instead he was given a £300 fine and an inordinately punitive eight-week jail sentence, whilst Loasby was given 14 days. Magistrate Eric Crowther had these words of wisdom for the pair: 'You are two intelligent men of mature years, who have a great influence on the lifestyle of teenagers and who should not cause damage to the moral and physical well-being of those who admire you. Both of you have a university education, which makes your involvement in the drugs scene even more contemptible. You have deliberately chosen to flout the law.'

Hugh and Loasby were released on bail, pending their appeal on 21 March. Paul's sentence was eventually quashed and replaced by a huge fine, but for Hugh, there was trouble ahead.

In the weeks before Hugh's appeal the band had been active recording tracks for the next album and for single release, and had shot a video for one of their best-ever singles, 'Bear Cage', released on 8 March. Also produced by Alan Winstanley, as a piece of music it maintained the high standards of *The Raven*. The song itself dealt with the ennui and corruption of Berlin, whilst the bizarre video saw Hugh incarcerated in a sort of Communist Germany Butlins' hell. Dave's synth riff, which ran through this rather slow-moving song, was also a delight. But reviews were mixed and the single was deemed plodding and ponderous by record buyers. It was the third Stranglers flop in a row, reaching a disappointing Number 36: a minor hit, achieving nowhere near its true potential.

The band continued making plans for 1980, including a gig at the Rainbow that April. When that sold out in double-quick time, a second was added for the following day, Good Friday. There was still no reason to believe that Hugh would eventually be 'banged up the slammer', since the variety of drugs in his possession might have been a shock to the police, but the quantities were negligible. And this was the tactic used by Hugh's defence lawyer, John Matthew QC, on the subject of Hugh's stash of heroin. Here's another extract from *Inside Information*: ' "I don't know if you take snuff, Your Honour, but it's the equivalent of that."

'The judge said: "You mean one good sniff?"

' "Yes, that's right. One good sniff." '

Hugh was bowled over by his lawyer's brilliant character study of his client and his noble advocacy ('I was going to get up and applaud after he had finished.'). But amazingly, after a short deliberation, he was instructed that his appeal had been unsuccessful. A high-profile media celebrity and well-known 'nefarious' rocker, Hugh Cornwell was to be made an example of. To this day, Hugh's sentence remains one of the most punitive ever handed down to a rock star for this type of offence. On 21 March 1980, he began the first day of an eight-week prison sentence at Pentonville Prison, London.

The imprisonment was not simply a severe personal trauma for Hugh. It also had obvious knock-on effects for the band and management. 'It will cost us £200,000,' Ian Grant predicted to the press. Grant was gradually becoming disillusioned with the band's progress, and Hugh doing time was another in a long line of set-backs. One bone of contention was the band's 'enthuzine', *Strangled*, which had been set up by Alan Edwards and Tony Moon two years earlier, then reactivated under the auspices of Jet Black. The band felt that their fans were due a proper information service, and prized their close links with them. *Strangled* gave Hugh, Jet and JJ the chance to extemporize upon lyrics and such like. When Jet took over the running of *Strangled* from Tony Moon in 1979 he found a situation of near-disaster as he now remembers:

> On close examination it was clear to me that we were on the verge of receiving some very damaging publicity if the 'fan club' was not given urgent attention. There were literally thousands of unanswered letters, some containing orders for goods accompanied by payment. Some contained orders and no payment. Others contained orders which had been dispatched but some hadn't, and to make matters worse, no records had been kept of any transactions. The whole business was a complete mess.

Over a period of several months, Jet turned *Strangled* into a viable concern:

> With the help of Suzanne Prior (my girlfriend who, as a professional secretary, was able to do masses of speedy typing), I composed a newsletter and mailed it to every address I could find amongst the pile of letters. I explained to the fans (under the pseudonym of Suze) about the problems that had arisen, and

invited anyone who had not received goods to write in. I also offered a 'new' subscription-service to *Strangled* magazine, a bi-monthly which would supply all the information that most of them wanted about the band, along with a properly controlled merchandizing service. I compiled and edited a brand-new *Strangled* Volume 2 Number 1 (Volume 1 being the few editions Tony Moon had issued). I personally wrote everything in the first three to four issues except the readers' letters and the credited articles. I was Suze.

But *Strangled* was costing large amounts of money to keep afloat, and some of the more extravagant requests from Jet and the lads angered Ian Grant, who regarded some of the wilder schemes as a drain on band finances: 'Jet did 10,000 *Strangleds* in French and had it freighted to France, unbeknown to me. Then I had to pick up the bill.'

Ian Grant had lined up a Stranglers tour of India, including a gig in the 14,000-seater Calcutta Sports Stadium, one at the 25,000-capacity Bombay CCI Stadium and another in Delhi. A show was also scheduled for Cairo. His vision was to break the band in hitherto virgin territories for rock, but he was beaten to the punch when the Police organized a concert in Bombay on 26 March, the first in the country since Hawkwind ten years earlier. The *Police In The East* film documentary released in 1980 completely queered the Stranglers' pitch.

But of most pressing concern were the two gigs scheduled for 3 and 4 April at the London Rainbow. Rather than cancel the shows, the Stranglers' management, now situated along with SIS in new offices near London Bridge, decided to turn them into something of a media jamboree. A list of celebs drawn up by Ian Grant and personal assistant Jane Gibb were asked to perform for free in Hugh's stead, in consciousness-raising concerts to make the media aware that Hugh had plenty of friends in the business who thought his sentence was unjust. As Ian Grant remembers, the two evenings were not without their little perks for those pop stars that way inclined: 'I remember buying £1000-worth of cocaine to pay the performers at the Rainbow for the gig that Hugh couldn't do. I don't know how many people know that. The band certainly did.'

John Ellis, then on tour with Peter Gabriel, filled in on guitar, whilst a variety of big names paraded on stage. From post-punk there was Toyah, Hugh's girlfriend Hazel O'Connor (soon to get her fifteen-minutes' worth as star of 'Breaking Glass' and subsequently to cover the band's 1977 song 'Hangin' Around'), Robert Smith and Matthieu Hartley from the creepy-crawly Cure, and Mr VH1 Richard Jobson from the Skids. The older set were represented by whizzo guitarist Robert Fripp, pub rockers Ian Dury and Wilko Johnson, Steve Hillage and Peter Hammill. Stranglers' compadres Steel Pulse added some tasty rhythms to the mix. With support groups like the then happening UB 40, and Manchester's seminal Joy Division, the gigs were a success. Jet: 'These were great evenings. It went down hugely well and we had an effigy of Hugh hanging from a rope. So he was there in spirit if not in person.'

Hugh the person was now a number, not a free man. In fact, rather than being a snappy Number 6, he was a more long-winded F48 444. Today Hugh is reluctant to talk much about his prison days, claiming it can all be found in the SIS book, *Inside Information*, which he put together with *Record Mirror*'s Barry Cain, one of the few trusted journos, who constructed the book out of a weekend's worth of interviews. From that source we can build up a picture of Hugh's prison days that spring.

The food was pretty terrible. His opening meal was 'really old, dry bread, a mug of horrible tea with no sugar, macaroni cheese, which was awful, a tiny bit of margarine, and a small dollop of jam'. At the weekend everyone was locked up: 'It's like two Sundays. Nobody works.' Hugh was a cleaner and spent a lot of time in the canteen serving food, washing up and scrubbing floors as well as cleaning the toilet. For this he 'earned' £1.30 a week. The secret of survival, according to Hugh, was to 'cut off all sensations': 'Anything that was going to happen to me physically won't take root inside me. It would not affect me. I must keep my mind lively and awake . . . Everything became like water off a duck's back.'

Hugh rolled with the day, kept his head down. He slept longer hours than ever before in his life, and learnt to live without the buzz of drugs and alcohol. He received a mountain of letters from fans and associates every day. At first this antagonized the authorities, as it marked Hugh out as a special person. He was allowed to open personal correspondence only; fan letters were kept with his personal belongings. There were restrictions on the number of letters which inmates could write too. Hugh was allowed to write one letter a week to an employer (Ian Grant) and one to a solicitor. This heavy-handed restriction in the flow of communication between prisoner and outside world was a deliberate tactic to demoralize those doing porridge. No phone-calls were allowed either. According to one press report at the time, a certain Miss Kate Bush actually asked Ian Grant if he had Hugh's phone number in prison! The screws could be stroppy and vindictive, but they were locked up too, and performed a joyless task. He enjoyed most prisoners' company, and being in a good mood was a prerequisite for survival. Being locked in a room from 5 p.m. to 8 a.m. with someone with a cob on was a recipe for disaster. Hugh busied himself reading the Bible, storing information which would be used for the next bout of band writing. Apart from a tummy upset and suspected lice, Hugh navigated his way through prison life admirably: 'You can get very healthy inside. A lot of people get into doing physical exercise in their cells. I ended up doing about 150 press-ups a day and 200 hand clenches . . . Once you get into a routine, time ticks by.'

Even an infestation of cockroaches failed to faze him. But no concessions were made to Hugh's artistic bent: 'I missed the guitar. I wanted to write and play music, but I couldn't. I didn't see what right they had to deprive me of that. I asked for a guitar and they said, "We've got bus drivers in here, and they can't have buses."'

Hugh was released on 25 April, having served five weeks of his eight-week jail sentence. A small contingent of Stranglers people including Ian Grant, and Jet Black – were there to greet him, together with girlfriend Hazel O'Connor. 'I know one thing,' Hugh told the assembled reporters, 'it's the end of my drug career and the end of my prison career.' Hugh was just making conciliatory noises, for if he had resolved to kick drugs that resolve was soon broken. In 1997 he confessed, 'I did as much drugs afterwards as I did before.' The custodial sentence had been a complete failure, it had only made Hugh more bitter, more resentful and more wilful with regard to drugs. A proud man, he wasn't going to be cowed into submission, to be dictated to on the ethics of moral righteousness by the Establishment he hated. His drug career wasn't over. And his prison career wasn't either . . .

Fresh out of prison, all Hugh wanted to do was work, to put his life on an even keel by doing what he did best. In June 1980 the band were embarked on yet another small-scale European tour. On 20 June they were scheduled to play in Cannes, on the steaming-hot Côte D'Azur, but at the last minute the gig was cancelled (the same old reason – media speculation about the band's punk credentials had frightened off the promoters) and hastily re-scheduled for Nice University. The band checked in at the 'resplendent Negresco'. In his laconic booklet, *Much Ado About Nothing*, Jet commented: 'There was, in retrospect, a certain irony in the way fate had coincidentally brought us to this, the most luxurious hotel we had ever visited, on this particular day, since it was to be only a few hours till we were to experience the worst accommodation of our lives.'

There was trouble ahead. Andy Dunkley, the tour manager, informed them that the University authorities wouldn't allow their truck into the grounds, with the result that the crew had to carry ten tonnes of equipment all the way up a footpath and some steps, across the quadrangle and down into an outdoor arena. No reason was given by the University for this. Then Andy told the band that the authorities wouldn't supply enough electricity to power the gig. It was a sold-out gig, but, for some reason, they were doing their utmost to stop the band from playing. At the sound-check the power cut out several times, but the crew boss, in an effort to save the gig, suggested that if the band cut down on lighting, they still might be able to play. At the band's behest, a generator was hired which would have provided adequate power for the night's festivities but, rather unhelpfully, the University authorities forbade them from using it as it might have melted the concrete! When they arrived for the gig they were told that the dressing-room door was locked and the key couldn't be found! When the band took the stage that night there was tension in the air. They played a brilliant gig. Hugh:

> We were really positive – we'd rather play than not play. We were really fed up with cancelling things, so we said that we'd take a chance. And we played for about half an hour and it was the best

gig we'd ever played. I thought we were shit-hot. I remember turning round and looking at the rest of the band after about two songs and thinking, 'Fuck, we're a good band. This is really excellent music and we're playing superbly.' But the power kept cutting out and it was dark for a long time. The crowd were getting really upset.

The road crew did everything they could to rescue the gig, but there simply wasn't enough juice to run a rock show. The power cut out after the opening three bars of the first number. So they continued with less lighting until the power failed again after two more songs. But when, after a further reduction in the lighting requirements (it must have been a seriously gloomy show), the power failed for a third time half an hour into the set, there was no option but to pull the gig.

The band rightly thought that they had some explaining to do. Jet made a speech in English, in which he alluded to the problems caused all day by the University authorities, and the particular handicap imposed by the lack of power facilities made available to the crew. JJ then made a speech in French. An element of doubt exists as to what was actually said. Jet comments, 'I didn't, and don't, and never will know what JJ said without a translation.'

A tape of the speech does exist and was used as evidence in the subsequent trial, but its contents have not been made public. Jet maintains that he merely took the opportunity to inform the crowd that the University had failed to honour its contract with the band by failing to supply adequate facilities for both crew and band and to provide enough electricity for the gig, even though they had it within their power to do so. As a result, it was impossible to continue: 'If I said anything more inflammatory than that, I honestly don't remember. None of us knew that a riot was going to happen.'

However, both Hugh and Ian Grant put a different spin on that night's events. Hugh:

I understand a bit of French. JJ did try and explain what had happened about the generator not being strong enough. But he wound them up a bit as well. He got a bit carried away in the situation. I think he said something like: 'Do what you want. But it's not our fault.' He's just a bit irresponsible. We used to get him off mic as soon as possible because he's not a dynamic performer with a microphone. He gets carried away. You've got to be very careful what you say to groups of people because you can actually blow a gig. He's got no idea about dynamics when he speaks into a microphone – he speaks for too long, he's got no idea about delivery. He said, 'Don't destroy our equipment', because we had already had our equipment destroyed by the Raggare and we didn't want a repeat performance. But they might have construed that as, 'You can do everything else but don't destroy our equipment.'

Ian Grant: 'They were guilty. Jet had said what they said he said. He had incited them. Jet said, "I know what I'd do around here. There's a lot of plate glass windows", and insinuated that they should smash them up.'

But what happened next completely bamboozled the band, who were sitting outside the venue in the tour bus. Jet remembers: 'At that point the entire audience, I can't remember if it was two or three thousand people, went totally berserk. We saw them charging at plate glass windows with these great barricades and they wrecked every window in the university. They set fire to palm trees and wrecked everything that they could.'

Provoked or not, the students had a list of grievances against the university authorities which dated back years. The Stranglers had unwittingly given them the opportunity to enact the final instalment of a long-running feud. Jet suspects that the band were simply duped, manoeuvred deliberately into the situation by local authorities in need of a scapegoat. After packing away their untouched equipment, the band split up for the evening, Hugh and Dave to a dinner party, Jet and JJ to the hotel. At 6 a.m., as Hugh and Dave returned to the hotel, they were arrested. Jet: 'We found out later that there was a huge political problem going on here. After the student riots in the 1960s the government brought in new laws which would enable them to nail the ring-leaders of riots and they charged us under that act with inciting a riot.'

The band were whisked off to Nice central police station and charged under Article 314 of the French Criminal Code, known as the 'anti-smashers' law. It was the first time that the law had been used to justify the arrest of a pop band, and was being used as a test case by the French authorities. The university had endeavoured to stop the gig because they could see trouble coming, and the students were looking for an opportunity to riot.

For the first part of their prison stay, whilst they waited to be charged (under French law there is no *habeas corpus*, so they were guilty until proven innocent and could be detained for 48 hours without charge), the band were held at the 'cockroach motel'. Jet:

We were held in police cells which were Napoleonic, literally. The place just stank of shit. There was a typical French toilet – just a hole in the ground. The walls were covered in shit. They hadn't been painted for perhaps 50 or 60 years, and it was appalling. There were huge cockroaches running around all over the floor and the temperature outside was about 90° in the shade. It was incredibly uncomfortable and we were kept in there for about two days being farted about with by the police, taken in for questioning, interrogated, then put back in this dump. It was all an attempt to soften us up, to keep us from sleeping, so we'd confess to something we hadn't done.

After two days of this charade, during which time the only thing to keep them occupied was the newly-discovered sport of 'cockroach stamping', a very smelly Dave was released. As the only member of the band who hadn't spoken at the mic during the gig, he couldn't be charged with inciting a riot, and so he made his way to Rome for a wash and plate of pasta. Here he hooked up with Steve Churchyard, who had worked with Hugh on his *Nosferatu* album and who had taken over as engineer and producer on the new Stranglers album after Alan Winstanley had to leave the project.

The rest of the band were moved from the shitty police cells to the Maison D'Arrêt, the main prison in Nice and, by all accounts, quite a swish little establishment to boot, with newspapers, showers, tea and coffee, and decent food. (Jet did, however, at one point suspect that the food was spiked in order to keep the inmates sleepy and docile.) The long-suffering Ian Grant flew to be with his charges via Nice, where he collected £30,000 in francs to bail them out. So far he had bailed out JJ and/or Jet in Glasgow, Newcastle, Brighton, Philadelphia, Brisbane, Örebro and now Nice. He found some of the band in dramatically desperate mood: 'Certain members of the band threatened suicide. JJ told me he was going to do it. Hugh said, "I feel so bad for you."'

Jet, as always, was taking it in his stride:

I was taking notes while I was in prison. From the very minute the riot started I thought, this is going to be serious. I was totally cool about it. Hugh was suicidal. He was in a dreadful state because he'd just come out of prison. By the end he was just a shivering wreck. He was really bitter and angry. I could see his point of view because he'd done absolutely nothing. I sympathized with him immensely because of his predicament, plus the fact that he couldn't handle it. JJ said he thought about killing himself, not because he was suicidal but because he wasn't prepared to tolerate somebody else incarcerating him. I don't think he ever came close to it, but he was badly freaked out. It didn't bother me at all. I thought, 'God, this has got to be so good for our career.' And it was.

The Stranglers had become the most notorious rock band in Europe, in part by default (half of what was written about them was untrue or greatly exaggerated, but, by this point, Jet didn't care). Sure enough, the French press, and of course, the press back home, were full of stories of the 'shock horror' type. The most boring had the headline 'Jailhouse Rock' (used by three different newspapers), whilst the best was 'Jail "medieval" says Stranglers' organist'.

But there wasn't much 'shock horror' going on back in prison. For the next five days the band were taken up with the crazily labyrinthine task of trying to find an *avocat* (barrister). Eventually Ian Grant managed to engage the services of a certain Monsieur Treal, one of these media-friendly hard-hitters who are often called upon to get 'fallen' celebs out of tricky situations. Eventually the band were freed on the afternoon of Friday 27 June, almost a week after the riot. Then it was back to the hotel Negresco for a celebratory glass of champagne. The band were to stand trial at a later date, and it was expected that they would be given a suspended sentence and fined. Another nightmare was over. Surely it couldn't get any worse?

By the time the band set off on yet another tour of the States that October, it had been all change in Stranglersville. There had been yet another 'internal rationalization' within the massive EMI structure. In July 1980 the company carried out phase two of its take-over of United Artists. The label was now known as Liberty Records, and its base moved from London's Mortimer

Street to EMI House in Manchester Square. This marked the beginnings of a frosty relationship between label and band. And within the Stranglers' team it was all change too: Paul 'Sheds' Jackson, the band's crew boss since 1976, had quit, to be replaced by Bruce Gooding. The band were now managed by the American Ed Kleinman, a New Yorker who had worked with them on their previous two Stateside jaunts. The split with Ian Grant was acrimonious. For Grant the band had become unmanageable. On the previous year's *Raven* tour Grant had actually been attacked by JJ: 'He was violent towards me once, and he threatened to commit suicide the next day and wanted me to book him into a mental home. He whacked me and I just walked out and said, "Goodbye, see you, have a nice life" and off I went back to the hotel. And the next day he was really apologetic and he was on his knees in the lobby of the hotel.'

But the events of 1980 – Hugh's imprisonment, the cancelled Asian tour, and then the Nice debacle – had a wearing, cumulative effect. Despite a number of attempts to clear the air with the band, including a trip round to Jet's place in the West Country to discuss the situation with the band's traditional 'voice of reason', the situation was hopeless. Ian Grant: 'They were so obnoxious, rude and cynical. You don't work with people when it's like that because it's pointless and you can't. That's why I quit, ultimately. It wasn't just obnoxiousness though – it was obnoxiousness mixed with heroin.'

Matters had come to a head at the end of the British tour when Ian informed the band of his intention to quit after the concert at the Lyceum. Surprisingly, Dave embarked on a tirade of abuse against his emotional manager, whilst the rest of the band affected an uninterested air. Jet: 'We didn't know what decision to make, but we knew it wasn't working. We'd gone on as far as we could with him, but we didn't want to throw him out because he was a nice bloke. So he sort of resigned and nobody said, "Don't resign." We were trying to part as friends.'

Jet adds, however, that Ian Grant simply couldn't handle the pressures of being a top rock manager any longer:

> We really focused ourselves on keeping our career going and we were all rather tense and very determined. We didn't suffer fools gladly. And that meant that there was a lot of pressure around. We

felt that everyone who was a part of the team should be doing equally as much. And we always felt that nobody was doing as much work as we were. Furthermore, we always felt that we could do other people's jobs better than they could! Sometimes we were right, sometimes we were wrong, and of course in that respect we were very self-confident. In Ian Grant's case, though, he went through a phase where he simply couldn't handle the pressures that we were throwing up.

Perhaps Ian Grant's main problem was that he identified too closely with the band. He was a rock-star manqué. Jet: 'Ian Grant was a lovely bloke, but untogether. He liked having a good time too much. He had all the best intentions but he was just untogether, he was always out of his head. And I think he's had a chip on his shoulder about the band ever since he left.'

Publicist Alan Edwards, who later went on to promote some of the biggest gigs of the 1980s along with Grant, had this to say about Ian Grant in his Stranglers days: 'He was a great bloke, but he was a wild one all right. Ian would be getting up to antics that the record label wouldn't believe.'

So Ian Grant retired from the Stranglers scene, to become very successful as the co-manager of the Cult with the same Alan Edwards later in the decade and to co-promote some of the biggest artists of the era. But it wasn't quite the end of the road for Ian Grant and the Stranglers.

Eleven nights into the American tour, the band were in New York to play four club gigs. The Stranglers were not big news in America: their real chance at Stateside superstardom already blown after they were dropped by A&M two years earlier, the band now reduced to playing clubs and small venues, the impetus of the new-wave long gone. Then, at the fourth New York gig at the Ritz club in Manhattan, disaster struck again. After the show one of the hired American hands was scheduled to drive the truck, which included all the band's equipment, to Atlanta. Hugh painfully recollects: 'He stopped off at his flat for a shit, shower and a shave, and the truck was gone! It all sounded very dodgy to me. He could have been in on it, that's what I'm saying. It was a big organization that did the lift. Two or three years later they

found this big warehouse full of equipment from loads of rock
groups.'

This was probably the lowest point of the band's entire career.
They were a third of the way through an extensive American tour
(which had so far failed to break new ground for them), they had
already endured imprisonment, loss of earnings, and a managerial crisis, and now all their equipment had been stolen. Jet Black
recollects: 'We sat in our hotel room extremely depressed, 3,000
miles from home, a tour lined up, and not a drumstick between
us, desperately trying to cheer each other up.'

Ironically, it was Hugh who saved the day. In a year in which
surely nothing more terrible could have happened to him bar a
public flogging, Hugh was the first to react positively:

> Everyone wanted to go back to England, except me. Andy
> Dunkley our tour manager, said, 'Well, I don't know what to
> do, boys.' And I said, 'I refuse to be beaten by this. We're still alive,
> we're still in one piece, we've still got all the crew and everything.
> Why don't we try and hire a bit of equipment in each place and do
> it like that?'
>
> We'd arrive in each town and we'd have to make do with what
> we'd got, but, by the end of the tour we were shit-hot because
> we'd learnt to play under the most extreme conditions. I ended up
> being very positive and it brought us all together again.

But there was still a dark shadow over the whole Stranglers'
operation. After the gig in Dallas, road crew member Alan
McStravich suffered a heart-attack. Hugh remembers: 'He was
clearing up the gear afterwards with the humpers, the local
muscle who'd help you load in the equipment, and they said,
"Do you want a line, Alan?" and he said, "Yeah, sure," thinking
they were going to give him a line of coke, but they gave him
angel dust, which is horse tranquilliser and extremely powerful.
He took a line of this and he was carried screaming on a stretcher
back to the hotel and was shipped back home the next day.'

Emboldened by their resurrected team spirit, the band returned
to the UK looking forward to a less traumatic 1981. The last
twelve months had been a macabre time of death and disaster. In
addition to the high-profile band catastrophes, those connected
with the band were suffering too: artist Kevin Sparrow, who had
designed the band logo, their first promotional poster and the

cover of the 1978 *Black And White* album, died accidentally on Christmas Day, 1979, after taking a Mogadon pill on top of a bottle of whiskey, and tour manager Charlie Pyle died of cancer at the age of 24.

There were some other very strange happenings too: Kevin Sparrow's portfolio of photographs, the Stranglers' songbook and a biography of the band he was working on all went missing, as did the tapes of *The Raven* album. An FM broadcast of a gig at Emerald City, New Jersey, mysteriously had the Meninblack voice missing. And in Munich during the recording of their new album, *(The Gospel According To) Themeninblack*, a telephone engineer came into the studio to do some routine maintenance. Although he went nowhere near the recording equipment or the power supply, while he was working, the whole studio blew up! In *Strangled* magazine in 1981, JJ wrote:

> An unusual chain of events. A more than usual number of coincidences, setbacks, downright bummers which can be traced back to the first day the Meninblack entered our lives. Maybe just an uncanny set of related incidents but ask any of the band and they'll tell you we're expecting a visit any day. Ready and waiting.

> P.S. One of the theories involving the MIB is that besides their awesome physical presence they are able to influence their contactees by thought transference and can influence events indirectly by communicating ideas to those around their contactees. Many of those who have been contacted by the MIB have been threatened with actual bodily harm and have also experienced headaches, nausea, various sicknesses and heart troubles, and, wait for it, have spent time in prison for no valid reasons!

'Headaches'? That was Martin Rushent's excuse for walking out when the band were recording the 'Meninblack' track. 'Heart troubles'? That accounted for Alan McStravich's heart failure. There was enough in the Men In Black myth to seriously spook out the band members.

But 1980 wasn't over yet. Because of their straitened finances, Ian Grant had arranged for band insurance to be paid in six-monthly instalments. Grant is adamant that the band knew that this was the case. But when Grant left over the summer, the second half-yearly instalment hadn't been paid. A mortified

Hugh: 'The fault lay in the management team. I won't say it was Ian Grant because he might have delegated it to somebody else, but, somewhere along the line, because everyone was so out-of-it, the responsibility got lost somewhere and the equipment wasn't insured.'

Whatever, it was a cataclysmic error. The equipment, including instrumentation, amplifiers, monitors and the like, cost around £46,000! The Stranglers were nearing bankruptcy. They needed a hit single, and they needed it fast.

8: THE MADNESS
OF LOVE

At least 1981 started off with some better news: the band would not be returning to the Côte d'Azur to do porridge. On 13 January they heard the news that Jet, JJ and Hugh had been given suspended jail sentences, as expected. In addition, they were asked to pay nearly £2,000 towards the cost of repairs to the windows. 'You mean to tell me that all that fucking about was just to get two grand out of us,' mused Jet at the time in disgruntled disbelief. The Stranglers had to be seen to be culpable; there was no way that the French authorities would share any of the blame for the Nice riot. But at least Hugh was spared a hat-trick of prison appearances inside a year. This might have had serious repercussions for an already freaked-out and embittered star. He might have got religion, or, even worse, become a blues singer.

Jet was later to find out that no less an authority than writer Graham Greene, then living in Antibes, had written about the corruption of the French authorities in a booklet called *J'Accuse: the Dark Side Of Nice* (published in 1982). In it Greene wrote:

> Let me issue a warning to anyone tempted to settle for a peaceful life on what is called the Côte d'Azur. Avoid the region of Nice which is the preserve of some of the most criminal organizations in the south of France: they deal in drugs; they have attempted with the connivance of high authorities to take over the casinos . . .; they are involved in the building industry which helps to launder their illicit gains; they have close connections with the Italian Mafia.

Greene goes on to describe a corrupt, almost impenetrable 'wall' in Nice, 'formed by the criminal *milieu*, by corrupt police officers and corrupt lawyers'. The Stranglers had run up against this wall of corruption and were powerless to do anything about it.

But with one on-going problem now resolved, the lack of chart success was still rumbling like a grumbling appendix. The Stranglers did not get that much-needed hit single, which would have kick-started their career after 18 months in the doldrums. The disco-influenced 'Thrown Away', recorded in Munich, possessed a childlike naïvety and a Costa-del-Sol synth riff which places it as the mad, bad brother of such wonders as 'The Birdy Song' and Whigfield's 'Saturday Night'. There was also a remark-able vocal delivery by JJ which Hugh would later accurately describe as reminiscent of Lee Marvin's drawlathon on the 1970 epic 'Wand'rin' Star'. It deserved to be a smash, but, despite a droll *Top Of The Pops* performance famous for Jet's sly smirk at the audience, it failed to break into even the Top 40. The album, *(The Gospel According To) The Meninblack*, which had been almost a year in production, and had utilized some of the top names and most expensive studios in Europe (at one stage the band had worked the producers in shifts while they, with the aid of coke, worked round the clock), was only a moderate seller, reaching Number 8 in the UK charts and shifting around 50,000 copies. This was yet another blow to band confidence, particularly since, at the time, they regarded the album as their masterpiece, their definitive statement. What made the album special, in the band's eyes, was the pioneering use of studio technology. JJ:

> The *Meninblack* album turned out exactly the way we wanted it. You listen to it now and it's very modern-sounding, almost like a techno album. But 17 years ago there wasn't much technology to play around with. Instead of sequencers we had tape loops, and we were holding pencils with tapes going round the whole studio and recording it to get that mechanical drum beat sound. We were making snares sound like drum machines and everything was looped. We were trying to make a techno album.

Conceptually, the album centres not just on the Meninblack myth but also examines religion, particularly the idea that God might be an alien intelligence and that the Bible's myriad miracles might simply be the demonstration of alien technol-ogy. This thematic thread runs through the Stranglers' work from the 'Meninblack' song on *The Raven*, and the single 'Who Wants The World', to the *Meninblack* album. 'Who Wants The World' was recorded just before Hugh's imprisonment in March 1980 and released that June. Again, the band had high hopes, but, yet again, the single stalled, reaching a disheartening Number 39. In truth, despite the band's bravado, it was only a mediocre track and lacked the production sparkle of the Stranglers/Winstanley material. The video, which featured Ian Grant as one of the Meninblack, was shot in the Kent countryside. The song itself centres on an alien visit to Earth and the idea that the planet is simply an experiment. After coming back to reclaim their inheritance, these extra-terrestrials are displeased by human-kind. Again, there are cannibalistic undertones to the lyric: 'Tasted flesh, tasted flea/Couldn't taste the difference'

With its wearied, embattled tone, 'Who Wants The World' also reactivates the idea of the Stranglers as a band of outsiders, the sewer survivalists who have turned their back on a disapproving world.

The *Meninblack* album proper continues these themes. 'Thrown Away' is also about alien visitation. JJ: 'It's Von Daniken meets Kraftwerk meets Giorgio Moroder meets the Stranglers' reinter-pretation of the Old Testament. The lyrics are being spoken by a spaceman who's just landed on earth and by doing so has created a new religion because he's so awesome – people immediately think he's a deity. But he flies off to another world leaving mayhem behind him.'

What makes this period particularly fascinating, and what makes the whole album something of a landmark, is the beguil-ing sincerity of the band's message. This was no simple exercise in arty pretension or some phantasmagoric reverie. The band were living out a cosmic crisis *in actuality*. They *believed* in the whole Meninblack idea (Hugh was wont to call himself Hughinblack, Jet, Jetinblack, etc.), arguing forcefully to incredulous journalists who quizzed the band that their idea of religion as some kind of primitive way of coming to terms with an alien intelligence was equally as valid as any other interpretation. The Stranglers were completely taken over by the Meninblack ethos, and it became something of a cancer, blighting their lives and inhabiting their thoughts constantly. The Stranglers were bewitched.

An interview with Lynn Hanna of the *NME* from January 1981

gives an indication of the Stranglers' siege mentality, and the reaction in the press.

> Jet: 'When Jesus came down in clouds of smoke, maybe he was just a mere mortal from another planet. I mean the Bible is full of stuff like that . . . Like everyone's sitting round waiting for The Messiah to return. Well, maybe when he does he might not turn out to be a bloke with a ring round his head and a white suit on. He might come down and start herding people into spaceships and take them off somewhere. I mean you don't know, do you?'
>
> It's about this time that I realize I'm smiling. My expression isn't complete cynicism so much as mild, well-meaning mockery of this earnest explanation of an outlandish idea. I'm also amused by the thought that such a sinister vision of the Second Coming seems so typically Stranglers in its tortured, determinedly pessimistic theorizing.

Of course, nobody can prove or disprove what the Stranglers held to be true. What's more interesting than assuaging the validity of their arguments is that they made for a great album in thematic terms. This was the Stranglers, and early 80s pop at their most bonkers, which, as always, has got to be a good thing. Although it was Jet who first became interested in material about alien visitations and subscribed to a publication called *Flying Saucer Review*, it was Hugh who made the connection between these themes and music. Speaking in 1997, Hugh explained that the main idea was that humankind:

> is a genetic experiment by some higher form of life and we're being monitored and watched. Occasionally, by accident, we see the species that has put us there. In the Bible there's lots of references to seraphims or angels in the sky and these are really ambiguously described. They could be flying saucers. Primitive people of the time would describe a laser exactly like this, in gobbledegook. The Catholic faith would end if all this were proved true and the world would be overrun with millions of nutty, crazed Catholics – who are pretty crazed anyway. If you took away their faith, their world would collapse.

Hugh wrote the lion's share of the lyrics for the album:

'Four Horseman' is about the fact that in the year 1999, or around 1999, there's going to be an occurrence which will completely stupefy all existing faiths. 'Manna Machine' is about the biblical story of the Jews living in the wilderness on manna from heaven – a kind of honey substance. And there's supposed to be a machine somewhere in the desert in the Golan Heights which actually made this substance. The Ark of the Covenant is missing and some researchers reckon it's the Manna Machine. 'Two Sunspots' is a song about tits, it's also about sunspot activity on the Sun which is supposed to make things happen on Earth. 'Just Like Nothing On Earth' is about a sighting, whilst 'Hallow To Our Men' is the alien version of the 'Lord's Prayer'. It's the only one of our albums which is a concept album.

The sound of the album has a real eccentric edge. 'Just Like Nothing On Earth' (the second single and a dismal flop – the first Stranglers single to not even nudge the Top 75), is almost like a white rap. 'Waltz In Black', which was slated as the follow-up to the gorgeous 'Thrown Away', has subsequently been immortalized both in the opening credits of the Keith Floyd cookery programmes and, in re-recorded form, in a Strepsils advert in the 1990s. It's the Stranglers best-ever instrumental and the essence of everything they're about. It is beautifully melodic, genuinely disquieting and, with its Pinky and Perky-style chuckles in the second half, completely barmy and (unintentionally?) silly. 'Turn, The Centuries Turn', is another top-drawer instrumental, pounding, ominous and begging to be used in a movie soundtrack. Everywhere the album sparkles with those strange, angular guitar riffs which were Hugh's trademark sound. Hugh's vocal delivery is also wildly eccentric, with 'a second co (pause) – ming will come in' taking the biscuit. It's all rather po-faced elsewhere, but the album draws most of its charm from its earnestness. The *Meninblack* is a flawed masterpiece. Its arty pretension links it with the then burgeoning new romantic scene characterized by the mock-operatic video and song 'Vienna' by Ultravox and the glam Europop of Visage. But the record company hated it. It was as far away from the melodic pop of the group's early material as one could imagine.

The final thing to say about the album is that its central concerns are quite prescient. The late 1990s are full of neo-paganistic doubt. As we reach the end of the millennium, part of the general dissatisfaction with the notion of progress and teleological betterment is reflected in an increasing interest not in the mundane and the everyday but the unknown and the unknowable. Hence the media fixation with sci-fi, the success of the *X-Files*, and the media brouhaha surrounding the footage from the Rockwell base in the USA of an autopsy performed on an 'alien' (which has been proved to have almost certainly been a hoax). Thousands of people have gone on record as having either seen, been contacted by, or abducted by alien intelligence. Have they all been duped, brainwashed, or hypnotized? Are they all lying through their teeth? Are they all the victims of some massive self-deluding prophecy? Wherever you stand on the 'we are not alone' debate, it's certainly true that the Stranglers were talking about these themes well before it became modish to do so within popular culture. It is no surprise that a 1997 film called *The Men in Black* was one of the highest-grossing films of the decade. The video for the theme tune, 'The Meninblack', included a phalanx of dancers in black suits gyrating Michael Jackson-style. This was genuinely ghastly and far more frightening than any alien abduction could surely ever be. At least the Stranglers can be content with the fact that they did it all much better, much earlier, and with a perverse panache.

But the critics generally thought the album contrived and lifeless, and the subsequent tour was also poorly received in some quarters. Adam Sweeting in *Melody Maker* wrote that there was 'no sense of warmth or purpose, and fun is certainly out of the question . . . the singing is indifferent to the point of apathy'.

Sounds turned the review of their Bristol gig into an epitaph: 'From where I'm standing The Stranglers have played themselves into a hole. The new stuff is practically worthless and the old stuff's been flogged to death. Where to now?'

Critically panned, commercially unsuccessful and with a less-than-supportive record company, the Stranglers teamed up again that summer down at Jet's place to write the make-or-break sixth album. And this time the topic was a most unexpected one – for the Stranglers it was time to think about 'lurve'.

But it wasn't until early 1982 that the last rite of the band's macabre fixation was finally played out. The band were asked by BBC South-West in Bristol to make a documentary for their programme *RPM*. Rather than simply coming up with a more spooky prototype version of *Bad News* (the famous *Comic Strip Team* spoof of a crap, heavy metal band on the road and forerunner of *Spinal Tap*), Jet and Hugh decided to use this opportunity to make a film about the colour black, and the phenomenon of the Meninblack. Jet:

> I wrote a script for a documentary on the colour black and how it's always associated with bad or negative things. And we got Professor Gregory, who is a professor at Bristol University and a world expert on perception, and interviewed him. Anyway, we started making this programme. The first half dealt with how people see the colour black in everyday life. Then the film started going off at a tangent to explore the darker areas of the occult and how black is associated with black magic, witchcraft and power – the subjects of the *Meninblack* album. They thought we were being a bit flippant and irrelevant, but we impressed upon them the seriousness of these themes. Anyway the programme went out and they got a huge public response. Teachers wrote in to ask for it to be re-shown for school projects and suchlike, and Professor Gregory told me it was the most exciting thing he'd seen in years, as there hadn't been any research into the colour black before. Then five or six years later the producer who made it was leaving the BBC and he was throwing a farewell party to which I was invited. The two blokes who we'd worked with at the BBC told me that they thought it was a really interesting subject and asked me whether I'd be interested in extending the idea and turning it into a 60-minute documentary. He said that he actually went down to the archives to get it out with a view to getting in touch with me and *the tape had vanished*! That hadn't happened to anything else in the BBC archives before and it was the last bad thing that happened in that whole range of events.

The Stranglers didn't write love songs. And their next album wasn't going to break with tradition. But after the gloom of the Meninblack period, the band wanted the next project to be something more life-affirming, more rooted in real emotion. After dealing with religion on *The Meninblack*, love as a theme was an obvious next choice. But it was to be an examination of love in all its myriad guises. In fact, the love which the Stranglers were to write about was the kind of love pop songs tend to obfuscate. In an interview with kidnap victim Ronnie Gurr in early 1982 Hugh had this to say: 'The next album will investigate another phenomenon called "love". We're going to investigate that and see what that consists of. I don't see much of the love that people talk about in 90% of songs, but I see people that love motor cars, people that love money, people that love power, people that love to hate people, people that love animals.'

Recording began in August 1981 at Richard Branson's studio, the Manor, in Oxfordshire, with Steve Churchyard engineering, and the Stranglers themselves producing. Whilst the new material still had a decidedly misanthropic and batty edge, the songs were more conventional than on the previous three studio albums. On *The Raven* the band had played around (successfully) with form. 'Ice', 'The Raven' and 'Sha Sha A Go Go' had long instrumental openings unusual in pop save for the likes of Bowie's 'Sound And Vision' or Gerry Rafferty's 'Baker Street', whilst 'The Meninblack' material was as quirky as mainstream pop ever got. But the new material positively swung along, with great choruses, nifty and memorable riffs, and some fine singing from Hugh. Whereas on previous outings Hugh had often shouted or half-spoken his way through a record, on the new album he actually *sang*. His voice was becoming one of the most recognizable in pop. Hugh was no great singer technically, but his vocal oozed personality. Like Lou Reed and Bob Dylan, Hugh was a great vocal *stylist*, with an odd attack on individual notes creating the impression that he was singing deliberately very slightly flat. On *La Folie* his vocal sounded great. This was undoubtedly due to the contribution of a very high profile mixer brought in to finish the job.

The American Tony Visconti was, by the early 1980s, probably the most respected producer in pop. His work with Marc Bolan had helped set the standard for British pop, introducing a kind of post-Spector symphonic sound which was the quintessence of early glam rock. But it was his work with David Bowie later in the decade, particularly on the peerless albums *Low*, *Heroes*, *Lodger* and *Scary Monsters*, which cast Visconti's star high in the firmament of greats. Bowie had a booming vibrato, and his vocal never sounded better than it did when Visconti recorded it. It was Visconti's talent for getting the pop vocal perfect that made him the obvious choice to mix the album. With hindsight, Hugh, however, is less than happy with the end result:

I thought that in all Bowie's work with Visconti the voice was really good. So I thought he'd be a good choice to mix the album. His forte is in mixing, he brings the voice up and makes it sound great. He's a lovely bloke, a very, very charming man. But most of *La Folie* I can't listen to. It just sounds too cantankerous. I listen to it and I can't hear the songs. I like to hear something honed and crafted and some melody coming through and some nice organic changes going on. But last time I put it on I listened to about half of it, and I thought this is awful, and I had to take it off.

There's a lovely bottom end on the *Meninblack* album. It's like wine, its rubiness, its warmth. It just says, 'come in', it just says 'invite me in'. But nothing on *La Folie* says 'invite me in', it says 'fuck off'. It's like two dogs barking. But the songs were great. These dogs, the songs they were barking were fine, it's just the delivery was bad. I don't think Tony did a good job on most of the songs.

Hugh's negative summation is a surprise as *La Folie* surely ranks as one of the best Stranglers albums. There really isn't a single dud on the whole album, save the rather plodding 'Ain't Nothin' To It'. 'Non Stop', with its cheeky organ run (the aural equivalent of pissing in the church pews), deals part tongue-in-cheek, part cynically, with the life of denial and love of God in the sisterhood.

> Dedicated, emancipated
> Claims she waited her life for her man
>
> Loves to pray every day
> Says she's not frustrated in any way
>
> Dressed in black cotton sack
> Pledges herself and she never looks back
>
> She's a non-stop nun.

If 'Non Stop' is typical Hugh, then 'The Man They Love To Hate' is far more under JJ's influence, brimming over with ominous riffs and that neo-new-wave surf guitar sound he was so fond of. Lyrically, it could almost be the band's signature tune. 'Pin-Up', which targets fan devotion, is almost deliberately cheesy bubblegum pop. 'It Only Takes Two To Tango', which looks at the cold war with typical cynicism, has some startling Beach Boys-style harmonies, startling since our two intrepid singers must have been way at the top of their ranges to hit the notes. 'Everyone Loves You When You're Dead' is an acerbic examination of how in death our icons become objects of devotion in the post-Lennon murder climate of pop intrigue, whilst the first single off the album, 'Let Me Introduce You To The Family', deals with familial devotion. Based on a friend's family, this song discusses an idyll that Hugh himself was denied, his family never having been particularly close. Its mafia overtones were not intended to be inferred. Rather this was a heartfelt lyric by a man alienated from the depth of love he saw in others.

'Let Me Introduce You To The Family' joined the now prodigious line of great, but commercially unsuccessful, Stranglers singles, peaking at Number 42. With its driving drum figure, jagged guitar line, and relentless attack, it now sounds closer to contemporary dance music than rock. It's one of the few Stranglers tracks to have a real groove. The Stranglers have always been a songs-based group, and if there is a real weakness in their armoury musically, it's in their decidedly unfunky and unsyncopated rhythm section. They were always danceable, but in a very orderly, on-beat fashion. But here there's a terrific groove which thunders home every time, and the song is still a live favourite 16 years on.

In thematic terms, *La Folie* was just as coherent an album as *Themeninblack*, if not more so. What it lacked in daring it more than made up for in sheer musicality. Reviews were again mixed, but generally critics were more approving of the new, more direct Stranglers' approach. Barney Hoskyns in the *NME* paid an accurate and eloquent tribute to the band's misanthropic designs: 'The Stranglers are the great exiles of rock 'n' roll, and for some time now they've been making records which sound both dispirited and resentful. That said, I still believe there is a place in our hearts for their curious blend of pessimism and romanticism. At times the sheer sense of fatigue and indifference in their music is almost cathartic.'

The slacker generation starts here!

But one track seemed to stick out right from the start: the beautiful, sensuous 'Golden Brown'.

Its musical origins date back to the pre-*Themeninblack* phase.

The basic 3/4–4/4 bit at the beginning of what is now 'Golden Brown' was Dave's piece which they had tried to fit into a number of songs without success, including – notably – 'Second Coming'. Jet later added the verse sections and the piece evolved into the now famous 'Golden Brown' as Dave eventually wove the pieces together on the harpsichord. During the writing for *La Folie*, Hugh heard the track again. But this time, in isolation, it sounded different, distinct. Before, Hugh had only heard this instrumental piece in 3/4 time in relation to other musical ideas which were being developed. But now he recognized it as a separate entity. Fifteen minutes later he had the lyric and tune for 'Golden Brown'. Dave was chuffed: finally he'd found somewhere to put this almost elegiac piece of music.

Jet for one was convinced that this was the hit the band needed. 'It's gonna be a fuckin' smash,' he told everyone. 'It's gonna be huge!' Whereas the rest of the album looked at the cruel downside of love – its unthinkingness, its blindness, its negativity – 'Golden Brown' celebrated sensuousness like no other song in the Stranglers' canon to date. Subsequent readings have caricatured it as a paean to heroin, but, as Hugh now reveals, it's a far more complex song lyrically than that: 'I was having an affair with a girl with golden-brown skin, and she used to have one of those gold chains round her ankles, which I found really enticing. I was snorting a lot of smack at the time too. So it's a very romantic song: women and heroin are both the ultimate escape.'

But 'Golden Brown' isn't a standard pop song. For a start it's in 13/8 time, three bars of 3/4 time (a key signature traditionally associated with the waltz form) and one bar of standard 4/4 time. There had been waltzes in the charts before, but not many. Kate Bush's haunting 'Army Dreamers', which took the troubles in Northern Ireland as its initial theme, from her 1980 album *Never For Ever*, was one contemporary example. But it was Dave's harpsichord that really gave the song its recherché charm and its real distinction. Although 'Golden Brown' is now popularly classified along with the MOR of the 1980s, a fresh listen reveals a real peculiar edge.

Amazingly, 'Golden Brown' might never have even made it on to the album in the first place. JJ hated it and bowed to band consensus only after voicing severe reservations. And when Tony

Visconti came to mix the album, he thought 'Golden Brown' was an excellent song, but not single material. So it was a real fight to get it released.

Even its release was not hazard-free. A limited number of copies was sent to the shops in the pre-Christmas 1981 period, prior to the official release date in early January. This was confusing: Christmas is one of the worst times for artists to bring out a new product, unless they've attained superstar status and can be confident of attracting the attentions of grannies looking for a stocking-filler, or teenagers with gift-vouchers to spend. But local radio and *Radio Luxembourg* were already playing the song to death, while 'Let Me Introduce You To The Family' was limping around the bottom end of the Top 50, and public demand for the single was building weekly. The single soon took off. Within three weeks it was in the Top 20 and after six it was Number 2, held off by the Jam's mod pastiche 'A Town Called Malice'. 'It's great to break new ground,' Hugh said at the time, 'I'm really excited that the single is David Hamilton's record of the week on Radio Two.' A video was made in early January at a house in Holland Park which used to belong to the royal painter Frederick Leighton, who'd had a fascination with the Middle East and Muslim artefacts. For Hugh, the video had to reflect the serenity and beauty of the song, with plenty of calming light browns in the use of colour, hence the shots of the pyramids, suntans, palm trees. Intercut with this skilfully edited library footage are shots of the band: Hugh in a dusty evening suit crooning into a thirties-style microphone with the legend 'Radio Cairo' added for extra exotic effect; Dave with his harpsichord, JJ playing a double-bass and a hilarious Jet coming on like a cross between a snooty butler and a mannequin of a 1930s palm-court style drummer, playing the snare like a wind-up doll.

The band were back on the road. A tour that autumn had met with a surprisingly muted response by critics and fans. This despite the Stranglers using the artiest opening segment in their career, The London Ballet Company performing a dance for the show's opener, 'Waltz In Black'. With 'Golden Brown' nudging Number 1, and *La Folie* climbing back up the album charts to a respectable Number 11, the band were at full throttle once again. And they still weren't averse to meting out some of the old-style

Stranglers ritual humiliation to the odd malcontent. At a gig in Swindon that January the band were once again the victims of a torrent of gob from one particularly over-productive salivary gland in the audience. The offender was duly hauled on stage, had his trousers pulled down and was given a good spanking.

Even with the song vying for Number 1, there were still major problems with distribution. EMI simply weren't pressing enough copies to keep up with demand, and Jet reported that the single wasn't even available in some of the major record shops. A bemused EMI sent the lads a case of Champagne to congratulate them on their chart resurrection, but it was cold comfort for a group who had been told only weeks previously that they were yesterday's men. They wanted off the label, and quick.

Whilst the Stranglers' legal team of Stephen Ross and Brian Eagles scrutinized the EMI recording contract for a loophole to get them out, the band had the task of cementing their newly-won British success with a hit follow-up. 'Tramp' was the outstanding candidate – another great Hugh song, catchy and dynamic. EMI thought it was bound to reach the Top 5. With two hit singles under their belt, the Stranglers' career would be well and truly resur- rected. In fact, the future promised even more than that. For the first time since 1977, they were on the verge of becoming one of the biggest band in the UK. But JJ thought that the title track was the perfect follow-up. 'La Folie' is a long, slow-paced monologue which possesses one of the most curious lyrics in pop history. JJ:

'La Folie' is a word which doesn't quite translate into English. It means a kind of madness, but not just of love; it signifies a temporary insanity and it's a word which alters its meaning in different contexts. The song itself is about a story I caught up with when we were making the album. Basically, it's about a student living in Paris called Issei Sagawa who ate a girl called Renee Hartman with whom he was obsessed. She was invited round for tea, not realizing that she was on the menu! Paris Match and Photo Magazine ran stories on it, and I got copies before an injunction was placed on them by Hartman's parents. I used to use the mags as a joke. At dinner with record executives I used to pass it round the table. Parts of her body were in frying pans, and there were reconstitutions of what was left. In the end Sagawa was transferred to Japan and released after two years. He's written two books on the murder and now has his own TV show. All that because his dad was a high-ranking Japanese businessman. It's a tale of how you can get away with murder, literally, just because your dad's a big-shot. And the French were complicit in the whole thing, just for business.

'La Folie' might have told a grisly and perverse tale, but it was housed, ironically, in some beautifully romantic music. Even so, it surely wasn't the obvious choice as a single, particularly since it was narrated in French! 'The least we could have done was to have had it translated,' Hugh commented in 1997. There is no direct, single translation for 'La Folie', but it means approximately 'the madness of love'. It was an intoxicating piece of music and its lyrical idea was later echoed (probably unintentionally) by the Rolling Stones for their actually very fine 1983 track 'Too Much Blood'. But both EMI and Hugh thought it was madness to release it as a single.

However, JJ managed to talk the rest of the band members out of having 'Tramp' as 'Golden Brown's' heir in favour of 'La Folie'. Hugh suspects that JJ was secretly annoyed that a Hugh song had been considered the natural successor to the Top 2 smash, and wanted a co-written track to lead the Stranglers' fight-back. A video was shot in Paris one freezingly cold early spring night with 'Golden Brown' director Lindsay Clennell. It was an unhappy experience for everyone. The band had been sent the wrong version of the track to shoot the video, and the French division of EMI managed to provide the correct edit of the song for filming to finally commence at midnight outside the Sacre Coeur Church. Tired, frozen and pissed-off, the band sloped around Paris looking more mournful than they'd ever looked before. It was a harbinger of things to come. The single stiffed at Number 47. Hugh had an 'I told you so' expression for weeks afterwards.

In the interim, the Stranglers' legal team had noticed that EMI had failed to take up an option to renew its contract with them. As a result the band informed them that they intended to leave the label forthwith. EMI were horrified and demanded that they record at least one more studio album before departing, but eventually a compromise was reached. The band would record one final single for the label, which would be included on a greatest hits package to be released later that summer.

Richard Branson's Virgin were hot favourites to sign the band.

At the time Virgin had a good reputation for looking after their artists, and after years of what the band deemed inattention from EMI, Virgin seemed an ideal choice. But, at the last moment, the major label CBS weighed in with a better offer. Under pressure from their accountants, who advised taking the CBS deal purely on financial grounds, the band signed on the dotted line that March. Hugh now regards this as a mistake, and feels that the band should have remained loyal to Virgin's initial enthusiasm.

The band's last projects for EMI was a final round of publicity photographs, which showed Hugh, yet again, displaying a perpetual two-day stubble, and the greatest hits album. The band chose the songs themselves, leaving off tracks such as 'Five Minutes' and 'Go Buddy Go' which had been UK hits, in favour of the excellent 'Bear Cage' and the never-was-but-should-have-been single 'Waltz In Black'. Again the project was not without its little hiccups. The original album cover, an innocuous enough crumpled black cellophane-effect shot with the band logo in white, was vetoed by the band, and, after several weeks of having their wires crossed, EMI eventually presented them with the worst album cover of their career – a girl with short-cropped hair in a black jump-suit, frowning to camera, with the Stranglers' logo in triplicate. It looked like one of those awful K-Tel 'Best Of' compilations, and became known, in band circles, as the 'keep-fit' cover.

The Stranglers' parting gift to EMI was the extremely wonderful 'Strange Little Girl'. Again, this was a Hugh idea: the very song which had been demoed back in 1974 and turned down by a host of record labels (including EMI) would be the band's swansong with the label. Their 1982 reinterpretation was fairly faithful to the original, and Tony Visconti once again added a distinctive commercial sheen, with Hugh's vocal and Dave's keyboard line high in the mix. A video, again shot by Lindsay Clennell, restated the central theme of the song. The idea behind the lyric was borrowed from *Gil Blas* by Le Sage, which centred on a country girl's loss of innocence in the city. The Stranglers put out an ad on Capitol Radio calling for the services of local punks. The video followed the simple storyline of a girl's transformation from provincial innocent to Mohican-coiffured urban punk. The single reached Number 7 in the UK charts that August. It was pure pop at its best, and put the band back on course.

By 1982 the band had a new label and a new manager too. In March of that year the Stranglers said goodbye to Eddie Kleinman. Contrary to some press reports at the time, he was not sacked. The parting was by mutual agreement, and relatively amicable. But the band were disappointed that Kleinman had not been successful in breaking them Stateside. A Bronx Cheer was all they were accustomed to on their American escapades. Kleinman's place was taken on a temporary basis by the affable Bill Tuckey, formerly the tour manager. Tuckey understood the wiles of the band's disparate characters, and what he lacked in imagination and original thought, he more than made up for by his caring stewardship. His 'caretakership' would extend for another six years, a period in which he would manage the band with active involvement from the four members themselves – a kind of managerial co-operative. The Stranglers didn't just kiss goodbye to another manager in 1982, they bade *au revoir* to the Stranglers 'sound' too.

Their next studio album, recorded in September 1982 in Brussels, produced by the band and Steve Churchyard, and mixed once again by Tony Visconti, marked a watershed in musical terms. Dave's end-of-Blackpool-pier organ sound, that topsy-turvy barrel-organ of a Hammond, had all but gone. JJ's aorta-thudding bass sound, on the way out since *The Raven*, was now absent from the sonic mix. It was to be replaced by something altogether more subtle and refined. Critics were keen to point out that the band were mellowing and, whilst this is undeniably true, the music on their next album, *Feline*, was far from standard MOR fodder. JJ:

> If you talk about success being when you have a vision and then you try and capture that vision on record, then *Feline* is our most successful album. For *Feline* the remit was to marry two big influences: Northern Europe (Protestant, industrial, hi-tech music) and Southern Europe (Catholic, agricultural, Spanish guitars, Moorish influences). So we had that Spanish, acoustic guitar sound set against Dave's keyboard work. He was using some of the very first computer samplers at the time. And we were using syncopated rhythms and electronic drums. For me, the marriage worked.

The new acoustic sound came courtesy of Jonny and Simon Kinkade from Bristol, whom Hugh had discovered and who made five black acoustic guitars for the band. *Feline* has a dreamy, even-tempoed, seamless quality to it, which is both the album's main strength and its main weakness. The album it was most reminiscent of in its overall feel was Roxy Music's *Avalon*. *Avalon* was, in its way, flawless. Beautifully played, it was an integrated package of soft grooves and bewitching songs, all rather effortless. But it was determinedly safe, and prefigured the rather noxious bland-outs of mid-80s cocktail bar music all too accurately. The same problem announced itself with *Feline*. Like *Avalon*, it came pre-formed, all the rough edges and quirky bits ironed out. 'Ships That Pass In The Night' builds to perfection; 'Midnight Summer Dream', with Hugh once again back on recitative mode vocally, has another sombre slab of Spanish guitar set against Jet's Simmons drums, whilst the first single, and the best track on the album, 'European Female', glides along with JJ's best 'Froggy' delivery and the best bass and acoustic guitar parts on the album:

> I saw her in the strasse
> And in the rue as well
> Pursued her in the high street
> She had me in her spell
> The European female she's here.

This was also the cleverest lyric on the album. JJ was writing about his then girlfriend, Anna Von Stern, whilst also personifying the European idea, turning his longed-for United States of Europe into a fictionalized female entity. JJ remembers his time with Von Stern, a dancer at the Paris opera when they met, not altogether fondly: 'She made my brain go berserk – a most beautiful woman. I was meant to go on holiday with her for a month to Sri Lanka but I only stayed a week, I'd had enough. I just wanted to murder her. So I came back!' Despite JJ's real-life romantic vicissitudes, *Feline* has more romance than the band's 'love' album, *La Folie*. It was the first Stranglers album which could be played at a dinner party, or could be put on after the hours of darkness without spooking out the rest of the family. 'Paradise' was very differently mixed and sounded more up-front, as JJ was struggling to hit the high notes and was using a spectrum analyzer to make sure he wasn't flat. It didn't altogether work, but 'Paradise' was still a fine track. The same couldn't be said of 'Blue Sister', the weakest track of the whole set and Jet's most unfavourite Stranglers' track of all time. 'I hated it,' confided Jet in 1996.

Feline's softer, more wistful tinge was apparently due to some lovie-dovey-ness in the recording studio, as Hugh remembers:

> It was a very funny period doing that album because John, Jet and Dave all had their girlfriends with them while they were recording, which I wasn't very happy about. I remember doing 'Midnight Summer Dream' and listening to it when Steve Churchyard was doing the rough mix. I'm sitting next to him and we look round and Dave's in one corner with his girlfriend, Jet's in another with his and JJ's in the third with his and all three of them are snogging and kissy-cuddly. And I said to myself, 'I thought we were making an album here, guys!'

However, the band members themselves were not on snogging terms. One incident when the band was recording in Brussels is indelibly stamped on both Jet and Hugh's memory, and its significance in the overall scheme of things was profound. Hugh:

> Jet and I stayed up very late one evening doing a lot of work in the studio on one of the songs, and John and Dave had fucked off somewhere. We thought what we'd done was turning out really good when we left at 4 or 5 a.m. John and Dave came in the next day, heard what we had done, took all the tape, fucked it up, stuffed it in an envelope saying something like 'This is shit' on it, and stuck it to the studio door. When me and Jet came in later that morning and saw it, I thought, 'I've stayed up all night working on something and this is what I get.' So I said to Jet, 'Fuck this, I'm off, I'm not working with people who do that sort of thing.' Jet said, 'Well. I totally understand, this is outrageous!' I went back to the hotel, packed my bags and booked a flight. Then I got a very worried John on the phone apologizing profusely, and Dave as well, and they persuaded me to stay on. Steve Churchyard told me later that both of them had turned up that morning at the studio out of their heads. But when people put work in, you want respect for it. If someone doesn't like it then that's something else. But I thought to myself after

this incident, 'What have we achieved as a band after all these years if this is the way people behave?'

The Brussels incident was the beginning of the end for Hugh as a Strangler.

PART THREE

Stigmata (1983–1997)

9: HUGH IN THE WALL

'Golden Brown' resurrected the Stranglers' career, reaching the Top 10 in the UK, Australia, Belgium, France, Holland and Italy. It would undoubtedly have also matched that achievement in Europe's biggest market, Germany, had EMI not cut off their nose to spite their face and stopped promoting it on hearing the band wanted off the label. Significantly, though, the group's commercial stock was so low in the States that the single wasn't even released there. 'Golden Brown' was, however, a watershed in their career in musical terms. Although itself a rather quaint, odd piece of music, the ensuing Stranglers material would be progressively more honed, more crafted and more melodic than their earlier work. By 1983 the band had entered the third phase of their musical development. Against the background of the new-wave/prog-rock of the first two albums and the more experimental left-field pop heralded in by *Black And White*, Hugh sees the post-'Golden Brown' Stranglers as a kind of Roxy Music for the 1980s (the real thing having disbanded in 1983): 'By then we'd become a sort of sophisticated Roxy Music-type band; a bit more adult, a bit more mature, but really cool. We weren't cutting edge, but we weren't reactionary either.'

The Stranglers were now craftsmen. The tongue-in-cheek manifesto, a spoof of the Surrealist manifestos of the 1910s, which accompanied the album on a free seven-inch single, was a deliberate swipe at some of the new synth-pop bands who, according to the Stranglers, were bastardizing pop: 'The musicians of our time are harlots and charlatans who use science without being scientists and abuse art without being artists. We are witnessing the demise of music. So be it.'

This is significant in that it is one of the first reactions by the older guard to the new mode of musical production (the movement away from 'real' sounds as performed by musicians in real time, to sampled, 'found' musical messages and collages of sound), a mode which, by the late 1980s and house, ambient and hip-hop, would come to dominate the mainstream. The

Stranglers could see it coming in 1982, and they didn't like what they saw. The 'song' as they knew it was under threat, as was the whole idea of rock performance on which they had based their whole career. In fact, it was the band's failure to contemporize their music in the light of these new developments, their failure to remain abreast of changes in the pop mainstream as they had until the early 1980s, which led them into a creative cul-de-sac at the end of the decade and allowed them to be marginalized as a result.

The Stranglers' music was now more *formed*, with all the loose ends tidied up. There were no more barking-mad organ frills, no more shifty little guitar lines, no more frequency snapping bass runs. From now on it was all good clean pop fun. It would be left-field pop played with a swagger, but no longer, as Hugh commented, cutting-edge. 'European Female', however, had done well, reaching Number 9 in the UK charts, and the album *Feline*, another UK Top 5 hit (and a massive hit in France, going gold in November 1989), was released at the start of 1983 to a generally favourable critical reaction. Simon Hills wrote in *Record Mirror*: 'There will be those who say the Stranglers have gone soft. Gone subtle is more like it. Underneath the smooth exterior, there is a core that is as hard and as unbreakable as before. Lap it up, but don't be fooled, the purr is really a softer growl.'

If, on vinyl, the Stranglers were new sophisticates, as people they were changing too. JJ was based in Cambridgeshire, but spending more and more time in France, staying with his mother in Grasse and writing material there during the summer. Dave lived near JJ in Cambridgeshire, whilst Hugh and Jet lived close to each other in the West Country. They were no longer the same band they were five years earlier, living, writing, eating, sleeping the Stranglers. They were now professional musicians, with successful careers, who met up at intervals to become Stranglers. But, from the early to mid-eighties onwards, being a Strangler, for whatever reason, was becoming less and less easy.

For JJ, karate was now more than a hobby: he was teaching it regularly, and eventually became a branch president of the Shidokan Karate Kickboxing Association, winning his black belt in 1989. By the late 1980s he was married to Corinne and had two children, Jeremy and Hannah.

Jet, always the most solitary Strangler (he hated the herd

mentality), was as committed to the band as ever, but he too had a life outside of music which he prized. Apart from running SIS until December 1986, when JJ took over, he was a keen gardener, furniture designer, amateur wine-maker, cook, and inventor, having a number of ideas patented. After his friend Sue Prior suffered a nervous breakdown, he attended an Exegesis seminar, having been told by a friend that the 'system' might help Sue. According to Jet, the result was an immediate and permanent cure for the condition. The controversial movement which accorded with the Thatcherite ethos of self-help and individual gain, had some adherents in the music world. Jet made this comment to the *Daily Mirror* in 1985: 'If all Britain's unemployed were put on this course, it would do them a lot of good – since it's all about personal achievement.'

His interest in Exegesis is unsurprising. Jet Black was a creation of Brian Duffy, and the ultimate in individual self-help. Brian Duffy had left school as a virtual illiterate, but by the time of his transformation into Jet Black he was an urbane, intelligent and cultured man. Jet was an individual with a quirky, genuinely off-beat personality and a self-made man three times over (first as a successful small-scale businessman, then as a major-league rock star, and lastly as an inventor). Exegesis worked for some people, but others gained little benefit.

Meanwhile, Dave was withdrawing from the present day and looking for inspiration in the past. In the 1980s, he developed an interest in fantasy role-playing, joining the Dark Ages Re-enactments Association mustering in his local Grantanbrycg (the old name for Cambridge) group of the *Regia Anglorum*, which put on mock battles for the public. Dave would make his own costumes, indulge in a spot of tablet-weaving, and drink mead round at friends' houses. He had remarried, and his wife Pam would become a regular on the Stranglers' scene, running SIS in the late 1980s. Together they grew to love that most stigmatized of animals, the rat. The Greenfields found rats adorable: their rodent chums were meticulously clean and came in all sorts of engaging shapes, sizes and colours, the agouti, and the silver fawn being particularly favourite breeds. Indeed, rats became a regular feature *chez* Greenfield. Locked in their cages by day, at night they would be allowed to roam free over the counterpane.

Dave is a curious mixture of the logical and the conventionally 'irrational'. A brilliant crossword puzzle solver and lateral thinker, and an outstanding musician, Dave has, despite his penchant for the past, always embraced technological change and the here-and-now. While JJ, for example, remained computer-illiterate for a decade, Dave could write programmes at the drop of a hat. And yet his theoretical interest in the occult went on unabated too. Dave thought of the occult not in terms of the popular caricature (seances, Ouija boards and black magic), but as having a positive role to play in understanding the real world and our own 'cosmic' existence. For Dave the occult was merely another word for 'unknown science', for phenomena which exist, which will be scientifically explainable in the future, but for which mankind today has no rational explanation. Dave:

> Trying to understand how the universe works, the material and the non-material side, the relationship between cause and effect, is at the centre of occultism. Whenever anyone asks me about the occult I always quote them a line from Alphonse Louis Constant, 'To know, to dare, to be silent'. The truth is different for every single person, depending on their degree of learning. If you pick up a decent book on the occult, 95 per cent is going to be rubbish, but the 5 per cent truth is going to be different for each person. I'm a theoretician rather than a practitioner – I read and study it rather than do things with it.

Although not a practitioner *per se*, Dave has put some of his learning to good use on the road: 'In the occult there are five elements, the usual four and an over-element, the "God principle" if you like, called the Akasha principle. This is the pure energy which the other four elements come from. Akasha is the element which keeps you awake for example. Before I go on stage I often draw in a certain amount of energy and flow the energy through my body, then when I've done, or when I go to bed, I pay it back.'

Hugh was broadening his horizons too, although on the terrestrial plane only. He had always enjoyed film and theatre, and during the 1980s he began to accentuate these extra-curricular interests more forcefully. His first acting appearance came with Bob Hoskins and Stephen Rea in the Almeida Theatre production of Gawn Grainger's play *Charlie's Last Round*, a 25-minute situation comedy. During the recording of *Feline*, he had also worked on Sam Fuller's small-budget film *L'Etoile du Sang (Bleeding Star)*.

Hugh now had a personal manager and stylist – Jackie

Castellano. He wanted to create a separate life for himself outside of the Stranglers and needed somebody to oversee his acting career. Castellano, who had been Musical Youth and U2's stylist, also acted as the band's stylist for a short while. Hugh:

> First of all Jackie was my acting agent. Then she became my agent for all my solo work, and she got me a deal with Virgin records to do my 1988 album, *Wolf*. She said to me, 'You could look a lot better than you do and she started giving the band some advice on clothes too. We were looking a bit scruffy and this didn't go with our mature, mid-80s Roxy Music-type thing, so she helped us pick some clothes to wear. It was still black, but a different cut of black! But it didn't go down too well with the rest of the band.

The idea of the Stranglers being a designer band was something the rest rejected vehemently. Jet:

> Hugh suddenly became fashion-conscious and he was always talking about 'Jackie this' and 'Jackie that'. On one occasion she came over to advise the band about their sartorial position in society and she suggested that she should kit us out. In my case she produced some ex-Army clothing, but I hated it. I never wore the thing and I got a huge bill for it. We'd never been a fashion-conscious band and JJ probably thought that the Stranglers in fashionable attire would become a sissy band. All this entered into the decline of our relationship really.

Hugh's new image-consciousness was seen by the rest of the band as a sure sign that he was growing apart from his colleagues. For JJ, Hugh was losing the plot: 'Hugh was a butterfly, really, depending on who was his latest sycophant, who was being obsequious and oleaginous to him. Hugh was never comfortable with people who liked the Stranglers. He used to mix in different circles. However, Hugh and I developed a relationship with Kenzo the fashion couturier in Paris, after we found out he was using our music during one of his shows.'

According to JJ, Hugh was becoming yuppified:

> He was willing to appear in *Cosmopolitan* modelling dodgy clothes, to drive up and down the M4 in a white Range Rover and appear on quiz shows and art shows – all things that had nothing to do with us. He was moving so far away from the things which initially

fired the group in the first place. You can't blame someone when they get money if they move in different circles, but you can retain some discernment. He was surrounded by sycophants. People actually told him, 'You don't need a band.'

Challenged by this ten years later, Hugh admits that he was 'rediscovering what I really was', adding: 'I'm not actually a tough-boy punk-rocker. I was being a bit more true to myself. But I think it is a bit like the pot calling the kettle black, because he was becoming yuppified as well. We both were. John was driving a Jaguar at the time. In fact, when I was banned from driving he actually sequestered my white Range Rover and wouldn't give it back when my driving ban was lifted!'

Hugh's 'diversification', was seen as symptomatic of a general malaise which struck the band round about the mid-1980s. But this torpor, this inactivity, was sharpened by the growing antipathy between the two leading men. After ten years of being together, Hugh and JJ were now slowly tearing each other apart. They seldom wrote together as in the early days, with Jet and Hugh demoing in the West Country and Dave and JJ working on tracks in Cambridgeshire. Now the generation of new ideas was reduced to the level of a musical correspondence course, as tapes were posted back and forth, and shaped courtesy of the Royal Mail, rather than direct contact in the rehearsal room.

Looking back on his time with the band, Hugh remembers that it was during this period that he felt that they were on automatic pilot:

Our lives were drifting apart, everyone was drifting apart. JJ is a very difficult man to be with and I found it increasingly difficult to work together with him from about *Feline* onwards. Everyone was losing enthusiasm for what we were doing. You start going through the motions and it all gets a bit wearing. The band were living on borrowed time from that point on, although we still made some good stuff, but we kept something going which none of us had the courage to stop. We got used to a standard of living and way of doing things which is difficult to stop, because if you suddenly say, 'Well, that's it', suddenly the standing orders stop coming in! But I was just going through the motions on the tours. I was enjoying playing the gigs, but I was getting more and more bored with John's posturizing and sloganeering. It was just too much exposure to someone. And it depressed me.

If all was not entirely well within the band then it certainly didn't show on the eighth album, which hit the racks in November 1984. *Aural Sculpture* was a positive, up-tempo collection of some of the finest songs of their career. The main difference between this album and previous outings was the commercial sound given it by Paul Young producer, Laurie Latham. Songs such as the first single, 'Skin Deep', were given a huge, almost overwhelming, storming, rich production (the twelve-inch mix is the best of their career), whilst on a majority of tracks a brass section was used to enrich the musical mix. *Aural Sculpture* is a synth-pop meets Stax soul hybrid. Whereas past albums had innovated, this one was state-of-the-art pop. But still the Stranglers could give even the most conventional of pop songs a dramatic or quirky turn. 'Ice Queen', for example, is a classic Stranglers song with a bewitching melody. 'North Winds', with its cold-war chill and vocordorized ending, is another strong track. 'Let Me Down Easy', with a lyric by Hugh dealing with the death of JJ's father and music by JJ himself, is as heart-rending as pop can get, whilst 'No Mercy' was an eighties update of the band's original misanthropic pose:

> Everyday your love is getting warmer
> Just look at her and love her did you get it right
> Will she soothe your brow with kisses
> Only meant for thee
> She'll show no mercy
> She'll show no mercy

This was written and sung by Hugh, against a gloriously catchy piece of instrumentation and some 'authentic' soul backing. Elsewhere on the album there's less sparkle: 'Uptown' is fun, but lightweight, whilst 'Mad Hatter' and 'Punch And Judy' show that the addition of a horn section to the Stranglers' sound was always going to be problematical; the mix somehow didn't quite come off, the Stax soul musical *leitmotifs* sounding unnecessarily backward-looking and safe at a time when the pop charts were full of the horrors of MOR white-boy pop crooners doing soul very badly.

Hugh, for one, was very pleased with Latham's work on the album:

We'd already recorded 'Skin Deep' and we gave it to Laurie Latham to finish off. We liked what he did with it. He brought in the backing singers, who would later form London Beat, and suggested that we used brass on the album. Laurie was a very gifted guy: he was a producer, but he was also an engineer. He was the man that Steve Churchyard and Alan Winstanley weren't; he was a very talented engineer who could do all the knob-twiddling, but he also had the musical sensibility with songs. I've never met anyone like that before. He was the perfect producer – two men in one, really.

For the photo shoot for the album, Hugh's brother-in-law John King, who was head of art at a North London school, assembled a team of pupils to create a huge fibre-glass ear, the 'aural sculpture' which graced the sleeve and the videos for the 'Skin Deep' and 'Let Me Down Easy' singles. A photographer friend of Hugh's from New York took the actual photograph used for the cover. It was striking, but a bit tacky too, and continued the run of blindingly obvious Stranglers sleeves (after the black-and-white photograph for *Black And White*, the raven for *The Raven* and the cat for *Feline*). Again, the Stranglers were simply too literal for their own good, subtlety or irony never having been their strong points.

Aural Sculpture, like every Stranglers album, split the critics. Long-time Stranglers supporters *Sounds* gave it four stars ('Overall . . . great listening') and *Record Mirror* went one better with a five-star commendation, whilst Robin Denselow in the *Guardian* wrote, 'Don't be put off by the cover: this is an excellent album.' But the rest of the music press were less than chuffed, and rather more direct. Sean O'Hagan in *NME* raged, 'I couldn't bear to listen to this unmitigated shite ever again', and Mick Mercer in *Melody Maker* concluded: 'celebrating your hundredth year in showbiz is no excuse; this is shocking'. If *NME* and *Melody Maker* were the barometers of teen and student cool, then the band's more listener-friendly music was a flop. Rather surprisingly for an album with such a modish mainstream sound, it fared slightly disappointingly in the UK charts, reaching only Number 14. But elsewhere in Europe, the album and concomitant singles did much better. In Germany the album became the group's first to reach the Top 20.

The input of the brass section was a turning point in the band's career as it meant that the touring party was now seven, not four. In Alex Gifford, who was brought in for the tour, JJ found a soul mate. They became inseparable and always hung out together. This helped diffuse the tensions between him and Hugh. The arrival of the horn section changed the focus on stage and added an extra attraction. The band were alive to criticisms that they were beginning to look static and undynamic. The brass pepped things up and re-vivified a flagging stage act, but the inclusion of a swinging, honking brass sound to new-wave classics such as 'Peaches' and 'Something Better Change' was bizarre to say the least.

Two incidents on the *Aural Sculpture* tour of 1985 showed how far the Burnel/Cornwell relationship had deteriorated. In Rome that April, what started as a petty minor incident blew up out of all proportion. JJ remembers this tragicomic event vividly:

We came off stage and Hugh and I were talking about what to do for an encore. During 'Hanging Around' Hugh used to try and jump. Now Hugh can't jump. I can jump five or six feet in the air, but Hugh can't. I use it to keep time with Jet, and if I miss my timing I just jump a little lower. Me and Hugh would always jump at the same place during the song, and he'd always be out of time. Hugh took himself very seriously in those days and he was up his own arse. I happened to say, as a bit of a wind-up, 'I see you jumped in time tonight Hugh' and he chucked his glass of champagne in my face. Now we were backstage in this big tent in this sort of cardboard hut room and *I put him through the wall!* It was a very thin wall, mind. But all you could see was like Hugh's silhouette in the wall – it was like one of those *Tom & Jerry* things. Anyway, he appeared on the other side and outside of our dressing-room were all the promoters! Of course, we had to go back on stage and do an encore. He didn't speak to me for about a week after that. I put chocolates outside his bedroom door that night to say sorry. But I think we both contributed to it.

Hugh denies ever throwing a glass of fizzy at JJ and at the time did not see the funny side to being attacked by his writing partner. The whole incident was another decisive moment in terms of his Stranglers career.

It was nothing to come to blows about, but he just attacked me and I just thought that this was another example of someone out of control, basically. From that moment on, I started worrying about my physical health. I said to him, 'I'm going to have to be very careful what I say to you, because I just can't tell how you're going to react.' If you're working with people and you're collaborating then you expect to be able to have heated words with someone and to get it off your chest and to get it all out in the open. But when that happens and you think, Well the guy might attack me', then that's something else. It was at this point that I started wanting to create an independent existence. I thought, I can't rely on a working relationship with someone who's going to attack me. It was in my mind to leave then.

But it would be JJ who would leave the band first. This, as the rest of the Stranglers know, is not, in itself, a cause for major anxiety. JJ often threatened to leave, only to return a few days later after conciliatory noises from the management. Hugh remembers JJ wanting to leave as early as 1976 after a gig at the Speakeasy, so disconsolate had his friend become about the band's lack of success. But his departure in 1985 was of a slightly different degree and a harbinger of the troubles to come.

The Stranglers had arrived back in Australia and were scheduled to play a gig in Queensland. Joh Bjelke Petersen, whom they had grown less than fond of back in 1979, was, to their dismay, still in power. It was at this moment that JJ's fears about Hugh's lack of conviction were made manifest:

We were playing a really big gig in Queensland to about six or seven thousand people. Before the gig we said, 'Let's say something, we've got 7,000 people here, let's cause some shit before we do the encore. We've played the gig, now that everyone's hot let's wind them up a bit, have a riot or whatever'. Hugh said, 'No, we can't do that, it'll cause shit' and he refused to talk about the political situation. I said, 'I thought "shit" used to be our middle name.' I thought he was just wimping out. He'd sold out by then. I think, in the end, Jet came to the mic to say something. But after that tour I left the band. Hugh just wanted commercial success to finance his lifestyle, and if you're going to think about the consequences all the time then you're never going to do anything, are you? You go for it and you reap what you sow. You don't achieve anything by sitting on the fence and that's just what I think he was doing.

Hugh thought JJ's resolve and fight merely a pretence. Times had changed and he wasn't willing to re-adopt the stroppiness of yore ten years past its sell-by date. But he still considered the Stranglers something worth saving, and after the tour he jetted down to Nice to persuade JJ to re-join the band. This show of affection was all JJ needed. He wanted to be told that he belonged to the band and that the writing partnership was still viable. So JJ and Hugh began work on the next album.

But it was a temporary reprieve; the *Aural Sculpture* tour had exacerbated tensions. In Hugh's eyes, JJ was increasingly an anachronism. Tired of JJ's aggression and his posturing, Hugh resolved to carve out a career without him. JJ, on the other hand, saw Hugh becoming less in touch with himself, less in touch with being a Strangler, and more of a phony poseur. Hugh and JJ's positions had become entrenched.

The second half of the 1980s didn't so much witness the band falling apart as sliding into complete inertia. Their next two albums, *Dreamtime* and *10*, took two years in production, and both had to be re-recorded before release. Of the two, *Dreamtime* is considerably the stronger, although nowhere close to being classic Stranglers material. Work on the album began with Laurie Latham again as producer, but this time progress was problematical. A lot of studio time was spent working on a Hugh track called 'You', which later ended up as a 'B' side only, whilst the best of a new crop of songs the band had demoed, 'Always The Sun', remained unrecorded. Two versions of events have been put forward by the band as to what happened next. Hugh, who has remained in contact with Laurie Latham (working with him on his 1997 album *Guilty*), maintains that the band simply weren't ready and didn't have enough strong material for an album. So Latham asked them to go back, re-group, and write some more stuff before continuing recording. Jet, JJ and Dave remember events entirely differently, however. Rather than Latham, in effect, sacking the band, he was told by the 'hirer and firer' Jet, unhappy at the way in which the album was shaping up, that his services were no longer required:

I spotted 'Always The Sun' immediately as having great chart potential. This song was the crisis point in the sessions with Laurie

Latham in Brussels. Now, I regard Laurie Latham as a complete professional, and his work was excellent, but what he was doing was changing the material so that we were being left with a Laurie Latham album. He was changing the songs musically and lyrically, and all the songs which I thought were the best, including 'Always The Sun', were at the bottom of his list. When we came to 'Always The Sun' he was changing the lyrics and the metre of it, and the chords were changed. One day I just said, 'Look Laurie, what you're doing is really excellent, but it's just not us. I don't know how we can continue making this Laurie Latham album', and he felt pretty shocked and he freaked out and we all went home.

Although Latham didn't know it, *Dreamtime* was the product of a disintegrating unit. He had enjoyed working on *Aural Sculpture* and admired the band's musicality and workman-like approach. He was even warming to grumpy Jet after a remark made by the drummer to Latham backstage after a gig: 'I remember Jet coming backstage and putting his arm round me saying, "Do you know, Laurie, when I first met you, I thought you were a complete wanker . . . But now, you're all right really aren't you?!"'

But this time, there simply weren't enough good, worked-out songs to make the project run smoothly. Laurie Latham:

I don't know what *Dreamtime* was. With *Aural Sculpture* there were songs, with substance. With *Dreamtime* what happened was that the demos were extremely sketchy and they handed them in like kids handing in shoddy homework! They probably thought because I'd had such an effect on *Aural Sculpture* that I'd sort them out and turn them into songs. This is what caused the problems because we were going into the studio without having done any proper pre-production and we were writing songs in the studio which is fatal if you've got one eye on the overall budget. Not only that but they didn't have enough material to start an album. One day, the day it all came to a head, Jet suddenly said, 'Ooh Laurie, I'm not hearing any hits.' He woke up one afternoon after being fast asleep and started whingeing. I said, 'The best bit of production I can do is to say, "Let's stop, go away, write some more songs and then come back."' The material wasn't up to scratch. If there was ever a song that didn't sound like the Stranglers it was 'Always The Sun'.

Latham did not want to be the catalyst who brought divisions within the band out into the open: 'My main worry was that I was going to be responsible for splitting up the Stranglers. I had already sensed that something wasn't quite right and that Hugh was a little bit detached. In the end, I suppose I was given the sack because I would have tried to have finished the record.'

'Always The Sun' wasn't in a fit state to be recorded during those sessions with Latham in Brussels. It took the band several months of hard work to transform it into what we know today. 'Always The Sun' is the last classic Stranglers single to date: a moving, soaring melody married to a life-affirming, optimistic lyric, it completely overshadows the rest of the album. The man brought in to produce the second lot of sessions for *Dreamtime* was Mike Kemp. Hugh: 'He was a very nice guy, but a bit conciliatory with us. He didn't force his ideas as much as he could have done. But he was sympathetic to us, which was nice.'

Surprisingly, 'Always The Sun' was not chosen as the lead-off single. That honour went to the breezy, infectious 'Nice In Nice', sung in cheeky style by a very breathy JJ. A fine single, it peaked at a disappointing Number 30 in September 1986. 'Always The Sun', though, surely couldn't fail.

The band entrusted Hugh with the task of generating ideas and story-boarding the video clip. But the process again brought nothing but grief for him: 'The others were quite happy for me to story-board the video. I spent a lot of time with the director making sure we got it right, following my brief. We finished the video and the others watched it and said, "It's shit." I thought, Well, that's nice. I put the extra work in so you can go and have your spare time and you've got the cheek to say you don't like it. They should have been involved. I thought that was ungracious and undiplomatic.'

The single was released in October 1986, but, despite a *Top Of the Pops* appearance, it stiffed at Number 30. For Hugh, this was yet another turning point: 'The CBS promotion people were very, very disappointed. They thought they'd really failed big-time because that was a Top 10 song. It was another nail in the coffin. I don't think the band were losing it creatively, we were delivering the songs, but CBS were certainly losing it promotion-wise.'

After two mediocre chart successes, CBS released a further two singles from the album, 'Big In America', a jokey swipe at the Yanks, and the cod-swing of 'Shakin' Like A Leaf'. But both were under-par songs and failed to make the Top 40. The *Dreamtime* album itself, released in November, only managed a six-week run in the charts, peaking at Number 16.

There were some choice moments on this, the Stranglers' ninth studio album. The title track is a splendid song, dealing tangentially with the Aboriginal cause. Hugh said in 1987: 'A lot of the songs are about lost ideals. It's very difficult in today's age of modern enlightenment and technology . . . for certain ways of living to survive and certain values to survive, and that isn't necessarily a good thing.'

'Mayan Skies' was also affecting enough, and JJ's 'Reap What You Sow', unwittingly both lyrically and melodically similar to Lou Reed's 'Perfect Day', is another moody, emotional piece of writing. But the band were obviously not firing on all cylinders creatively, and part of the reason was that the writing unit of JJ and Hugh had all but broken down. Most of the *Dreamtime* material had originated separately from the two main songwriters themselves. It was obvious that for the Stranglers to produce their best material both Hugh and JJ would have to invest more in generating songs together rather than individually. For them to produce fine songs, they needed each other. But, by now, they were palpably unable to forge the same creative bond that existed ten years before. Some of the critics picked up on the collective stasis which had hit the band. Mat Smith in *Melody Maker* wrote: 'Everything here is so lacklustre, so devoid of the merest hint of life, so overwhelmingly . . . knackered.' But there were still supporters in the media. *Sounds* came up trumps again with a four-star review, whilst Chris Roberts, writing in the same publication, had this to say about the 'Nice In Nice' single earlier in the year: 'The new music is fine. Conventional, intelligent soft rock-pop, laced with Stranglerisation. When Jean-Jacques Burnel opens "Nice In Nice" with "Hey [sic], look at that gurl", it's still very different to, say, Owen Paul doing the same. It's still lustful and a mite wicked.'

The Stranglers still possessed that 'wicked' edge. But it was obvious to Hugh that JJ could stomach more quantities of old-fashioned bile than he could. Hugh suspects that round about the mid-1980s, JJ became totally dissatisfied with the new 'mature' stance the band had adopted and, in interviews and in the writing process, started to try and re-inject some of the angst of yore. JJ told *Melody Maker*'s Stud Brothers in 1986: 'Of course we're outsiders. They never invited *us* to Band Aid, so let 'em starve . . . We used to think that the Marxist philosophy . . . the *Groucho* Marxist philosophy that I wouldn't want to be a member of a club that would have *me* as a member was great.'

While working on material for the band's next studio album, *10* (a further example of the band's penchant for the mind-numbingly obvious: yep, it was their tenth studio album), JJ penned the following lyric: 'Jesus Christ wasn't a Christian/He was a good-ole Jewish boy'.

JJ remembers with a certain amount of disgust that the couplet was vetoed by Hugh: 'Hugh said, "You can't have that! The music business is owned by Jewish people in the States." I thought, Why has he wimped out? What's so offensive about it anyway? I really started having my doubts about Hugh at this stage.'

For Hugh, however, the line was simply another hollow attempt at controversy for controversy's sake. JJ was living in the past:

> That lyric had no place in the song it was supposed to go in, and I didn't see what it was going to achieve other than upset a lot of people and make our progress even more difficult. John has a certain amount of destruction and hell-bent drive about him. He'd flirt with disaster, court it, and not worry about the consequences. This is OK sometimes. But when you're trying to make a living it doesn't make sound business sense. The days of all that were over. He was getting unhappy with our profile being more mature, which he was quite into a few years earlier. Whereas I was quite happy with the way we were getting this great profile of being these mature but cool songwriters. It had longevity about it.

The *10* album was the work of a flaccid, directionless unit and it was prefigured by three years of aimlessness by the band. Jet: 'By this time the band were pretty knackered, after a tumultuous decade. It might have been more sensible to have taken a year out instead of making a half-hearted effort during that period.'

The band were still regarded as a big draw, big enough, for example, to play support gigs in Spain to Bowie during his *Glass Spider* extravaganza of 1987. But in the late 80s the individual members seemed to be interested in anything as long as it wasn't to do with the Stranglers. JJ and Dave, together with ex-Vibrator

John Ellis, formed the good-time r'n'b band The Purple Helmets, recorded two albums and played some low-key dates. JJ himself recorded a second solo album in 1989, *Un Jour Parfait*, a dreamy, wistful blend of chanson and Europop. It was a pleasing enough record and consolidated his position as a talented songwriter outside of the band. The previous year Hugh had released his second solo album, *Wolf*. Neither were great commercial successes. In addition, Hugh contributed the catchy 'Facts And Figures' to the soundtrack for the 1986 Raymond Williams' animated anti-nuke film, *When The Wind Blows*. Hugh's daftest team-up unfortunately never saw the light of day. He recorded a song with cook Keith Floyd, then television's foremost media culinary celeb, called 'Give Geese A Chance', in which the famous 'gastronaut' rapped a recipe for that most neglected of Yuletide fayre, roast goose. It was a great idea for a Christmas single (and had Vicky from We've Got A Fuzzbox And We're Gonna Use It on vocals too) but, according to Hugh, Floyd's 'advisers' at the BBC cautioned against the project as it might tarnish his impeccable media image. The single was pulled at the last moment.

Meanwhile, the band's extremely uncreative period was camouflaged by the success of their Kinks cover, 'All Day And All Of The Night', which reached Number 7 in January 1988 (and is their last Top 10 hit to date). The track had been played by JJ and Dave on their Purple Helmet tour and was previewed by the band in their co-headlining slot for Alice Cooper at Reading Festival in 1987. They even managed to whip up some old-style controversy, when the cover had to be withdrawn not once, but twice! The original cover showing Monica Coughlan, the call-girl at the centre of the Jeffrey Archer 'sex-scandal' that wasn't, was withdrawn by a jumpy CBS after noises from the band's lawyers. The second, depicting a brothel with various naughty bits illuminated in the bedroom windows, again had to be redesigned, with a few of the more explicit scenes replaced by less 'corrupting' parts of the anatomy. The band, now a fully-fledged mainstream pop act, performed the song on the high-rating *Wogan* show just before Christmas and watched with obvious relief when it stormed the Top 10 in the post-Christmas period. It was indeed a career-saver, and bought the band time. The success of the band's second live album, *All Live And All Of The Night*, followed; it reached Number 12 in February 1988. On balance, this is a more successful album than *Live X Certs*. The material is stronger, the performances more assured, and the bonus of the Kinks cover (surprisingly not included in live form, but in its studio manifestation) was an added incentive to buy. The only thing wrong with the album was its truly dreadful cover, a complete artistic catastrophe which showed up a woeful lack of ideas on the part of the band.

With the band's commercial star once again in temporary ascendance, they retreated with local engineer Owen Morris to JJ's newly-built 16-track studio to record the *10* album. (Incidentally, the studio was designed and built by Jet, with the assistance of Sil Willcox, in two weeks flat!) Morris was later catapulted to fame in the mid-90s as Oasis' engineer and producer. In the late 1980s he worked on Stranglers and Stranglers-related projects to good effect. The original version of the album was incredibly rocky in comparison with the existing catalogue and the band thought that it would be released in spring 1989. But Muff Winwood, the A&R man at CBS, was unhappy with the production and suggested they re-record it.

Roy Thomas Baker, the man behind Queen's 'Bohemian Rhapsody', was brought in for the job. Hugh remembers that the process of getting the big sound associated with Thomas Baker was a far from easy task: 'It was incredibly painstaking recording, with loads of over-dubs. It was so unusual, as it wasn't how we were used to working at all. When we'd worked with producers in the past we'd always had some input.'

Today, the band view the album as their least favourite: 'overproduced' (Dave), 'pretty grim' (Jet), 'the physical sound of it is awful' (John Ellis). For JJ ('I got the mixes when I was up in Scotland and it spoilt my Christmas'), the album was the surest indication yet of Hugh's quiescence: 'The album definitely demonstrated that it was time for something to happen, because Hugh thought it was the best album we'd done. I thought it was totally directionless and atrophic. It was the sound of Hugh trying to be middle-of-the-road.'

The problem wasn't so much the production by Roy Thomas Baker (although it has to be said that the original version with Owen Morris was considerably better), but the fact that the material was simply stale and boring. The one quality track was the cover version of ? & The Mysterians' 1966 hit '96 Tears', which had not even been the band's idea in the first place, suggested as it was by Thomas Baker during recording of the album. This was a splendid single, and became a Top 20 UK hit in February 1990, but the album itself fared no better than *Dreamtime* three-and-a-half years earlier, reaching a respectable Number 15, but charting for only a month. The second single, 'Sweet Smell Of Success', barely dented the Top 75. The best feature of the album was undoubtedly the cover, which stands as one of the finest of their career. The band are in panto-mode, with the lads impersonating some of the leading political figures of the day. Hugh is George Bush and Colonel Gadaffi, Dave, Rajiv Gandhi and a rather sombre Gorbachev, JJ, Pope John Paul, Benazir Bhutto and a rather too-pretty Margaret Thatcher, and Jet steals the show as a brilliant Yasser Arafat, Fidel Castro, and a Joshua Nkomo resembling an overweight Harpo Marx. Reviews of the album were again mixed, but there were some encouraging noises from the most unexpected of quarters – like the *NME*'s Stephen Dalton, who gave it a very charitable 7 out of 10. Roy Wilkinson in *Sounds* summed the album up like this: 'Undemanding, mildly cantankerous and as laid back as hell, *10* is the sound of four seasoned pros cracking a few tinnies and knocking out a slice of vinyl for God knows what reason. The cash, force of habit? It's often mediocre, but there's something undeniably likeable about *10*.'

The *raison d'être* behind the album was to have one last attempt at cracking the States. Fifteen years together, and with one of the finest back-catalogues in pop, there was still not even a sniff of a hit single in the States. Of course, the Stranglers were in good company when it came to lack of success across the pond. The history of British pop is littered with deserving UK chart acts, from T. Rex and Roxy Music in the seventies to the Smiths in the eighties and Blur in the nineties, who failed, for whatever reason, to establish themselves in the US. But with a big-name producer, and an equally big guitar-rock sound, it was hoped that this, the most mainstream of the Stranglers' albums, would make an impact. Hugh:

The whole reason behind making the record was to set up a tour of America. I went over and did some pre-release publicity in New

York with the management. We came back, and while we were rehearsing for the British tour they said, 'Sorry boys, we can't get an American tour together, there's no interest.' I thought, Well that's fuckin' great, we've just released an album for America and we can't even get the chance to play it over there. Well, that's got to be it. That really is the last straw.

As far as Hugh was concerned, there was now nothing keeping him in the band. There were no plans lined up for after the British tour, which was scheduled to end at a big gig at Alexandra Palace on 11 August. For the first time in his life as a Strangler, there was a yawning gap in band duties, and it was this that gave him the window of opportunity. For Hugh the decision to leave 'was getting closer and closer and higher and higher on my list of priorities. Before there was always some band commitment to keep me from leaving, there was always something to stop me. But after the Ally Pally gig there wasn't anything planned for months.'

As the *10* tour started, it was a question not of *if*, but *when* Hugh would decide to call it a day.

10: EXIT, STAGE LEFT

Paradoxically, the Stranglers circa 1990 seemed in no worse shape than they had been five years earlier. True, their recent album was the weakest of their career. But they could still shift enough units to make the UK Top 20 in both the singles and albums charts, and were still, in the UK at least, a sizeable live draw. For the *10* tour, ex-Vibrator guitarist John Ellis was brought into the starting line-up. The pretext was that there was so much guitar on *10* that Hugh couldn't possibly play it all *and* sing lead vocals. The real reason, however, according to JJ and Dave, was that Hugh wanted to become a cozy lead-singer without any other extraneous musical duties. In reality, his guitar playing was backsliding. JJ:

> I got John into the group and me and Dave were very pleased with his playing. Hugh was playing less and less guitar anyway. He was actually regressing musically as a guitarist and we all thought he was losing it. It was obvious that he just wasn't interested. It wasn't difficult to convince even Hugh that we should bring him [John] into the group. In fact it suited Hugh down to the ground. John could take over the guitar playing and Hugh could stick his fingers in his ears and sing.

Dave: 'John can play the solos a lot better than Hugh could in some cases. Hugh was an inventive guitarist, but never fast. For example, I don't think Hugh ever played the solo on "Golden Brown" right, apart from when he was recording it, and that took several takes. He could never play it at full speed.'

John Ellis was temperamentally quite different from the rest of the Stranglers: more reflective, more sensitive to other people, less given to outrageous strops and prima-donna behaviour, and hungrier for success. Like the rest of the Stranglers (with the exception of Jet), he came from a middle-class background. John William Ellis was born on 1 June 1952 and spent his childhood years in Kentish Town and Kingsbury

near Wembley. He attended Orange Hill County Grammar
School, where he met Pat Collier, who would be the bassist
in the Vibrators. After school John went to Chelsea College of
Art and Design with the intention of working in film. For three
years he worked as a film librarian for the British Institute, and
afterwards took jobs as a tree surgeon and a warehouse man
before returning to the art-school milieu at Hornsey College,
where one of his classmates was Stuart Goddard (Adam Ant).
Whilst at Hornsey, Ellis formed a band, Bazooka Joe, which
would later feature Dan Barson, the brother of Madness's Mike.
In fact, many of the boys who would later form Madness would
hang around with them, and Bazooka Joe's North London art-
school tomfoolery was a major influence on them. Then in 1975
Ellis formed the Vibrators, one of the least-lauded but most
influential new-wave bands of the day. Like JJ and Hugh, John
was a blues devotee and disciple of Peter Green, and also
enjoyed the hippy-era Hendrix and Pink Floyd. Like the
Stranglers, the Vibrators pre-dated the media fascination with
punk, but were happy to be bracketed with the movement for
commercial reasons. And just as the Stranglers were ostracized
by punk, so too did the Vibrators find themselves marginalized
by the punk orthodoxy after they signed to anti-Christ Micky
Most's RAK label. Duly tarred and feathered, the Vibrators have
been forgotten ever since. After leaving the Vibrators in 1979,
John Ellis formed REM, an arty, experimental, mixed-media
rock band, toured with JJ's Euroman band, and then forged a
partnership with two of rock's leading lights, Peter Gabriel and
Peter Hammill. By the mid-80s Ellis was one of the most
innovative but unsung guitarists in the business. His time on
the road with JJ was not an altogether happy one, as John
remembers:

> I thought the music we played on the *Euroman* tour was quite
> interesting, but it was a shambles of a tour. Hardly anyone
> bothered to turn up, and JJ was taking a lot of drugs at the
> time. We all were really, I guess. He was being a particular pain in
> the arse though, and I vowed never to speak to him again after
> that tour. In fact during the last gig we had some fisticuffs and JJ
> ended up in the audience! I walked off and didn't see him again for
> ten years. Then I got asked to work on a single that JJ was
> producing for Laurent Sinclair, then I worked with JJ and Dave

on the Purple Helmets project, which I enjoyed, and then I was the second guitarist on the *10* tour.

Unlike the rest of the band, politically and temperamentally he was a socialist who automatically empathized with people on a no-frills, common-sense level. He didn't deal in the mind games and contrivances that the four original members were wont to deploy. Unlike the rest of the band, he was not financially secure and had never enjoyed the level of success the others had. His 1970s band, the Vibrators, had garnered a certain amount of success, and Ellis had been active on the scene, most notably as Peter Gabriel and Peter Hammill's side-kick. But, at 38, Ellis knew time was running out if he was to make the break into major-league commercial and artistic success. Nevertheless, he did not take on the gig with much relish:

> I'm going to be completely honest with you. I didn't want to do it because Peter Hammill had just asked me to go on tour with him. I knew it would be grief. There's a certain aspect of the Stranglers that is surrounded by darkness and there's a lot of heavy vibes in the band. It's not a gig for an over-sensitive person and it's not a gig for someone who can't deal with a lot of emotional and psychological stress. But I managed to side-step most of the stress on the *10* tour. But my feelings were that it was a big career move and I had a lot of respect for the music they were creating . . . And I needed the money!

Although he managed to get through the *10* tour without a great many alarms, he remembers that Hugh was becoming increasingly unpleasant to be around. And, not only that, his right-wing political credo soon began to cause offence:

> Hugh was a bit stand-offish sometimes. When we were touring I'd often find myself at breakfast with him and he could be very nasty to people. He could come on as a regular pop star, which I think is unnecessary. He could be very rude to staff in hotels and demand things unnecessarily and be very cutting and sarcastic. At times he could be quite pleasant, but I remember having a heated conversation with him before a gig in Switzerland. Hugh was defending the Tories simply because it meant he had to pay less tax, which I thought was a disgusting thing to say. He'd worked out that, under Labour in the 70s, he had to pay 101 per cent tax.

Now I don't know how anyone can pay 101 per cent tax. And Dave always used to say, 'If we were under a Labour government now, I'd be paying out all my money in taxes for education and I haven't got a kid (which, of course, he has; he's got a teenage daughter). Why should I have to pay money for schools?' Virtually everyone in the band was right-wing when I joined. JJ was very definitely pro-Tory.

But, as ever, it was the relationship between the two front-men which was so precarious, and so crucial to the future of the Stranglers. It didn't take long before Hugh and JJ fell out yet again. This time it was in Paris, on 30 May. The pre-gig meal had seen another blazing row, and that night, JJ and Hugh took the stage with evil in their eyes. Sil Willcox, then the band's production manager, remembers: 'There was a horrible tension on stage, you could cut it with a knife. Hugh broke a string on four different guitars. It was a great gig because the audience thought, Fuck, these guys are going to kill each other in a minute. You didn't pop back-stage for a chat with the band after the gig that night!'

Personal and political differences aside, the *10* tour was, artistically, an improvement on the album. The addition of John Ellis not only fleshed out the band's sound, but made them a tighter, more threatening entity. Always a fine live band, they sounded even bolder; less quirky maybe, but certainly more powerful. Although it was now desperately unhip for a journalist to admit to liking them, the Stranglers still had the odd supporter willing to stick his or her head above the parapet. For example, this is how the *NME*'s Stephen Dalton described the last Hugh-era gig: 'Hugh becomes more and more like a pervy civil servant every day, JJ works his rent-boy pout and karate kick once too often, Jet engulfs the drum riser and Dave's *Name Of The Rose* hairstyle is no substitute for keyboard solos that once killed at 50 paces. But, even when they make me yawn, I will always love them.'

Stagecraft couldn't totally paper over the deep divisions within the band, and the redundancy of the new material. It was time for a change, for all concerned. On the afternoon of the band's Alexandra Palace gig, Hugh finally made up his mind to go: 'After the soundcheck I was watching the Test Match on the television in my hotel room and Devon Malcolm hit a six off a

JJ and Dave flash some leg to promote
'Fire and Water', 1983. (*Photograph:
courtesy of Epic*)

JJ at the Astoria, April 1988. (*Photograph: © Richard Bellia*)

Promo shot for '10', 1990. (*Photograph: Claire Muller © Epic*)

The new Stranglers line-up, 1992. From left:
Dave Greenfield, JJ Burnel, Jet Black, Paul
Roberts, John Ellis. (*Photograph: © Jill
Furmanovsky*)

Paul, JJ and Stuart 'Psycho' Pearce, 1992.
(*Photograph: courtesy of The Stranglers*)

A fresh-faced Paul, 1992. (*Photograph: ©
Jill Furmanovsky*)

A statesman-like Jet, 1992. (*Photograph:
© Jill Furmanovsky*)

Dave and rodent chum, 1992.
(*Photograph: © Jill Furmanovsky*)

Bosnia, 1997.
(*Photograph: courtesy of The Stranglers*)

Fancy-dress time for Dave as Jack the Ripper (with SIS's Marian Shepherd as Puss in Kinky Boots), and authentic costume for Dark Ages re-enactments. (*Photographs: courtesy of The Stranglers*)

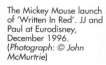

The Mickey Mouse launch of 'Written In Red'. JJ and Paul at Eurodisney, December 1996. (*Photograph: © John McMurtrie*)

Hugh Cornwell at the 100 Club. (*Photograph: © 1997 Shoko Fujiwara*)

Dave at the Royal Albert Hall, June 1997. (*Photograph: © John McMurtrie*)

John Ellis at the Royal Albert Hall, June 1997. (*Photograph: © John McMurtrie*)

Paul Roberts, the first man to stage dive at the Royal Albert Hall?

The truly crap Johnny Rubbish, the first 'alternative comedian', pictured at the Royal Albert Hall, 1997.

'Good cop, bad cop', Sil Willcox and Trevor Long, the band's current management team. (*All photographs this page:* © John McMurtrie)

Hugh Cornwell, 1997.
(*Photograph: Tim Kent ©
Snapper Music*)

The Stranglers,
Hammersmith Bridge,
1997. (*Photograph:
courtesy of Eagle
Records*)

West Indian fast bowler, and I thought, It's got to be tonight. I can't keep this up any longer. So I went to the gig and thought, make this the best gig you've done, play your heart out, which I did. I felt a sense of freedom which was great, and that's why I enjoyed the gig.'

After the gig, Hugh left immediately to get drunk with friends. There would be no fraternizing with the band after this show, no end-of-tour celebrations. At that point he was the only person who knew that he had played his last gig with a band he had helped to form over 16 years earlier. He knew also that his decision would almost certainly finish the band that he had helped to create, would mean the end of the road for his fellow Stranglers. He resolved to break the news the next day.

The way he did it left a bitter taste in the mouths of the rest of the band. Rather than confront them face to face, Hugh decided to use the impersonality and safety of the phone to break the news. This was an understandable demonstration of human frailty. But it was again seen, particularly by JJ, as another example of Hugh 'wimping out', of him not being man enough to tell the band in person. For Jet, the first to be contacted, the news of his departure did not come as a big surprise: 'I had no inkling he was making other plans but when he phoned me to say, "Jet, I don't want to be a Strangler any more," I wasn't in the least surprised. In my subconscious I knew that his tether was wearing thin, and the minute he said it I didn't bat an eyelid. I said, "I understand, Hugh."'

Hugh then rang Dave, who was totally shocked. Hugh remembers that Dave's first reaction was: 'Does that mean that we're going to have a band meeting?' JJ was told last, and, in a long, emotional and tearful conversation, Hugh and JJ discussed their futures. Asked what was next for the band, Hugh remembers JJ replying, 'We always said we'd split up if one of us left.' It seemed like the Stranglers, one of the most successful and certainly the most controversial bands of their era, were finished.

According to one source, Sony were actually far from heart-broken at the news of Hugh's sharp exit. Marian Shepherd, who would later perform a sterling job running *Strangled* magazine, was working in the international A&R section of Epic at the time: 'The Managing Director at Epic, Andy Stephens, took great delight in breaking the news to me that Hugh had left the band. A few weeks later he came in with the Stranglers' recording contract and proudly showed me that the option clause for ''Drop'' had been circled. We all thought it was the end for the band.'

When asked about the events of August 1990, it's clear that the three original members of the line-up are still, to varying degrees, upset and bitter over Hugh's departure, or rather the manner of his leaving. For Jet, losing Hugh was like losing a comrade-in-arms. They had always got on well. But, in Jet's eyes, Hugh was turning into a very different person to the young eccentric he had met all those years ago in 1974. It was Hugh's personal rivalry with JJ which caused the split. Jet:

> It had been apparent to me for a year or two that Hugh was beginning to look old and to move and think like an old man, whereas at the beginning it was like 200 per cent enthusiasm and he was the funniest man I'd ever met. Over the years he was becoming less and less funny and less and less enthusiastic, and in the last couple of years his level of enthusiasm took a noticeable nose-dive. This coincided with the personality clashes with JJ. JJ and Hugh didn't see eye to eye, and JJ used to think of him as being a bit of a wimp. The reality was that he *was* a bit of a wimp, but was also nevertheless a very talented man, no doubt about that. But Hugh was finding it very difficult to spend five minutes in the same room as JJ, and I knew that, although nobody would admit it. I just felt he reached a point where he said, 'Well, this is it. I just can't go on with pretending to like somebody when I don't.' And he wasn't man enough to stand up and fight his corner when that might have been the sensible thing to do. He just upped and left. I think he'd had enough of this band and wanted to experiment with music on his own, and to try his hand at acting. I think he had around him a circle of friends who were saying, 'You've got the talent. You're finding it hard work. Why not go out on your own?'

Dave is now more succinct and terse about the events of 1990: 'Personally, I put the blame on Hugh.' In Dave's eyes, Hugh simply abandoned ship and, regardless of his motives, he was totally culpable. It was JJ who took Hugh's departure really to heart. It was, in a way, like losing a brother. Hugh might have fallen out of love with JJ, but JJ still had a lot of affection for

Hugh. In 1997, looking back on his relationship with Hugh, JJ had the following to say:

> I was in Hugh's shadow for quite a while. I looked up to him, and I respected him, *and I loved him*. But even from quite early on I started bringing songs into the band, and eventually journalists were starting to ask for my opinions as well as his. I had a look, and people liked that look, so he lost his monopoly on the band fairly early on. But he was my mentor – he taught me loads of things about modern music. I was relatively green and he was worldly and smart, and very quickly I created my own shadow. My solo albums sold more than his did, and that really pissed him off because he wanted to be more cutting edge than I was. I just did it, and it turned out that way, more by luck than design. I think Hugh always had more design. He planned things. Slowly I admired him less and less, and I think he lost touch. He was embarrassed by our fans. He wasn't hanging out with the Finchley Boys, he was hanging out with people from TV down the Groucho Club, which he still goes to today. If you deny the past, or the things that have given you strength, then that's wrong.

In the seven years since Hugh's departure JJ has tried to talk to his old sparring partner, but with no luck: 'Hans Wärmling died last year, so I did my usual trick and left a message on his [Hugh's] answerphone because, you know, the past is the past. But he never returns my calls. He's a total arsehole.'

Hugh's official statement on his reasons for leaving, as printed in *Sounds* that September, was either suitably diplomatic, or a cowardly fudge, depending on your point of view: 'We've just released what I think is one of the band's strongest albums – *10* – and the gig at Ally Pally was so good I thought, well, if I'm ever going to go, I should go now while I'm ahead.'

The truth, which Hugh knew only too well, was that he was not ahead. The Stranglers were not on an artistic or commercial high at all. Hence the band's annoyance at the timing of his departure. They felt Hugh was kicking them in the teeth just when they needed to launch a fight-back. But for Hugh, time was up: 'The final straw was being at that gig at Ally Pally and seeing this big expanse of space afterwards and nothing planned. Everything else I could deal with apart from JJ. To me it had burnt itself out, it really had. It was well past its sell-by date. We had one hit single from *10*, and that wasn't even a song we'd written. That does wonders for your writing confidence, I can tell you.'

In Hugh's eyes the Stranglers were a spent force creatively. Tired of the arguments, the incessant hassles, the touring, the boredom and the frustrations of the rock 'n' roll circus, he wanted a more varied artistic life which did not revolve around keeping up an increasingly untenable charade of rockiness. Hugh wasn't really comfortable as a rocker, and, at 41 years of age, he wanted to indulge his own interests in film, theatre and art, as well as make music on his own terms.

The three survivors of the original line-up accuse Hugh of premeditation, of having planned his escape for months in advance. He had already been writing with Roger Cook, ex-Blue Mink, a songwriter formerly based in Nashville hoping to re-establish himself back in England (he also created that seemingly omnipresent and insidious seventies MOR tune, 'I'd Like To Teach The World To Sing'). The speed with which Hugh moved after the ending of his Stranglers days to set up a writing and recording arrangement with Cook cast the latter as the malevolent outside force who broke up the internal 'harmony'. Jet:

> Hugh wouldn't stay another five minutes. He'd made a whole string of plans because he went straight into working on stuff he'd obviously been working on for months and months, and he wasn't going to be talked out of it. The only people who really resisted it were our managers, who could see that our record company would probably dump us because they always regarded Hugh as the Stranglers. Nobody ever knew the truth behind this band. Just because he was the lead singer, it didn't mean that he wrote all the songs. I thought the very least they could do was to talk him into staying with the band another six or nine months so that they could pull together some end-of-period deals like a last album or a greatest hits collection.

Hugh vehemently denies that he had some grand Machiavellian plan, that he'd planned a new career to the extent Jet and the lads thought. The truth is, though, that, although Hugh did not have any firm plans to write and record after his split, he had already started a songwriting partnership with Cook. But Hugh did not have the sort of head-start his ex-band-members accused him of having. He would beat them to the punch with his first post-split solo work by barely four months.

What strikes the outsider as the most peculiar aspect of the whole episode is that nobody, apart from managers Colin Johnson and Ron Brown, made any real effort to persuade Hugh to change his mind. Jet made a half-hearted attempt to keep Hugh in the line-up, thinking as ever about the commercial factor – a valedictory tour, perhaps, and a greatest hits album, with Hugh kept on board to see out the 'farewell' period. But nobody in the Stranglers entourage did the sensible thing, which would have been to offer Hugh a sabbatical.

Jet has often commented that one of Hugh's major weaknesses is his over-confidence. Hugh is a self-motivated person, who can easily psyche himself up for an artistic endeavour once he's made up his mind to follow the project through. But, according to Jet, this often made Hugh overestimate his own worth. The omens for a successful solo career were not good. In terms of records sold, JJ had fared considerably better than Hugh, and neither of his two solo albums *Nosferatu* and *Wolf* had been total artistic triumphs. If Hugh thought that he could simply tap into the Stranglers' fan-base and continue with the same level of success, then the portents were not exactly encouraging.

When Hugh left for a holiday in Japan in August 1990 the last thing he considered was that the band would brush themselves down, take a deep breath and carry on without him: 'I was quite shocked that they carried on because it showed they thought Hugh was replaceable, and I didn't think I was. They showed how much they cared about me leaving by carrying on. Everybody's replaceable. Even Hugh.'

And carry on they did. A new phase in the band's career was about to start.

'This really looks like the end of the road. The Stranglers without Hugh is like the Rolling Stones without Mick Jagger – finished.' So claimed an anonymous insider to Gill Pringle of the *Mirror* on 28 August. Indeed, the band did consider splitting in the late summer of 1990. Hugh's exit was a very high-risk strategy. Very few artists who have broken away from successful groups have ever made it solo, unless of course they happen to be the major (or only) songwriter in the band, like George Michael, who left Wham! in 1986, and Sting, who left the Police that same year. Genesis have seen both their lead singers, Peter Gabriel and Phil Collins, leave, and have endured nevertheless, whilst Pink Floyd, against all the odds, maintained their status as a huge stadium rock draw in the 1990s without Roger Waters. But the Waters parallel is telling. Despite his obvious talent, and despite being the dominant force in the group at the time of his departure in terms of songwriting, he has been unable to build anything approximating the success he had while part of the Floyd, whilst his old band has remained in the big league. Pop is littered with groups who have soldiered on beheaded, their lead singer and figurehead departed, and neither side enjoying the same level of success. The 80s band Marillion is a cautionary case in point. Although they never had the status of the Stranglers, by the mid 1980s their following was sizeable. But since the departure of lead singer Fish, both have been struggling to break the Top 20 for a decade. The lesson is that fans will often shirk bands which move away from their original blueprint and formation.

As professional musicians there was very little alternative for the Stranglers but to continue in some form or another. What else could they do if they called it a day? JJ was still only in his late 30s and thus relatively youthful compared to the seriously doddering rock circus, in which the likes of Cliff Richard terrorized the charts and Keith and Mick were still bashing out those sly, sloppy grooves on the Stones' tours. Dave had known nothing else but music since his teens, and Jet wasn't going to throw away a career he'd sacrificed everything for. Their first act was to make affable John Ellis a permanent Strangler. Indeed, there had already been talk of this as far back as the car journey to the Alexandra Palace gig, when JJ made this very suggestion to Jet. Ellis would give the band another writing source to tap in to. And, having worked with JJ before, he would know what to expect in terms of band life. JJ had this to say in 1996 about the reasons for carrying on:

> I think I was ready to finish the band, but we sort of talked
> ourselves into trying it out again, seeing if there was anything left
> to save. It took us a long time to re-group. We had to see if it was a
> viable proposition and if we were really a group, not just a bunch
> of blokes going through the motions. Then the sap was rising and

we thought, Hugh was doing less and less for this band, the band was less and less Hugh. People's opinion of the band was that there were *two* front men, myself and Hugh, which was fortunate.

The only real discussion was over whether the band should alter their name or not. JJ had, even before Hugh's departure, suggested they drop the 'L' and become 'The Strangers', on the basis that the band had altered so much since its new-wave inception that a name change would signal their new status. But Jet, who had spent 15 years trying to raise the band's profile, would have nothing of it. 'Stranglers 2', and 'More Stranglers' were non-starters too.

The main problem facing the band, however, was that, from the mid-1980s onwards, they had failed to keep abreast of pop fashion, or rather their brand of menacing macho pop had never really come back into vogue. The Indie scene was getting hip to dance grooves, while the Stranglers' music was, in the main, resolutely unfunky. Although their spokespersons have always taken pride in the Stranglers' devil-may-care and unmodish ways of working, the truth is that every album up to and including *Aural Sculpture* had at least sounded of its time, had been part of the pop mainstream (and in some cases had helped to define it). But from *Dreamtime* onwards, their music possessed a faintly anachronistic quality. Their significance in the pop scheme of things had been in decline (arguably) since *The Raven* album. The days of *Melody Maker* and *NME* front covers, of a high media profile, had long gone, despite their sizeable following. Hugh, as we have seen, was almost happy to be sidelined as a curio, a supercool songsmith. But the rest of the band weren't. They needed a relevance beyond their past exploits. Other figures from the new wave had made the transition into either critical respectability (Elvis Costello) or huge commercial success (Sting). So the task for the new Stranglers wasn't simply to replace what many considered to be the irreplaceable. It was to create a new buzz about a band which, in the eyes of the media, had everything to do with the past (the constant necrophilism of the press concerning punk hardly helped) and nothing to do with a pop present dominated by Madchester, Baggy and dance music.

The task of finding a replacement for Hugh was accomplished surprisingly quickly. Hugh himself considered it strange that the multi-talented Alex Gifford was not asked to join full-time, but he and the brass section would be dropped from future projects. The Stranglers did consider some big-name replacements, and there was talk of bringing in the Damned's Dave Vanian and Ian McNabb (ex-Icicle Works). But, in the end, only four singers were actually auditioned. The lead singer from the Scottish group the Bible, the singer from the seventies soft-rock group Medicine Head, Sil Willcox, the band's production manager and possessor of a fine voice himself, and a 30-year-old total unknown by the name of Paul Roberts.

Paul was born in Chiswick on the last day of the 1950s. Unlike JJ, Dave and John, Paul was a self-educated working-class London kid, streetwise, intuitive and cocky. His father, a Labour Party man, worked as a guard on London Transport trains. His mother was a housewife and mother to Paul's elder brother, younger sister and baby brother, who was born with a hole in his heart. From an early age, Paul was a creative, artistic person, whiling away the hours with his watercolours. But he felt all the attention was being lavished on his sick younger brother and his more academically-minded elder brother and soon developed an independent, rebellious streak. He was a gifted footballer and played for the Middlesex county team. As a child Paul was also interested in pop music, but never got off on chart material. His initial loves were King Crimson, the MC5, Alice Cooper, Led Zeppelin and Jimi Hendrix – 'stuff with an edge', as he now calls it. The only British icon Paul had any real interest in was David Bowie:

> Bowie made a massive impression on my life, no doubt about it. I was always thinking about my sexuality. I was a small, blond, blue-eyed guy and I used to get a lot of problems with that. I started wearing make-up when I was 13. I didn't know if I was gay or not, and I lost my best friend when I was 16 because I told him I thought I was gay. I really got off on dressing as a woman and I used to enjoy upsetting people at work by wearing socks up to my thighs. Something definitely happened to me round about that time which made me realize that I possibly wanted to be a woman, or wanted to be beautiful. Before Bowie men had to accept that they were men and had to hide behind shirts and suits and ties and cloth caps. I didn't want to do that. I could never be a bog-standard man. I enjoyed being mistaken for a woman.

Paul was around a generation younger than the rest of the Stranglers and had been influenced by the outrage of glam and punk during his teens. But he was also the one Strangler with an authentic street-level druggy past. By the end of his teens, Paul not only had a son, but also a drug habit which was escalating all the time:

> I started taking drugs when I was about 13, started drinking when I was 12. First of all I was smoking marijuana heavily, and within 18 months I was taking LSD. I started doing everything excessively. By the time I was 15 I was taking all sorts of things through needles. At that point I realized I wasn't going to be a professional footballer and I tried to get my parents to send me to art school after my mother had told the school that I wasn't capable of taking 'O' levels (thank you, Mum!). I was a registered drug addict by the time I was 16 and only really cleaned myself up when I was 21, by which time I'd had a child accidentally on purpose.

From the late 1970s onwards, Paul began putting bands together with his mates, starting off his musical career as a drummer. His early bands included The The (before Matt Johnson got round to calling his successful 80s band the same name), Who Shot Susan, and Alternative Rabies. Paul was looking to marry rock with dance music such as that of Sly & The Family Stone, and Funkadelic – or 'Hendrix Dance', as he christened it. In the 80s he also flirted with reggae, before ending up deputizing for a lead singer with a sore throat in a band called The Word.

In the late 1980s Paul worked with songwriter Nick Graham, whose song 'The Flame' had resurrected Cheap Trick's career in the States, and with the Mark Shaw-less Then Jerico. These various projects also foundered before reaching fruition. By 1990 Paul had still to break into the big-time, although his most recent band, Big Wheel, had come close to being signed by Dave Ambrose at London Records. Paul had made the acquaintance of Colin Johnson, unbeknownst to him part of the Stranglers' management team, and had invited him to a gig that August at the Mean Fiddler. Paul takes up the story:

> We played this gig at the Mean Fiddler and I asked Colin Johnson to be there but he didn't show up. Ironically he'd been put on the

support band's guest list but hadn't shown up. This was on a Sunday night, and on the Monday I had planned to see him to try and get a management deal. I had no idea that he was the Stranglers' manager. When I rang him up on the Monday morning he said, 'What do you do?' and I said, 'I'm phoning about my band to see if you're interested in managing us.' Then he said, 'Well I'm looking for a singer for the Stranglers.' I said, 'Has Hugh left the band?' I had no idea. Anyway, it turned out that this guy Colin Johnson had been supposed to be coming down to the Mean Fiddler to see our support band with a view to putting their lead singer into the Stranglers. But, through a twist of fate, he asked me to audition instead.

A flabbergasted Paul was in a curious position. He was in a band he truly believed in and so still felt duty-bound to push his own group with Colin Johnson. But on the other hand, the chance of auditioning for the Stranglers was too good to turn down. A meeting was arranged between Paul and JJ at a local restaurant. As ever, JJ came along in combative mood. It was time for the potential new recruit to be tested out. Paul remembers:

> He tried to vibe me out, but I'd been around too long for that. It's a very pseudo-intellectual thing, getting the better of an individual. As I walked into the restaurant the first thing I thought was, 'God, you look pale and fat!' He looked like someone who had muscles but they'd turned to flab. The first thing he did was throw me a copy of the all-hallowed *Strangled* magazine and say, 'Can you read?' I said, 'Can you write?' My initial impression of JJ was 'Who is this arrogant person?' The last thing you need is some bloke in your face when you're trying to replace an enigmatic front man. You just want a decent conversation with someone. So we're there, the two of us, in the corner of the restaurant, me with a white T-shirt on and hair down to me arse. And I said, 'I'll do the gig, man.' It was a really flippant answer. I said, 'I really love the band, I'll do it!'

Talking to *Sounds* on the subject of Paul's recruitment, JJ, with tongue firmly in cheek, said: 'First of all I tried psyching Paul out and discovered he had a bit of front. We tested him intellectually to see if he could think and obviously checked his voice. In the end, I liked the ideas he came up with for songs, and then one day we gave him a good kicking – which was the initiation ceremony. After that he had to felch me, which is licking my bottom after I'd had a curry.'

For Paul, this was indeed *the* dream gig. The Stranglers were his band. JJ gave Paul a cassette of music and asked him to go away and write some lyrics. The next stage was to meet the band's elder statesman, Jet, who, one suspects, would have the ultimate say in any hiring and firing of new recruits. Jet was immediately impressed, and suggested that Paul spend a week rehearsing with the band in the Nomis recording studios. Paul's very uncool, almost ankle-length blond mane did however cause JJ a certain amount of consternation, and Paul was ordered to shave his head – a directive he refused to comply with, although he did compromise by lopping at least half of it off.

It was clear to the band after the initial vocal test that they had almost certainly found their man. Paul:

> We rehearsed for four days before they auditioned the other singers. These guys were heroes of mine. JJ, for example, was a bass-playing hero of mine when I was a kid. Lots of kids would never have picked up a bass guitar had it not been for JJ. When I walked into the rehearsal room, Jet was leaning on the drums, which is quite an awesome sight. All at once I was hit with this band that I used to put money in juke-boxes to listen to, and whose records I bought, and who I went to see. I wasn't particularly impressed with the music they were doing at the time, though, and I remember thinking *10* was dreadful. There wasn't that much music after *The Raven* which was great, although I did like 'Golden Brown'. Actually I remember doing 'Golden Brown' in that first rehearsal and saying, 'You're playing that bit wrong, it doesn't go like that!'

Not only did Paul know all the songs, but his vocal at times sounded uncannily like Hugh's. Paul was adept at dropping in and out of other vocal styles too. What's more, he was young, enthusiastic, and a showman. The band had grown increasingly dissatisfied with Hugh's rather static stage persona. Paul, on the other hand, was more in the rock tradition, a mixture of punk's Jimmy Pursey and the Godfather of new-wave, Iggy Pop. He was lithe, loose and angular, and a completely different sort of singer to Hugh. Whereas Hugh was most un-rock 'n' rolly, Paul's performances mined rock legend. Many fans revelled in the band's new energy and loved the power-house performances of a singer who mirrored the potency of the material and who lived the words he sang on stage. Others baulked at Paul's (over)enthusiasm, mourning the nuanced sinister presence of a man who didn't have to *try* to achieve stage presence.

It was the trick of impersonation which marked Paul out from Hugh. For Paul was a singer-fan. Rather than create a distinctive stage persona for himself, Paul at times seemed merely to parody existing performance styles, whether it be Iggy or Bowie, or Jimmy Pursey or Hugh Cornwell. His performance was a brilliant high-speed display, but the effect was often curious; the new Strangler was almost like a rock-star impersonator who played at being an 'authentic rocker', right down to the cool shades, tambourine, and bare-chested playfulness. If they'd lost the 'real thing' with Hugh, they'd gained a jack-the-lad whose forte was the way he played around with iconography. Paul was a rock ironist, a ventriloquist, producing and recombining the stage acts and sounds of others and forming one parodic whole.

Paul was also a much more upbeat person than the often morose and cynical Hugh. Paul was open and forthcoming about himself, his opinions and others. He was a chatterbox and liked playing the fool. But this was just on the surface. Deep down he was sympathetic to others and thirsty for knowledge. Like Jet, Paul is an autodidact. What he lost in formal education he has more than made up for since. From the outset Paul was temperamentally closer to Jet, and especially John, than to JJ and Dave. Like John Ellis, Paul was not afflicted by the rock-star double-speak used at times by the rest of the band. Like John, he had never really tasted major league success, and hadn't had his personality formed in the cosseted environment of the rock world. He hated the bullshit and double standards he saw in operation. And yet, paradoxically, the Stranglers became a more rock-dominated band with Paul as leader, the material more guitar-dominated, and the beginnings of a more rhythmic, groove-based sound. With Paul the band lost any arty pretensions and became a fully-fledged rock band, if with an ironic edge.

Paul was confirmed as the new Strangler in November 1990: 'I remember the phone call came from Colin Johnson one Friday and I was elated. I just ran round my house saying, "Yes! Yes! Yes!" After all these years I could stop pissing around with part-time work. I suddenly realized I was going to get paid and that I was going to be with a band with a great following, a great history and a lot of integrity.

In amongst the feelings of elation, there were nagging doubts about his newly won position as a Strangler: 'Because of the band's past reputation, I was a bit concerned about being labelled a woman-hater. This did start to affect me a little way into things.'

An announcement was scheduled for January 1991. Over the Christmas period the band signalled to the media that they hadn't bit the dust by performing on Channel 4's *The Word*, with JJ on lead vocals. With a new line-up now finalized, it was time to slowly feel their way back into the scheme of things with some low-key dates and some writing and recording. After five years of stasis the band was alive again.

Paul's settling-in period was brutally short. A 17-date tour was arranged for February and March 1991, and 36 songs were rehearsed in two weeks. The band already had some strong material waiting to be recorded, including the excellent 'Wet Afternoon', an old-style piece of quirky Stranglers stuff, and a big rock ballad brought in by John Ellis, 'Heaven Or Hell'.

The Stranglers unveiled their new line-up at the Rodon Club in Greece on 22 February 1991, six months after Hugh had quit. Paul soon got a taste of what to expect from those who still held a candle for the old band: 'After the first night the promoter told me over dinner I was crap,' remembers Paul.

From this lowest of low-key starts the band hit the UK for a small club tour. For Jet, Dave and JJ, it was, as the old John Lennon song went, just like starting over. From the Ally Pally to the Town & Country in six months. JJ: 'People said, "Don't you feel degraded playing pubs?" and I said, "We're not worth anything anymore, we have no value. If you're talking in commercial terms, then we've got it all to prove again."'

But the response from a fan-base keen to show their loyalty was positive. Paul:

You could get them on your side if you sang the right songs. So we put the message out straight away that even though the line-up had changed, it was still their band, by opening with 'No More Heroes' and 'Threatened'. Most nights, within the first verse of 'Heroes' we had the audience, and I think they were over-whelmed anyway because it was the first time they'd seen the band that close. Every club was sold out and packed to the hilt. We were doing places like the Boardwalk in Manchester that were holding 450 people and we had 750 people in there. Peter Hook of New Order was there that night and he voted us the best new band of 1991 in the *NME*!

The addition of Paul Roberts meant that the Stranglers now had a showman amongst their number. Technically, he was a fine singer, possessed with a deep, growly vibrato – an Iggy Pop/David Bowie super-hybrid. The Stranglers were now much closer to their new-wave roots. Gone was the sophistication of the late 80s, Hugh-era Stranglers, and in its place was the sort of hard-rocking, no-frills, hi-energy band that JJ, one suspects, had wanted all along. But the critics noticed that, although the band looked as if they'd been given a transfusion of new blood, Paul was simply trying too hard to make an impression, where his predecessor didn't have to try at all. Reviewing their Brixton Academy gig in June 1991, Dave Jennings wrote in *Melody Maker*: 'They're doing their damndest – and at the start they're embarrassing. They *sound* fine, opening with a storming stomp through "Five Minutes". But new lead singer Paul Roberts is making an utter prat of himself, striking ludicrous Freddie Mercury poses with the mikestand. Thankfully, he soon calms down, but it's still clear that The Stranglers' infamous machismo has been redoubled by the upheavals.'

The first few months of 1991 were a time of optimism as well as nervousness about the future. Dave, Jet and JJ felt as if they had recovered from a five-year spell in the doldrums and John and Paul were brimming with enthusiasm. The new greatest hits package, which had been released the previous autumn, had defied all expectations by reaching Number 4 and becoming the band's biggest-selling album since *Rattus Norvegicus* thirteen years earlier. In June 1991, the band were asked by the French government to play at the Palais Royal in Paris for their French National Music Day on 21 June (a UK equivalent, masterminded by Mick Jagger and Harvey Goldsmith in the nineties failed to catch on). After the gig, the band were fêted by French ministers and dignitaries. From the horrors of the Nice jail to a slap-up five-star red-carpet treatment in just over a decade. The band's profile had indeed changed. But elsewhere all was not well. The first indications of a mutiny in the ranks of Stranglers fans were felt when the management received a number of threatening letters directed against Paul. At one stage they took the hate-mail so seriously that special protection was arranged for Paul at gigs. At one venue on that first club tour in 1991, the hecklers were very vocal in their support for Hugh. Paul: 'I had one bad night at Goldmans in Birmingham when I was almost involved in a punch-up with some guys in the audience. There were about ten blokes in front of me chanting Hugh's name. First of all I took it as a joke, but then it really got to me. I just went off the mic and said, "Why don't you fuck off then?" and I really wanted to take one of them out. JJ was quick to kick me up the arse, which I appreciated.'

Rather as expected, Sony/EMI did not take up their option on the band. A Hugh-less Stranglers was, for them, an unsaleable commodity. For the first time since December 1976, the band were without a label. Their solution was to invest heavily in a label of their own, Psycho, a subsidiary of China Records. As the band gathered to record their first post-Cornwell album in the spring of 1992, they knew that they had everything to prove.

11: OLD DOGS,
NEW TRICKS

At a time when any band as long-lived as the Stranglers would
have been entering their dotage, taking the stage as venerables of
a bygone era like a smaller-scale Who or Rolling Stones, the
Stranglers seemed to be entering a second childhood. This was
partly through necessity rather than design. Even when Hugh
was in the band, the Stranglers had never had the critical or
commercial respect some of their music deserved. Rock acts with
the puniest of back-catalogues were being lauded in the pages of
the monthly music glossies, but the Stranglers were conspicuous
by their absence. They were stigmatized as ruffian outsiders,
desperately macho and unhip in a period before *Fever Pitch*-style
'New Laddism' came into vogue in the mid-90s. And even when
the times seemed more propitious in the climate of post-Hornby
thirty-something male angst, still the Stranglers remained out of
bounds. All this despite a string of 21 Top 40 hits.

Paul in particular was enjoying his first few months in the
limelight. With his shoulder-length shock of blond hair, dark
shades, drainpipe trousers and athletic look, he cut a very different
figure from Hugh's Lothario. The band could still count on some big
name personalities for those important photo opportunities. Hearing that England full-back Stuart Pearce, or Psycho as his friends call
him, was an ardent fan, playing their music before matches to get
the adrenalin flowing, JJ and Paul were duly dispatched by the
management to meet the epitome of footballing 'all-out commitment': the no-frills punk-obsessed man of action. Paul:

> I interviewed him for *Strangled* and he was a really good bloke. He
> showed us round the City Ground, and when we played in
> Nottingham we met up with some of the Forest players. Although
> it has to be said that he and his mates trashed our dressing-room at
> Leicester De Montfort Hall one night. I think it was because I asked
> him the burning question: 'Was that "back pass" which led to San

Marino taking the lead in the World Cup qualifier a deliberate
attempt to get Graham Taylor the sack?

Paul Roberts and John Ellis had completely changed the band
dynamic, and as the 90s wore on it would be these two new
recruits who would be its most active contributors. JJ emerged as
something of a lion in winter: the addition of a bona fide lead
vocalist made him withdraw from any lead vocals on vinyl, and
even in concert the sight of him breathing his best Froggy all over
'European Female' is the rarest of birds. So, not only did
Stranglers fans have to deal with the loss of Hugh, they had to
live without JJ's voice as well. The band that emerged on their
autumn 1992 release *Stranglers In The Night* was a very different
beast from the outfit which made *10*.

The chief thing to say about the first post-Hugh outing is that it
is far and away superior to almost all of *10* (save '96 Tears' and a
couple of others) and most of *Dreamtime* (save the glorious
'Always The Sun' and a few other gems). The songs have a
new life, a new design about them, and Paul's vocal is recorded
with clarity by a re-called Mike Kemp. The opener, 'Time To Die',
with its mock-portentous lyrics (a parody of *Blade Runner*), a
brilliant Shadows-style guitar riff and sweeping synth line, is
undoubtedly classic Stranglers. It also evidences JJ's continued
knack of coming up with excellent, well-structured, almost neo-
symphonic pieces of melody. 'Heaven Or Hell' is one of those
anthemic Stranglers' songs which really powers home. 'Wet
Afternoon' is possibly the best track on the album. A jokey
description of a seance, it's in the classic mould of British pop
suburban angst, dealing as it does with the extraordinary behind
the mundanity of everyday life.

There are some real surprises too: 'Grand Canyon', a John Ellis
lyric about social and racial inequality, is the first ever Stranglers
song to attempt straightforward social reportage. Under the influence of John Ellis and Paul Roberts, the Stranglers would become a
more demotic, grass-roots group, less blind to social realities:

> I've been standing on the poor man's side
> Looking across the great divide
> At the people with the money
> But they never look across at me.

'This Town' is a gay-pride anthem, the sort of song which would have been unthinkable in the old days of the Stranglers. Not that any of them were homophobes; it was just that social and political comment was largely off the agenda, save for a few wry comments on political situations in far-off places such as the USA and Australia:

> And I don't give a damn
> Whatever anyone might say
> And it's not gonna be
> A love that dare not speak its name

'Southern Mountains' has a lovely rolling instrumental backing, and 'Leave It To The Dogs', although corny and clichéd lyrically, is as affecting a piece of music as the Stranglers had written for a decade, and a precursor to the classic Britpop ballads by Blur such as 'This Is A Low' or 'The Universal'.

Some of the other material was less successful however: 'Sugar Bullets' is a serviceable rocker, but elsewhere, when the band try to change gear, they often do so with little spark. 'Laughing At The Rain', 'Brain Box', 'Never See' and the parodic piece of Americana, 'Gain Entry To Your Soul', sung by Paul as high-school spotty to his amour, show up their limitations. What was more worrying was that, for the first time in their career, the Stranglers had, for whatever reason, become 'Yankified'. Paul's vocal accentuation and John Ellis' guitar runs had the twang of middle America. Whereas before, the Stranglers had possessed a cosmopolitan swagger, a European melodic touch, now they were starting to sound in places like an American arena rock act. It was this that tarnished what might have been a very successful comeback album.

Paul also found some of John Ellis' songwriting contributions unnecessarily doleful: 'I think "Leave It To The Dogs" is a good song, but it's almost like a Lionel Bart kind of thing. John used to write a lot of songs in D minor and they all felt rather negative. They were always clever/sad, not like a good ballad.'

The other emerging feature of the new Stranglers was their unashamed poppiness. There were no 'difficult' tracks on *In The Night*. This was melodic pop, well-crafted, excellent in parts, but anachronistic and middle-of-the-road in others. Mat Snow, in his three-star *Q* review, was suitably cordial about the album and the new line-up:

> Few groups survive the departure of a long-standing front-man, never mind thrive, so it will be more with trepidation than expectation that Stranglers fans will greet the band's first album, happily entitled *Stranglers In The Night*, since the replacement of Hugh Cornwell by guitarist John Ellis and singer Paul Roberts. They do not pale in comparison, the former echoing the Bunnyman's Will Sergeant while the latter offers two kinds of fruitiness: distinct echoes of Julian Cope and Erasure's Andy Bell. Moreover, at a juncture more likely to break the band than propel them to new heights, they have responded with an album of such quality as to shame old fans who might desert and quite possibly attract a few new ones with an accessible blend of various post-punk psychedelic styles.

A prerequisite for the Stranglers' comeback was a hit single. It had been two-and-a-half years since '96 Tears' had skirted the Top 20 and almost eight since the last Stranglers-penned single had reached the Top 20. In 'Heaven Or Hell', the Stranglers team thought they had a winner. But it disappointingly failed to break into the Top 40, stalling at Number 46. This was not a disaster – Stranglers singles had disappointed before and some had fared worse – but bad enough to give everyone the jitters about the new album's prospects. In the end, *Stranglers In The Night* spent just one week on the album chart that September, reaching a creditable, though underachieving, Number 33. This wasn't the stuff of great commercial comebacks, and Paul, for one, was disheartened. He had underestimated how Hugh's defection would affect the public perception of the band:

> Up until that point I thought everything would go reasonably smoothly. I always thought the Stranglers were more than one man. In fact, I remember when I was in my teens thinking that the Stranglers were a French band, that's how strong JJ's influence was. So I never really considered it to be a problem for the band and I thought we'd have more success. We didn't, and I was very, very disappointed. I was disappointed mainly because I didn't have the control over the album I wanted.

Looking back on the *In The Night* album, some of the band are dissatisfied with Mike Kemp's production. Paul in particular felt at times peripheral. Some of the songs had been written before he joined the band, and he was disappointed with the overall sound, and Kemp's painstaking approach with regard to his vocal:

> I should have kicked the producer up the arse, occasionally. I should have said, 'Hey listen man, I don't fucking care about what you say about what I've done. I want to do it like this and I think it's right.' And it was a mistake to use a computer Cuebase to put an album together when we're a rock 'n' roll band. I was a new boy and I couldn't believe that we were using someone with no track record to do a very important album. I didn't think it was my place to say anything but I thought we would have been much better off using someone well-known. He hadn't had his hands-on since *Dreamtime* in 1986. If we'd have used someone like Stephen Hague then it would have been awesome.

John Ellis, who had originated the majority of the songs with JJ, was also displeased with the sound of the album:

> The trouble with Mike Kemp was that he hadn't produced anything for a very long time. I don't like the album very much. I don't like the sound of it. I think the songs are very good, but it wasn't a good mix. For example, 'Grand Canyon' didn't turn out as well as it should have done. That was one of my songs and I did a fantastic demo with another singer. I don't think any of the songs reached their full potential. That album could have been 100 per cent better if it had been re-mixed.

Conversely, Jet was well pleased with it ('pretty damn good' was his comment in 1996), and liked Mike Kemp's work. In truth, it is a solid production, nuanced and intricate, but unsuited to the more rock-oriented numbers (which turned out to be the least successful in any case). The problem was that the band was moving towards a more full-out-rock 'live' sound, and saw Kemp's more state-of-the-art approach as unnecessarily fussy.

Despite the moderate success of their album and single (the album would go on to sell a modest 40,000 copies worldwide), the band were still doing well on the live circuit and, more importantly, were beginning to get some belated success on the Continent, particularly in Germany.

Life on the road was still not without its little problems. An incident at a gig at the Brixton Academy in 1991 lingered long in Paul's memory:

It was a bad night. My monitoring was crap and I was a little flat in places. We'd done about nine gigs in a row, and I think someone was staring at JJ all night saying, 'It's not the same without Hugh, it's not the fuckin' same without Hugh.' And then JJ kicks me in the head because he was so frustrated with the audience! I think it was just a moment of madness, but I didn't forgive him for a long time. In the end JJ went to the mic and said, 'There's been someone standing in front of me all night saying, "It's not the same without Hugh . . ." Of course it's not the fuckin' same without Hugh, you fuckin' idiot. If you don't like it, fuck off!'

Jet, now well into his fifties, endured not one but two periods of incapacitation. At a Kilburn gig a stage light had by accident been put too near the plastic back screen projection of the *In The Night* cover, and potentially deadly cyanide gas was blown through Jet's fan straight into his face. At the end of the gig he felt a bit unwell, but after a few beers and a sandwich he thought no more of it. But back at the hotel, disaster struck. His breathing became laboured and he became weaker and weaker.

I ended up feeling worse and worse. I'm an asthma sufferer anyway, and I was puffing away on this Ventalin inhaler but I wasn't feeling any better. I started to feel a temperature coming on. Some time in the middle of the night I started to feel paralyzed. I couldn't even get off the bed to get help! I wanted to get to the phone to get some help and I couldn't even reach the phone. Before I knew where I was it was 9 a.m., and eventually I got the strength to get off the bed. I managed to lie next to the phone and wait for it to ring, which it would have to do as our tour manager, Bill Tuckey, would be ringing to tell us we were leaving. When eventually the phone rang I made an enormous effort to pick it up and mumbled something like, 'I'm dying!' I was having serious difficulties even speaking too and I think the tour manager either thought I was taking the piss or I was still pissed from the night before.

Jet was rushed straight to hospital, where his lungs were pumped out and various chemicals pumped in. Ever the trouper, Jet rejoined the group that night for the gig in Cambridge, and then a few days later travelled over with them to play at the Nachtwerk in Munich. However, by this stage, he was ill and weak. At a club gig in France the audience were even asked not to smoke (which, amazingly, they complied with), so weak was Jet's condition. To make matters worse, Paul now had the flu. In the end Jet collapsed and had to be flown back to London. His place was taken by Rat Scabies of the Damned before more shows had to be cancelled due to Paul's illness. Jet made a full recovery, but his condition sent alarm bells ringing: 'Everybody thought I was dying of old age and most of the band didn't attribute any significance to the incident at Kilburn, but I'd been desperately ill. I had a bit of time off, but the rest of the band were paranoid about doing another gig with me and so they got a mate of Paul's, Tim Bruce, rehearsed up in case I died on them! But he wasn't called upon in the end, I just got better.'

Then hardly had Jet got himself healthy again when further calamity struck. This time it was nothing so rock'n'rolly romantic as cyanide inhalation during a gig, but a surprisingly painful tug-of-war with a mysterious object in the garden: 'I was tidying up in the long grass one summer's day. I grabbed hold of something and thought I'd pick it up and pop it on my wheelbarrow. I went to pull it and it didn't come, so I gave it a big tug, not knowing it was a great big cast-iron thingy, and I put out a disk in my back quite seriously.'

Jet was to endure a year of pain while specialists, chiropractors, acupuncturists and purveyors of 'alternative' medicine all wrestled with his back. For his part, Jet spent most of his time trying to ease the excruciating pain, either by lying on his stomach, or walking about. He was advised not to drum, so for the majority of gigs in 1993, his place was taken either by the already genned-up Tim Bruce or a Japanese drummer called Keith Tobe. However, he still toured with the band (but didn't play drums), and actually appeared on stage, as a singer for the first time since 1975, when he had growled his way through Telly Savalas' 'If', singing 'Old Codger' to an ecstatic audience. At least they knew he was still around.

This wasn't the first time he had been ill during his time with the Stranglers. In 1987 his place had to be taken by Robert Williams after he had fallen ill with shingles in the States. These two serious health problems started to try the patience of some of the band, and the thought crossed everyone's mind that Jet was not up to the rigours of touring and might have to be pensioned off. But neither Jet, nor the band, were ready for the knacker's yard just yet. By 1993 they had a new record label, a new management team and a new direction.

If the Stranglers' new line-up was suffering some teething problems, then their ex-lead singer Hugh Cornwell was having it far worse. Before leaving the Stranglers, Hugh had been writing songs with Roger Cook with a view to getting them recorded by other artists, as Cook had a reputation for providing hit material for other singers. There being no takers, Hugh resolved to record the material with Cook and a local musician and songwriter from Bath called Andy West. The result was his first post-Stranglers album, and a most odd thing it was too. CCW (Cook, Cornwell and West) was a mixture of country, folk and melodic MOR, as different from the Stranglers as one could imagine. The idea was to form a kind of nineties version of Crosby, Stills and Nash, hence the title of the band, but the whole project lacked any real spice. The marketing was a disaster, the album wasn't promoted and wasn't even given a release outside of the UK (even in Britain it was given a limited-edition release only). By indulging in some low-key frivolity with his mates, Cornwell had sent exactly the wrong type of message to future managers, promoters and record labels – that he'd gone into a kind of semi-retirement.

The first positive decision Hugh made, nearly two years after leaving the band, was to re-employ Ian Grant as his manager. Grant had unsuccessfully attempted to manage the Stranglers again in 1988. According to Grant, his offer was accepted by all the members except Hugh, although Jet vehemently denies this, saying, 'No way did everyone want Grant and he wasn't even considered by me.' Grant now thinks the reason for this was that Hugh had it in mind to split in 1988 and wanted Grant to manage his solo career.

Either way, Grant, who was by now Big Country's manager after a productive time with the Cult, was back in the frame. But he had a desperately hard task rebuilding confidence in Cornwell after the CCW album: 'No one wanted to know. Period. Except Dave Robinson. Muff Winwood, who'd had them at Sony, said, "You put them back together and I'll sign them tomorrow, but Hugh on his own? No way!" He did a lot of damage by doing that CCW album. There was no A & R, no producer, no one overseeing it and it wasn't what people expected. Everybody thought he'd lost it. The follow-up album, *Wired*, was a love album, and on stage he was crooning on a stool!'

The main problem for Hugh was that all the time he was trying to concentrate his efforts on writing and recording solo material, his manager was working behind the scenes to get him back into the Stranglers. Hugh was supporting Big Country at the Corn Exchange in Cambridge in 1992, and JJ came along to check out the 'opposition'. Grant arranged for the two to meet. JJ: 'I saw Hugh backstage and it was very embarrassing because Hugh hugged me and he'd never done that before in 20 years. Normally I'm the hugging kind, but somehow it wasn't right.'

Ian Grant:

My idea was to get Hugh to rejoin them, because I still feel they're not the same band and that he won't do it without them. Unfortunately, in pop you're always remembered for what you do first. I always wanted them to make *Rattus Part 2* – the Stranglers album which should have been made in the 90s. He should have rejoined the Stranglers, and he was up for it, but JJ intimidated him. When we were standing in the corridor at the Corn Exchange JJ was banging the wall all the time with his fist as he was talking to Hugh. Now that might have been totally innocent, but it made Hugh feel really uncomfortable.

Ian Grant was even contacted by the Stranglers' manager, Colin Johnson, asking whether Hugh would still write for the band, even if he didn't rejoin! By the end of 1992 there were definite moves to break up the new line-up and to restore Hugh. How far this ever got is open to conjecture, and the extent to which the band were aware of it is uncertain. Hugh himself is adamant that he was never 'up for it', to quote his manager Ian Grant and wasn't ready to rejoin the band at all. But Paul does remember JJ telling him about an idea for a concert where Hugh would perform with the band for one half and Paul would play the other half of the gig, as if to show the audience that Hugh was passing the baton on to Paul. Dave remembers that 'at some point' the Stranglers' management approached Hugh to do a reunion concert, but that 'the time wasn't right' or 'Hugh was busy'. For Hugh, the question of rejoining was, in effect, a non-starter: 'How can I rejoin a band who haven't split up?' he told Ian Grant. But, of course, a band doesn't have to split up for someone to rejoin.

If the moves by the respective managements to re-employ him in some sort of capacity weren't unnerving enough, 1993 saw yet another commercial disaster for Hugh. His album *Wired* was to be released in the UK and France only, and promotion of it stopped in the week of release because of a contractual wrangle between Hugh's label Transmission, and Phoenix, run by ex-Stiff's Dave Robinson. Robinson footed the bill for work to start on the album but midway through recording his company had gone bust. On the release of the album, Robinson brought out an injunction claiming that he owned the rights to it and that Cornwell had broken his contract by recording with another label. The injunction severely affected distribution and promotion. One track, 'The Story Of He And She', was picking up air-play on Virgin FM, but ended up as a single only in France.

On *Wired* Hugh had dabbled in ballad and funk material but the production was lightweight and the songs, for Hugh, very substandard. The material and the backing sounded very dated. Only 'Hot Cat On A Tin Roof' had that earthy push and its countdown 'ignition-sequence starting' intro was later echoed by Barry Adamson on his excellent 'Set The Control For The Heart Of The Pelvis' three years later. But the strangest thing was that his songwriting seemed muted and subdued. He wrote and sang of love and relationships, and this struck longtime Hugh-watchers as odd and unconvincing. Hugh had always been associated with taboo-breaking and outrage, not with the subtleties of romance.

He was trying to move away from his Stranglers image and present a more nuanced performance: 'I didn't really want to play guitar any more. I thought it would be nice to just write something and sing on the *Wired* album. I got two guitarists to play lead for me. At the time I thought the album was quite well done, but in retrospect I don't like it much.'

Wired was not well received by the press. *Q*'s Andrew Martin gave it a lukewarm two-star review: '. . . a determinedly commercial affair with lots of bustling, vaguely danceable beats and big, oft-repeated, not to say flogged to death choruses. It reveals a new, questing and vulnerable Cornwell who – in songs like the mellow ballad "Love In Your Eyes" – occasionally verges on the sensitive.'

It was after the release of *Wired* that Ian Grant once again decided to call a halt to proceedings. Grant was by now disillusioned, his attempts to rekindle some sort of liaison with the Stranglers stymied and, with the *Wired* release a shambles, horrified by the lack of interest in Hugh as a live act: 'We toured France and we toured England and it was disgraceful. We were playing to 50 people. I couldn't get Hugh a record deal. No one was really interested at all.'

Indeed, attendance at the shows was often derisory, and of the few in the audience, many would be calling for old Stranglers favourites, while Hugh was striving to create a new, distinctive vibe about his music. In the end Hugh would bow to public pressure and play a few Stranglers numbers, such as 'Strange Little Girl', 'Golden Brown' and a re-worked and extended version of 'Grip'. But the going couldn't have been tougher. Hugh was frustrated, but put the poor attendances at gigs down to the promotional shambles that were the campaigns behind his two post-Stranglers projects. Hugh still had not had an international release with a proper promotional budget. And it was that goal that he would devote himself to in the years to come.

In Ian Grant's estimation, Hugh needed the Stranglers and the Stranglers needed Hugh. Neither could function properly without each other and, in this, Grant's views accorded with those of many fans and critics. As with the ending of his Stranglers managership in 1980, the manner of Ian's departure from the scene was once again inconclusive and, according to Hugh, something of a farce:

All the time he was managing me he was trying to get a re-formed Stranglers back together. After the debacle with *Wired* he couldn't handle things and fired himself. He resigned again! He told me it was giving him sleepless nights and stress and stuff. So he left and I got together with David Harper, who was the manager of UB40 and Robert Palmer. The next thing Ian is on the phone and he says, 'Why are you with David Harper?' and I said, 'Well, because you resigned.' And he said, 'No I didn't!' I thought to myself, I can't believe I'm hearing this! So I made a few phone calls and spoke to a few people and they all confirmed that Ian had actually said he had resigned.

The David Harper stewardship was not long-lived. According to Hugh, Harper had all the best intentions, but was often impossible to get hold of and was simply too busy to devote the time needed to get Hugh's career back on track. Then, in 1995, Hugh was put in touch through his lawyer, Alexis Grower, with an old acquaintance, David Fagence, who had been one of the first ever Stranglers fans and who had run the local record shop down in Guildford in the mid-1970s. Fagence, who at the time was managing the Orb, became Hugh's third manager, and it was with renewed confidence that Hugh set about working on new material.

The Stranglers were working on new material of their own. In fact, they had been in the same grotty dungeon of a rehearsal room in south London, just across from London Bridge, on and off for almost a year, and they were beginning to get right up each other's noses. They were, however, learning to write and record together again. The new line-up was learning to be a band, demoing material, playing it live, testing the water, then re-writing. The new Stranglers were forming. Whereas *In The Night* had been started before Paul joined the band, their next album, *About Time*, would be the first release from the Hugh-less band which showcased the new writing team of JJ, Paul and John.

Marooning five often extremely temperamental individuals in Southwark Street Studios, which was originally a debtors' prison, was the collective bright idea of the band's new management team Sil Willcox and Trevor Long who, according to *SPL* magazine, were the Morecambe and Wise of pop management. Sil Willcox had already been working for the band for nearly 15 years, initially as a member of the road crew, and latterly as production manager. He knew the band inside out and was the perfect choice. In fact, he'd been given his first band-related job by Hugh, and lived only a few minutes' drive away from the ex-Strangler in the West Country. It was do-or-die time for a band whose career was undoubtedly in the doldrums, at least commercially, if not creatively. Willcox remembers:

I thought I'd better make a decision here, so I went into JJ's office and said that I wanted to take the band over. He looked really surprised. But I gave him the reasons why: 'I know exactly where you're coming from and what the punters want, which the current managers don't.' Obviously I knew that my job was on the line anyway, so I thought I may as well get in there first. So we arranged a band meeting, I put over my ideas and they all said, 'Let's go for it.'

Willcox was also a sound choice because he was extremely good at making money. In the 1980s he had the idea of marketing Christmas crackers with actual games in them (not the usual tacky Yuletide crap) using TV quiz shows such as *A Question of Sport*, *The Generation Game* and *Telly Addicts* as their basis, and adapting them for home entertainment. It was an idea which brought in tens of thousands.

Top of Willcox's list of priorities with the Stranglers was to tell the band not to release any more records on their own label. Their finances were already in such a straitened state that they could not afford any more commercial failures. Also, they needed new ideas in promotional terms, stories for them to approach the press with. So in 1994 they embarked on the *V* tour, signalling to their audience that they were now five, not four. But Willcox knew that he needed somebody else in the 'steering committee' to help him create more distance between the management side and the band. That someone was Trevor Long: 'Trevor and I first met up when he was working for China Crisis and I was in the support band Big Square. We were hard-up musos and he screwed me for £50. I called him a bastard for years and that's what made me think he would be a good partner.'

Long had made his mark early in his career with bands such as Duran Duran and Dexy's Midnight Runners, and had also managed Haircut 100 and the Fall. After Long had done such a good job as tour manager on the Stranglers' 1993 live outings, Willcox called him for a crisis conference in his room at the Adelphi Hotel in Liverpool and put the idea to him that they should approach the band with a view to managing them. This was, of course, a high-risk strategy, as Willcox had no previous experience in band management, and, as a confidant of the band, knew that it might be difficult to say 'no' to a bunch of mates when the next crazy unworkable scheme came up (which it was surely bound to do). Long, however, a lovable Brummie rogue but a good man to have on your side, was a past master at haggling. He knew perfectly well that temperamental stars had to be told off from time to time. They were a good partnership: Willcox, the band man, a talented musician in his own right (he had come second to Paul Roberts in the vocal test to replace Hugh!) and Trevor, the businessman. So Sil and Trevor, 'good cop, bad cop', became the next in the long line of managerial partnerships to tackle one of the most notoriously shirty bands in rock history. Mainstreet Management, as they called themselves, took over at a very tricky time, as Trevor Long remembers: 'It had been a long time since the band had had any real fun. As a unit, back in 1993, when I was touring with them, they were despondent, like a ship without a captain. They needed direction.'

The Stranglers had grown extremely disillusioned with previous managers Colin Johnson and Ron Brown. Today, they are forthright in their condemnation. Paul too, was angry at the way they treated the band's affairs: 'They probably would have been fine with the band twenty years ago, but I think they were scared of the band, which doesn't help. In the end things started going amiss.'

Indeed, the major problem for Johnson and Brown, or 'The Rons' as they inexplicably became known as, was in trying to manage what was by now a non-original line-up. Trevor Long: 'You must remember that when you have an original band it's very rare for people to say no. But when you've got a non-original band, then it's virtually a new band and you have to start from scratch. And that's what management's all about. That's when you have to get your thinking cap on and start getting it bloody right.'

Within a year the five Stranglers had gelled into a tight live unit, powerful and hard-rocking, playing small auditoria and clubs. It wasn't big-league by any means, and the band's set became punchier and less arty as a result, although their first gig with Long and Willcox was a support slot (or 'special guests' slot, as it was euphemistically called) at Wembley Arena in March 1994 with the Kinks, a hugely successful night which virtually financed the rehearsal and recording of the *About Time* record. Willcox: 'Most managers' first gig is usually the local pub. It makes me smile when I think that mine was Wembley Arena!'

There was, however, a real dilemma facing Mainstreet Management. On the one hand the new line-up had to win artistic and commercial approval for their new material: on the other hand the new management also knew that the band's glorious past was there to be traded upon. With new bands such as Therapy covering a Stranglers song, Britpoppers Elastica forking out royalties to the Stranglers after their 'Waking Up' single lifted the riff from 'No More Heroes', and 'Always The Sun' and 'Waltz In Black' blaring out every day on prime-time telly for car and Strepsils ads, it was apparent that the band's past was as, if not more, marketable than its present. This angered guitarist John Ellis for one; Ellis wanted to make new music and throughout the 1990s wrote a selection of new-age, plunderphonics and jazz-influenced instrumental music to accompany art exhibitions of paintings (a selection of which was collected on his intriguing album, *Acrylic*, in 1997). To John Ellis, the Strangler probably most open to new musical ideas, including avant-garde electronic music, dance music and pop, this incessant toting of the band as 'the legendary Stranglers' was most disillusioning. Particularly since this was a past in which he and Paul, now the dominant songwriters in the band, had had no say in:

> Every time I'm playing a concert I'm making more money for Hugh Cornwell than I'm making for myself. It breaks my heart when every two or three months there's some new re-release. What that does is to divert attention to the old band, and it underlines attitudes in the media along the lines of 'the Stranglers were great, but they're no good now with the new line-up'. That's bollocks. The new line-up is good, and if you talk to any hard-core Stranglers fans, they'll tell you it's better than the old line-up. But the media don't want to know, and as long as you keep churning out the old stuff, you'll always reinforce that attitude.

And sooner or later the two Stranglers singers, old and new, were bound to meet up with one another on the liggers' circuit. Paul:

I met Hugh at Madonna's party about three-and-a-half years ago and he was very nice. I've got no criticisms of the guy as he's done nothing wrong to me and I'm not in the business of putting people down. But it was fucking terrifying because I was as high as a kite and Hugh was there 'cos he likes to be around, he's quite a ligger. I'm standing in the hall at the ICA and this lady says, 'I've got someone to meet you' and I knew the minute she said it what was going to happen next. I saw it all happening like an accident and this hand came down the stairs and shook my hand and I thought, 'Oh wow!' I remember saying to him, 'The last time I saw you was in a coffee bar in South Kensington and I was with a girl. I walked in and you were the first person I saw. We just froze and I walked to the back of the coffee bar thinking, what the fuck do I do now! I don't remember what he said, but he was very pleasant to me, which was difficult to reciprocate because of his acrimonious departure and the feeling which still existed amongst the other members of the band.

It's as well to remember that Paul is a fan of Hugh's music. And although Paul and Hugh couldn't have been much more dissimilar artistically or temperamentally, they both, according to JJ, enjoy amusing band members and roadies with that quintessentially laddish (and British) 'trick' of setting fire to their farts. Hugh, apparently, was the Stranglers' 'le pétomane', and could fart with the best of them, occasionally setting them alight for good effect. But it was Paul who turned out to be the past master. In the nineties the band would travel on the tour bus in an orgy of dope-smoking, boozing and partying. Paul's ignitions, again according to a flabbergasted JJ, were outrageously impressive and were more akin to the flame of a Bunsen burner set on maximum than anything biological in origin. On one occasion, he suffered a deadly sideways blow-back and set fire to the trouser leg of his pyjamas. What great rock 'n' rollers these Stranglers are!

There were still obvious tensions between the two new members and the 'originals'. Both Paul and John were delighted to be working with an established band they admired, but it appeared to them that their enthusiasm quotient was higher than that of some of the other members, who had tasted superstardom and for whom continued success was not such a matter of artistic and commercial life or death. Being cooped up in that rehearsal room month in, month out, led to some personality conflicts.

Not the least of the tensions was caused by the new recruits' more left-wing political persuasions. John Ellis had been press secretary for the 'stop the M11 link-road' campaign. In fact, his house was due to be demolished if plans for the motorway went ahead. Together with Paul, John did some gigs as the Road Breakers to raise funds for the campaign. Paul: 'It took me fuckin' ages in the car one night to get to one of the Road Breakers gigs. I remember saying to the audience, who were made up of the campaigners, when I took the stage, "I hope they get this link road ready soon, it'll be much easier to get here when they do!"'

The political differences kept bubbling over into acrimony. Paul remembers a heated exchange between JJ and the two new recruits:

> We got into a heated argument at a recording session one night at Jacobs Studio for the *In The Night* album. What happened was that we saw Norman Tebbit getting pelted with eggs on TV and me and John shouted 'Great!' Suddenly JJ took it upon himself to have a go at us about it. I said, 'How the hell can you even talk to us about it when you're a rich kid. You don't understand anything about where I come from and you don't know anything about what this guy's done to destroy this country.' JJ told me to shut up because I didn't know what I was talking about. Now JJ's a great socialist . . . which is interesting.

JJ, however, vigorously denies being either a traditional Tory or a Labour man, arguing that his politics are far less simplistic than that – far right in some areas (economic policy, for instance) and resolutely left in others. He regards any attempt to bracket him in one camp as intellectual laziness.

Every band has its problems, but the completely different mind-sets of Paul and John resulted in the Stranglers becoming a far less cohesive group ideologically. According to those who had known him for a long time, Jet was becoming more withdrawn, less affable, and still given to stroppy 'impresario' behaviour, nit-picking, and ridiculous demands, whilst JJ, the doyen of the outrageous strop, was about to go on walk-about yet again. Jet remembers:

We were in this rehearsal room writing songs and JJ was just farting about, and behaving like a cunt. John had just had enough of it and he tore into him verbally, absolutely terribly. JJ couldn't handle the verbal abuse and said he was leaving the band. He made his protest for about five or six days, then Trevor spoke to him and he came back. I'd seen it all before. The first thing JJ did when he joined the band was to split. But John hadn't seen it all before. I didn't like the fact that we had to have this sort of thing.

The Stranglers without Hugh and JJ wouldn't have lasted five minutes, and it didn't take a genius to work out that, from the commercial point of view, JJ had to stay put. Of course, this puts JJ in a very powerful position. Without his presence there would be no band. Indeed, any further diminution of any kind would lead to its demise. Without Dave, the band would lose that air of eccentricity which makes it special and without Jet, it would lose its soul.

Jet was ensuring that he wasn't going to be out-done in the temper-tantrum stakes. Again, JJ was the catalyst. At a gig at Glasgow Barrowlands, JJ was of the opinion that Jet wasn't having a good day keeping time, which was crucial if he, JJ, was to get his bass in time. He told Jet backstage before the encore that his drumming was off. Jet, a trifle miffed, demanded an apology, and when none was forthcoming, Jet squared up to JJ face to face, 'pressing his nose up against mine', as JJ remembers. Despite a chronic back problem, a less than sylph-like figure and his advancing years, Jet was actually challenging JJ, a karate black-belt, to a fight! It was at this point that JJ saw the absurdity of the situation and started to take things more lightheartedly. The band finally came back on stage for the encore thirty minutes later. Most of the audience had, of course, left. It could only happen with the Stranglers.

By the time recording went ahead for the next album, the band had regrouped. *About Time* was put together with a re-called Alan Winstanley during the early months of 1995 and was a very different beast to *In The Night*. It was more organic-sounding, less 'produced', more like a rock 'n' roll band playing together than the 'artificiality' of Kemp's production. Jet saw it as a retrograde step: why try and re-create the vibe of *Rattus*? Surely the band had moved on from trying to sound like a live band on a studio album? But the rest, particularly John and Paul, were very happy with the *About Time* sessions, and with Alan Winstanley's genial air in the studio. John:

> I think *About Time* was great because I think we did it right. We decided that after *In The Night*, which was so technology-based, it would be a good idea to go back to having a more live band feel. We rehearsed for a long time and in the end had twenty tracks to choose from. The versions on the album are basically live versions with some overdubs, and I think it was a very good way of getting those tracks down. When we play together live in a room, we're pretty unstoppable, so it makes sense to do something you can do really well rather than something you don't do well. What we don't do well is dealing with electronics.

The result was a solid Stranglers album containing guitar-based pop played with gusto. It still wasn't classic material, but there was enough on the record to keep the listener's interest. That cool, assured, melodic sweep was still present. Again, some of the material didn't quite work, the opener, 'Golden Boy', being a case in point. But 'Money' and the fabulous 'Face' (with 'Time To Die' the finest post-Cornwell song) had brilliant guitar riffs from John Ellis. 'Sinister' was a creepy song in an older vein, 'Paradise Row' centered on John's experiences losing his home to road developers, and 'As The Ship Sails By' was a surprisingly jaunty light weight summery piece of exotica. But the epic was 'Still Life', replete with string quartet, haunting melody and powerful vocal from Paul (in terms of technical range and virtuosity, if not in terms of actual *style*, Paul far outstripped the previous incumbent in the lead-vocalist's chair). Marian Shepherd who was running the Stranglers Information Service at the time remembers that it was this track which affirmed her faith in the new line-up: 'I was gobsmacked when I heard "Still Life". I thought, this could be a classic. It had that timeless appeal and it really caught you at the back of your throat. It was definitely the strongest track from the new line-up.'

About Time contained the first, and as yet only, song completely courtesy of Jet Black. At 56, Jet was finally finding his song-

writing touch. 'Lies And Deception' depicted two real-life incidents, completely unconnected, when Jet had made a phone call
to friends and the receiver had been left off the hook, leading him
to eavesdrop on a conversation. Jet showed himself to be
unexpectedly poetic and succinct. No longer did his lyrics read
like letters to the bank manger! Finally 'Face' contained the silky
touch of punk violinist Nigel Kennedy. He was, as Paul Roberts
remembers, wilder than the band:

> Nigel Kennedy, apart from the fact that he supports Aston Villa
> which is very sad indeed, was real laugh actually. He's a big fan of
> the Stranglers. He was much grosser than us when we went out to
> eat that night and he upset more people in the bar we were in! In
> fact, he was the only one who got recognized in the street in
> Liverpool when we got to the recording studio. He warmed up
> with *The Four Seasons* and then did two takes (the first one was flat
> – we had to tell him but he was quite cool about it). He's a brilliant
> eccentric. We tried to get him to play with us in London but he
> blew us out.

Alan Winstanley found the whole recording process far easier
than the previous time he had worked with the band, at the
height of their coke period. This is his honest assessment of the
'new' Stranglers:

> I enjoyed making the record and I liked the material. I like Paul
> and I think he's a good vocalist, but he does sound like Bowie
> though! But I think they miss Hugh. As much as they miss his one-
> note guitar solos, they miss him vocally as well. For me the
> Stranglers were always the sound of Hugh's voice. I loved the
> naïve sound and the way he played his guitar. I think that's what's
> missing in the band. I think if it was five of them in the band now it
> would be really good because John Ellis adds to them.

Like *In The Night*, *About Time*, despite containing at least six very
good tracks (as many as *Aural Sculpture*, for example), nevertheless sounded a tad anachronistic musically. But even when
they were a little too intent on resurrecting the Stranglers classic
sound, they still knew how to write an excellent melody. It was in
the lyric department that the band was struggling. *About Time*
lacked any real lyrical focus. For Paul, who was trying to give the
project a more coherent lyrical theme, the album was intended to

be about madness, paranoia and suicide – topics which had continually fascinated him. But these ideas don't (or weren't allowed to) come through. Whereas past Stranglers albums had either dealt with very definite themes such as women (hatred of), love, religion, the occult, etc., *About Time*, like *In the Night*, seemed rather careless and haphazard and not bound together by either a musical or lyrical unity. The band needed some concepts, and this was obviously where they missed Hugh. Even though Hugh himself was recording the worst material of his career, producing work of a far inferior standard to that of his old group, his lyricism *was* missed. At times the band's lyrics were a strange mixture of the mundane and the overly ornate, dealing in abstracts, personifications, and classical allusions, or were simply heavy-handed. Again, the old Stranglers fault of making things too literal was the main problem. So we get a sinister record called 'Sinister', and the worst cover artwork of the band's career (save 1988's *All Live And All Of The Night*), with some stereotypical pouting from JJ and some time-warped grumpy looning from Jet on the back cover and an unimpressive shot of a rope about to snap against a horrid blue background on the front cover, again simplistically commenting on the equally woolly title. It also seemed clear that some members of the band were either becoming out of touch with contemporary musical styles, or simply didn't like them. Jet has always remained constant here: apart from very occasionally having the radio on, he doesn't listen to pop music at all. And, since a burglary at his house in 1995, he doesn't even have a CD player. This, Jet maintains, keeps his own music fresh. It is different from the mainstream and thus interesting because he has no idea what the mainstream is. At home the last thing Jet wants to do is listen to music. That would be a busman's holiday. Dave, on the other hand, just doesn't like what he hears: 'I only have music on in the car as a rule and there's nothing that sticks out above the rest. Up until very recently pop music seemed to consist just of rhythm tracks and samples. It's not music to me. It's just stealing something from someone and putting it on to a heavy beat. It may be exciting and it's fine if that's what you like. I'm sure my parents said the same thing about music when I was a kid!'

To JJ the band would always have to be a song-based rather than a groove- or rhythm-based outfit if it was to remain true to itself:

Now we're much more self-conscious and we're much more aware of who we are and where we are in the firmament. Not to sound like other people is an advantage. We're sufficiently confident in ourselves, to come out with what we have inside us. If that doesn't appeal to anybody, then that's fine. That's happened to us before, it doesn't bother us. We've created our own cutting edge. But I'm still keeping my ears open for anything that takes me by surprise. The most important thing, though, has to be the song, because rhythms come and go every few months, every few years. Whatever rhythms you want to dress the song in is entirely up to you. The rhythms are the clothes you wear but the person is the song, and what's more important, the person or the clothes?

But it's hard to avoid the suspicion that, without fresh impetus, new musical ideas and a cognizance of the new and the now, pop simply becomes an exercise in the art of pastiche. The band needed to contemporarize their sound, and for their next recording project they would attempt to bring in some nineties production techniques.

Despite some good reviews and, again, successful tours of Britain and the Continent, *About Time* only marginally improved on its predecessor, selling a very moderate 60,000 copies worldwide. Phil Sutcliffe's review in *Q* pointed out the record's undoubted charm:

> Unloved, but durable and sporadic hitmakers regardless, The Stranglers have re-emerged in the pink following a long fallow period since the departure of Hugh Cornwell. *About Time* recaptures their sound of '77 to the life: sneakily hypnotic organ and guitar, a fetching mood of melancholy enhanced by their own husky back-up vocals over which Cornwell's equally basso replacement, Paul Roberts, sings full of grand, dark passion, moderated by a touch of British reticence and a hint of boyish twinkle.

But for every convert there seemed to be a doubter challenging the band's credibility, such as *Mojo*'s Sylvie Simmons: 'The Stranglers, 20 years old this year, have denied rumours that original vocalist Hugh Cornwell will rejoin. Shame. Cornwell's sensuous, brooding jazz sensibility fits the menacing music far better than replacement Paul Roberts' mannered pop vocals.'

The single, 'Lies And Deception' was given no airplay at all on

Radio 1. In the eyes of radio programmers the band were has-beens, and without Hugh there was simply no chance of getting a single played. Ten years ago, the single would undoubtedly have reached at least the Top 40, but now the Stranglers were stigmatized. Despite the validity of their current material, to the media they were too old, and had upset too many people in the past. The old line-up had caused a lot of ill-feeling on the way up. Now that the band were struggling commercially they had too few supporters in the media to ease their passage. The new line-up had restored a lot of faith through their friendly professionalism on the live circuit and, in spreading their sphere of operation to the club scenes of Europe and the USA, had built up some confidence in the band after years of being dubbed too much trouble to take seriously. But in Britain, their career, apart from as a live act, seemed almost dead. 'We have to clear 100,000 sales with the new album,' Sil Willcox claimed after the band had just finished recording their thirteenth album, *Written In Red*, 'and we have to break a Top 20 single.' John Ellis, in the middle of recording *Written In Red* in 1996, was equally gloomy about the continued viability of a band struggling to make ends meet:

> *About Time* has done about 60,000 worldwide, *In The Night* about 30,000: it was a fucking fiasco. That amount of sales impacts on the amount of money you make from gigs and things. So every time we go out and play a gig Paul and I make less money than the rest of them. So while JJ, Dave and Jet are earning income, as they should be, from fucking great records, Paul and I don't get a cut of that. So we have a different hunger about making great music. These guys have been doing it for 20 years and have been at each others' throats for 20 years. Basically, if you really want my opinion, a couple of the guys are going through the motions. Paul and I primarily love making music and love writing songs. When we came to rehearsals for this album, Paul played a dozen songs, I played a dozen, and JJ said I've got a few ideas and played them on his acoustic guitar. Now on this album there's probably going to be only two songs that aren't generated by anyone other than Paul and myself, apart from the cover of 'Summer In The City'.

Paul, annoyed that the band had all but deserted the project, leaving John and him to carry the can, said:

I agree with that in part. Jet is more interested than the others. Some people are going in one direction and some are going in another. There's a different kind of hunger going on. We've had two phone calls during the whole of this session from certain members of the band. JJ popped his head in yesterday to say hello, for example. We seem to have been given artistic control by proxy. For me, this is brilliant, because I've put so much of myself into it anyway. You listen to Dave's playing on the album, for example, and it reflects his feelings inside of him at the time – it's not there.

John and Paul, frustrated and knowing themselves to be potentially expendable, viewed the future of the band with less than all-out optimism. Yet the future of the band, in artistic terms, seemed to belong in their hands. They were in a predicament, but both of them still loved being Stranglers and knew that, live, they were all but unstoppable. But there was internal disharmony of a sort. As the band put the final touches to their new album in the summer of 1996, the stakes had never been higher.

12: 'IT'S NEAR ENOUGH 21, FOR FUCK'S SAKE'

As work progressed on the *Written In Red* album during the hot summer months of 1996, and a disgruntled Paul and John bemoaned the lack of interest from some of the other members of the group as they frantically worked with producer Andy Gill, who was running out of studio time, it was hard to imagine that little under a year later, the Stranglers' career would be, if not resurrected, then certainly back on track. But before their triumphant return to the public eye at the Albert Hall on 'Black Friday' (13 June 1997), the band had several wobbles to overcome first.

The Stranglers Information Service (SIS), run by Marian Shepherd and overseen by JJ, was struggling, and by the beginning of 1997 had ceased operations altogether. The reason was simple: there wasn't the money to run it. Marian Shepherd:

> I had a great time running *Strangled* but financially it was a complete nightmare. SIS used to get money thrown at it when the band were signed to a major label. In the past organizers could rely on £10,000 being donated by the label for every major release. We had about 18,000 'live subscriptions' but the problem was that there were long gaps between albums and tours and the band weren't as successful commercially. We started manufacturing our own CDs and videos to pay our debts, but then, in turn, we'd be running up huge debts with the suppliers.

Not the least of their troubles, however, was the new album itself, which, even at the recording stage, was proving problematical. The band decided that, despite the quality of much of *About Time*, they needed to give themselves a sonic kick up the arse and to go for a more contemporary sound. Rock music was leaving the Stranglers behind. In the nineties, thrash, grunge and industrial had largely replaced the more melodic rock associated with the Stranglers with their huge walls of eerie discordant sound, screamed vocals and dark, black themes of emotional deprivation. In Britain, rock and dance had become cheery bedfellows as first the Madchester groups such as the Stone Roses and the Happy Mondays and later Primal Scream tore up the rule book, marrying trip-hoppy rhythms with funky rock guitar. All these developments seemed to pass the band by. In one sense, of course, this was a good thing, as they developed a style which was very different to the more danceable rock sounds of the day. But the downside was that it made the Stranglers even more difficult for promoters and pluggers to fit in to a recogniz-able style – to package the band as something vibrant for the nineties.

For *Written In Red* the band took on Andy Gill, ex-Gang Of Four, who had a reputation for a more sentient experimental approach and an interest in the textural side of music. Gill adopted a number of new (to the Stranglers) production tech-niques. From the outset, though, this meant that, whereas on *About Time* the band had played together as a band, now the five individuals would lay down their parts separately, on different days, under different conditions, without any direct contact with the other band members, and these parts would then be treated and fitted into the overall picture like a mosaic. This was how a lot of bands had been produced for the last decade, but it was a novelty for the Stranglers, and there was resistance from almost every quarter. For Dave the album was undoubtedly the most dispiriting experience of his career. He felt supernumerary in terms of the music, an anachronistic appurtenance rather than, as in the past, perhaps *the* central player, and he disapproved of the way in which songs were now being generated by the band: 'I feel I've been marginalized to a degree. I've put in so much more that isn't there. John and Paul now come in with completed songs and want them done as is. In the old days the songs were catalysts.'

Dave does have a point. His trademark keyboard work is becoming less and less prominent. JJ suggests that the reason for this is that the function of the instrument has been redefined. The keyboard is now for layering sound, for textural importance, and it would be impossible to have Dave's arpeggio solos on every song, particularly since the main songwriters in the band aren't keyboard specialists and thus find it difficult to make space in the sound for Dave. Dave implies that his role is being marginalized because the new recruits John and Paul are not as open as Hugh was to their songs being shaped over a period of time. John Ellis, however, disagrees: 'This album makes me more determined to make more records with the Stranglers and more records on my own, because I've seen songs to a certain extent compromised, and I don't like that very much. One pure vision gets diluted and affected by other people, and I think most of the time your own personal vision is right really. I don't like the way my songs have come out on this album.'

Some members of the band point out that Dave is now more marginal to the band sound because he's simply not as committed as he used to be. They can't put in what's not delivered on to tape in the first place. John Ellis: 'I have a feeling that JJ and Dave aren't as committed as they could be, and I personally hear it in the tracks.'

John Ellis thought the album was flawed as soon as it was completed. Listening to the mixes in September 1996 he said:

> I think it's very interesting and it's got some good moments, but I think it's flawed in many ways. There's a lot of things wrong with it. One of the problems was that Paul and I were left alone to finish it with the producer, which is mad. Andy ran out of time so a couple of the tracks aren't as finished as they should be. I think that this is an album where the bakers attended more to the icing on the cake than to the cake itself. In other words, Andy's strength is in the sonic landscapes he creates using samples, synths, loops and effects on guitars. I think the songs are good, but I wish we'd had another month to work on it. If we make another album I think you need a kind of Alan Winstanley/Andy Gill approach, because the best of what they do well is perfect. Andy Gill is a great man with sound, but with the Stranglers you can't ignore the band's strengths, and that includes the band playing together *as a band*: bass, guitars, keyboards and drums working together in unison. They don't if you record them all separately and people aren't in the room together and people aren't even talking to one another. How can you have a band making an album when they don't even see each other during the recording?

The album had to be totally re-mixed, so dissatisfied were the band with the original sound. The re-mix was completed at very short notice by Cenzo Townshend, who had also engineered some of the tracks on the album. Despite Andy Gill's work, the one thing that *Written In Red* isn't is a state-of-the-art album.

When it was released, JJ claimed that it was 'off-the-wall' and very different for the band, but on repeated listening this is simply not the case. They are still playing songs with conventional structures, their penchant for melody above texture and rhythm is still in evidence, and the material, in the main, is pretty conventional in structure. There's nothing, for example, as odd as the starkness of *Black And White*, the surprising, almost punk-prog-rock material of *The Raven*, or the battiness of the proto-techno *Meninblack*. Somehow, *Written In Red* sounds like a fudge, as if Andy Gill (who, according to JJ, didn't like some of the material he was recording) wanted to really contemporize the sound, whilst the band (or sections of it) wanted to retain a more conventionally melodic, hard-rocking vibe.

The one song all the members find radically different, and very contemporary-sounding, was their ill-judged cover of the Lovin' Spoonful's 1966 hit 'Summer In The City', replete with a half-time verse and a trip-hoppy rhythm. But this would only have been seen as state of the art in 1992, not 1997, and the cover itself is not successful compared with the joys of '96 Tears' and 'Walk On By'. It was commercially a rather daft thing to do in any case. Spurred on by the record company and the management who, perhaps rightly, thought that a cover version was the only way the band could break a single on ageist British radio, they chose a record which had just been covered by Joe Cocker (and had been a sizeable European hit). Someone, somewhere, wasn't thinking straight.

Written In Red contains plenty of old-style melodic pop. 'In Heaven She Walks', a Paul song, is a great track, and, subsequently released as a limited-edition media-only single, it is surely as strong as anything the band has put out in the last 10 years. Catchy, and riffy, it is a classic piece of Stranglers pop. But again, there was no consistency behind the project. The accompanying video showed the band surrounded by several scantily-clad, gyrating girls in 'kinky' gear before being killed off in not-terribly-good special effects at the end. It was the band's corniest moment ever. Elsewhere on the album there was plenty to remind listeners how adroit the band still were at producing eminently hummable choruses. 'Joy De Viva' is another fine pop song with a soaring, if rather traditional, melody. 'Here' is a dark, effective piece of pop; 'In A While' a breezy, summery song. 'Blue Sky' saw the addition of some inventive percussion set against another slab of pure pop, whilst 'Valley Of The Birds', with its sampled 'bird noises' at the beginning (another example of the Stranglers' 'obvious' imagery), is a more old-school Stranglers song which allows Dave full rein to mark the mix with some trademark keyboards (unsurprisingly, this was his, and many others', favourite track). Once again, though, the band sounded at their most ham-fisted when it came to the rockers (a perverse state of affairs considering how brilliant the band rock out in concert). Once more the problem was that the corporate rock pose they adopted musically was ill-suited to a band traditionally more subtle than that. 'Silver Into Blue' and 'Miss You' are the biggest culprits, sounding like late-period INXS.

Overall, *Written In Red* was another sporadically good album. In melodic terms it kept up the standard of pure pop the band had been perfecting since *Aural Sculpture*, and every song has a catchy, well-honed melody. But the promised sonic development was a chimera. The music was a little more nervy and trip-hoppy in places, and there were some interesting musical interludes where, one suspects, the band pulled back from further experimentation fearful that they might lose their market altogether (unsurprisingly these are the most intriguing parts of the album). But these interludes are few and far between, and there is none of the darkness, the arty-forbidding climate of nastiness, which infused some of the tracks on *In The Night* and *About Time*. At least the art work, literally an exercise in the bleeding obvious (a red cover for *Written In Red*), was a marked improvement on *About Time*. Abstract and arty, it depicts a miscegenation of water, fluid and blood. It was an abstract cover for an album which promised to be less literal and more multi-layered than it eventually turned out to be. Rather than re-invent their sound altogether, and marry grooves and pulses with the conventional trappings of pop-rock, the band had simply dressed their songs in some more contemporary-sounding rhythms. The material was essentially the same as on any other late-period Stranglers album.

Despite being flawed, according to band sources the album did better business than *About Time*. The industry jargon used to describe the sales pattern by manager Trevor Long (or 'Snogger' Long as his close pals call him) was that it was 'selling through'. But it wasn't a hit in the UK. Finally released after the Christmas retro-rush in January 1997, six months after it had been completed, it reached Number 52, the lowest chart position for any Stranglers studio album ever. It did reach Number 7 in the Indie chart, a feat which pleased the Stranglers entourage no end, particularly JJ, who had always considered the band, in spirit at least, to be more an indie band, and less part of corporate rock/ schlock. Elsewhere, the pre-sales had by the beginning of 1997 already matched the total sales of *About Time*. So the commercial meltdown, the disaster scenario which the band had contemplated after *About Time*, failed to materialize. But neither had the album broken the band back into mainstream pop in the UK, despite a very high-profile launch in December at that most un-Stranglers of places – Eurodisney.

The management shuttled over a select band of fans and assorted media people for a Saturday night special, where the band played the whole album, minus 'Wonderful Land' (paradoxically one of the best tracks on the album), and a selection of oldies. According to JJ, they weren't on top form, and Jet was in yet another grumpy mood throughout the trip. The cod-Americana and glitz of 'Eurodismal' was never going to be to his liking:

> We were not on form. Jet was being crap. Sometimes he throws a wobbler and he's very rude to people. On the boat he was just an arse-hole, demanding 60p back on a Coca-Cola bottle. He just made a spectacle of himself because he was so aggressive – much more aggressive than me. He's very precious about small things. We were trying to launch the new album in a pretty spectacular way and trying to do something that hadn't been done before. In the music business there are standard routines which have become so hackneyed and clichéd. We've been in the business for twenty years and we don't want to go through all the same routines. If I can avoid them, I will. That's why I didn't want to do a British tour in 1997 until they had convinced me that we would be playing places that we'd never played before.

The launch seemed to have little effect either on sales or on creating a buzz about the album. Reviews in the British press were almost wholly negative. Here's *Q*'s Paul Davies: '. . . devoid of anything remotely resembling a memorable crunchy tune. Messrs Burnel, Greenfield and Black are assisted by the deadpan vocals of Paul Roberts and the understated guitars of John Ellis, but they struggle to make sense of an anonymous raft of unconvincingly delivered songs . . .'

Another problem, as ever, was that the Stranglers simply couldn't get any airplay at all in Britain. Even when they attracted the attention of a journalist to review a live gig, they didn't even get a write-up, let alone a bad review. Paul Roberts:

> An *NME* journalist was told to give us a shit review and he said, 'I can't do it cos it was so fucking good, I've got to write a great review!' They didn't put it in, of course. Two years ago a *Melody Maker* journalist followed us round for seven gigs. He didn't want to leave, he thought it was so brilliant. Did we get a write-up? Did we fuck. He wanted to do a two-page feature in *Melody Maker* and his editor told him to stand back, to lay off, allegedly. The only things they allow in the papers are negative things.

This was a form of stigmatization, if you believe what Paul says (and since the inkies haven't done a feature on the band for years, there are no real grounds to disbelieve him). The British media, particularly the weekly mags and the style guides such as *The Face*, are notoriously wary of old-generation artists trying to make a living on the rock circuit. With good reason, of course: for every one over fifty still cutting the mustard, there are a thousand fallen stars trading on a more glorious past. To be old and liked is certainly more common in the nineties than it was a decade earlier. Indeed, the post-Britpop cultural terrain seems to be populated by twenty-somethings who actually like their dads' record collections. But it helps if these past masters and mistresses are either long-dead (Jim Morrison, Jimi Hendrix), only ever attained cult status (Lou Reed, Iggy Pop), or have disbanded. Almost all of those still on the circuit who have actually built up a career have had to suffer the same knee-jerk reaction of loathing and mockery from the press, regardless of the actual merit of the music. The Stranglers were caught in this trap: too uncool to be loved, too politically incorrect to be cherished, they could be side-lined in a way the Sex Pistols could not.

What made matters worse was that, in direct proportion to the lack of interest in their new music, the Stranglers' back-catalogue was being lauded at almost every turn. Since the departure of Hugh, the band had been re-mixed, re-packaged and re-sold every which way. The market had been flooded with 'new' Stranglers material. As a salutary reminder of past 'glories', the *Saturday Night, Sunday Morning* video of the 1990 Ally Pally gig was re-released as the band were putting the finishing touches to the new album. Here's a sample from *Q*'s review by John Aizlewood, which has gone down in band legend, coining as it did a rather uncharitable nickname for John, the unidentified second guitarist at the gig: 'There's no rapport with the exclusively male audience, the sound is tinny, the brass section and extra, lard-arsed guitarist are wholly unnecessary. Little wonder all four parties fared so dismally post-split.'

Neither the band nor Hugh have had any say in these reissues, and every year brings a new compilation somewhere across the globe. In 1997 it was the turn of the (actually pretty comprehensive and unstoppable) 43-track double CD *The Hit Men*, released by EMI Gold. The critics loved it. Here's *Mojo*'s Sue Smith: '. . . this collection is a reminder of just how chart-friendly and tuneful they were too. Hit men indeed . . . And it all sounds remarkably fresh – just ask Elastica.'

Whilst John Aizelwood was again in fine piss-taking mode for *Q*:

> Funny lot, the Stranglers . . . they were (they're still just about going) a cuddly, if dysfunctional bunch. Jean-Jacques Burnel did his martial arts, embraced right-wing causes and got the girls; Hugh Cornwell, the most gauche man in rock, aspired to acting and thought the way forward was to become Nigel Planer's chum; Dave Greenfield had an unpunk moustache and looked slightly retarded; while Brian 'Jet Black' Duffy will next year become punk's first 60-year-old . . . For a while The Stranglers were fantastic.

At the end of 1996 the band also discovered that the song which had by now become their own 'My Way', 'Golden Brown', was being sampled by the dance/rap act The Kaleefs, and moves were made by his management team to put Hugh in the video – a plan quickly scuppered by a Stranglers management keen to sabotage any attempt by Hugh to hog the limelight. (Hugh and his entourage were to get their own back when they objected to 'Golden Brown' being used to promote the band's 1997 Albert Hall gig – a live version with Paul singing was substituted posthaste.) The single reached the British Top 30 in early 1997. It was the first Stranglers song to reach those giddy heights since the reissued 'Always The Sun' made Number 29 in early 1991. For 'new boys' Paul and John this must have been an unutterably dispiriting statistic.

The band were still busy playing dates on the Continent in clubs and small halls. And there was still a goodly quotient of high jinks too. Dave remembers a rather unconventional start to a gig in Holland, for example:

> We come on stage to 'Valley Of The Birds'. The first part is played from the CD to get the sound of the birds flying around, then we come in at a set point in the song and the tape stops. This night we're on stage with our head-sets on already, and unbeknownst to us Paul is still backstage having a dump! So we start off and all the rest realize there's no Paul, but I'm looking around trying to catch my roadie's eye to try and get my monitors balanced, and don't realize he isn't on stage. When we get to the chorus I start singing and then suddenly notice no one else is. I look around and notice Paul isn't there. We had to keep going round and round, playing the instrumental section until he finally came on stage looking baffled, wondering why we'd started. That shows how much I can normally see of a gig, and how much attention I normally pay as a rule!

The band had always been infamous for on-stage cock-ups. In the eighties they were notoriously good at cocking up 'Golden Brown', the rhythm section collapsing due to the odd time-signature of the song combined with monitoring problems which by the 1990s had been ironed out. It used to be desperately embarrassing for the band, but great fun for the punters, who loved it. At times they could have been said to be the Eddie 'The Eagle' Edwards of rock.

But their next major gig had to be a cock-up-free zone. Bowing to commercial pressure the band decided to go back to the future for their next project. JJ had always wanted to put on an orchestral evening, when the band would play a selection of new songs and 'classics' complete with a full orchestra. The Stranglers had used string sections before, most recently on *About Time*, so it was nothing new for them. What was new was the scale of the next project.

The band had left their record label Castle and had signed a contract with Eagle Rock. Twenty-three years into their career, they now found themselves under the BMG umbrella, with potentially the biggest distribution capacity of any label they had ever been signed to. Eagle Rock agreed to finance a special 21st anniversary concert at the Albert Hall, from which a live album and video would be culled. This was yet more retro-active marketing by the management, linking the present line-up with its more saleable past incarnation. But why yet another anniversary tie-in? The band had already toured in 1995 to celebrate their 20th year in the music business (it was really their 21st). Now they were doing a gig to celebrate their 21st (it was actually now 23 years since the band got together). 'It's near enough 21, for fuck's sake,' commented Trevor Long after the show. In fact, the (rather tenuous) commemoration was of the 21st anniversary of the band's UA deal in 1976 (and even this was six months too early). Whatever the anniversary (perhaps the next one will be Jet's 60th birthday?), it gave the band a big gig to focus on that spring and, for the first time since the departure of Hugh, they were guaranteed sizeable media coverage. Seven years too late, the new line-up was being launched.

But first there was a special tour to get under their belt. In April 1997 the Stranglers went out to play for the British troops serving in Bosnia. Not only was this a brave and highly comradely action, it also proved to be one of the most moving experiences the band have ever had. JJ:

> What a very beautiful country, and what a fucked-up place it is too. We played five dates over an eight-day period. Bosnia is fucked forever. It's mined, and I was told that even if they knew where all the mines were it would take 120 years for them to make them safe. Every day people, mainly women and children, are losing their limbs or dying. You go past a row of houses and one house is left standing with a satellite dish and a Merc at the front, and the rest of the houses are shelled to fuck. Of course, those people were the same ethnic group as the people coming through so they were allowed to live. It was a very worthwhile experience and a real privilege, in a way, to be in the Stranglers and to see it at first hand rather than in the papers, because the

papers desensitize you. You can't get the full impact unless you go there.

Of course, the Stranglers' visit went completely unreported in the press.

The Albert Hall gig exceeded the band's expectations. A lot, some might say everything, was resting on it. Despite a few technical hitches, the evening was an unqualified success, even if it was yet another back-to-the-future exercise in nostalgia. Johnny Rubbish was brought back as one of the 'warm-up' acts, and was suitably rubbish as usual. One of his 'jokes' ran: 'I heard Camilla Parker-Bowles has been in a car accident. I thought she'd already *been* in an accident!' Then the band (well, JJ, John and Paul at least) took the stage in stylish black suits. Paul looked perfect as the bony, slightly cheesy, wide-boy, whilst JJ was suitably Continental and slightly crumpled, puncturing the proceedings with the odd 45-year-old karate kick into thin air, breathing his way through 'European Female' and looking every inch the star he is. The audience lapped it all up. Paul lost his shoe after a stage-dive (surely the first ever at the Albert Hall – I can't see Eric Clapton doing one), hobbled round, took his shirt off and had a ball. As a promotional exercise, it was a complete triumph. The Stranglers, backed by the excellent all-female Electra Strings Orchestra, cruised through standards like 'Golden Brown' and 'Down In The Sewer', newer material perfect for the orchestral backing such as 'Still Life' and 'Heaven Or Hell', and forgotten gems like 'Skin Deep', 'Ice Queen' and 'Let Me Down Easy'. Manager Trevor Long on the Royal Albert experience:

> The band had never been on stage with an 18-piece orchestra before, and to do a full one-and-a-half hour show with the strings incorporated was a nightmare. It's nothing to do with the band, or the orchestra, it's just the logistics of having 18 people and the specialist equipment they had to use. You couldn't keep dragging an 18-piece orchestra into rehearsals, so we had to do it in sections. In fact, before the show the whole orchestra only played twice with the group. But the gig was completely sold out. The touts were selling £18.50 tickets for £75. We've been getting letters from the 'lapsed' fans saying they thought the gig was great, which is exactly what we wanted. The gig was such a 'one-

bite-at-the-cherry' lark that everyone was under pressure, but it was amazing. We got a standing ovation. Typically, we got the usual press. The *Independent* review mentioned that we did 'Peaches', so they obviously weren't even there, because they never played that song!

For JJ, whose idea it was to do the event in the first place, it was one of the most special gigs of his entire career:

That was the one Hugh should have left after. He phoned me up in Nice after the Ally Pally gig to say *10* was our best album, that we can't do better than that, and that last night's gig was just about the pinnacle and we couldn't top it. But the pinnacle, as far as I was concerned, was the Albert Hall. Symbolically, it was probably the best gig I ever played. For the Stranglers to start off as a new-wave group and then to play with a classical orchestra, to show that our material, both past and present, could be played in any way, was a fantastic achievement. And it was the first time I'd ever worn a suit on stage!

While the Stranglers were back in the big time yet again, Hugh too was resurfacing after a seven-year creative hibernation. Despite him having been the main contributor of ideas to the Stranglers (although, as we have seen, certainly not to the extent the band's media profile has tended to suggest), and undoubtedly crucial to them in terms of generating ideas, concepts and eccentric schemes, his own solo work was, rather surprisingly, surpassed by the quality of JJ's extra-curricular work. His more recent solo albums lacked the conceptual framework he had always brought to the Stranglers. In his Stranglers manifestation, Hugh's great strength was his ability, like the best of the post-Beatles suburban Britrockers, to frame music, to give it some thematic clout. Curiously, this was once again missing from his most recent album, *Guilty*. There's no unifying theme in the work, although the title wryly pokes fun at the post-Stranglers popular construction of the man. Hugh: 'Everyone accuses me of so many different things. So I'll just admit guilt to everything and then I can get rid of that and get on with doing the music.'

The songs themselves don't so much deal with guilt. Rather, they show Hugh, once again in bittersweet mood, telling tales of love and redemption in a manner the cynical, scheming eighties

Hugh would have found unimaginable. The one exception, lyrically, is the totally bizarre, musically infectious 'Snapper'. That most rare of rock 'n' roll birds, it is a song about fish:

> If I could have just one more wish
> It would be for a fillet of fish
> You wouldn't have to take out the bones
> You could even serve it up on its own
> I'd call it snapper
> Just give me snapper

With this track Hugh successfully regains his sense of the surreal, something that had left him in latter days. But if, thematically, there is no real unity to the album, in terms of the overall sound there is a great deal of congruence. The message, whether intentionally or not, is plain: this is a solo Stranglers album. For a start, it is produced by *Aural Sculpture* producer, Laurie Latham. Also, *Guilty* sounds more like the old-style Stranglers than any post-1990 album by the band itself. Hugh's vocal was clear and assured, and his band – bassist Steve Lawrence, drummer Chris Bell, keyboard player Phil Andrews and Hugh himself on lead guitar – was, on the face of it, a simple reconstruction of the classic Stranglers ground. Hugh was taking the feet from underneath the band he left. For those still keen on the classic Stranglers sound and unhappy with the way in which the current line-up has moved away from what they believe to be the essence of the band, *Guilty* is the antidote. Comparing it with the post-Cornwell Stranglers' *oeuvre* is insidious, but it is back-ward-looking in terms of its overall musical direction (in fact it sounds like the kind of album the band might have made five years before *Rattus Norvegicus*) referencing as it does the post-psychedelic rock styles still beloved by Hugh, with its guitar-rock punch closer to the band's traditional sound than *Written In Red*.

Hugh's *Guilty* is determinedly organic. The vibe is rich and energetic, the playing is good, the singing is sweet, and the songs, for the most part, work well within the limitations Hugh has set up, sometimes excellently. It was definitely the best work he had done since *Aural Sculpture*. 'One Burning Desire' (the best track on the album), 'Black Hair Black Eyes Black Suit' and 'Nerves Of Steel' (Stones' 'Satisfaction' meets Dylan's 'Like A Rolling Stone') are fine songs – well-crafted and punchy. The creepy 'Torture Garden' is like Portishead without the samples, whilst the opening to 'Stravandrabellagola'/'Long Dead Train' naughtily out-Greenfields Dave Greenfield, and the surf-style guitar sounds just like the sort of thing JJ might have come up with. The psychedelic leanings and the late-sixties/early-seventies musical references ride the mid-nineties *Zeitgeist* along with bands such as Oasis, The Verve, Kula Shaker and Ocean Colour Scene. Hugh himself is quite content to re-trace his musical roots (a covers album of old Love, Dylan, Lennon, even Sammy Davis Junior songs is planned somewhere down the line), finding contemporary music simply too time-consuming to invest his interest in. Like some other members of the Stranglers, Hugh seems to have rather shut up shop when it comes to contemporary pop: 'I don't go to gigs. I haven't bought any new records. You do end up listening to it by default, walking into shops you hear it. I've heard a lot of great stuff recently, I have to say. But to begin to collect it, or buy it, is counter-productive, because you're going to end up losing your own identity because there's so much out there. I like Radiohead and Supergrass, but I'm not that convinced about Oasis. Music is about energy and I find Oasis a bit slowed down.'

Producer Laurie Latham was trying to convince Hugh that the more discordant, the dirtier his sound was, the more chance he would have of being played on Radio 1:

> On 'Black Hair Black Eyes Black Suit' I originally had his vocals going through an amp and it was really distorted but Hugh was a bit nervous about using it, so for the final mix we ended up using a combination of a normal vocal and this more unusual take. I was saying to him, the grittier and nastier it is the more likely it will be played on Radio 1. People have got so used to looping, sampling and distortion from dance music that they expect rock to be the same. Or else you're destined for Radio 2.

In fact, Hugh admits that the new-style Radio 2 is perhaps the natural home for both his and the Stranglers' music. *Guilty* is far and away Hugh's best solo album, as Paul Davies noted in his three-star *Q* review:

> Whilst his ex-colleagues have struggled to keep The Stranglers aboard the squalid nostalgia merry-go-round, Hugh Cornwell has

ferreted out a useful solo career for himself, despite less than record-breaking sales. The vocals may have lost some of their snaggle-toothed edge and the lyrics walk a fine line between wit, whimsy and callow reflection, but guitars are clipped and treated in time-honoured fashion and with songs as up front and melodically charged as 'One Burning Desire', 'Endless Day Endless Night' and 'Long Dead Train' we may yet see that sneering face on *Top Of The Pops* again.

Paul Du Noyer for *Mojo* also noticed that *Guilty* paraded a far less bile-ridden Hugh than of yore: 'Melodicism rules at every turn of the track-listing – tuney guitar parts peal like bells – while Cornwell's delivery is so low-key that he's practically intoning like a London Lou Reed . . . This grim outsider has rarely sounded so mainstream, nor more at ease with his job.'

It was this lack of energy and attack which old mate and ex-manager Ian Grant thought slightly marred the set: 'It's really good but it needs Burnel's driving bass, it needs Dave's keyboards, it needs Jet. For me, Hugh should have rejoined the Stranglers.'

Both Hugh and the band, however, are still unable to regain centre stage, to make music that people not only buy but think of as vital and important. The Stranglers are perhaps in a better position to launch a comeback. They have the name, the back-catalogue (Hugh now refuses to play Stranglers songs in his set), and a loyal, though small, fan-base. But what lies in the future, and how do they all feel about their rather glorious past?

In 1997 the future for the Stranglers looks rosier than it has done for seven years. There are still tensions within the band, but this is hardly a surprising state of affairs after so many years together. Now that the whole Stranglers operation has been scaled down since the glory days of the eighties, travelling from gig to gig means the delights of the tour bus, rather than the first-class jet. It would be hard enough for a saint, let alone Cliff Richard, to keep totally cool and aggro-free. Ninety per cent of the time it is a riotously silly mode of travelling, but for those such as Dave and Jet who like a bit of privacy, it's wearing too.

JJ is at pains to point out that he still has a great deal of affection for the original Stranglers. He's probably closer to Dave than

anyone else in the band, and considers him to be a good person
and a friend. Despite the many set-tos down the years, Jet is also
close to his heart: 'Dave is very strange. But he's also very kind.
And Jet, although he can be the raging bull and the biggest cunt
on the earth, is also the anchor in the band.'

JJ is the songwriter with the proven track record. Some of the
best melodies in the Stranglers' canon are his. 'Hallow To Our
Men', 'Down In The Sewer', 'Let Me Down Easy', 'Toiler On The
Sea', and 'Time To Die' all show off JJ's almost symphonic
melodic sweep. When he is going through an uncreative period, the band necessarily suffers. The popular perception of the
group was that Hugh was the dominant talent and the main
songwriter. This was always a bit of a distortion. Whilst it is true to
say that Hugh was crucial to the band, and originated the
majority of the Stranglers' material, JJ was contributing around
40 per cent of the total recorded output and sang a quarter of the
songs. For the band to be a success in the future JJ has to fire on
all cylinders.

All the band members are a mass of contradictions, and that's
what makes them special: Dave is a genuine eccentric, distant,
inhabiting a special secret psychic space that few are ever invited
into. At times he is withdrawn and quiet, and yet he is also witty,
friendly and considerate, particularly to those who take an
interest in his range of activities, from the occult to Dark Ages
re-enactments. According to some of the band, both past and
present, Dave has opted for a quieter life, and most forms of
publicity, avoiding the aggro. Hugh: 'Dave is a very private
person. He's got it sorted because he doesn't do any publicity.
He doesn't get involved in a lot of the writing. He is quite gifted, so
he can quickly put his mark on something. He manufactured this
perfect life for himself where he could be very private and still be
part of this band, *and* have a lot of free time! But he was very easy
to work with, most of the time.'

Marian Shepherd regards Dave as a very special person: 'I have
a great deal of affection for Dave. But it's almost like the logical
side of his brain has crushed the emotional side. If we opened up
the logical side, I'm sure we'd find diodes and wires!'

John Gatward (a.k.a. Johnny Rubbish) also remembers Dave
with affection as a completely bewildering person, a genuine,
one-off, English eccentric: 'Dave I've never really understood.

Actually I thought they would find something about him when that probe landed on Mars recently. I mean, he's a spaceman! I remember back in the seventies knocking on his door one morning back when he was married to Jackie and he came to the door looking really terrible and he said, "I was up until four in the morning." I said, "What were you doing?" and he said, "Oh, Snakes And Ladders".'

But for JJ, Dave is often in a state of psychic turmoil, unhappy, even fearful of his own thoughts: 'Dave cannot sit in the same room with his own thoughts. I get the impression that he's afraid of his own thoughts or his own company. He's always got to be playing games, or doing crosswords, anything to occupy his mind.'

And, at the time of writing, Dave feels dissatisfied in particular with the manner in which his own role in the music has been successively downgraded over the years. His sonic absence, for whatever reason, makes for a less quaint, less individual sound.

Jet's temper is legendary, and he can be sullen and grumpy. According to some he is also something of a control freak. Yet for the most part he's a down-to-earth, regular nice guy, avuncular, supportive and still very creative. Both Dave and JJ have noticed, though, that, as Jet approaches his 60s, he's becoming more withdrawn, more insular and less cheerful. JJ attributes the sea-change in Jet's personality to the Exegesis programme he underwent in the early 1980s: 'It makes him get very extreme and not accept that he's wrong, and behave totally irrationally sometimes. Once you've been indoctrinated, your life changes and you behave in a different way. Before, he was more easy-going and not so selfish. Something happens to people when they undergo Exegesis and they think they're the centre of the universe, which, of course, you're not. None of us are.'

Jet denies vehemently that he was ever an ardent exponent of Exegesis and points out that his involvement was restricted to attendance at one three-day seminar, during which he liked what he saw.

Yet, to Paul and John, who see Jet as something of a comrade-in-arms, he is the member of the original line-up who still has the sparky enthusiasm, boyish twinkle and sheer industry to make the band work. He is the custodian of the Stranglers, and the two new recruits have naturally graduated towards him.

Jet the inventor and businessman also has been making something of a comeback in recent times. In 1997 he was granted a patent for an invention he had been working on for two decades, with the invaluable help and technical assistance of research scientist Dr B.R.A Wybrow, which Jet hopes will revolutionize drumming in the future. Jet saw that the conventional set of the drum-kit was impractical, uncomfortable, and limiting. His new invention, the 'Power Bass Drum Pedal', enables the bass drum to be removed from the kit altogether (leaving a space which could be used for a variety of other drums – some maybe yet to be invented), and played at a distance using an electrical signal operated by the drummer. Multiple bass drum sound is now feasible; several bass drums, of varying sizes, and in different sites in the auditorium, can be played in unison, or in sequence, all operated by one drummer. Indeed the drummer could be in a different hall altogether and still operate the drums at the gig! Jet has also patented a 'footplate module' which accounts for the up and down motion of the foot used by most drummers, replacing the conventional pedal configuration which often causes the foot to slide down the pedal. Jet calls his idea 'Power Assisted Drumming' and hopes that his new invention will, in the years to come, lead to a revolution in drumming. So the frightening prospect of Phil Collins simultaneously drumming at Wembley Stadium and at JFK Philadelphia, (whilst at the same time giving an interview for Paul Gambaccini in Moscow) for *Live Aid 2* is now a real possibility.

JJ remains the dominant character in the band and his personality is the most problematic. His manager, Trevor Long, calls him a 'pussy cat', claiming he's had to deal with far more temperamental bastards than him. JJ is extremely intelligent, sporadically still very creative, and overwhelmingly charming. The wilfulness of youth, the devil-may-care attitude to life, has never left him. He approaches life like an assault course. Whether it be personal or professional relationships, he goes for it and damns the consequences. This makes JJ endearing. But JJ has also never lost his ability to wind people up something chronic, and it is this trait which his confrères regard as his biggest weakness. He still plays mind games, and will doubtless continue to do so. Marian Shepherd: 'JJ is one of life's situationists. He loves to inspire a reaction in people either by shocking them or by charming them. The biggest insult to JJ is indifference.'

John Ellis, however, has identified something altogether more sinister at the core of the band, a pall of darkness created when Dave, JJ, Hugh and Jet got together. The tension between Jet and JJ both drives the band, and gives the outfit its negativity. John Ellis is convinced that when the four Stranglers came together in 1975, something truly dark and evil was created:

> Dave is completely eccentric, but there's no ill-will in him at all. He hasn't created any of the dark moments as far as I can tell. The dark moments of the band have come from elsewhere. That's where the darkness is. It's clearing now, but it's still there. I'm not saying that the devil was riding out on the Stranglers but sometimes there are situations which have aspects of negativity surrounding them. It feels to me like, when the Stranglers came together, some negative energy was created which occasionally bubbled up pretty big. I think it's dying down now, and that may be because the original band are not in existence any more.

To some, it is rather ridiculous and outlandish, to find menace in one's own shadow. But John for one is adamant that this negativity has rubbed off on both himself and Paul, making them prone to dark moods. It has been claimed that anyone who gets close to the band is susceptible to these doomy vibes. There is something undeniably macabre about the band, a black hole of negativity. One only has to look at their career to see a configuration of evil happenstance and the genuinely bizarre (plus one genuinely frightening experience concerning one member of the band, which has been omitted from the narrative to respect the individual's wish for secrecy). But according to John Ellis, this negativity still exists. Jet's bouts of bleakness and aggression are merely a reactive defence to JJ's obsessive and voracious appetite for mayhem of all sorts. Jet has, in fact, made the startling claim that JJ is a schizophrenic:

> I've got no medical training, but I've observed that he's a very complex person. One day he can be an absolute bastard and impossible to be with, and then on another day he can be the life and soul of the party, witty, wise, intelligent. After seeing this over the years I came to wonder perhaps whether he was a schizophrenic, if that is what schizophrenia is, I don't know.

But he's a difficult man to know. He's extremely talented. He can come up with the most moving piece of music like 'Reap What You Sow', that was one of his creations, beautiful melody, and then he can write something dark and aggressive like 'Ugly', and that's a wide spectrum of talent. He's obviously educated, but then he can be completely illogical. Sometimes I think that that's the French side of his personality, when his words and his behaviour don't make sense to an English mind.

And what of the man who some would say was most likely to be the new lead singer of the Stranglers? Today Hugh, physically, seems to be in an eternal state of non-ageing, as if he's starring in his own private version of *Cocoon*. Looking at pictures from the mid-70s and comparing them with the man today, there's hardly any difference save for a creeping bald patch which seems to be taking forever to creep. While Jet, and even JJ, have piled a few pounds on, Hugh remains wiry and angular, still rather gauchely making his way through life with the gait of a born eccentric. He's still coming up with new theories, maxims and apothegms (dietary obsessions are part of his character – apparently for months he maintained that parsley cured colds, now it's fresh ginger and lemon tea for the liver!), swearing blindly that this or that is a great cure for some ailment or fantastic for some aspect of the metabolic process, before moving on to the next obsession at a later date. Hobby-horsing is one of the characteristics of the born eccentric. Hugh is the Tristram Shandy of rock 'n' roll. Dave: 'Everyone in the band has mellowed – that happens automatically with age. But Hugh was a bit different. He would change like that, up and down. He'd come out with weird theories and swear by them and then change his mind.'

To be thought 'different' by Dave must be a special commendation indeed.

Many people have remained loyal to Hugh and value his friendship. Ex-publicist Alan Edwards maintains that, without Hugh, the band is simply a non-starter:

It was just chemically right before. Hugh is irreplaceable. They played off each other so well. You had the weirdo, trippy, Doors-like keyboards going on. You had Jet, salt of the earth, straight-forward drummer; JJ knocking out the great bass rhythms looking the pin-up, the hunky-punky, and then Hugh, a sort of slightly deranged, moody intellectual. It was a fantastic combination.

You'd have to put it in a computer to get that. I don't think any of them are replaceable. Without Hugh fronting it, I wouldn't cross the road to see it, frankly. No offence to the others but . . . Good blokes. Talking about it, I miss them all. They were great times. It was like family really. You can't put it better than that.

For some, though certainly not all, Paul Roberts is no substitute for the real thing. One long-standing fan told me:

When I saw the new line-up without Hugh at the Town & Country Club, I have to admit to being very disappointed. Somehow the band didn't look right being fronted by a 'Rod Stewart'-type singer. The new boy Roberts gave it everything he had, but it wasn't right. I think they would come across much better, or more in the style of the band, if he were taught some basic chords and given a guitar as a prop, in much the same way as Strummer used one in the Clash.

In the eyes of some, Hugh *gained* credibility leaving the Stranglers when he did. He was realistic enough to see that the rich seam of creativity had played itself out, and he was willing to forgo future financial security as a Strangler in order to try something different. Yet those who have known him for some years comment that, particularly towards the end of his time in the band, he'd become sullen, sarky and downcast, inveterately rude to people and verbally highly provocative. Hugh is very wary of anybody delving deeper into his emotions. He is an intensely private man, single-minded, and totally committed to his art. Whereas fatherhood has changed JJ and made him less self-obsessed, for Hugh, life still revolves around writing, recording, gigging and ligging. He's a free agent, still very creative, but, to some, rather detached and austere, as if trying to cover up the unacknowledged bitterness he feels about his predicament. He knows, as do those who care about his career, that, like the Stranglers, he is at present under-achieving. His current work, like that of the band he left, deserves more attention, and his sometimes brilliant past has seldom been given the praise it deserves. Over-confidence is, as Jet remembers, his greatest weakness. Today Hugh remains convinced that his solo career will eventually take off, and until that moment there can be no chance of a reconciliation with the Stranglers. He has something to prove to the doubters first, and he's never doubted his own ability. Although surprised, and a little offended, that the band decided to carry on without him, he bears them no ill-will. Is he a bitter man?: 'No, I think it's great. It's all good sport, part of the rich tapestry of life. It's fun. I really hope they do well. Because I'm going to do fantastically, so I hope they do well too.'

Does he miss JJ, does he miss the creative input from his old mate?: 'I don't need a writing partner. I'm writing so much better now than I've ever written before. I know that I'm good at what I do because enough people have told me that for me to believe they're not bullshitting me. I know they're not bullshitting me, because results speak for themselves. I'm totally secure professionally. Enough critics have said that I'm a songwriter of a certain standard for me to reasonably assume that I've reached a certain level of competence.'

And no, despite the nudge-nudge, wink-wink rumours in some quarters surrounding JJ's sexuality (he was spotted all those years ago with a transsexual in his bedroom), JJ and Hugh never got it together. Hugh: 'We used to like each other emotionally and respectfully, but it's the hairy back that I can't stand. That's why I've never been homosexual, can't stand the hairy back!'

JJ's shag-ability is something the man is still at pains to show off. 'Have you got loads of pictures of me with pretty girls?' was one (possibly tongue-in-cheek) comment made by him to the author.

Hugh is missed by almost every Stranglers fan, even those who have fallen in love with the new line-up. They miss his creativity, his vitality and his humour. Despite the harsh words and the acrimony surrounding the split, Jet, for one, remembers him fondly:

> I feel rather sad about Hugh because in those early days together, when we started to build up the band, he had an immense amount of energy. It's sad that after all that work he's not here anymore. He really went downhill, lost his sense of humour and became very difficult to be with at times. He became quite depressing, and gave short shrift to questions put to him. He thought we were going to fold up, and he didn't think he was going to have to compete with us. I think he's angry we're still doing it. I might be wrong. I always thought him to be a pretty honest man . . .

Following the clichéd maxim of 'never say never', both Dave and Jet fail to completely rule out the possibility of working with Hugh again. Dave: 'It may happen in the future. We'd all have to agree. Whether it would be to re-form the old band for a one-off, I don't know. I can't possibly say that it won't happen because people's minds change and situations alter. Doubtful but possible, I'd say as of this moment.'

Jet:

> By and large there's still a great deal of confidence within the band and in our ability to be successful. But there's no reason why a reunion could never happen, because we're all just human beings and we're all fumbling our way through life. I wouldn't care to predict one way or the other. All I can say, is that as long as he's capable of doing what he does, and as long as we're capable of doing what we do, there's always the chance. Maybe we might become a six-piece, I don't know!

Would Hugh consider joining the new line-up? 'Paul Roberts isn't going to be very happy having the guy he replaced coming back in, is he? Not very fair on him, is it? But again I say, how can a group re-form that hasn't split up? There's no dynamic there. If we'd all stopped and split up, then we could have got together and done an album and a tour five years down the line, or something. Had they done the honourable thing and stopped then, yeah, it was a possibility.'

Hugh has cut himself off from the Stranglers. He has never seen the new line-up perform, and doesn't have any contact with the band apart from the occasional accidental meeting with JJ, when the two are polite, but not friendly. Hugh doesn't rate the Stranglers material he's heard since leaving the band: 'I thought the two I'd heard weren't that novel. It sounded like they were re-covering old Stranglers' ground. But I wish them all the best.'

JJ also remembers their most recent meeting at their mutual accountant's, Stephen Ross: 'In the old days he was wonderful, he was lovely. When I saw him at Stephen Ross' offices he came up to me and shook my hand as if he was some politician and I was some OAP in the crowd. "Hello, how are you?" he said. It was like meeting John Major. Then I said we were playing the Albert Hall, and he went white. His face dropped and he said, "Got to go, bye!" '

There is, of course, an enormous financial carrot dangling in front of the Stranglers. Re-forming the old line-up (with or without John Ellis) would undoubtedly be a very sound commercial move. Would the present management ever consider it? Sil Willcox: 'I wouldn't sow the seed to try and get it to happen, due to personal contact I've got with the band. But if all parties wanted it to happen, then you'd be obliged to do it. But I don't think the band would do it, to be honest.'

Trevor Long: 'From a commercial angle, if it was actually said, "We are going to re-create the old Stranglers", then we'd be bloody mad not to do it. But the only way the band would do it would be if the present line-up disbanded.'

Both John and Paul are only too aware that their positions are potentially vulnerable. Interviewed in 1996 John even went so far as to say: 'I reckon right now if Hugh Cornwell phoned up and said, "I want to join the band", I think they would go for it!'

What does the present management team expect from the Stranglers in commercial terms in the future? Trevor Long:

> The Stranglers are never going to be doing Wembley again, or Ally Pally. But, that said, the level of business they did on *In The Night* and *About Time* is far below what they should be doing and what they're entitled to. We've had to go through a transitional period to try and turn things round, which we obviously are. I think the Stranglers will reach a level of business which will be very good business, but they won't be a stadium band again because there isn't the interest there.

Faced with the question as to why the band have not been successful recently, JJ points to two major factors:

> Firstly, we've had terrible distribution in the last three years. We initially thought it was a great idea to go through an indie, as we've always liked lots of control over things, but now we realize they don't have the distribution. We've got a new distribution deal now. Eagle Rock, our new label, is going through BMG in most countries in Europe, so that's the biggest distribution deal the band

has ever had! Secondly, our fans might not be buying the records because they might think that the band are not the real Stranglers. I mean, God knows what will happen when Shearer's not playing for Newcastle this season. Are the Newcastle supporters going to think it's not the real Newcastle out there? From the artistic point of view it is a bit different and I understand that. But I think a lot of people thought Hugh was more important to the band than he really was. He was important but the band didn't rest on Hugh.

JJ pinpoints the problems the band have had with distribution. Indeed the marketing and the whole packaging of the band since 1990 has often been less than spectacular, and some of the decisions with regard in particular to single selection, were thought of by those close to the band, but excluded from the decision-making process, as suspect. There was a bit of a bunker mentality within the Stranglers' operation as any constructive criticism tended to be brushed aside: 'What sounds like negativity', Marian Shepherd opined, 'is positivity. It's positive to point out things which you know are going to go wrong.'

It was not always so. In 1990 Neil Martin at Sony had won an award for the marketing and sales campaign for the Stranglers *Greatest Hits* collection. But since then, the band's work simply hasn't been promoted extensively. Very often there has been no pre-promotion leading up to the release of a single or an album, no television shows, sometimes not even a video available for a single release. 'Heaven Or Hell', the first single off the *In The Night* album, was a strong pop song, but when Simon Bates on Radio 1 started playing the up-tempo 'Sugar Bullets' (a song which some considered the more obvious single), China rush-released the track and the single flopped badly. At this point fans wrote in to SIS claiming that it was actually impossible to even buy a Stranglers single in the shops so poor was the distribution. And with *About Time*, a video was made for 'Golden Boy', but the song wasn't even put out as a single, whilst 'In Heaven She Walks' from *Written In Red* was limited media-only release. The promotion and distribution of the band, regardless of the antipathy shown by the music press and Radio 1, has been so patchy, Marian Shepherd at SIS even noticed that a lot of rock fans actually thought that the band had split up and were totally unaware of the new line-up's existence.

The new line-up makes for a very exciting live band which, after the Albert Hall gig, has regained a certain amount of media confidence. Jet still looks a picture behind the drums, head turned to one side, gruffly powering his way through the set not unlike a wilder version of Chas from Chas and Dave. John Ellis is a beautiful guitarist who prowls the stage with his mock show of menace making him look cuddly rather than creepy. Dave looks even more maniacal behind the keyboards, with his dyed hair in a pony tail, playing the keyboard instrumental break in 'No More Heroes' with one hand whilst affecting the air of a tripped-out toff and downing a pint of warm beer with the other. JJ's still doing those karate kicks, still has that special crouched way of playing his bass, and still does his little dance, cocking his leg at alternate steps like a dog having a piss. Paul is still whirling across the stage, bare-chested, cheeky – the consummate show-man. Live, the band are an amazing match of the bizarre and the brazen, the youthful and the near pensionable. Together they are a cross-generic, cross-generational super-hybrid. In contrast, the 10-era Stranglers were almost dead on their feet creatively, and, up until his *Guilty* album, there was little at all to suggest that a creatively somnambulant Hugh could bring much into the band. But the chance of a lucrative reunion is always, if not on the agenda, then in the minds of all concerned, whether they voice it publicly or not. For those who know the band, it would be very hard to see the Stranglers' new recruits hounded out in some sort of bloody coup. This is not simply because they are two of the nicest people you could ever meet in the rock business (they're a collective bullshit-free zone and seem to actually *care* about people), but also because they are now the dominant song-writers within the band.

In all probability both Hugh and the band have left it far too long to effect any sort of rapprochement. Had Hugh been reinstated in the first few years after the split, then perhaps the band might have been able to recapture their creative spark. But that spark was, by the 10 album, burnt out. The new line-up has been together now for seven years, almost a third of the band's total life-span. And yet when their name is mentioned in the media, it's almost always in terms of the past. Pop can't get enough of nostalgia: anniversaries of great albums, re-formations of classic line-ups, endless re-packages, re-recordings, and great-

est hits tours; the language of pop which ultimately kills pop. Pop
has a history, and a great history too, which fulfils an important
function in creating our identity as past, present and future
consumers of pop music. But if we dwell too long on the past,
then the future seems frightening, and we're all dead well before
we're old. Both Hugh and his ex-friends in the Stranglers have to
find a way of creating a future for themselves which does not rely
on selling nostalgia and which re-establishes pop's truest code:
the celebration of the perpetual now. The kindest future for both
Hugh and the Stranglers would be more success, more great
music, *but on their own terms*, not by resurrecting their pasts. The
Cornwell camp and the Stranglers camp have become entrenched. Any reunion would involve a huge loss of face on
both sides. As the book was going to press, JJ decided to quash
speculation once and for all: 'There is no way that the old line-up
would re-form. You know what happened to Lot's wife when she
looked back?'

There was much to find distasteful about the Stranglers: they
had (have?) an image of irretractable white machismo. A
research project carried out on the band by Paul Holland showed
that their fan-base, circa 1993, was overwhelmingly male (84 per
cent) and almost 100 per cent white (of the 268 people contacted
in the study there was only one non-white Stranglers fan). The
new line-up has helped destroy this tiresome machismo. Even if
the band have become more rock-oriented, both Paul and John
are progressives, libertarians.

But the band enjoyed, and still enjoys, a cross-generational
appeal. Peering out from over his drum kit, Jet sees a positive
cornucopia of ages and styles in the audience of pogo-ing punters:
'We get punky types, denim types, your thirty-somethings, your
forty-somethings, and then you get people in suits at the back!
You get all strata of society, it's most peculiar. At the beginning it
was all these crazy kids with torn clothes. Now you see people in
their sixties who were forty when they first liked us. Fans who
have been fans for a long time even bring their babies and hold
them up. It's bizarre, and the baby's wearing a Stranglers T-shirt!'

This is the secret of their appeal: the Stranglers have made
music which has crossed the generations. The key is melody. The
Stranglers have written some of the best melodies in pop since the
Beatles. Their songs sound intelligent and well-crafted. They

were the new-wave band that produced not only the energy but also the honed and fine-tuned melodies. They were also the new-wave band for those who wanted their pop to carry with it more than the common currency of pop platitudes. Finally, their songs appealed to that classic constituency of male, suburban angst: the would-be hep, cool cat; the frightened bookish teenager.

At their best, the Stranglers are one of the élite live bands on the circuit, entertaining, eminently danceable, technically brilliant and occasionally genuinely enthralling. Their music doesn't seem to have dated. They have seldom been musically predictable, and always more intelligent than most critics made out. At times, they have been possessed with a barmy genius. Ex-publicist Alan Edwards: 'The band are one of the most under-recognized and undervalued, British bands full-stop. I think they had an incredible ear for melody. They were good songwriters and were a great live band. They made seven or eight good albums, and there's not many people who can claim that. The Pistols managed one, the Clash about four, the Damned only one. The Stranglers were far more musical and had far more depth.'

They were also, as JJ is the first to admit, inconsistent: 'I don't think our current material is that bad now. None of our albums have been universally brilliant. There have been glorious moments on each album, apart from, perhaps, *10*, although I think "In This Place" is pretty amazing.'

JJ is right. The band never made one truly great album. *Rattus Norvegicus* is a powerful record, but sounds dated. *No More Heroes* is too much a deliberate wind-up. *Black And White* is brave, *The Raven* yearning and melodic (and for most of the band their finest hour), *The Meninblack* top-drawer craziness, *La Folie* a super collection and probably the closest they got to marrying crankiness and tunesmithery. Thereafter begins a slow decline. *Feline* is conceptually the most unified the band ever got, and is a beautiful, if inconsistent, album. *Aural Sculpture* is the poppiest they ever got, and boasts the finest Side 1 of any Stranglers album (shame about Side 2). *Dreamtime* is patchier still, but nevertheless great in places, but *10* was their creative nadir.

The post-Cornwell Stranglers, despite their media detractors, have made some fine music and may, for all we know, go on to even better things. *In The Night* showed them back to near top melodic form; *About Time* was a dashing, occasionally excellent set; and *Written In Red* a necessary experiment which failed. But it's the great singles which the band will be remembered for. For a while they were Britain's premier singles outfit, before Madness and then the Smiths took over the mantle. Almost every Stranglers album is littered with should-have-been singles ('Hangin Around', 'Ice Queen', 'Waltz In Black', 'Tramp', 'Wet Afternoon' . . . the list goes on) which never made it on to 45. The band's Achilles heel has always been their lack of grooviness. If only they'd contemporarized their sound with a few dancey beats when the rest of rock did so in the late 80s, then maybe they'd have continued their success story into the 1990s in the UK.

Their career has been one of the most genuinely outrageous in the post-Beatles pop era, if not *the* most outrageous. But the infamy has been a double-edged sword, both a great selling-point and a handicap. JJ: 'It's been an amazing 25 years. Very few bands could equal it. But on the whole I think all the outrage has affected our success. We would have been mega, mega, mega if we'd kept a lid on these things or not done them at all. But then we wouldn't have been the band that we were/ are.'

The Stranglers took the rock cliché, the unholy trinity of sex, drugs and rock 'n' roll, and lived it with more panache and more downright silliness than any other rock band of their time. It's been a career full of fine music, genuinely frightening and bizarre episodes, hilarious incidents, and also moments of personal tragedy. No band of their stature could have dreamt of matching them in the bad-taste stakes, of emulating their utterly monstrous lapses in public decency, the crass behaviour. But they did all this with a very wicked sense of the ridiculous too. Their 1979 *Willesee At Seven* interview with Howard Gipps on Australia's Channel Seven should be required viewing for all comedy script-writers. In it our four lads crucify a particularly under-researched, strait-laced Aussie interviewer in an ill-fitting shirt, and reduce him to tears, whilst remaining in obnoxious, tongue-in-cheek *Spinal Tap* mode throughout. It makes the Pistols' appearance with Bill Grundy on *Today* look completely tame.

They're still doing it, still winding 'em up and still making fine music. For too long the Meninblack were pop's abductees, having

their own sort of missing-time experience, their names removed
from the annals of pop history. But now they're back.

They've created untold mayhem, untold anguish, and bucket-
loads of fun, along with some of the most resonant pop of their
day. Meninblack, welcome home.

SELECT BIBLIOGRAPHY

Most of the information for this book came from the hundreds of hours of interviews conducted by the author with the band members past and present, and with those who have worked with them. This invaluable exclusive material was supplemented by material from rock periodicals such as *Sounds*, *New Musical Express*, *Melody Maker*, *Record Mirror*, *Music Week*, *Trouser Press*, *Zig-Zag*, *Rolling Stone*, *Mojo* and *Q*, as well as hundreds of articles in the international, national and regional press. *Strangled*, the band's 'enthuzine', set up in 1977 by band publicist Alan Edwards and Tony Moon, was another invaluable source of inside information. From early 1979 to December 1986 *Strangled* was overseen by Jet Black, and from 1987 to 1997 it was run by JJ. Both relied on a succession of hard-working editors: Suzanne Prior, Paul Roderick (a.k.a. Paul Duffy, Jet's brother), Nick Yeomans, Pam Greenfield, Gary Lucas, and Marian Shepherd.

The punk era is undoubtedly one of the most written-about eras in pop history. The best introduction to it can be found in a superb, accessible academic book by Dave Laing which contextualizes the era perfectly. *One Chord Wonders: Power and Meaning in Punk Rock* (Open University Press, 1985) is essential reading. Another academic work, Iain Chambers' *Urban Rhythms: Pop Music and Culture* (Macmillan, 1985) also contains some very good writing on punk. Lucy O'Brien's excellent *She Bop: The Definitive History of Women in Rock, Pop and Soul* (Penguin, 1995) is a salutary reminder of the often misrepresented or forgotten role of women in pop.

Of the many punk biographies, the best is Jon Savage's lauded *England's Dreaming: Sex Pistols and Punk Rock* (Faber, 1991), which marries top-class investigative journalism with socio-political critique to good effect. Its only drawback is the crucial omission of an index, although the discography is comprehensive. Marcus Gray's *Last Gang In Town: the Story and Myth of the Clash* (Fourth Estate, 1995) is extremely detailed, while John Lydon's 'autobiography' (mysteriously, for one so eloquent, co-written with

Keith and Kent Zimmerman), *Rotten, No Irish, No Blacks, No Dogs* (Hodder & Stoughton, 1996), is a rollicking read.

Two anthologies by famous writers on punk are also worth dipping into. Tony Parson's *Dispatches From The Front Line Of Popular Culture* (Virgin, 1995) is provocative about the punk era and much besides, and Jon Savage's collection of classic writing, *The Faber Book Of Pop*, co-edited with writer Hanif Kureishi, has essential background material not just on the punk era, but also on the relationship between pop and culture from the 1940s to the 1990s.

The most vehement recent critique of the band and its misogyny is contained in Simon Reynolds and Joy Press' thought-provoking survey, *The Sex Revolts: Gender, Rebellion and Rock 'n' Roll* (Serpent's Tail, 1995).

DISCOGRAPHY

ALBUMS

Title	Catalogue No.	Label	Date	Format	Highest UK Chart Position	Weeks in Charts
Rattus Norvegicus	UAG 30045	UA	1977	LP, CD, CAS	4	34
No More Heroes	UAG 30200	UA	1977	LP, CD, CAS	2	19
Black And White	UAG 30222	UA	1978	LP, CD, CAS	2	18
Live X-Cert	UAG 30224	UA	1979	LP, CD, CAS	7	10
The Raven	UAG 30262	UA	1979	LP, CD, CAS	4	8
The Meninblack	LBG 30313	Liberty	1981	LP, CD, CAS	8	5
La Folie	LBG 30342	Liberty	1981	LP, CD, CAS	11	18
The Collection 1977–1982	LBG 30353	Liberty	1982	LP, CD, CAS	12	16
Feline	Epic 252337	Epic	1983	LP, CD, CAS	4	11
Aural Sculpture	EPC 26220	Epic	1984	LP, CD, CAS	14	10
Off The Beaten Track	Liberty 500I	Liberty	1986	LP, CAS	80	2
Dreamtime	EPC 26648	Epic	1986	LP, CD, CAS	16	6
All Live and All Of The Night	EPC 460259	Epic	1988	LP, CD, CAS	12	6
Rarities	EMS 1306	Liberty	1988	LP, CD, CAS	–	–
Singles (The UA Years)	EM 1314	Liberty	1989	LP, CD, CAS	57	2
10	4664831	Epic	1990	LP, CD, CAS, PD	15	4
Greatest Hits 1977–90	4675411	Epic	1990	LP, CD, CAS, PSD	4	47
All Twelve Inches	4714162	Epic	1992	CD, CAS	–	–
The Early Years – '74, '75, '76	SPEAK 101	Newspeak	1992	LP, CD, CAS	–	–
Stranglers In The Night	WOLCD 1030	Psycho	1992	LP, CD, CAS	33	1
The Old Testament	CD STRANG 1	EMI	1992	CD/Book	–	–
Saturday Night, Sunday Morning	ESS 194	Castle Communications	1993	LP, CD, CAS	–	–
Strangled: From Birth & Beyond	SIS CD001	SIS	1994	CD	–	–
The Stranglers & Friends	RRCD 195	SIS/Trojan/Receiver	1995	CD	–	–
About Time	WENC001/MC001	Castle Communications	1995	CD, CAS, LP	31	1
Written In Red	WENCD009	Castle Communications	1997	CD, CAS, LP	52	1
The Hit Men	EMI CDEMC 3749	EMI	1997	CD, CAS	–	–
Friday the 13th (21 Years at the Royal Albert Hall)	EAGCD006	Eagle Rock	1997	CD		

SINGLES

Title	Catalogue No.	Label	Date	Format	Highest UK Chart Position	Weeks in Charts
Grip	UP 36211	UA	1977	7"	44	4
Peaches/Go Buddy Go	UP 36248	UA	1977	7"	8	14
Something Better Change/ Straighten Out	UP 36277	UA	1977	7"	9	8
No More Heroes	UP 36300	UA	1977	7"	8	9
5 Minutes	UP 36350	UA	1978	7"	11	9
Nice 'N' Sleazy	UP 36379	UA	1978	7"	18	8
Walk On By	UP 36429	UA	1978	7"	21	8
Duchess	BP 308	UA	1979	7"	14	9
Nuclear Device	BP 318	UA	1979	7"	36	4
Don't Bring Harry	STR 1	UA	1979	7"	41	3
Bear Cage	BP 344	UA	1980	7", 12"	36	5
Who Wants The World	BP 355	UA	1980	7"	39	4
Thrown Away	BP 383	Liberty	1981	7"	42	4
Just Like Nothing On Earth	BP 393	Liberty	1981	7"	–	–
Let Me Introduce You To The Family	BP 405	Liberty	1981	7"	42	3
Golden Brown	BP 407	Liberty	1981	7"	2	12
La Folie	BP 410	Liberty	1982	7"	47	3
Strange Little Girl	BP 412	Liberty	1982	7"	7	9
European Female	EPCA 2893	Epic	1982	7", PD	9	6
Midnight Summer Dream	EPCA 3167	Epic	1983	7", 12"	35	4
Paradise	EPCA 3387	Epic	1983	7", 12"	48	3
Skin Deep	EPCA 4738	Epic	1984	7", 12"	15	7
No Mercy	EPCA 4921	Epic	1984	7", EP, SPD, 12"	37	7
Let Me Down Easy	EPCA 6045	Epic	1985	7", 12", X12"	48	4
Nice In Nice	EPC 650055	Epic	1986	7", SPD, 12"	30	5
Always The Sun	SOLAR 1	Epic	1986	7", SPD, 12"	30	5
Big In America	HUGE 1	Epic	1987	7", SPD, 12"	48	6
Shakin' Like a Leaf	SHEIK 1	Epic	1987	7", SPD, 12", X12"	58	4
All Day and All of the Night	VICE 1	Epic	1987	7", SPD, 12", CD	7	7
Grip '89	EM 84	Liberty	1989	7", CV, 12", CD	33	3
Nighttracks Session	SFNT 20	Strange Fruit	1989	12", CD		
96 Tears	TEARS 1	Epic	1990	7", 12", CD, PCD, CAS, X7"	17	6
Sweet Smell of Success	TEARS 2	Epic	1990	7", 12", X12", CD, CAS	65	2
Always The Sun	6564307	Epic	1990	7", 12", PCD, CD, CAS	29	5
Golden Brown	6567617	Epic	1991	7", CAS, CD	68	2
Heaven Or Hell	WOXCD 2025	Psycho	1992	12", CDX2, CAS	46	2
Sugar Bullets	PSYCD 002	Psycho	1992	CD, CAS	–	–
Lies And Deception	WENX 1007	Castle Communication	1995	7", CDx2	–	–
In Heaven She Walks	WENX 1018	Castle Communication	1997	CDx2, CAS	–	–

SELECTED VIDEOS

Title	Catalogue No.	Label	Date	Format
The Collection	TVE9010322	EMI	1982	PAL VHS
Screentime	357750	CBS/FOX	1986	PAL VHS
The Old Testament	MVN 4910463	PMI	1992	PAL VHS
Saturday Night, Sunday Morning	CMP61031	Castle Communications	1993	PAL VHS
Friday the 13th (21 Years at the Royal Albert Hall)	QLG 5013	Eagle Rock	1997	PAL VHS

SELECTED SOLO RECORDINGS (Albums only)

Title	Catalogue No.	Label	Date	Format	Highest UK Chart Position	Weeks in Charts
(i) JJ Burnel						
Euroman Cometh	UAG 30214	U.A.	1979	LP, CAS, PD, CD	40	5
Un Jour Parfait	5ISCD002	SIS	1988	CD	–	–
(ii) Hugh Cornwell						
Nosferatu	UAG 30251	U.A.	1979	LP, CD, CAS	–	–
Wolf	V 2420	Virgin	1988	LP, CD, CAS	98	–
CCW	UFO9	UFO	1992	LP, CD, CAS	–	–
Wired	TRANSCDI	Transmission	1993	LP, CD, CAS	–	–
Guilty	SMACD 501	Madfish	1997	CD, CAS	–	–
(iii) John Ellis						
Acrylic	OPT4.00	Optic Nerve	1997	CD	–	–
(iv) Dave Greenfield & JJ Burnel						
Fire And Water	EPC 25707	Epic	1983	LP, CAS	40	5
(v) Purple Helmets (features JJ, Dave & John)						
Ride Again	ROSE 160	New Rose	1988	LP, CV × 2, CD, CAS	–	–
Rise Again	GRAM 42	Anagram	1989	LP, CD, CAS	–	–

INDEX

'S' indicates the Stranglers; 'JJ' indicates Jean Jacques Burnel.